Best wishes and all the best

W0006185

Alibi for an Alibi

The Detective Inspector John Cahill Series, Volume 2

John O'Donovan

Published by Castley & Fox Publishers, 2023.

ALIBI FOR AN ALIBI

First edition. September 5, 2023.

ISBN: 979-8223316039

Written by John O'Donovan.

Also by John O'Donovan

The Detective Inspector John Cahill Series
The Deadly Steps
Alibi for an Alibi

Watch for more at https://johnodonovanbooks.blogspot.com.

Table of Contents

FOR: Declan, Shane, Kevin and Claire

Epigraph

E very society gets the kind of criminal it deserves. What is equally true is that every community gets the kind of law enforcement it insists on.

Robert Kennedy

---

*EVERY INVESTIGATIVE **technique** described in this book is based on some of the experiences of the author.*

Also by the Author

T*he Deadly Steps*

Volume 1, of the Detective Inspector John Cahill Series.

John and Jules Cahill move to Belfast, from Cork, when John begins a new career with the police in Northern Ireland. Several years later, he is seconded to the Garda Siochana, the national police force in the Republic of Ireland, back in his native Cork City, where he tackles some of the most complex homicide investigations to hit the city.

Distributed by Draft 2 Digital

Prologue

From Volume 1 of the D.I. John Cahill series,
The Deadly Steps

J ohn Cahill grew up in one of Cork City's oldest neighborhoods, Blackpool, situated in the heart of the North Side. Unlike most kids in the Blackpool area, John did not play the traditional sports of hurling and Gaelic football. Instead, at an early age, he got involved with horses and ponies. In his late teens, John Cahill entered the world of horseracing.

John Cahill, his wife, Jules, and their young family enjoyed a moderately successful lifestyle, training young horses, (and a few older ones), at Inchydoney's twin beaches, on the west coast, near Cork City.

After sustaining a life altering injury on the racecourse John Cahill needed a new career with a secure future for his family. He decided to become a police officer, but in 1994, at the age of thirty-three, he was too old to join Ireland's national police force, 'An Garda Siochana.' So, he crossed the border, into Northern Ireland and joined the Royal Ulster Constabulary.

- Life could not have been more different for the young family from the Republic of Ireland, working and living in Belfast during the final years of 'The Troubles.'
- John Cahill was promoted to Detective Constable in 1997 and assigned to the Criminal Investigation Division, (CID), in Belfast.
- The Royal Ulster Constabulary was rebranded in 1999 after

the Good Friday Agreement and became the Police Service of Northern Ireland. John Cahill's career flourished in the new police service.

- After working on his first homicide investigation, John Cahill was promoted to Detective Sergeant and transferred to the Serious Crime Unit in Belfast.

- Detective Sergeant John Cahill successfully investigated many complex cases, while assigned to the Serious Crimes Unit, such as homicides, kidnappings, robberies and the case of an international gun-runner and bomb maker. It wasn't long before he was promoted to the rank of Detective Inspector.

- With promotion came transfer, within the Police Service of Northern Ireland and Detective Inspector John Cahill was transferred to the Professional Responsibilities Unit, the forces Internal Affairs unit.

- During this assignment, D.I. Cahill ruffled some feathers with some senior ranking officers and the police union when he investigated two officers for failing to carry out their duty. The officers' negligence led to the death of young man from a marginalized community.

- With the Assistant Chief Constable as an ally, Detective Inspector Cahill was transferred again. He was seconded to an Integrated Fugitive Squad, working with An Garda Siochana, in his native Cork City, south of the border, in the Republic of Ireland.

- John and Jules Cahill moved back to their homestead in Inchydoney in West Cork. After two extremely successful years leading the Integrated Fugitive Squad, D.I. Cahill was parachuted back into the world of Serious Crime when his boss in the Garda, Superintendent Paddy Collins asked him to lead a difficult and complex homicide investigation.

- Using extraordinary investigative techniques, D.I. Cahill led a small, dedicated team of investigators in the newly formed Serious Crime Unit in Cork City, tackling the notorious street gangs, the Independent Posse and the Mahon Warlords.

- Like any city, where drug fuelled violence terrorizes the normal citizens, The Serious Crimes Unit in Cork City, were kept busy and nothing was straight forward. The investigations became more complex and challenging.

Chapter 1

S <u>unday December 21st.</u>
  Four days before Christmas, John and Jules Cahill were busy packing their suitcases for their trip to Northern Ireland. They went there at least twice a year, ever since John had been seconded to the Garda from the Police Service of Northern Ireland. Although technically it was work related, it was an opportunity for the Cahills to have a break and visit with their friends, Fred and Janet Nesbit, who lived in Belfast.

Fred, now a superintendent with the PSNI, met John in the 1990's when they were both recovering from life-altering injuries received in their respective workplaces. Fred, a member of the Royal Ulster Constabulary. was the victim of a terrorist bomb blast and John fell from a racehorse during a steeplechase race at Down Royal Racecourse, near Belfast. Constable Fred Nesbit and John Cahill became great friends, encouraging each other through weeks of painful physiotherapy and rehab. With his horseracing career in tatters and facing a bleak future, thirty-three-year-old John Cahill, was convinced by his friend, Fred Nesbit, to move his family to Northern Ireland and join the Royal Ulster Constabulary. Their wives also became close friends and allies.

December 21st was a typical winter's Sunday afternoon at Inchydoney Beach. There was a bite in the air and the wind swirled in from the Atlantic Ocean, across the sand dunes, up the cliff face to the front of the Cahills' homestead. Jules was in charge of all the planning and organizing for this trip because John, as usual, was completely focused on his work. They had to pack up their two retired racing greyhounds, Lucy and Molly, their large wire dog crates and the dog food. The dogs were to be boarded with Jules' aunt, Nan O' Regan. Nan ran a pub in the small town of Bandon, situated between Clonakilty and Cork City.

"We're only going to be in Belfast for a week. It just takes five or six hours to drive each way. Why, in the name of God, do we need two huge suitcases?" John asked his wife.

"You want me to look nice while I'm there?" Jules shot back with a smile. "What's the itinerary for the journey?"

John rolled his eyes but he would do anything just to please her.

In the early 1980's, after riding the winner in a steeplechase race at Cork Race Course in Mallow John met Jules, the love of his life. Jules had bet on a winning horse that just happened to be ridden and trained by John. A whirlwind romance commenced. They soon married and over the next ten years John enjoyed moderate success as a racehorse trainer and jump jockey in their small training yard near the twin beaches of Inchydoney in West Cork, on Ireland's south coast.

"We leave here tomorrow morning at 7. With a stop for lunch in the Midlands, we should be in Belfast around 2. We're staying at the hotel near the waterfront. Only the best for government employees," John said with a sarcastic grin.

"One stop in the Midlands!" Jules interrupted him. "Typical, you think nobody needs a bathroom break, just because you can hold it for hours. It's a good job we're not bringing the dogs. Lucy would demand a stop every hour," she teased.

"All you have to do is tell me you need to stop. I can't read your mind," he fired back defensively.

"Are you going to be working all the time while we're there? I really want to see the Titanic Museum again."

"It's literally around the corner from the hotel. I only have a few days' training. I have my yearly firearms qualification and am due for first aid training again but that only takes a few hours. I also have defensive driver training, that's it really. Maybe two and a half days' work during the week."

"Don't you have a meeting at headquarters as well?" Jules enquired.

"I have to go and see the new boss in Personnel."

"They call it Human Resources now. In fact, they've called it that for the last twenty years," Jules smirked, knowing what was coming.

"Personnel is for assholes. That's a direct quote from one of my favorite movies, 'Dirty Harry.' These people in HR go there to avoid working nightshift and doing real police work. Sometimes that means dealing with the scum of the earth but most of them are afraid of the dark or allergic to the moon. Then they design the promotion process to suit themselves and get promotion after promotion. So they end up in senior positions, making decisions about a job they know absolutely nothing about," John vented in a usual rant that Jules expected.

"Step off the soapbox! You'll only upset yourself and raise your blood pressure," Jules said laughing, knowing she had purposely set him off on his pet peeve. "Now you can stop sighing and rolling your eyes. Get the dog crates and the dog food ready. "Should we drop them off at Nan's tonight or tomorrow morning when we're on the way?"

"I'd prefer to drop them off tonight, but I really don't fancy driving to Bandon now."

John set about his next task when the familiar sound of his cell phone rang. He looked at the call display, '*Superintendent Collins Work.*' "Oh, for fuck sakes," John muttered under his breath.

"You are not going in! I don't care who's dead or how many have been killed. YOU ARE NOT GOING IN!" Jules glared at her husband. She stormed off and left John to deal with the call.

John Cahill had been a police officer with the Police Service of Northern Ireland for almost seventeen years. For the last three years he was seconded to the Garda Siochana, the police in Cork City and the rest of the Republic of Ireland. John was initially seconded to the Garda to run an Integrated Fugitive Squad but his direct supervisor, Superintendent Paddy Collins, saw an opportunity to re-assign him as the Detective Inspector in charge of the Serious Crimes Unit, in Cork City. Business was brisk and John was always on call, although his official working hours were Monday to Friday, 7AM to 4PM. When new business came in, John and his team regularly worked around the clock. Jules was annoyed about the call from Superintendent Collins as she worried about the long hours her husband worked and how seriously and personally he took his job.

John answered the phone, "Hi Boss, what's up?"

Superintendent Paddy Collins was the Commanding Officer of all the Investigative Units and Support Units, including Forensics, in Cork City and County. Before the arrival of Detective Inspector John Cahill in Cork City, all homicide investigations were overseen by detectives from the National Bureau of Criminal Investigation, situated in the capital, Dublin.

However, Paddy Collins saw an opportunity to form a Serious Crimes Unit in Cork City and with the backing of the Assistant Commissioner, he put the officer from the Police Service of Northern Ireland in charge of the new unit. The superintendent knew that John, who was born and raised in Cork City, knew the subculture that existed in the city and because of his homicide investigation experience in Northern Ireland, he was the obvious choice to head up the new unit. Almost none of the other Garda officers in the city were originally from Cork. It was both tradition and a rule in the Garda that you could not serve in your home town.

The Serious Crimes Unit was one of the busiest Garda units in Cork and also one of the smallest units, with only eight full time investigators including their detective inspector, who ran the unit. The DI made all the investigative decisions; senior officers like the superintendent and the chief superintendent were the administrators.

"Hi John, I'm sorry to bother you. I know you're getting ready to head up to Belfast, but I need a favour," the superintendent said sheepishly in his strong rural Kerry accent. "Remember that fella, Pierce Alfonso, the guy you spoke with last week? Well, he just walked into the station and asked to speak with you. He claims he has more information on the Killen homicide. The duty officer called me because he didn't want to call you directly. Can you come in? It shouldn't take very long. I promise that you'll make it home in time to drive to the North."

"Let me call you back," John answered as he thought about the best way to break the news to his wife.

Jules didn't overhear the conversation but she looked at her husband and guessed what was coming. John was now fifty years old and he was working an average of one hundred and twenty hours overtime every month. She worried about his physical and mental health. "What now?" Jules groaned.

"Paddy wants me to interview someone. Remember the Killen homicide back in August. We haven't made any headway and it's gone stone cold. We have nothing; no suspects whatsoever. It shouldn't take long. I've already spoken to this clown twice and I don't think he has anything to offer, but according to Paddy this fella thinks he has more information," John answered sheepishly.

"Well, you better go in," knowing that he would go anyway but wanted her blessing. "DON'T BE LATE! We must be on the road before 8. Put the dogs' crates and food in your car now. You can drop Lucy and Molly and all their gear off at Nan's on your way to the city. I'll take them out for a quick walk on the beach while you're getting ready and I'll call Nan and tell her to expect you."

John and Jules had kept their home at Inchydoney's twin beaches in West Cork as a holiday let when they moved to Northern Ireland in 1994. Now that John was seconded to the Garda in Cork City, it was the perfect place to live as it was only a forty-five-minute drive to the city.

John smiled at Jules; he knew he could not do his job without her support. Jules headed down to the West Beach with the two large dogs. The wind had picked up and the mercury had dropped; it looked like it was going to be a cold windy night on Inchydoney's twin beaches. According to the latest weather forecast, it was supposed to snow shortly after Christmas. Snow was an anomaly in West Cork and if there was any serious accumulation, it would cause havoc for drivers. Jules had bought warm coats and boots for the greyhounds. The two dogs loved to go walking on the beach, but the skinny athletic dogs certainly were not built for cold snowy weather. She tried walking through the sand dunes but the damp sand was being blown in her face, so she turned back and headed home after a few minutes.

JOHN CALLED HIS BOSS back, showered and changed into his business suit and began the forty-five-minute drive to Garda Headquarters on Anglesea Street in Cork City. He stopped at the pub in Bandon and delivered his two dogs, their wire crates and food. John knew the dogs would not get very many walks while they stayed with Nan but they would be spoiled rotten and probably put on some weight during their vacation.

During the drive from Bandon to the city, John thought about this tough investigation. In early August, Stuart Killen, a twenty-six-year-old man was found dead in his own home, in the quiet suburb of Ballinlough. John had attended the scene and it was one of the most violent and bloody scenes he had ever encountered.

Killen had been savagely bludgeoned around the head with three golf clubs. At first glance, his body looked as if it had been staged as it sat upright on his living room sofa, with his arms calmly by his side, palms facing up. But the blood spatter told a different story. Stuart Killen had been beaten to death where he was found. Both the sides and the top of his skull had large deep holes created from the impact of the golf clubs. Blood and brain matter had oozed out of the cavities when the next strike landed.

When one of the golf clubs snapped after the impact with his smashed skull, Killen was then impaled through the stomach with the broken shaft of the club. And for some strange reason, the index finger on his right hand had been hacked off with a big kitchen scissors. Although this was a brutal crime scene and there was blood spattered everywhere in the living room, there was no physical evidence left behind by the assailant and the investigators had no clue how many people had been involved in the death of Stuart Killen.

Early in the investigation, John had learned that Stuart Killen was gay and frequented clubs and bars where he met random men. The Serious Crime Unit investigators had canvassed all the usual clubs and bars. The victim was well known in most establishments but nobody remembered seeing Stuart Killen the night before he was found dead. Detectives also canvassed the immediate area near the victim's home. A waitress in a coffee shop reported that a man came into the shop the day that Killen's body had been found. While this man was in the shop, there was a news story about the murder broadcast on the radio. Then this man told the waitress that Stuart Killen was his friend and that Killen had been beaten to death.

Detective Inspector Cahill found this information to be particularly interesting because when the police told the media they were investigating a homicide, they never mentioned the cause of death or the weapons used. This was hold-back evidence. However, the investigators had failed to identify the mystery man in the coffee shop.

In early December, with the investigative trail growing colder, just like the weather, John decided to make a plea to the general public through the media asking for the mystery man to come forward.

FLASHBACK TO MONDAY December 15th.

On the previous Monday, thirty-two-year-old Pierce Alfonso walked into the foyer of Garda Headquarters on Anglesea Street and went directly to the front counter.

The foyer was dull and cold. The walls were painted an institutional creamy grey and the red tiles on the floor needed a good scrub after all the foot traffic in and out of the place. Pierce Alfonso approached the semicircle counter where three young officers sat in front of computer screens. Two of the officers appeared to be speaking on the phone so Pierce walked up to the third.

The young officer looked down at his keyboard and although he was well aware of the man standing in front of him, he did his best to ignore him. Alfonso was not to be deterred. He cleared his throat and shifted from foot to foot until the young officer looked up.

"Yes?" the officer said in a bored tone.

Pierce thought it interesting that as soon as this young man spoke to him, the other two officers finished their phone calls. Pierce introduced himself to the young uniformed Garda. He told him that he had seen the media report about the Stuart Killen homicide and thought that he may be the man the investigators wanted to speak with.

The young officer was relieved. He didn't have to take some stupid report from this person at the counter. All he had to do was phone upstairs to the Serious Crime Unit. The officer asked Pierce

Alfonso to take a seat along the wall by the front door while he made the call to the Incident Room on the second floor.

Pierce Alfonso took his seat under a memorial for police officers who had died in the line of duty. Every time the automatic door at the front slid open, the bitter cold air blew into the foyer and wrapped around him.

Detective Inspector John Cahill took the call from the young officer at the counter. John looked around the Incident Room to see who was available for the interview. The only detective present was the youngest member of the team, Detective Garda Tim Warren.

"Tim, what are you doing right now?" the inspector called out.

"Not a lot, what do you need?" the detective answered.

"With me! We got a potential witness in the Killen homicide."

Tim rolled his eyes and picked up his suit jacket from the back of his chair. Tim stood over six-feet tall and had an athletic build. He kept his hair very short and always had a slight stubble on his face. Although Tim always wore a tie, he never did up the top button on his shirt. John believed Tim got his dress sense from an old TV show, "Miami Vice."

Tim followed his boss down the single flight of stairs to the foyer and glanced at the officer behind the counter. The officer nodded his head towards Pierce Alfonso, the only person sitting in the cold, bleak foyer.

John stood in front of Pierce and extended his hand. "Hi, are you Pierce?"

Alfonso nodded and answered "Yes" in a hushed voice.

The first thing that John noticed about Alfonso was that he was very quiet, even shy. He was soft spoken and presented himself as a gentle individual. Pierce Alfonso was tall and lanky with a thin build. He was well dressed in beige corduroy pants and a pale blue sweater, under a green quilted coat. John observed how extremely well groomed the man was as he introduced himself and Tim Warren to Alfonso.

"We'll go upstairs to our office to talk." John motioned for Alfonso to follow him and turned towards the bank of elevators across from where he sat. It wasn't an invite or a suggestion. It was an order.

"If this guy has something to say, he's going to say it on my terms," John thought.

When they reached the second floor and got off the elevators, John produced his pass card and held the card to an electronic box next to a door. A light on the box turned from red to green and the lock on the door clicked. As he opened the door, they stepped through the doorway and Alfonso looked around in awe. Several men and women were walking around a large office area. Some of them wore guns on their hips and some carried papers. None of them paid any attention to the three people who just walked in. Alfonso had never been in contact with the police prior to this day; he had never even received a traffic ticket. Pierce felt that he had just walked onto the set of a cop movie.

John led him down a corridor. On their right they walked past a closed door, with a sign that read 'Serious Crime Unit.'

"That's our office, Pierce. But we will speak in a room down here."

Another fifty steps and the corridor opened up to another large work area with work station cubicles on the right, each one separated from the other by a grey portable partition. Each cubicle had a wrap around desk, two computers and two chairs. On the left side were eight steel doors with a sliding steel shutter about forty-five centimeters by thirty centimeters in the middle of each.

"These are our interview rooms, Pierce," John announced as he pointed to the row of steel doors.

There were seven interview rooms and a toilet in the middle making up the eighth room. The first door had a large white number

1 above the steel shutter. John slid back the shutter and glanced into the room. Seeing it was unoccupied he slid back the heavy bolt, opened the door and invited Pierce Alfonso into the room.

Pierce's heart rate began to quicken as he stepped inside the small concrete room. He quickly surveyed his surroundings. Three of the walls were painted in the same institutional cream/grey as downstairs. The other wall had some form of grey wallpaper torn off in places. The floor was concrete but painted a glossy dark green. There was only one seat in the room, a plastic cushioned steel chair and a steel table, both bolted to the floor. The table top was covered in graffiti. Pierce looked up at the ceiling, The bright fluorescent lights blinded him momentarily but he noticed that they, too, were covered by a steel grate to protect them from prying hands.

John saw the look of sheer horror on his guest's face and smiled. "I must apologize for the surroundings, Pierce. It's all we got. We interview everyone in these rooms...victims, witnesses, suspects and some very bad and dangerous people too. Please have a seat and Tim and I will be back to speak with you in a few seconds, I just have to pick up my notebook. Is there anything I can get you, tea, coffee, a bottle of water?"

Pierce Alfonso asked for water as the detectives left the room. He felt a little at ease after the detective spoke to him. He liked these detectives and did not feel intimidated by them.

When John and Tim returned, they pushed two chairs into Interview Room 1. Pierce Alfonso sat with his knees together and his legs under his chair, crossed at the ankles. His hands were in front of him between his thighs. Pierce looked down at the table top and spoke in such a low hushed voice that the detectives had to ask him several times to speak up.

After John had collected some tombstone, background information from Alfonso, they got down to business.

"How long did you know Stuart Killen?" John asked.

"About three years," Alfonso answered as he looked directly at the inspector.

"How well did you know him?"

"Pretty well," whispered Alfonso.

John asked "How well is pretty well? He exhaled slowly through his nose.

Alfonso's gaze dropped to the floor again. There was an awkward silence in the room. At least it was awkward for Alfonso. The detectives just stared at him waiting for his response. 'Spit it out man!' John thought and he felt like shaking the other man.

After what felt like an hour, but in reality was less than thirty seconds, Pierce Alfonso felt he had to answer, "I'm gay." He took a deep breath, still staring at the floor and continued. "Me and Stuart would hook up every few months and spend some time together. It was very casual, nothing serious. Stuart liked that. He didn't want a steady partner."

"As long as nobody was getting hurt, Pierce. I'm not going to judge you." John smiled reassuringly, and immediately Pierce felt slightly more comfortable as his tension eased.

At first John and Tim thought Alfonso was trying to be evasive because he said "I may be the person you spoke about in the news!" Alfonso claimed that he hadn't seen Stuart Killen since the beginning of the summer in June, but he may have been the man who spoke to the waitress in the coffee shop.

After a couple of hours of questioning and going over the relationship a few times, John and Tim left the room and discussed the interview.

"I don't know what to make of this guy, Tim." John commented as he shook his head. "He definitely knows the victim and claims to know where he lived but he doesn't know for sure if he was the person that spoke to the waitress. He's a weird duck!"

"Do you think he's fishing for information, trying to find out what we know?"

"I thought that too for a while, but I don't think so. He appears to want to help but has nothing to offer. He is actually a nice guy. You can't get mad at him. If you did, he would break down and cry." John was frustrated. "Let's test him. We'll ask if he'll give us a copy of his fingerprints to compare to the crime scene and for a D.N.A. sample. We should also ask him to point out the victim's house and the coffee shop where Mr. X went and spoke to the waitress."

"All right! But you do remember, we don't have any unknown fingerprints or D.N.A. at that scene," Tim replied.

"I'm guessing that he doesn't know that!"

John and Tim returned to the interview room and asked Pierce Alfonso to voluntarily provide his fingerprints and a D.N.A. sample so they could compare it to evidence from the crime scene. Alfonso agreed without any hesitation. He was only too happy to assist the officers.

The detectives then drove Alfonso to the area of Stuart Killen's home in Ballinlough. There was no doubt that Alfonso had been there before as he had no problem directing them and pointing out Killen's house. But Alfonso failed miserably in pointing out the coffee shop. The detectives did not tell him he had failed that test.

When they returned to Garda Headquarters, Pierce Alfonso was asked to wait again in the dingy interview room.

"I'm pretty sure this fella has nothing to offer this investigation, Tim. But something doesn't sit right. I don't know what it is."

"Do you want to take another run at him? Maybe turn the heat up a bit?" Tim suggested.

"No, I don't think that is the way to approach this guy. What about a polygraph?"

"Why not! We got nothing to lose," Tim agreed.

John returned to Interview Room # 1 and asked Pierce Alfonso if he was willing to take a polygraph test in order to rule him out of the homicide investigation. Again, without any hesitation, Alfonso agreed to the test. Tim Warren contacted the polygraph examiner and the appointment was made for the following Wednesday.

WEDNESDAY DECEMBER 17th.

On Wednesday morning, John and Tim met Pierce Alfonso outside his place of work on Washington Street and drove him to the polygraph appointment. Alfonso was nervous as he did not know what to expect. His only knowledge of polygraphs was what he had seen in movies.

On arrival at the office, Alfonso was directed into the room where the examination would take place and was left alone. Alfonso's anxiety level was rising as he looked around the room, taking in the computer equipment strategically placed next to his chair.

The polygraph examiner met with John and Tim and explained that he wanted Alfonso's anxiety to rise as this would give him a clearer result in the test that was to follow. He did not want Alfonso in a relaxed state. The examiner explained that after setting a baseline with basic questions, he would present Alfonso with ten different weapons that could have been used to kill Stuart Killen.

- Gun
- Knife
- Baseball bat
- Hammer
- Golf club
- Saw
- Rope
- Crow-bar

- Axe
- Hands and Feet.

If Alfonso has any knowledge of what was used to kill the victim, the results would show in the polygraph test.

The polygraph examiner, Sergeant Donald Caufield, was a tall, thin man, with an outgoing personality. When he met with Alfonso in the examination room, he immediately put him at ease but didn't allow him time to calm down. Alfonso liked Caufield and again it appeared that he wanted to cooperate with the investigators.

Alfonso answered all the examiner's introductory questions truthfully.

When it came to the ten assorted weapons, the examiner asked; "Did you kill Stuart Killen with a gun?" and so on.

Alfonso answered" NO" to all the questions and at the end of the four-hour test, the examiner met with the investigators.

"Well, John, Pierce Alfonso passed the polygraph test. In my expert opinion, Pierce Alfonso knows absolutely nothing about the murder of Stuart Killen."

"Thanks, Donald. We'll get him out of your hair," John replied.

John and Tim thanked Pierce Alfonso for trying to assist them and decided to write him out of this investigation. They drove Pierce back to work and never expected to hear from him again.

PRESENT DAY, SUNDAY December 21ˢᵗ.

After abandoning his packing and leaving all the travel preparation to his wife, it was now mid- afternoon. John pulled into the carpark at Garda Headquarters on Anglesea Street. The weather was worse in the city than on the coast and the rain poured down so hard that it was actually bouncing off the ground. The wind, blowing from the north east, had picked up. John pulled his collar close around his neck as he felt the ice in the wind and the cold rain running down his head.

"Maybe for once the weatherman has got it right and this could easily turn to snow," John thought.

John made the short walk to the Garda Station, and as he ran up the steps he met his partner, Detective Garda Tim Warren.

"I got to ask Boss, what the hell are we doing talking to this moron again? He passed the polygraph. What more can he tell us?" It was plain to see that Tim was quite frustrated

"What did you have going on, on the Sunday before Christmas?" John asked.

"My daughter had dance practice and then we were going to finish off some Christmas shopping. But here we are on another Sunday, talking to assholes!" Clearly, Tim was not impressed.

"I am well and truly in the doghouse too. I was actually putting my underwear and socks in a suitcase, packing to leave for Northern Ireland in a few hours," John grumbled. "We have to be on the road first thing in the morning and the weather doesn't look like it's going to cooperate."

The two detectives walked up the stairs to the second floor where the Serious Crime Incident Room was located. They shared the second floor of the Garda Headquarters with CID and The Organized Crime Unit. The Forensic Identification Unit was also located on the second floor but in a completely separate wing. John unlocked the door to the Incident Room and Tim walked over to the thermostat and turned up the heat.

"It's like a butcher's walk-in freezer here. It's colder than a witch's tit!" Tim muttered. It was obvious he was going to complain about everything today.

The detectives walked to their desks and started up their computers when Sergeant Ken Scott, from the Criminal

Investigation Division knocked on the door, opened it and walked into the Incident Room.

Before John could say a word, Sergeant Scott spoke, "Don't start!" as he held up the palm of his right hand. "He is in Interview Room # 1. He says he remembers some other things about the last time he saw Stuart Killen and he only wants to speak to you. No one else will do,"

"So let's get this over with as quickly as possible!" Tim Warren stood up, ready to go.

Both John and Tim knew that it wasn't CID's fault. Sergeant Scott was on duty and would have gladly spoken with Pierce Alfonso. However, Alfonso was, after all, a 'different' individual. John quickly checked his email, saw that there was nothing urgent, grabbed his notebook and walked directly to Interview Room # 1, followed by Tim. They didn't bother to turn on the recording equipment. They did not think it was necessary and this interview was not going to be worth recording.

Interview Room # 1 was the closest room to the Incident Room. Each of the seven interview rooms was approximately four meters by four meters and wired for audio and video recording because the rooms were used for both suspect and witness interviews.

The detectives brought two regular office chairs into the room. Pierce Alfonso sat in the only other chair in Interview Room # 1, the one that was bolted to the floor. He had spent his time waiting by reading the graffiti that had been etched into the top of the steel table.

"Well Pierce, what brings you back here today?" John asked in a tone that suggested he wasn't in the mood for socializing. He sat down, putting his closed notebook on top of the table.

Pierce Alfonso actually squirmed in his seat. He turned slightly sideways in his chair. His legs were crossed at the ankles. Pierce placed his joined hands between his knees and looked at his feet.

"I've remembered some more details about the day before Stuart's body was discovered," Alfonso whispered.

"You are going to have to try to speak up, Pierce. The boss is getting old and he's getting hard of hearing," Tim joked as his boss shot him a dirty look across the room.

Pierce Alfonso looked at Tim and tried to smile. He continued in a low voice, "I met Stuart that day. I picked him up at his house and drove him to the supermarket to get some groceries. I know that because I paid for them. Fifty-eight euros. I found the transaction in my bank statement for August."

"How is it that you are only remembering this now?" John silently scolded himself for the stern way he asked the question.

"I don't know. This has been bothering me since last week, when I saw the news report about the coffee shop. I believe that I must know something about this and last night I remembered going to the supermarket. I dug out my old bank statement and there it was, Fifty-eight euros at the grocery store."

"Do you have the bank statement with you?"

Alfonso said he had left it at home.

"Pierce, were you in Stuart's house that day when you took him to the supermarket?" John enquired less harshly.

Pierce Alfonso looked very uncomfortable as he glanced around the room; it was as if he was checking to see if anyone else was listening.

"I went over there in the morning and Stuart and I were starting to fool around. He told me he needed groceries, so I said I would take him to the supermarket and after we could fool around again."

"What do you mean, 'fool around'? John had to know. He had to get Pierce to be specific. "Do you mean to be intimate, even have sex?"

"Yes," Alfonso blushed as he answered in a whisper.

"It's okay, Pierce. We are not here to judge you or make fun of you. This is important. We just want to know what you know," John reassured him. "Did you go back to his house after you took him shopping?"

"When we went back to his place, we went to his bedroom and 'made out.' But then we started to argue." Alfonso was barely audible. "I don't remember much more than this. It's all a blur."

"That's okay. You're doing really well." John smiled at his witness, trying desperately to keep him calm. "Why were you arguing?" John asked, keeping his voice low and unintrusive.

Pierce Alfonso felt very much at ease speaking with the inspector, listening to the North Side Cork City accent. "Stuart told me he had AIDS. I was shocked when he said this. I asked him why he hadn't told me before. I would have used protection." Pierce, upset, pleaded for sympathy and understanding.

"Of course, you were shocked, Pierce. I can see why you were annoyed, even hurt and betrayed. Tell me about this argument. Were you yelling at each other? Or did it get physical? You know, pushing and shoving." John wanted to keep this conversation rolling.

"It was mostly yelling. But I did shove him."

"So, tell me now Pierce, where did this argument happen? Where did it take place?"

"It was all over his place. We started arguing in the bedroom and then all over the house."

John looked Pierce Alfonso in the eye, "Where did it end, Pierce?"

Pierce paused for a few seconds while he thought about this question.

"On his sofa," he whispered and his eyes filled with tears.

John looked across at his partner. The detectives could not believe what they had just heard from this man. This man who had passed a polygraph a few days earlier. Now Pierce Alfonso was telling his interviewers that he was with their homicide victim the day before the body was found. Pierce argued with the victim about AIDS after they had unprotected sex. And the argument ended on the sofa. The same sofa that the victim was killed on. A piece of holdback evidence that was only known to a handful of police officers and the killer.

"We're going to stop you here for a few minutes, Pierce. Tim and I are going to step out and when we come back, we have a few things to go over with you and we can continue this discussion if you want. Is that okay?" John was trying hard to hide his excitement.

John and Tim left the interview room and went to find Ken Scott. Scott was in his office, surfing the Internet. He did not want to delve into any work four days before Christmas. John asked him if he could help them out for a few hours; they had to record the rest of the interview with Pierce Alfonso and now treat him as a suspect.

"Holy fuck, Ken! He just told us he was with Killen the day before his body was found. After they made out, they had a huge argument that turned to pushing and shoving and the argument ended on the sofa. That's where we found Killen's dead body," John was speaking quickly, eager to finally close this cold case.

"Glad to help. There's only so much solitaire and online shopping I can do," the sergeant replied.

John and Tim returned to Pierce while Ken Scott turned on the recording equipment in Interview Room # 1. Before entering the room, John told Tim that he didn't think that Alfonso was smart enough or experienced enough to try to fool the police and deliberately lie. John really believed Alfonso was responsible for the death of Stuart Killen but for whatever reason, Alfonso was having trouble remembering all the details.

With the recording equipment now turned on, John and Tim entered the interview room, with the intention of arresting Pierce Alfonso for murder.

"Pierce, there are a few very important things I have to tell you before we continue with our conversation." John remained very calm and relaxed.

"I told you everything I remember," Pierce said in his usual murmured voice, barely making eye contact.

"I know you did. And I believe everything you told me," John reassured the scared man. "But I think there is more. You just haven't remembered it yet. Listen now very carefully. I have turned on the recording equipment in this room, so everything we do and say in here from now on will be recorded. Are you okay with that?"

Alfonso nodded in agreement.

"Pierce, right now, I am arresting you for murder or a similar offence. Do you understand?" John asked.

Alfonso squirmed in his chair and brought his hands up to his face, "Oh my God! Murder?"

"Yes, Pierce, murder." John provided Alfonso with his legal rights and the usual police caution.

Alfonso looked completely overwhelmed but told John and Tim that he understood his rights. He didn't ask to speak with a lawyer so John continued his gentle interrogation.

The first thing the detectives had to do was get Alfonso to repeat everything he had told them earlier, so it could be recorded under charge and caution. Alfonso did not hold back; he repeated everything and added more.

"When Stuart told me he had AIDS, I focused on his index finger. He had a big open sore on that finger. It had been there for months. I started to panic. I really believed the reason it hadn't healed was because he had AIDS. It made sense to me." Alfonso was almost in tears, recalling this detail.

"When you were making out with Stuart, did he touch you with that finger? Did he put it inside you? It's okay to be embarrassed, but like I said before, we are not here to judge you. You are still the same

Pierce Alfonso we spoke with last week." John was trying very hard to sound kind and caring.

"Yes. He touched me with his finger. I couldn't get it out of my head. I was so angry. I remember being angry, I was never that mad before in my entire life," Alfonso sounded more determined than he had in any of his previous conversations with these officers.

"And you will never be that angry again, Pierce. But I get it, anyone would have been angry. Stuart let you down. He should have told you he was ill." John was blaming the victim, making his prisoner feel more at ease with the situation. "What did you hit him with?" John thought it may have been a bit early to ask a direct question but he did it anyway. He could always work back to it again and again if need be.

Alfonso told the detectives he could not remember if he hit Stuart Killen with anything. John looked over at Tim and nodded his head slightly. This was a signal for Tim to ask a few questions. Tim Warren went over the entire story from the start. Alfonso didn't falter. Nothing changed in his story. But when it came to striking the victim with a weapon, Alfonso claimed he could not remember.

Throughout the entire interview Alfonso never denied that he was responsible for killing Stuart Killen, He simply said he could not remember if or how he killed him. After over four hours of constant conversation, it was time for a break. The detectives left Pierce Alfonso alone but he remained on camera.

"What do you think?" Tim asked his boss.

"I don't know what to think! Actually, I really think he doesn't remember everything that happened that day. It's like he is struggling with his memory or he could have blanked it out. He could have some form of post traumatic stress after the murder. I'm going to make a call."

John called the police psychologist, Dr, David Wilson, who was contracted to assist officers with their personal problems but was also open to assisting in investigations. John explained to the doctor the scenario he was facing with a very mild-mannered, shy suspect, whom he believed in a fit of rage had killed his sexual partner. John asked Dr. Wilson if Pierce Alfonso's lack of memory could be a case of post traumatic stress.

"It's impossible to say without speaking with the man for several hours," Doctor Wilson responded as he pondered the situation. "But you are describing a normally gentle, quiet, shy individual who claims that he felt his life was threatened because his sexual partner disclosed that he had AIDS. It is possible that your suspect flipped out. He could have lost his temper beyond all control and flew into a violent rage and now has pushed that memory to some dark corner of his brain." The psychologist blew out a long breath and continued, "It's a fascinating scenario. I wish I was able to interview him."

Dr. Wilson thanked the detective for consulting with him and asked him to let him know the outcome as he wished he could be present or at least watch the interview. The psychologist also advised John to continue with easy questions for Alfonso such as the color of the walls in the deceased's house and the type of flooring in different rooms. This line of questioning would assist in memory recall.

John called Jules; she didn't answer and he was slightly relieved because he knew she would not be happy that he was still at work. He left a message, sounding rather sheepish, "This is taking a bit longer than we expected but it's going very well. We should be wrapping it up soon. Tim and I are going back into the interview room so I won't be able to answer if you call. Love you, bye!"

John and Tim returned to the interview room. They quickly recapped everything that had been discussed earlier. Then John introduced some memory jogging questions.

"What kind of covers did Stuart have on his windows? Blinds, drapes or net curtains?" John knew the answer but hoped it would help his suspect with his memory.

The look on Alfonso's face changed as he was genuinely searching his memory, "He had heavy, dark brown drapes in the bedroom, blue drapes and net curtains in the living room and a roll-down blind on the kitchen window." Alfonso looked pleased with himself for remembering.

"That's very good that you remembered that, Pierce. Well done," John congratulated him. "Now the sofa in the living room. Was it a two-seater, a three or four-seater or one of those sectional sofas that fit in a corner?"

That was an easy one for Alfonso. "It was a three-seater sofa."

"Was it leather or cloth or something else?"

"It was a tan colored imitation leather thing. It looked really cheap." Alfonso was really chuffed with himself for answering all the questions.

It was time to steer Pierce Alfonso back to the subject of the murder. "How did you feel later that day? How did you feel when you got home?" John asked.

Pierce paused and appeared to search his memory. "I felt an evil presence. I have never felt such a strong evil presence,"

"Have you felt an evil presence in other situations?"

"My family is very religious and they don't know that I am gay. Sometimes I feel that evil presence when I am not being truthful to them."

"I'm sure they would understand and accept you for who you are. There is nothing wrong with you and you are not doing anything wrong because you are gay," John replied as he leaned into the man and patted his shoulder.

Pierce smiled at the detective.

Now was the time to try to return to the subject of the murder weapon. Again, John asked Alfonso what he used to kill Stuart Killen.

"I keep thinking about the list that the other detective had on Wednesday."

"Do you mean the list of weapons that Sergeant Caulfield mentioned in the polygraph exam?" Tim asked.

Alfonso nodded in agreement.

"Well now, lets go through the list of weapons," John suggested as he pulled his chair closer to Alfonso, looked him directly in the eye and held his gaze. "You list the weapons off and I'll ask you questions."

"I don't remember them all, but there was a gun," Pierce said in his usual whisper.

"Did you shoot Stuart Killen with a gun?"

"NO! Definitely not!" Alfonso looked horrified at the thought. "There was also a knife."

"Did you stab or slash Stuart with a knife?"

"NO! I did not...there was a crow-bar too."

Did you hit Stuart with a crow-bar?" John asked calmly.

Alfonso paused and looked down at his feet, then up at the ceiling. "No," but he paused and looked the inspector in the eye. "I think I swung something at him."

"And to be clear, Pierce, you don't think it was a crow-bar that you swung at Stuart?"

Alfonso sat silently, squirming in his chair, with his hands joined between his legs. Then he pulled his hands up to his face. "OH MY GOD! I HIT STUART WITH A GOLF CLUB." That was the loudest Pierce Alfonso had ever spoken to the detectives.

John flashed Tim Warren a quick smile. Ken Scott, who had been watching the interview on a TV in the monitor room, stood up and punched the air. "YES!" he yelled. It was as if his favourite soccer team had scored a goal in a championship match.

Pierce Alfonso was close to tears as he had just realized that he had killed his lover. John and Tim wanted more details from him.

They asked Alfonso how many times he hit the victim with the golf club.

"Three of four times I think," Alfonso whispered.

"What else did you do to Stuart?" Tim Warren was now asking the difficult questions.

It was a tactic the detective team had developed over the last year. One of them would get a confession but still appear to be on the side of the suspect, while the other asked the more difficult questions after the initial confession.

Tears flowed freely down Alfonso's cheeks. His upper lip trembled. He tried to speak but gasped as he sobbed loudly. "It's too awful to say."

"I think you need to come out and say it, Pierce. I know it sounds awful. I will not judge you. As far as I am concerned you are still the same Pierce Alfonso that I met last week. But you need to say this out loud. Do not let it beat you. Do not keep it inside," John stressed in his soft Cork accent, urging the man to say more, as he leaned over and reassuringly patted Alfonso on the knee.

"I chopped off his finger with a scissors," Alfonso blurted out between deep sobs. "And I stuck the shaft of the golf club into his stomach. OH MY GOD! WHAT HAVE I DONE?"

The detectives didn't need any more. Pierce Alfonso had confessed to killing his lover and disclosed information about the death that only the killer and the police knew. When Alfonso had calmed down a little, he was left alone in the interview room.

It was nearly 9:00 PM when the detectives left the interview room. Ken Scott met them outside the room.

"We need to get that bank statement that he mentioned earlier. It shows that he was at the supermarket buying groceries for the victim," John said.

Sergeant Scott nodded in agreement.

"For fuck sakes, Boss. We need a search warrant to get that and you have to go to Northern Ireland in a few hours and I have to finish my Christmas shopping...IF our wives don't kill us first," Tim groaned.

John called Jules and he explained that he had to get a search warrant but it shouldn't take long. He would be home in a couple of hours and told her not to wait up. She slammed down the phone!

John, proficient in applying for search warrants and other judicial authorizations, started to prepare an affidavit for a search warrant for Pierce Alfonso's apartment. No matter how capable he was, he knew it would take at least six pages of information to get all the appropriate material down for the on-call judge.

Shortly after midnight, John called the on-call judge. He woke her up at home and requested an audience. She wasn't too pleased with him either.

John asked Sergeant Scott to continue to monitor Pierce Alfonso in case he tried to kill himself and he and Tim drove to the judge's home. She opened the door in her housecoat, showed them into her kitchen and excused herself as she went into the living room to read the affidavit.

"I guess it's too late for tea and dainties," Tim whispered to his partner.

Fifteen minutes later the judge granted the search warrant. The officers left the judge's home and drove at warp speed to Alfonso's apartment. On the way they activated the emergency lights and siren in their unmarked police car to avoid any further delay.

Pierce Alfonso had provided them with a key and told them where the bank statement was stored. At the residence, they met an officer from the Forensic Unit. Once inside the apartment, the forensic officer took some photographs and seized the document. Then they raced back to the station.

On the journey back, John called the senior on-call prosecutor on his cell phone. After waking the lawyer up, John told him about the circumstances of the confession. The prosecutor authorized a charge of murder for Pierce Alfonso. Tim Warren finished the necessary paperwork to lock up Alfonso and delivered him to the police lockup in the basement of the Garda station.

John ran to his car. It was now 2:15AM; he planned to be on the road in less than five hours. He prayed his car would start as it was now bitterly cold. It did. He raced home to Inchydoney, making it in record time. He crept into the house at 2:50AM, slid into bed next to his wife, without making a sound.

"Thank God, she's asleep," he thought. He closed his eyes.

"ABOUT FUCKING TIME!" she snapped.

"Sorry," was all he could manage and they caught a few of hours' sleep.

Chapter 2

Three and a half hours later the alarm clock rang. Jules jumped out of bed and although still angry with her husband, she let him sleep for another half hour.

Jules started on breakfast; she was glad that the dogs were with her aunt and she didn't have to let them out as it was freezing. She brought her husband a cup of coffee and gently woke him.

John dragged his ass out of bed, shattered and drained after the effort he put into interviewing Pierce Alfonso. He glanced at his wife who wasn't saying much, still annoyed at him for getting home so late.

Jules eventually broke the silence. "So, what was so important that you couldn't get home at a reasonable hour?"

He chose his words carefully before answering as this was not the day for an argument. "After the first couple of hours, speaking with this guy, I realized he had killed Stuart Killen. But I had no physical evidence to link him to it. I had to get a confession and it took a while. I've never had an interview like that before. It was so weird. I think he had blanked out his memory and we had to coax the confession out of him."

"I don't know why you couldn't beat it out of him!" Jules teased said with a glint in her eye.

"Somehow I don't think that would have worked on this guy."

"You got him now? It's all wrapped up? Paddy Collins won't be pestering you for the next few days on the phone or through emails?" Jules said setting the ground rules for their trip to Northern Ireland.

"Tim can tidy up any loose ends that pop up, but it's not really a vacation in Belfast. I have to do some work while we are up there and if someone from here needs to ask me something, I'm technically on the clock."

"Whatever!" Jules sighed. "Now get your ass in gear! The dogs knew there was something going on last night, before you took them to Nan's. They were looking at the suitcases. I think they wanted to come with us and not go to Bandon."

By 9:15 the Cahills were on the road. They had driven through Cork City and were on the M8, towards the toll booth at Watergrasshill. John checked his mirrors, looking back towards the city. Part of him was hoping he would not miss any new homicides and another part of him was dreading what could be waiting for him upon his return to Cork.

BACK IN CORK CITY'S North Side, five men sat around the kitchen table in a compact townhouse in Manor View Estate. All five were members of one of Cork's most notorious street gangs, the Independent Posse.

Like most of the homes in Manor View Estate, this one was small with three compact bedrooms and one bathroom upstairs. The main floor had a small sitting room leading into the efficient kitchen that doubled as a dining room. This home was the last house in a row of four townhouses.

Manor View Estate was built in the early 1970's, among much fanfare, when the Irish Prime Minister, known as the Taoiseach cut the first sod. There was no manor to view, only the large ugly concrete water reservoir in Knocknaheeny. Manor View Estate was built to provide affordable housing for working class families, in the hope of establishing a strong sense of community. However, many people looked at the estate as a public housing experiment gone horribly wrong because of the terrible social and economic problems that existed there. As time passed and unemployment in the area grew, gangs and drug dealers were the only ones thriving.

This particular home in Manor View was well kept. Trish Langford lived here with her three children and her mother. Most people in the neighborhood knew her as Trish Galvin. Her common-law husband, Georgy Galvin, was one of the top men in the Independent Posse. Georgy and Trish had a strange relationship. He did not live with her but came around whenever he felt like it. She was fine with this open arrangement as Georgy was a good provider. Trish knew where the money came from and didn't care; she too, had been entrenched in the gang lifestyle in her younger days.

Today, Trish, her mother and the kids made themselves scarce. Her brother-in-law, Mikey Galvin, was holding a council meeting in her kitchen. Mikey, known to everyone, including the police as 'Mikey G', sat at the head of the wooden table. The kitchen was bright and clean, with pastel blue walls. Ironically, in the midst of these evil drug dealing gangsters, a crucifix hung on the wall behind Mikey Galvin.

At thirty-three years old, Mikey G stood five feet eleven inches and weighed around eighty kilos. He had a muscular build, dark curly hair and liked to wear snappy, expensive casual clothes. Although he lacked education, he had a magnificent mind for business and was the 'President' of the Independent Posse street gang. Mikey G had a reputation for being ruthless; he had a propensity for violence and nobody crossed him. Mikey was in a common-law relationship with Tess Rutherford. They had two children, a boy, aged eight and a five- year- old girl. Tess was terrified of Mikey although they had been together for years.

Mikey G's brother, Georgy, sat on his right. Georgy was shorter and heavier than Mikey with long greasy hair, usually worn in a ponytail. Georgy dressed like a slob. He was a follower, not a leader but Georgy was very dangerous and would do anything his brother asked without question or considering the consequences.

On Mikey G's left sat Johnny Johnson. He was thirty-four years old of average height with a thin build. Johnny also had long greasy hair worn in a ponytail. He had a pock-marked face and walked with a limp. A couple of years earlier, Johnny shot himself in the left leg when he grabbed a gun from his waistband, pulled the trigger and shot himself in the upper thigh, causing significant permanent ligament damage. Johnny was an enforcer for the Independent Posse.

Next to Johnny Johnson sat Tyson Rolland. Tyson, only twenty-four years old, was tall and well built. He kept his fair colored hair short and neat. He dressed well but could tone it down if needed. Tyson's arms and body were covered in tattoos and each told a different story, mostly tales of violence. Tyson was a loyal Independent Posse member and had a very dangerous look about him. What made him even more dangerous was he was very ambitious!

Across from Tyson sat his close friend, Darryl Lyons. Darryl, the same age as Tyson, was also tall and well built. He kept his hair in a buzz cut and had a birth mark under his right eye resembling a tear drop tattoo. Darryl was also very violent but unlike his best friend Tyson, had no ambition to rise within the organization. Darryl was a loyal soldier. However, Darryl was more loyal to Tyson than to Mikey G.

TO OUTSIDERS, THE INDEPENDENT Posse appeared to be a disorganized street gang that fought with other rival gangs for inches of territory. However, the Independent Posse controlled over one third of all the drug trade in Cork's North Side.

Mikey G, with his brother Georgy by his side, ruled with an iron fist. Mikey had several lieutenants including the ones who sat around the table with him. Each of these lieutenants ran part of the illicit drug and prostitution/human trafficking trade but all major decisions were made by the gang president, Mikey G.

The Independent Posse's territory encompassed most of the North Side of Cork City. They were strongest in Manor View Estate, Knocknaheeny, Churchfield, Farranree, Blackpool and The Glen but also operated in Mayfield, Dillons Cross and Ballyvolane. Some of the poorest people in Cork City lived in these areas and Mikey G knew exactly how to take advantage of them and their desperate situations.

Rumor had it that Mikey G moved around ninety ounces of cocaine and crystal methamphetamine every month. His cost on this was somewhere in the region of 145,000 euros. But after he cut it down and converted it into crack cocaine, he easily tripled his cost, earning him 445,000 euros, tax free before expenses.

Mikey ran a very smooth operation because nobody would ever dare rip him off. To do so could be fatal. Had Mikey G gone to business school, he would probably be the chief financial officer of a large corporation. On any given day he ran between ten and fifteen crack shacks throughout the gang's territory. Crack shacks are like twenty-four-hour storefronts, where the addicts can walk up to the door, day or night and purchase their drugs. Cork had been a cocaine town for years, but crystal methamphetamine was starting to edge its way into the drug subculture.

But being the businessman that he was, Mikey G had several different ways to peddle his venom. He also ran mobile sales units, commonly known as a Dial a Dealer. This was not Mikey G's preferred sales outlet as it was less profitable to operate. He had to recruit drivers with valid licenses and properly insured vehicles. He also had to supply cell phones and pay for phone plans.

Mikey preferred female drivers; they didn't draw as much attention from the police as male drivers did. Nothing drew attention from the Garda quicker than three or four young guys driving around in a vehicle. But the Garda would rarely give a second glance at a woman driving with one or two male passengers. And Mikey didn't discriminate by age either. Drug addicts came in all shapes, sizes and ages. Mikey had often put a grandmother driving one of his mobile distribution units and had children as young as ten years old as runners in his crack shacks.

Mikey G's point of sale preference was the crack shack operation. He had less overhead and there was never a problem finding suitable real estate. He would select an addict who had a home, a suite in an apartment block or a bed-sit in a rooming house. Then he would move the gang in and set up shop. Mikey would provide the official residents of the shacks with a little bit of crack cocaine or crystal meth to feed their own habit, just enough to keep them happy and quiet. Mikey G had no problem piecing off some drugs on a daily basis for the occupants. There was never a complaint from the residents because they were getting free drugs and they knew Mikey G's reputation of being a vicious tyrant who was not to be crossed.

To operate a crack shack, Mikey G appointed a manager, sales people and a security staff. The manager was responsible for keeping the drugs in stock and was also accountable for the money. The manager could buy the drugs directly from Mikey G and sell them at a profit; however, he had to pay 'tax' to Mikey G on the profit as well.

The sales staff were usually kids, between the ages of ten and sixteen. Their job was to run the drugs from inside the shack to the customer and collect the money. Nobody would dare short change even a ten-year-old in this business.

The security staff were always thugs...low level gang bangers who liked to play with weapons and had no issues using them. Most of them had been in prison at one time or another.

The security staff wasn't in place just to protect the drugs and cash. They often had to defend the crack shack from a raid by rival gang members. This type of raid could consist of an all-out attack by armed thugs who would invade the home, steal as much merchandise and cash as they could and beat up anyone that got in their way. Gunfire was often exchanged in these encounters and occasionally people had been killed.

The Independent Posse's biggest rivals were the Mahon Warlords. This ruthless gang operated a similar drug enterprise in the South Side of the city. The River Lee that ran through Cork's City Center formed a natural boundary. The Independent Posse members referred to the Mahon Warlords as Guppies, (little fish in the big pond), and the Mahon Warlords referred to the Independent Posse as Slobs, (because of their scruffy appearance). This childlike name calling sounded like something from the elementary school playground but often led to extreme violence which had resulted in the death of a gang banger on more than one occasion. This rancorous rivalry was not only prevalent on the streets of Cork, It was also rampant throughout Ireland's prisons. Prison authorities had to take extreme measures to separate these gang members in the different institutions especially around Cork.

Georgy ran the sex trade / human trafficking side of the business for the Independent Posse. Georgy managed around thirty girls at any given time. He 'allowed' these girls to work in the Independent Posse territory and they had to pay him fifty percent of what they earned. Georgy referred to this as a tax. Several of these women were nothing more than slaves, having ended up in Ireland from as far away as Eastern Europe and North Africa. Georgy had an arrangement with another gang in Dublin who sent these unfortunate souls to work in Cork. None of the girls would dare to rip Georgy off as he often parked on the street and watched them ply their trade. Georgy and his thugs would thump anyone who crossed him, be it one of the girls or one of her customers. The most unfortunate thing about the plight of these girls was they were all addicted to drugs and spent any money they had on the poison that they had to buy from Mikey G's crack shacks or Dial a Dealer. The Independent Posse and Mahon Warlords preyed on some of Cork's most vulnerable citizens.

TODAY MIKEY G HAD CALLED his lieutenants together to discuss a problem that had arisen with two of his soldiers in one of his crack shacks.

"Do you all remember last week, when one of our shacks on Blarney Street was raided by the Mahon Warlords?"

The others all nodded and grumbled.

"We lost a lot of product ...at least six ounces of crack and another six ounces of meth. and a chunk of cash. A couple of the little kids got roughed up too. What have you heard?" Galvin quizzed his audience as he looked around the table at each one of them.

"It was the M-W! We'll just raid them back next week," Johnny Johnson laughed, sticking his tongue out as far as he could and went "AHHH HAHA"! in his unique way of laughing.

"Too right, Johnny. We'll raid them next week, maybe even this week. The M-W did raid us, but they did not rip us off!" Mikey sounded very serious and again looked around the table, slower this time and held the gaze of each of his lieutenants.

"What the fuck?" Georgy asked as he sat up straight, holding his arms in front of him and clenching his fists.

"One of your girls, Rosie, the Nigerian chick, was crashing on the sofa, when the M-W came in. The Guppies slapped a couple of the kids around and punched out some old guy who was buying crack. They got scared and ran off when Eddie Flynn came charging down the stairs. Eddie chased them up the lane with a machete. That's when Rosie saw Julian and Alvin steal the cash and the stash. When Eddie came back, they told him that the M-W got everything."

"Rosie's a fucking crack head. Do you believe her?" Georgy asked.

Mikey grinned at his brother, "Do you think she would lie to me? I'd fucking kill her and cut her up into little pieces. She knows that I would do that! Plus, she has no reason to make that up."

"What are we going to do about it?" Tyson Rolland asked, in a low but serious voice. It was the first time he spoke during this meeting.

Mikey G looked at his young ambitious lieutenant. "What are you going to do about it, Tyson? Half a key, if you take care of the problem," Mikey G said with a sly grin.

"Problem solved." Rolland laughed as he looked across at his best friend and rubbed his hands together.

Half a kilo of cocaine was worth 32,500 euros, Rolland and Lyons would cut it down and cook it into crack cocaine and sell it in a week, earning a sweet 100,000 euros

"Get it sorted. I don't want to know anything about it until it's done. Make sure they know why this is happening and before they move on to the next life. You better make sure it doesn't come back to me or you'll join them." Mikey G didn't smile when he said this. He wasn't known for his sense of humor and stared at Tyson as he spoke.

That was the end of the meeting. Not all the counsel members were present; they didn't need to be. They would find out soon enough that a hit had been ordered on two greedy gangsters.

Mikey G was the first to leave the meeting. He put on his black winter parka and pulled the hood up. He walked outside and sat behind the wheel of Georgy's green Volkswagen passenger van. Before he drove off, Johnny Johnson walked out the front door, also wearing a black winter parka, with his hood up. Johnson walked around the back of the house to the back lane. Seconds later, Tyson Rolland and Darryl Lyons walked out, also wearing black winter parkas, with the hoods up. One walked east on the street and the other walked west. If by chance the police were watching, they would have to pick a target and it was difficult to tell who was who. This was the curse of trying to do surveillance in Cork during the winter.

AFTER SEVERAL STOPS along the way for lunch, coffee and bathroom breaks, John and Jules finally arrived at their hotel in Belfast by 3:30.

"Holy Christ, I don't know which is worse. The nonstop lashing rain in Cork during the winter or the freezing cold and sleet here in Belfast," John grumbled as he shook the wet snow off his coat once inside the hotel lobby.

"You should be used to it, you worked here long enough. And it's not a very long winter compared to some places. Maybe if you got a full night's sleep before we left you wouldn't be so cranky," Jules shot back.

John didn't answer. He knew he had that one coming. They checked in at the desk and made their way to their comfortable room on the third floor. John kicked off his shoes and lay across the bed. "What's on the agenda?" he asked.

"Shut your eyes for half an hour, I'll call Janet and Fred and let them know we've arrived safely."

Jules didn't have to tell him twice. Within minutes John was sound asleep.

Jules called the Nesbits and arranged to meet them for dinner at the hotel restaurant. John and Jules were regulars at this hotel and tried to stay there every time John had to return to Belfast for training or meetings with his commanding officers in the PSNI. Jules looked forward to catching up with Janet as they had been friends and neighbors for several years. When John and Jules initially moved to Northern Ireland in 1994, they lived near Fred and Janet in (police) force housing, in a safe environment within a compound. Now that the 'Troubles' were over, Fred and Janet had moved to North Belfast, near Helen's Bay Beach.

With her husband sleeping, Jules studied the restaurant menu. After forty-five minutes she brewed a cup of coffee and woke John. A few sips later the caffeine kicked in and John started to slowly wake up. He freshened up and they made their way to the restaurant where they met their friends, Fred and Janet.

John and Fred met in the mid 1990's, when they were patients at the Royal Victoria Hospital in Belfast, both suffering from very serious injuries. The bond they had formed, all those years ago, was stronger than ever. Both men had faced extreme challenges, when life as they knew it, had been altered for ever.

John returned to his home in Inchydoney Beach, in West Cork. Prior to his accident he had trained a few racehorses and often rode them in races. However, the fall at Down Royal had ended that career. Despondent and facing an uncertain future, Fred Nesbit convinced his friend to join the Royal Ulster Constabulary, where he had a very successful career. John and Jules and their two young children moved to Belfast, where John's police career took off.

A few years after John joined the RUC, the police force transitioned into the Police Service of Northern Ireland. John was made a detective and was eventually assigned to the Serious Crime Unit. He quickly progressed through the ranks and while holding the rank of Detective Inspector, he had an opportunity to work in an Integrated Unit with the Garda in the Republic. With their children now grown up and living their own lives, John and Jules were lucky that they kept their home in Inchydoney, renting it out as a holiday home, while they lived in the North. When the opportunity arose to work in Cork City, the Cahills just went home. After two years with the Integrated Unit, John's boss in the Garda managed to transfer the policeman from Northern Ireland into a newly formed Serious Crime Unit in Cork City.

Fred Nesbit's life had also changed and he was now the Superintendent in Charge of Training for the PSNI. John and Fred talked shop during dinner, while Jules and Janet caught up on the normal things in life. After supper the Cahills returned to their room with the promise of visiting with Fred and Janet over the holidays.

As they walked past the front desk, the hotel receptionist acknowledged them, calling them by name and recognizing them as frequent visitors to this hotel. When they got back to their room John turned on the television and sat on an armchair.

Jules looked over at him, "You look exhausted, you should go to bed. I'm going to freshen up. If you're still up when I come out of the shower, maybe we'll go for a short walk."

Jules gave him a kiss on the cheek. He smiled back at her and closed his eyes, glad of the rest.

An hour later, Jules shook her husband awake. For a few seconds, he did not know where he was but as soon as he smelled the fresh brewed coffee, he quickly remembered he was in a hotel room back in Belfast. John sat up in the armchair, turned up the television and sipped the coffee Jules had poured for him. His senses felt numb. His head felt like it was in a vice and his eyes were heavy and burning. His sinuses were stuffed and he felt just awful. It was a feeling he had become all too familiar with since he started working in Cork's Serious Crime Unit. This time, he didn't know if it was the long day's journey followed by the big meal or the long hours he had put in interviewing Pierce Alfonso... or a combination of everything. John didn't say anything. While drinking his coffee, he just stared at some show on the local Northern Irish television station. Jules knew what he was going through and just let him be.

"I'll just jump in the shower. I'll be two minutes." He headed into the bathroom.

John stood under the steaming hot water with his hands on the wall, steadying himself. "I'm tired of being tired," he thought. "Why do I do this to myself?" He held his head up and let the hot water bounce off his face forcing the tiredness away. Ten minutes later he was dressed. "Okay, I'm ready, where are we going?"

"Are you sure? If you're are up to it, we can head over the bridge and go into town for a look around. The air will do you good," Jules suggested.

Jules loved Belfast's shopping area now compared to what it was like when they first moved to the North. Back in the 1990's there were security checkpoints everywhere, soldiers and police were all around and still there was danger lurking everywhere. During the 'Troubles,' almost 90% of all bomb attacks happened in Belfast. John knew it could still be a scary place and there were paramilitary subversives still skulking around but it was a million times better than it had been.

Belfast's city center was vibrant and alive despite the late hour. Some of the stores were still open, giving people a chance for last minute Christmas shopping. The sleet had stopped but the wind was bitterly cold with the temperature hovering around one degree. Belfast was usually about five or six degrees colder than Cork mostly due to its geographical location.

Jules and John walked across one of the many bridges over the River Lagan and down Ann Street. They turned onto Corn Market Street and then along Donegal Place. They came around to the shopping mall on Victoria Square and Jules went into a few of the stores and they soaked up the atmosphere. There were buskers on some of the pedestrianized streets and even a few carol singers.

"As much as I love Cork City at Christmas time, Belfast must be a very close second," Jules commented as she held her husband's hand and walked, happily smiling.

They were both enjoying the Christmas spirit in the city. They walked to the Cathedral Quarter and went into Saint George's Market. Jules loved this market as it reminded her of the English Market in Cork. She bought fresh Irish soda bread, cream cakes and flowers to bring to the Nesbit's.

"How about we go back to the hotel, eat the bread and the cakes, put the flowers in water and bring the flowers to Janet tomorrow? Fred doesn't need any cakes and he'll never know the difference," John suggested with a mischievous grin.

"Not a bad idea, but you don't need any more cream cakes either," Jules answered as she patted his stomach.

They walked back to the hotel. Jules asked the concierge for plates, margarine and a butter knife. After devouring half a loaf of soda bread, John finally ran out of steam and lay on the bed and fell into a deep well-earned sleep.

The next morning, Christmas Eve, John, wearing dress pants, dress shirt and sports coat, went to his meeting with the officer in charge of Human Resources at PSNI Headquarters on Knock Road. The headquarters were a series of buildings in a compound type setting, surrounded by a security fence. After identifying himself to the sentry at the front gate, John parked and walked into the office. The receptionist didn't recognize him and asked if he could help.

"I'm here to see Superintendent Nash, the OIC of Personnel," John stated.

"Do you have an appointment?" the young man asked.

"Not really, tell him DI John Cahill is here now. If he can't see me, I'll be back in a few months," John told him, checking his watch, giving the receptionist the idea that he wasn't going to waste much time here. John looked around the office, taking in the new modern tubular and leather furniture. The carpeted floor also looked new. "Hell of a budget here," he thought.

The young man phoned Superintendent Nash. Moments later, a door opened and Superintendent Nash walked out of his office. "Cahill?" he asked as he looked at the Detective Inspector.

"Yup," John replied and walked past the superintendent into the office and sat in a chair by the desk.

Superintendent Nash followed and sat on his chair at the other side of the desk. John watched him move. "A career administrator," he surmised. "Thank you for coming in. I thought you might call to make an appointment," Nash began as he picked up a folder from his desk and started to read. "I see you have been seconded to the Garda for almost three years now."

John nodded but did not answer.

"You were initially seconded to the Garda to work with an Integrated Fugitive Unit; however, I see that the squad has been disbanded. What are you doing now?"

"I'm surprised it doesn't say in your notes," John answered as he pointed to the folder in the man's hand. He could see this annoyed Nash. "I'm the officer in charge of the Serious Crime Unit in Cork City."

"Surely someone from their own police service could fulfill that role?"

"I don't doubt there are lots of people in the Garda that could do that job and probably way better than me," John replied.

"Maybe we should pull you back up here, where you belong," Nash said as he peered over the top of the file.

"Maybe YOU should," John said with a grin, stressing that it would be Nash's decision.

John knew that the reasons he had not been sent back to the PSNI were politically motivated and the chief constable of the PSNI and the Garda Commissioner both wanted him to remain in the Republic as long as he was doing great work there.

"You know I can arrange that transfer?"

"Yes, I know. We can all be transferred anywhere anytime that the chief decides. Now, we are here to discuss my Mandatory Inservice Training. If you think I should be transferred, sign the form and put in the appropriate paperwork. Who knows? Maybe we'll both end up working nightshift in Ardoyne or Divis Street."

Superintendent Nash backed down and addressed the Mandatory Training courses that John had come back to Northern Ireland to complete. After the meeting and shortly before noon, John drove back to the hotel. Jules had just returned from the Nesbit's' home near Helen's Bay Beach, where she and Janet had brunch.

"It's not as nice as Inchydoney, but it's nice enough," Jules told her husband. "The wind was howling out there. I thought Janet's little dog would blow away."

"It is the North Sea! And it's on the top end of the country. You can't get much farther north on this island."

"There are no palm trees here, that's for sure," Jules answered, referring to the short stumpy palm trees growing along the coast in West Cork as the Gulf Stream brought warmer air flows.

The Cahills headed into the city center to do some shopping as they would spend Christmas Day with their friends, the Nesbits.

JULIAN HODNETT AND Alvin Pomeroy lived with Julian's girlfriend, Crystal Mannering. Crystal had two young children, a boy aged five and a girl of three. They lived in a cozy two-bedroom apartment near The Lough. Julian and Crystal shared one bedroom; the kids had the other room and Alvin crashed on the couch. The Lough is a suburb in the South Side of Cork City, situated near University College Cork. The suburb derived its name from a shallow spring fed, freshwater lake that has been a wild bird preserve since the 1880's. The outer paved foot path around the lake is a little over one kilometer long, and usually frequented by walkers and joggers. This Christmas it was unusually cold and there was a thin sheet of ice forming on top of the lake.

Crystal Mannering was in her mid twenties. She had long black hair and piercing blue eyes. She worked part-time in a supermarket and had a bad habit of picking up losers for boyfriends. Although Julian was not the father of her children, he really liked the kids and was good with them. On Christmas Day, Julian and Alvin took great pleasure in showing the kids how to play with the X-Box. It was a very happy scene; anyone looking in from the outside world would never have guessed these young men were drug dealers and gang members.

A couple of days before Christmas, Julian and Alvin had been Christmas shopping using the money they stole from Mikey Galvin's crack shack. They bought a gently used sixty-inch plasma television from North Side Rentals, a store on Shandon Street that sold, leased and rented electronic equipment. Because the TV was second-hand and had been previously rented, the name 'North Side Rentals' was engraved into the back of the television. The two lads had also bought an X-Box video game system. Julian felt like a real provider because he gave Crystal money to buy Christmas dinner, a turkey, ham and all the trimmings. On Christmas Day, Crystal Mannering cooked a beautiful meal for all of them.

For the first time in years, Cork City had a white Christmas. It had snowed on Christmas Eve and although it was wet, heavy snow, it remained on the ground and accumulated to nearly five centimeters. Georgy and Mikey Galvin, with their wives and children, went to their mother's house on Fair Hill for dinner on Christmas Day. It actually looked like a normal family setting. There was no shortage of food and nobody had too much to drink.

Also, in the North Side of Cork City, Christmas Day meant nothing to Tyson Rolland and Darryl Lyons. They were hanging out in Tyson's house on the edge of Churchfield, situated in Cork's North Side between Farranree and Knocknaheeny.

Tyson's two-story terraced house was situated at the end of the terrace. There were four small windows at the front of the house, two up, two down. Inside, it was reasonably tidy and clean. The best way to describe it was as 'practical!'

Being a very smart operator, Tyson didn't sell anything illicit out of his home; he only conducted high level business from there. This was a day like any other day and he had work to do. If he could arrange the assassination of Julian Hodnett and Alvin Pomeroy he would be well on his way to one of the top spots in the Independent Posse. The two young men sat on a sofa in front of an oversized flat-screened television, playing Grand Theft Auto. Darryl paused the game.

"Who can you get to do this so it doesn't come back to you?" Darryl Lyons asked.

"How about you? Those two pukes would invite you into their home and you could cap them both in no time," Tyson said, fishing for an answer to see if his cohort was interested or not.

"Fuck that! If I get caught, I'm never getting out of prison with my record," Lyons said, shaking his head vigorously and having no part of the deadly plan.

Tyson took that as a no! In a way, he admired Lyons's lack of ambition and sense of contentment with his position within the gang.

"I have an idea. Hear me out and let me know what you think. Do you know my brother, Kenny?" Tyson Rolland had a half brother, Kenny Rolland. They had the same mother, hence the same last names, but different fathers.

"Isn't he in prison in England? Manchester or somewhere?" Lyons acknowledged.

"No, he got out last month. He did eighteen months of a three-year bit. Then they kicked his ass out of the country and told him not to come back. He's hunkered down in Galway or somewhere in the back of beyond. I was talking to him online last week."

"Is he coming back here?" Lyons asked.

"Not permanently. He was with some bizarre dudes in Manchester. He was hanging out with a crazy gang of Asians. He's hanging with some of their buddies in Galway and crashing with some chick. I think Kenny would do this for us. We wouldn't have to pay him much as he would do it just for the street creds." Tyson was very excited and looking for approval for his idea. "Do you have a burner phone? I'll call him up."

Lyons reached into his backpack and removed a brand new, cheap cellphone. He fished around in the bag for an envelope with a new SIM Card. These were tools of their trade and necessary for selling drugs. These phones and SIM Cards would only be used for a couple of weeks and then dumped in case the police were zoning in on their deadly venture.

Tyson inserted the card into the phone. There was a little bit of life in the battery, just enough for a call. Tyson pressed the numbers and waited for his call to be answered. "HO, HO, HO, Merry Fucking Christmas, Bro."

Kenny Rolland answered, "Merry fucking Christmas to you too! What do you want?"

"I got a job for you Bro. Two of our own guys ripped off one of Mikey G's shacks. They must pay. Are you up for it? You could slide into town; nobody would know you're are here. Take care of business and slide out again." Tyson made is sound so easy.

Kenny was interested, "Are these Warlords or our own guys? I'm not moving back to Cork. I don't need anything from Mikey G." Kenny tried to sound bored and tough.

"They're not Warlords. They're I-P. You probably know these two. They were hanging around the shacks before you went across the pond to England. Julian and Alvin, two skinny kids," Tyson answered.

"Don't know them! What's in it for me?".

"Seven ounces. That is ten grand...you cut it and turn it into thirty grand. But I want it done right away."

"K, man. Anything for my little bro. I'll borrow a car here and drive down there tomorrow or the next day. I'm too drunk to drive there now." Kenny accepted the contract.

"K, Bro, call me when you get to town. Did my number show up on your phone?"

"I got it. I'll see you before the end of the week."

IN BELFAST, NORTHERN Ireland, John and Jules spent Christmas Day with Fred and Janet Nesbit. Both couples were now empty nesters. Janet had gone all out to make a huge dinner and afterwards, the two couples sat around talking.

"What should we do tomorrow?" Janet asked. "You two are only here for another couple of days and John has to go to work for a few days."

"How about the races at Down Royal?" Fred suggested.

Jules glanced at her husband. Down Royal was where John's horseracing career ended when he fell from a horse named Cottagetime. The Cahills had not set foot on a racecourse since that day.

John caught his wife's glance and winked at her. "That might actually be a really good way to pass the day," John said, his voice full of confidence.

Later, on the ride back to the hotel, Jules asked if John was okay with going to the races, especially at Down Royal.

"It will be fine. I really never gave it a second thought. It's not like I was avoiding going to the races, I just had no interest in going back before now, especially when I didn't have a horse running."

At around 3:45AM, John sat up in the bed. For an instant he was in shock and the unfamiliar surrounding of the hotel room didn't help. He had been awakened by his recurring nightmare. He knew it would happen sooner or later after he wrapped up the Stuart Killen homicide. The nightmare usually came when he was investigating a new homicide or when he had wrapped one up. The only difference between this nightmare and the last time was that now Stuart Killen appeared in it.

John had dreamt that the mutilated corpse of Killen, with the shaft of the golf club protruding from his stomach and his brutally amputated finger, led a line of other grotesque zombie like corpses into his bedroom. All the other corpses were victims of homicides that John had investigated and all were in the same state that their bodies had been discovered. Over thirty mutilated homicide victims walked up to John and muttered something to him. After they mumbled their incoherent words, they turned and disappeared. John could never catch what they said. He had been having this nightmare regularly for over a year and it still scared the living daylights out of him.

As soon as he realized where he was, he looked over at his wife who was sleeping soundly. He shook himself, lay down and went back to sleep.

On the morning of Boxing Day, John and Jules drove the short distance to Helen's Bay Beach. The beach was almost deserted and the weather had not improved since Christmas Eve, still blustery and cold. There was a solitary dog walker who had two greyhounds in his care. John and Jules had to stop and watch when the dogs were let off their leashes and started to race along the beach, nipping at each other when one would try to get ahead of the other. They spoke with the dog's owner and told them about their two greyhounds in Cork. These two dogs on the beach were living their best lives after retiring from the Shelbourne Park Greyhound Racetrack, in Dublin.

Afterwards, as they walked to the Nesbits' home, John was having second thoughts about the races. "I don't know if I want to go. It's cold and damp here and I really don't want to run into anyone that we know from the past.

"Give your head a shake! It was arranged last night and I'm looking forward to it now. It's an hour's drive from Fred and Janet's place. We don't have to stay for all the races. You won't melt in the rain and nobody will recognize you. You haven't been around the racetracks for twenty years." Jules reassured him that it would be a good day.

An hour later, the four friends were walking into Down Royal Racecourse.

Jules looked across at her husband. He remained very quiet. She knew this was a very nostalgic visit for him.

Finally he felt her watching him and he spoke. "It is a long-ways from Inchydoney, isn't it? It's like a different world, a whole different universe and a step back in time," John said, smiling at his wife. "Not much has changed since the last time I was here. The course looks good. You know, I don't remember leaving here the last time."

Jules smiled as a tear formed in her eye and she squeezed his hand.

There were seven horse races on the card, four hurdle races, two steeplechase races and one flat race at the end of the day. Down Royal Racecourse is an almost square right-handed track nearly two miles around with ten fences. The feature race was a Group Two race, a Novice Steeple Chase. This race was reserved for high class horses that had never won a steeplechase race. The race was two and half miles long so the horses would run one full lap of the track plus another third with eleven fences to be jumped.

The foursome watched the horses being led around the parade ring. They all looked stunning.

Jules studied the program. "I like the look of Top of the Hill. I'm going to put a bet on him. What do you like, Fred?"

"They all look the same to me. I'm going with Gimli Gangster because I like the name," Fred replied.

John laughed at his friend, "What's a Gimli Gangster?"

"Gimli is a small town in the middle of Canada. I guess it's a gangster from there," Fred laughed.

"Farranferris Lad is the favorite. He looks amazing and he is literally jumping out of his skin. I'm going to play it safe and go with the favorite," John stated. "This is a really good galloping track and anyone in a good position coming into the last three fences has a decent chance of winning."

"How much are you going to bet?" Jules asked.

"Five pounds, maybe."

"Oh my God, you are playing it safe. That will break the bank if you lose. Chicken!" Jules laughed, teasing him, as she walked off towards the bookies at the railing next to the racecourse. "I'm going to live dangerously!"

The jockeys walked from the weigh room to the parade ring. John stared at them; some were chatting and others were deep in concentration thinking of the task ahead of them. Most of them weighed around sixty-four kilos. John looked at his shadow on the ground, smiling, remembering he used to be that weight. The last time he stood on a scale he was a cheeky eighty-five kilos.

The race started and Farranferris Lad was in contention for the entire race. Top of the Hill was placed well in the middle of the field but never looked like he had a chance of hitting the front. Gimli Gangster was within the front runners throughout. With two fences left to jump, Gimli Gangster smashed through the top of the fence and flipped head over tail through the air landing on the other side. The jockey came down with a bone crushing crash next to his horse. Miraculously, the other horses managed to avoid the man and the horse on the ground. A few seconds later, the horse got up, shook himself and ran off after the rest of the field. The jockey looked to be okay as he also staggered to his feet and waited for a ride back to the changing rooms. John shuddered as he looked on from the stands.

At the last fence, Top of the Hill was only two lengths behind Farranferris Lad and the leader, Rock'n'roll Kid. Top of the Hill took a huge jump and landed next to the leader, Rock'n'roll Kid. Top of the Hill began to pull ahead on the short run into the finishing post. Rock'n'roll Kid began to fade but Farranferris Lad wasn't ready to give up yet and now challenged Top of the Hill for the lead.

John and Jules were cheering their horses as loud as they could. In the end, Top of the Hill hung on by half a length. Jules was ecstatic. John looked over at the bookie's boards.

"He finished up at 9/2. How much did you win? he asked

"I got him at 5/1," she laughed. "And never mind how much I won."

A few minutes later, Top of the Hill was confirmed as the winner. Jules walked over to the bookie's stall.

She returned and waved a wad of bank notes at her husband. His eyes widened, "How much did you win?" he asked in shock.

"Five hundred pounds. I put a hundred on him to win! You and your five quid. Chicken!" she teased him. "Maybe I'll buy you dinner later."

That was their one and only bet for the day. Although John and Jules had known a great many people in the horseracing industry, they didn't run into one person from their old life. John recognized a few of the names; some of the jockeys he competed against were now trainers but if they walked past him, he did not recognize them.

When they returned to Belfast, they stopped at a magnificent restaurant on the outskirts of the city and had a wonderful meal, compliments of Top of the Hill.

Chapter 3

A fter dinner the couples went back to the Nesbits' home for a short visit before John and Jules returned to the hotel. The next couple of days went by quickly, with John attending to the Police College on Garnerville Road and the firing range there to qualify with his Glock pistol and the Heckler and Koch MP5 carbine rifle. John carried the Glock 27, a ten shot, snub-nose pistol, with a short barrel of under four inches. Most of the other officers in both PSNI and the Garda carried the regular fifteen shot Glock 23. John liked the smaller gun because it was lighter and easier to carry and conceal.

Jules spent most of her spare time in Belfast, visiting with Janet Nesbit and some of her other old friends and neighbors. On December 30th they packed up their car and headed back to Inchydoney, in West Cork.

OVER THE BORDER IN the Republic, Kenny Rolland had borrowed a car and made his way to Cork from Galway. After the two-and-a-half-hour drive Kenny met with his half brother, Tyson, in Cork's North Side. Following a somewhat awkward reunion, the brothers drove across town to The Lough. They drove north on Barrack Street and as they approached the fish and chip shop on the Bandon Road, Tyson instructed his brother to pull over.

"Park here, near 98 Street," Tyson directed. "See that small block over there?" Tyson pointed to a small building. "There are only four apartments in that block, two on the ground level and two on the second level. Each suite has its own entrance. Those two thieves live on the second floor in the suite on the south side. There's the entrance, facing south."

Kenny Rolland was taking it all in. "Is that a common entrance to the block or is that the entrance to the upstairs suite?"

"I've never been there but Darrell said he was there once. That door opens up to a small hallway. Directly opposite that door is the entrance to the ground floor suite. Also, just inside the door is a staircase that leads to the entrance door of the upstairs suite. That's where Hodnett and Pomeroy live," Tyson answered. "Hodnett lives with his old lady. It's her place. She has a couple of kids too."

"What do you want to do with them?" Kenny asked.

"I don't give a fuck Bro! You don't want any witnesses so figure it out. If you grease them, I'm not paying more for extra bodies!" Tyson sneered.

"There's no point in complicating this," Kenny said as he ran through his plan in his mind. "I'll run into them on the street and get acquainted. Then I'll take them out, get them drunk and slash 'n stab and the job's done." Kenny clapped his hands and grinned at the simplicity of his plan. "I'll use a knife cos it's quieter and will draw less attention. If by chance I get caught for this, I'll say it was self defense. But if I executed two of them with a gun, even the cops wouldn't believe that one. When does this have to happen?"

"Soon, real soon. How about New Year's?" Tyson suggested as he looked at his brother with admiration.

Then the two sociopath brothers switched gears as if the planning of a double assassination was nothing more than planning an evening out.

"Do you smell that fried chicken from that place back there?" Kenny pointed towards Bandon Road, with his chin as he jerked his head backwards. "Buy your bro some chicken, man. Fuck, that was the one thing I craved when I was locked up!"

The brothers pulled in behind the fast-food takeout and picked up some fried chicken and chips.

Later Tyson went to visit Mikey Galvin. "Everything is in place. Our problems will be over by New Year's."

"Good job. I don't need to know how you're are taking care of it as long as it gets done. Don't fuck this up!" Mikey said with his customary sly smirk.

"We should have a New Year's Party in the North Side! Get lots of people to come so they all see us there. A perfect alibi," Tyson proposed.

"That's not a bad idea. Good thinking. I'll get Georgy to set it up. So, are you getting somebody to do this?"

"Don't worry about it. I'll be at the party," Tyson sniggered. "Remember, you said you don't want to know as long as it gets done."

That evening Kenny Rolland sat in his car near The Lough, watching the small apartment block where his targets were staying.

After an hour of watching, he was rewarded with his targets walking out a side door on the south side of the block. They walked towards Bandon Road. It was a brutally cold night with the temperature hovering around -4 degrees Celsius. It had snowed again and the sidewalks were covered. Julian and Alvin wore heavy black parkas but their hoods were not up. Kenny got out of his car and walked behind them.

Kenny Rolland was a huge man, standing almost two meters tall and weighing one hundred and ten kilos. He had long black straight hair past his shoulders. He occasionally tied it in a pony tail but preferred to just let it hang loose as he looked tougher. He always wore dark clothes which complemented his dark complexion. Kenny Rolland looked the part of an intimidating gangster.

Julian and Alvin walked into the fast-food takeout restaurant.

"Perfect," Kenny thought as he walked in. He could eat fried chicken and chips all day long.

Alvin and Julian were in line and Kenny stood directly behind them in the queue. At first, they didn't take any notice of Kenny but then Alvin spotted him. He didn't stare but nudged his partner and pointed.

Julian was the first to speak. "Hi," and he nodded his head in recognition of the other man.

Kenny looked at him and grunted as he also nodded. Kenny knew he had been recognized. His plan was coming together.

"You're Tyson's brother," Alvin said as he fist bumped Kenny.

"Kenny asked, "How do you know Tyson?"

"We work for him," Julian replied, showing tattoos on his knuckles with the letters "I-P."

"I'm Ken Rolland. What are you doing over here? If you're North Side boys it's not safe being around this neighborhood."

"My girlfriend has a place just around the corner. We come and go all the time. Nobody bothers us. This is really Bloodz turf, not M-W, but we're good here and they leave us alone. They're all scared of Mikey G," Julian grinned.

When Alvin and Julian got to the counter, they ordered four meals to take out. Kenny also ordered his and offered to pay for everything. Julian then invited Kenny back to the apartment.

While they were waiting for their food, Kenny asked, "Do you have anything to drink there?"

"Not much...a couple of King Cans in the fridge, that's about it," Alvin replied with a slightly embarrassed laugh.

"Grab my meal when it's ready and I'll just run across to the liquor store at Lough Road and grab a case of Bud."

Alvin and Julian were impressed by Kenny. "He's a good guy," Alvin commented. "Way nicer than Tyson. Tyson's a real scary hard-ass."

"Yeah, he only cares about making money and doesn't know how to have fun," Julian laughed. "We took care of his money and stash."

"Alvin shushed his partner, putting his finger to his lip and hunkering down, "You'll get us killed," he said smiling.

Outside the take-out, Alvin and Julian met up with Kenny Rolland and they strolled back to the apartment. They walked to the side door and Julian unlocked it. Kenny was surveying the place. Inside the door was the short hallway with another door at the end of it and a stairway leading up to the second floor, just as Tyson had described.

Kenny was taking it all in as he analysed the layout of that side of the block. Julian led the way up the stairs to another doorway. He unlocked this and walked into a spacious two-bedroom apartment.

There was a young woman standing by the sink washing some dishes. Two young children sat in front of the sixty-inch plasma television.

"We got supper!" Julian announced as he placed the bag with the boxes of fish and chips and fried chicken on the table in the kitchen area. "Hey Crystal, we have a visitor for supper. This is Kenny Rolland, Tyson's brother. Kenny paid for the food and bought a case of beer. Kenny, this is Crystal, my girlfriend and these are her kids, Zack and Ellen."

The kids looked up from the television for a second and smiled at Kenny.

Kenny was taken aback by how pretty Crystal was, with her high cheekbones, large blue eyes and long wavy black hair.

Crystal smiled at Kenny, "Thanks Ken, are you going to join us?" she asked shyly as she looked back at the sink full of water.

Kenny grinned back, nodding his head. He hadn't thought about Crystal being so friendly. She was different from the usual gang skanks. For a split second, Kenny had second thoughts about taking on this job but those feelings quickly passed.

Kenny sat at the kitchen table and unpacked one of the chicken dinners from the bag. Crystal grabbed a few plates from the sink and opened another dinner and divided it up for her children. Alvin and Julian joined Kenny at the table and Crystal moved onto the sofa. Her first impression was to not like or trust Kenny Rolland. There was something about him but she could not quite put her finger on it.

"Why is he being so nice? I know it's Christmas time but he doesn't strike me as the kind of person who gets all mushy around Christmas time," Crystal thought to herself as she stared at the back of Kenny Rolland's head.

"That is some television you got there. What is it, fifty-five inches?" Kenny asked.

"No, it's a sixty. Julian and I bought for Christmas," Alvin bragged

"Business must be good," Kenny mocked as he helped himself to a bottle of beer.

Julian and Alvin exchanged glances quickly and both had the exact same thought, "If Kenny only knew!"

After a few more beers each, Kenny Rolland was acting the big shot in front of the two younger men.

"I did time in the UK. 'Strangeways,' in Manchester. That's a huge fucking prison. One of the biggest in England. There are over eight hundred prisoners and about ten different gangs running that joint. I hooked up with a crew of Asians, The Yardies, they call themselves. Biggest gang in the country."

"Is it maximum security"? Alvin asked as he and Julian were completely enamored by Kenny and the garbage he was spouting. They thought he was the real deal.

Oh yeah, It's a max alright. The walls are sixteen feet thick," Kenny bragged to his two admirers.

"Are you going to come back to Cork and work with us?" Julian asked.

"I'm not coming back to Cork full time. I'll be back a few times a year to do business and hang out with Tyson. Maybe I'll do a few deals with Mikey G. I suppose I have to come and see me mam sometimes too. She still lives here," Kenny said sheepishly, regretting adding the part about seeing his mother. "But I'm going to establish myself in the Limerick and Galway area. I made some really solid contacts with those guys in Manchester. I got a job coming up and once I take care of that, they'll know I'm serious." Kenny stared into the eyes of Alvin and Julian; they didn't know that they were his job and his pass into The Yardies as a serious gangster.

Julian and Alvin looked starry eyed at their new hero.

"Does your mother live near here?" Crystal asked from the couch. She desperately wanted to change the subject from gangs and jail and hopefully not let Julian get too excited by this thug.

Kenny snapped out of his gangster role and looked directly at Crystal, "On Sharman Crawford Street, near the girls' school."

"Oh, that's nice and not too far from here," Crystal said.

"What is the plan for New Year's? Are you having something here with the family or are you heading out on the town?" Kenny directed this question to Crystal.

Crystal was shocked that Kenny was engaging in a somewhat normal conversation and she appeared flustered when she answered, "I'm going to my mom's in Mitchelstown with the kids. I don't know what these two have planned." Crystal waved her hand at Julian and Alvin.

Kenny looked at his targets, expecting an answer.

"We're going to one of those clubs on the Grand Parade," Alvin replied. "Why don't you come with us? It should be a great night."

Alvin looked at Julian who looked back approvingly, while he nodded and smiled. Someone was bound to see them out partying with Kenny Rolland on New Year's Eve. That would be really good for their reputation.

"Yeah, that sounds like a good idea. I've no other plans. What time are you heading out on New Year's Eve, Crystal?" Kenny replied.

"I'll be on the road after lunch. I don't want to be driving too late. Too many drunks around on New Year's Eve." She didn't sound thrilled because she wasn't overly excited about Julian hanging out with Kenny Rolland, especially on New Year's Eve. She knew nothing good would come from it.

"Sounds like a plan. I'll come over around supper time and we'll grab some food and hit the town," Kenny slapped his knees with the palms of his hands, sealing the deal.

Kenny had one more beer with his targets and left. He felt good about the plan. If he had to kill Crystal and the kids, he would have done it, but he knew killing kids at Christmas time would have brought a lot of attention from the cops. It would have certainly brought him the fame he desired but that would have been unnecessary.

Kenny wandered back to his mother's place on Sharman Crawford Street and texted his brother. "*ALL GOOD, MAKE SURE YOU CAN PAY ME.*"

Kenny Rolland's mother, Cecilia Rolland was a tough streetwise woman. At fifty-two-years old, she looked good for someone in her late sixties. She smoked a pack of cigarettes a day and drank as often as she could get the booze. You could not describe her as skinny but one could say she was wiry and had long unkempt salt and pepper hair. Cecilia Rolland was no stranger to violence, especially when she had been drinking. Cecilia, like Kenny, had spent time in prison for violent offences and she was well known to the police.

"You want a beer, Kenny? They're in the fridge. Get me one too," Cecilia yelled at her son in her raspy voice when she heard the front door.

"Jeez, gimme a chance to get my fucking jacket off!" Kenny answered as he took off his plaid lumber-jack jacket and thick grey hooded sweater and hung them on top of his mother's coat on a hook in the hallway.

Kenny didn't have a proper winter parka like the other gangsters. He didn't need one; he knew the snow wouldn't last and he didn't intend to hang around Cork more than he had to.

AT 6:15PM, JOHN AND Jules Cahill called at the pub in Bandon and collected their dogs from Aunt Nan.

"What's with all the snow here?" John asked.

"I know. We had a white Christmas, first time in years. It's freezing cold too. The weather is crazy. Those two dogs don't like the snow. They're too skinny," Nan said as she laughed.

"I don't ever remember snow at the beach. That will be something new, snow in the sand dunes," Jules added. "It was awful driving down from the city with black ice everywhere. I see the council spread some sand around at a few corners but that's about it."

"Are you coming here for New Year's Eve tomorrow?" Nan asked. "I'm having some live music and I'm making up a big pot of Irish stew."

"Will you be closing on time?" John enquired, smiling slyly.

"Are you joking me?" Nan teased. "I'll close when the taps run dry."

Nan had a habit of opening her bar late and closing long after the official closing time of midnight.

"We'll all end up in prison for being caught in a licensed premises after hours," John joked.

"Sure, isn't that why I'm inviting you. The local cops won't bother with me if they know the Detective Inspector from Cork is here."

"And I thought you wanted me here for my charm and good looks," John teased.

"We probably will come here if this fella doesn't get called to work," Jules added, giving her husband a soft punch on the arm.

They loaded the dogs in the back of the SUV and drove west towards Inchydoney. The road from Bandon to Clonakilty was particularly icy. However, once they hit Clonakilty and the coast, the salt in the air from the ocean helped improve the road conditions.

When they eventually arrived at their home at Inchydoney, the entire area was deserted. The sky was beginning to clear and the stars and a crescent moon were peeking through the clouds. There were a few parked cars in front of the luxury hotel, situated between the two long sandy beaches. All the holiday cottages were in complete darkness. Nobody had ventured to the beach for New Year's because of the treacherous road conditions.

John unlocked the house, turned up the thermostat and unloaded the dogs. Lucy, the bigger greyhound, didn't care how cold it was as she headed towards the road and for her evening walk.

"No way, old girl. It is too damn cold. You can go in the back paddock. We'll take you both on the beach tomorrow," Jules told Lucy.

Lucy looked dejected but made her way to the paddock behind the house, followed by Molly, the smaller brindle greyhound.

"You're not going back to work before Monday, are you?" Jules asked when John had the car unloaded.

"I hope not. Paddy Collins knows I'm back in town tonight, but I asked him not to call unless it's really urgent. Otherwise, I'm back on Monday."

The clear sky did not last long and it snowed again on the morning of New Year's Eve. The temperature dropped to -5 degrees Celsius and the wind picked up. John cleared some snow in the paddock to allow the dogs to run around so they could take care of business. When that was done, he let the dogs out. Lucy hobbled around doing what looked like a three-legged dance. She could not keep all four paws on the ground... it was just too cold. As soon as she had completed her task, she ran to be let back inside. Molly, as usual, dutifully followed.

John and Jules decided to go to Nan's bar to celebrate New Year's. It was always a lively evening and hopefully it would not go on all night.

IN CORK'S NORTH END, Georgy Galvin and Johnny Johnson were carrying cases of beer into Trish Langford's house in Manor View Estate. Trish told Georgy that if he wanted to throw a party at her place, he could only have canned beer. No beer bottles allowed.

"Not the way your family behaves when they've been drinking," Trish sternly ordered.

When Georgy asked why, Trish replied, "You know why! Someone always gets a bottle in the face or over the head when the Galvin's throw a party. I refuse to clean up blood again!"

Georgy grinned but saw Trish didn't crack a smile so he decided to leave it. He knew she was right and was not going to argue because he would lose. This was going to be a good night. They had invited about forty people to the tiny house. It was going to be a night for fun and not for business.

"Who's living in the blue house across the street?" Johnny Johnson asked.

"Just some young couple and their baby. Why?" answered Trish.

"Looks like they're having a party too. A bunch of people are going in and they're all carrying bottles and cases of beer."

"The whole fucking city is having a party tonight, Johnny. It's New Year's!" Georgy laughed.

ON SHARMAN CRAWFORD Street, Kenny Rolland was looking for his plaid lumberjack jacket as he was leaving the house. His mother Cecilia walked in from the backyard wearing it. Kenny scowled at her.

"I just threw it on so I could take the garbage out. It's not a very warm jacket," Cecilia said in her hoarse voice as she took it off and handed it to Kenny.

Kenny didn't answer her, put on the jacket, buttoned it up and headed out into the bitter freezing wind that howled through Cork's city center. Kenny strolled up Gilabbey Street with his head down and his hands deep in his coat pockets. Although the vicious cold wind blew in his face, it didn't faze him. He plowed ahead. The hoody was his only head covering, Under the coat and the hoody, strapped to the small of his back, Kenny carried his razor-sharp hunting knife, tucked away carefully in its leather sheath. Kenny's demeanour was stoic; if he was nervous or excited about the task ahead of him, one would never have guessed.

Kenny had deliberately left it close to supper time before heading over to the apartment near The Lough. He wanted to make sure Crystal Mannering had left. Just as he went to bang on the side door, it flew open and Crystal was standing in the doorway. She had one kid by the hand and the other in her arms, both wrapped up in coats, hats and mittens.

"Oh, hi Kenny. I should have left two hours ago but this little one fell asleep," Crystal was flustered as she nodded at the child in her arms.

"Are you leaving now?" asked Kenny.

"Yes, Julian and Alvin just finished packing the car. They're upstairs so go on up."

"Thanks, drive carefully, I hope the road isn't closed and not too icy," Kenny said as the girl stepped out of the doorway.

"Oh Kenny!" Crystal yelled from her car, "Can you make sure Julian doesn't get too drunk? He's a mess when he gets too drunk and you and Alvin will end up carrying him home!"

Kenny smiled at Crystal and as he lumbered up the stairs he thought, "Oh don't you worry, Crystal, I'll take good care of him."

Julian and Alvin were playing video games on the sixty-inch television when Kenny walked in. The two younger men were excited to see him, paused the game and beamed at their new found hero.

"Hey Kenny, are you ready for a fun night out?" Alvin asked.

Kenny made himself at home and helped himself to a can of beer. "I saw Crystal and the kids just heading out," he said. "Are they gone for the whole night?"

"They're gone until Friday night or Saturday morning. We got the place to ourselves. We got some cans in, some rum and there's pizza on the counter," Julian replied.

"Sounds good! Any more thoughts on where we should go tonight? We have to go out. I spent last New Year's in prison and I'm not sitting in playing video games this year with you two," Kenny said, smiling mockingly at the two younger men.

"I heard Mikey G is throwing a big party in the North End," Julian piped up. "But it must be family and full patch members only because we didn't get an invite."

"Yeah, I heard something about that too. Tyson mentioned it. I didn't get invited either. I don't think we should crash that party. Probably not the smartest thing to do," Kenny said, deflecting that idea before it was proposed.

"You're the guest, what do you want to do?" Alvin responded. "Every club in town is open but they're all going to be packed."

"Have you ever been to the Mirage on Castle Street? It's pretty exclusive but I know the doorman and he owes me a favor," Kenny suggested, knowing the other two wouldn't decline the chance to go to an exclusive club with him.

Kenny also knew that he could bring his knife into that club as the doorman would wave him through the metal detectors.

"The Mirage! Wow!" The other two were impressed that Kenny could get them into one of the top clubs in the city.

"Let's do it!" Alvin said. "We'll have a few bevies here before we go and have a really good night. I'll order a cab to pick us up around 9."

Alvin ordered the taxi and Kenny produced a forty-ounce bottle of rye from his coat pocket. Kenny intended to get his targets really drunk; they would put up less of a fight that way.

JOHN AND JULES DROVE to Bandon to ring in the New Year. New Year's Eve was one of the busiest days of the year at Nan O' Regan's bar, along with Boxing Day and Saint Patrick's Day. Nan hired musicians to entertain the crowds that would pack in to her little bar. By 10 that night there would be dozens of people singing out of tune rebel songs with the musicians.

Jules loved her aunt Nan; she was a great character, fun to be around and hadn't a mean bone in her body. She scraped a living out of the small pub in the small town with as many pubs as grocery stores. But the competition for customers did not deter Nan. Her friendly demeanor and live Irish music brought a reasonable crowd in once or twice a month.

Nan, born in the 1940's, was the younger sister of Jules' mother Elizabeth. From very early in Nan's life, she had a tough time as she was born with a cleft palate. Because of this, her parents pulled her from school in grade six until a maiden aunt took pity on her and left her the pub in her will in the 1970's. Nan and Jules were great friends and although it made Jules sad to admit it, she loved Nan more than her own mother.

"The only thing that could go wrong tonight is my mother showing up," Jules thought to herself.

In the late afternoon of New Year's Eve, Nan and Jules were in the small kitchen putting the finishing touches to the Irish stew. The heat in the tiny room was intense and water from the condensation ran down the stone walls and the window. As always, Nan had a cigarette with a huge ash on the end of it hanging out of her mouth. Jules was fixated on the ash. She knew what was going to happen as she had seen it before. The ash was going to fall into the pot of stew. Nan squinted through the smoke as it rose into her eyes. Right on cue, the ash fell from the cigarette but this time Jules caught it before it hit the pot!

The musicians set up at 7 and within an hour the tiny bar was packed. Jules and Nan were busy pulling pints behind the bar and John was on clean up duty, picking up empty glasses and washing them.

As midnight approached, the music stopped. All of a sudden there was a calm in the place as everyone started to countdown from ten. At the stroke of midnight, John and Jules hugged and wished each other a Happy New Year. Seconds later Jules' phone rang and their kids called from opposite ends of the planet to wish them all the best and a Happy New Year.

At the stroke of midnight at Trish Langford's home in Manor View Estate, a huge cheer went up from the forty-five guests at the Independent Posse party. Mikey and Georgy Galvin were in the center of the floor. Tyson Rolland was yelling, cheering and hugging everyone. Darryl Lyons and Johnny Johnson were also keeping a very visible profile in the large group.

At the Mirage Nightclub, balloons and glitter fell from the ceiling at the stroke of midnight and a loud cheer went up on the crowded dance floor. Kenny Rolland handed Julian Hodnett and Alvin Pomeroy doubles shots of rye. Julian and Alvin were really drunk by this time and hadn't noticed that Kenny was having one drink to their every three. Crystal was right. Julian was a real mess and could barely stand up on his own.

At 12:30AM some of the crowd left the bar in Bandon and the musicians were starting to wind down. Nan, Jules and John were glad of the change of pace after the mayhem during the night.

At the same time, Kenny Rolland told his soon to be victims that it was time to head home. "This place is getting dull now after midnight. We should head on back to your place and finish the bottles of rye and rum."

Only in Manor View Estate was the party still going strong. Tyson Rolland waited to hear from his brother before that party could break up.

Kenny walked out the front door of the Mirage Nightclub and looked for a cab. There was none in sight. He smiled as he knew this would be the case. "Fuck it boys! Let's just walk back to your place and if we see a cab on the way, we can flag it down," Kenny suggested.

Kenny planned to kill Julian and Alvin on the way. What Kenny didn't count on was the number of people who were also walking the streets at this late hour on New Year's Eve. There were not enough taxis in the city to supply the demand for a New Year's celebration.

The bitter cold hit both Alvin and Julian like a ton of bricks when they stepped out of the nightclub. They had too much to drink but the sharp cold air took some of the edge off. Julian was actually able to walk a reasonably straight line.

The three men walked along Castle Street and turned onto Liberty Street, around the back of the courthouse, heading to Washington Street. All the time Kenny was looking for a quiet alley to execute his targets. His last chance came after they crossed Washington Street, walking along the South Main Street, and Julian turned down the narrow Hanover Street.

"I got to take a piss. Hang on," Julian announced.

Julian unzipped his fly and pissed down the leg of his jeans. Kenny opened his jacket and started to reach towards the small of his back for his hunting knife. Just then, four people stumbled out of an apartment block heading off after a night of celebration. Julian zipped up his pants and turned back towards South Main Street. Kenny did up his lumberjack jacket again and the trio continued their journey.

It took a little over an hour for the two drunks and Kenny to walk up Barrack Street and Bandon Road to reach the apartment near The Lough. Barrack Street and Bandon Road were just too busy as it was so close to University College Cork and all the rental properties that went with it. It was also one of the main routes to Cork University Hospital, Cork's largest hospital. There were ambulances and cop cars driving by all day and night. Now Kenny was determined to complete his mission inside the apartment.

Across the city in Manor View Estate, nobody was leaving the Galvins' party early. Some of the older people who were friends of their mother and Trish Langford's family were not giving up the opportunity to indulge in the free booze. Nobody was in a hurry to shut this party down.

Mikey Galvin looked at Tyson Rolland and then looked at his watch.

Tyson shook his head and mouthed, "Nothing yet."

Mikey shrugged his shoulders and rolled his eyes.

Tyson nodded. "It will be done tonight."

THE ONE GOOD THING about the live music session at the bar in Bandon was that once the music stopped playing, the crowd ran out of steam and started to leave. By1:30AM the bar looked like a bomb had gone off, There were dirty glasses everywhere and empty plates and bowls from the Irish stew were stuffed into every nook and cranny. Nan said she would tackle the cleanup in the morning and sent her volunteers, John and Jules, home. By 2AM they were both fast asleep.

Chapter 4

Outside the entrance of the small apartment block, Julian Hodnett fished his door key out of his pocket and tried hard to focus on getting the key into the keyhole. He was still feeling the effects of all the liquor Kenny Rolland had fed him during the night, but not as drunk as he was an hour ago when he left the Mirage nightclub.

"Hurry up. Fuck!" Alvin Pomeroy giggled as he watched his best friend use both hands to steady his grip on the key and take aim at the keyhole.

Finally, Julian gave up. He stood back and charged the door with his shoulder. The lock gave way and the door frame shattered as the door burst open. The three men stepped inside to the warm hallway.

"That's one way to open it," Kenny said and he grinned as he looked at the badly damaged door and frame.

Julian grimaced and rubbed his shoulder.

"That's going to hurt tomorrow!" Alvin said, still sniggering, as he jammed a large splinter of wood from the broken door frame under the door to keep it somewhat closed.

The three men stomped up the stairs to Crystal's apartment. At the top of the stairs Julian again fished out a key but, sheltered from the brutal freezing wind, he had less trouble opening the door. They walked into the apartment and immediately hit a bank of warm air from the central heating. Julian and Alvin immediately stripped off their warm parkas, threw them on the floor in a corner and sat on the sofa. Kenny Rolland walked into the kitchen. He looked around.

He walked to the bathroom, looked in and then peeked into the two bedrooms. No one else was in the suite.

Julian and Alvin turned on the television and kicked off their heavy winter boots. Kenny flushed the toilet and walked back to the compact living room. He left his coat and boots on.

"Is there any beer left?" Alvin asked as he got up and walked to the fridge.

"Get me one too," Julian slurred as he stared aimlessly at some show on the television.

"How about you Kenny"? Alvin asked as he leaned into the open fridge and grabbed a couple of cans of beer. Alvin stood up, opened one of the beers and had a long drink. He reached in again and picked up another can, turned around and closed the fridge with his leg. Alvin staggered a little, feeling the effect of the beer on top of the copious amount of liquor he consumed earlier in the evening He liked the buzz in his head as he made his way back to the living room.

Kenny stood directly in front of Alvin, towering over the skinny man. Kenny had his hunting knife in his right hand, holding the deadly weapon low and behind his right leg. He was no less than fifty centimeters away from Alvin. Kenny looked directly into Alvin's eyes with a determined, diabolical stare.

Alvin looked puzzled but his drunken brain was slow to process anything. Alvin was about to speak when Kenny struck with the speed of a king cobra. Kenny lunged quickly, three thrusts of the knife into Alvin's soft stomach. Alvin dropped the cans of beers and tried to yell but all that came out was a blood curdling scream. Alvin reached out for Kenny and grabbed hold of his long hair. Kenny responded with a fourth thrust of his blade across Alvin's throat. The entire attack took less than five seconds. Alvin dropped to his knees. He couldn't breathe. All he could feel was the hot blood running down his chest from his slashed neck and the burning sensation of his ripped open stomach.

Julian, still sitting on the sofa fighting to keep his eyes open, heard the commotion in the kitchen. He leaned forward and looked through the doorway. Julian saw Kenny standing over Alvin, now lying on the floor, face down in an enormous pool of blood and only seconds away from dying. In that split-second Julian saw the blood dripping from the blade of the hunting knife in Kenny's right hand. Kenny turned around and looked right at Julian. Kenny still had that unwavering demonic look in his eyes. Julian immediately put two plus two together, and sobering up instantly, knew he had to get out of there. Julian had no intention of trying to fight the bigger man. Instead, he ran for the door. He didn't stop to grab a coat or his boots, despite the fact that outside it was freezing and the ground was covered with snow.

Kenny had every intention of finishing his task. The huge man ran through the small apartment like a wild animal. Alvin's blood still dripped from his blade. Julian screamed as he was half way down the stairs. At the same time Kenny was at the top of the stairs. Julian made a fatal mistake. He slowed to look behind to see if Kenny was coming. All the liquor had made him clumsy and losing his footing on the stairs, he rolled down the last four steps. Julian tried to stand up but Kenny jumped the last four steps and landed half next to Julian and half on top of him.

Julian panicked; he was so close to the outside door. He tried to push the big man away and reach for the door but at the same time Kenny overpowered him with a left hook to the side of his head, stunning him briefly. That was all the distraction Kenny needed. He quickly followed up with a stab wound to Julian's throat severing his jugular vein. Thick red blood squirted out of Julian's wound onto Kenny's jacket. Julian grabbed his throat trying to save his own life. Kenny roared in anger. He went into a frenzy and stabbed Julian twenty more times in the chest, stomach, neck and face. Half a minute later, it was all over. Julian and Alvin were both dead.

Kenny caught his breath and looked around the narrow hallway. Nobody was around. He looked up at the corners, checking for security cameras. There were none.

He smiled, thinking, "I should have checked for cameras before this. I will the next time!"

Julian's head and shoulders were on top of the last step. The rest of his body was on the floor and one of his legs was outside the broken, open door. Kenny peered out the door into the lane. There was no one around. He could hear the sound of traffic on Bandon Road and 98 Street, but nobody could see into the side door of the small block.

Kenny texted his brother Tyson, two words, "*I'M DONE.*"

It was now 1:45 AM, on January 1st. The party at Manor View Estate was still going strong. Tyson Rolland heard his cell phone ping. He looked at the screen and saw the message, "I'm done." Tyson called over to Mikey Galvin and gave him the thumbs up signal. Mikey G smiled back and immediately offered everyone another drink.

Back at the apartment block, Kenny pulled the outside door shut, stepped over Julian's body and stood looking at his handiwork. Julian's head was almost detached from the rest of his body and it looked freakishly weird.

"You lost your head, buddy," Kenny laughed as he looked down at the dead man.

Kenny continued up the stairs. He walked through the living room and into the small kitchen. He stood over Alvin who was lying in a large pool of deep red, almost black blood.

Kenny looked around the kitchen. He decided to get rid of any evidence that he left behind. He piled a bunch of garbage and papers and the empty pizza box on top of the stove.

Kenny eyed the sixty-inch plasma television that was still on. "Why not?" he thought. "I can sell it for a couple of hundred quid."

Although he was trying to establish himself as a killer for hire, Kenny Rolland was still a small-time crook who could not resist stealing something that was out in the open.

Kenny unplugged the power cord of the television and struggled to pick it up. He forgot to disconnect the antenna cord. It was still connected to the back of the television and to the cable box. Kenny gasped as he stood up with the television. He took a half step to turn around and wrenched the antenna plug from the back of the television, ripping the connector away from the plastic, leaving a hole about two centimeters in diameter in the back of the television. The television wasn't too heavy but it was extremely awkward to carry because of its shape and size.

Kenny stepped over Alvin's body and the large pool of congealing blood and headed down the stairs, balancing the huge television as he went. Sweat rolled off his brow after he struggled to carry the television to the bottom of the stairs. He carefully balanced the set on top of Julian's corpse and peeked out the door to ensure there was nobody in the lane at the side of the door. Once the coast was clear, Kenny carried the television outside and placed it between a fence and large steel garbage bin. Kenny was still sweating profusely as he went back into the block, carefully stepping over Julian again and returned upstairs. Again, he stepped over Alvin and went into the bathroom and splashed some water on his face, attempting to cool down.

When Kenny looked in the mirror, he saw Julian and Alvin's blood splashed over the front of his plaid lumberjack coat. "For fuck sakes!" he groaned.

THE FAMILY, FRIENDS and associates of the Independent Posse gang were enjoying a friendly night out at the party in Manor View Estate. There had been no issues, unusual for this tough crowd.

Eddie Flynn, who was known by everyone as BIG-E because of his enormous size, was standing outside the Langford home having a cigarette. He was joined by his younger brother, Bertie. Bertie Flynn was a 'full-patch' member of the Independent Posse. Bertie was a very successful drug dealer and had made a lot of money for himself, Mikey Galvin and the gang. BIG-E was not as smart as his little brother and liked to use drugs more than sell them. Nevertheless, Eddie Flynn was tough, fearless and loyal to the gang.

Three young men exited the big blue house across from Trish Langford's house. The three men were wearing red sports jerseys over their coats. They were supporters of the 'Churchfield Reds' soccer team as were everyone at that New Year's party at the blue house.

The three young men laughed and joked as they walked along the sidewalk to a parked car. What they didn't know was the Flynn brothers were watching and taking offence to the red jerseys. Red was the gang color for the Independent Posse and often members wore red baseball caps or red bandanas to show their affiliation to the gang.

"Hey! Who said you can wear red on this street?" Bertie Flynn yelled out.

The three men looked puzzled for a second and one then yelled back, "Happy New Year!"

"BIG-E stepped out of the shadow and shouted, "Get those fucking shirts off and bring them here, NOW!"

"Fuck you! We're going home," one of the men called out.

BIG-E could not let it go and rushed at the man. He looked like a charging bull elephant as he ran across the road. The three young men stood their ground. The liquor they had consumed made them braver than they should have been.

BIG-E didn't slow down. He charged straight into the group who were young, fit, well built and ready to fight back. Bertie Flynn saw that his brother might need help and ran in to join the fight that had begun. One of the three men stepped out of the scrap for a few seconds and pulled out his cell phone to call for backup. Within seconds about forty people piled out of the blue house, most of them wearing red jerseys. At the same time somebody raised the alarm at the I-P party and about twenty-five people appeared. There was an absolute brawl in the middle of the street in Manor View Estate.

Georgy Galvin, Tyson Rolland and Johnny Johnson armed themselves with baseball bats and hurley sticks from a stash in Trish Langford's yard and started swinging wildly, hitting anybody they didn't recognize. Tyson Rolland was enjoying himself as he selected a target and crashed the hurley stick onto a head or face. Two of the soccer supporters in red jerseys got the better of Bertie Flynn and knocked him to the ground. One of the men pulled a knife and went to stab Bertie in the chest. He held the knife with both hands and put all his weight on top of it, desperately trying to drive it into Bertie's heart. Bertie started to grapple with his opponent and tried to push the man's hands away from his chest. Bertie was strong but the soccer player had his entire body weight behind the knife. Bertie was wearing a thick leather biker jacket but he could still feel the tip of the blade starting to bite into his flesh. He thought he was going to die. Just when he couldn't hold on much longer, out of the blue came Mikey Galvin and he kicked the soccer player in the side of the head as hard as he could. The young man's head jerked backwards, the knife flew out of his hands and the man rolled off Bertie Flynn and lay on the cold road in a complete daze.

Mikey Galvin looked around like a general on a battlefield and saw that he was outnumbered and starting to lose this fight. He yelled at Johnny Johnson, "Get the strap and finish this NOW!"

Johnny knew immediately what he had to do. He backed away from the battlefield, threw his hurley stick down by the side of the house and ran back into Trish Langford's house. Some of the older people were standing in the front yard looking out. Some of the younger women, Trish included, were fully engaged in the fracas, punching, kicking and grabbing their enemies by the hair.

Johnny ran through the house and out the back door, through the yard and into a dark dusty old shed. There was no light, except from the light at the back of the Langford house, but Johnny didn't need light and he knew where to go. Johnny reached up into the rafters and fumbled around. Then he pulled out a burlap sack. Inside was a solid object a little over sixty centimeters long, a dark coloured twelve-gauge sawed-off Remington shotgun. The weapon had been sawed off at the stock and the barrel making it compact and easy to carry and conceal.

Johnny slid the slide back slowly until a shell appeared in the ejection portal. He pushed the slide forward again, this time faster, "Good...it's loaded," he said to himself.

He reached into the sack and found another four shotgun shells, each one a different colour. He shoved the shells into his jeans pocket and ran back through the house and out the front door with his unusual gait and slight limp, took up a position at the end of the front yard, near the street.

Johnny looked for a group of people that he didn't recognize. Finding his targets, he placed his left leg slightly in front of his right leg and braced himself. He raised the deadly weapon a little higher than his hip. He placed his left hand around the stumpy barrel of the gun, felt above the trigger guard with his right hand, pushed the safety button off, put his finger back inside the trigger guard and fired the gun from his hip. A burst of orange and blue flame flashed out of the short gun barrel. The gunshot sounded like a cannon had been fired on the street. Everybody stopped what they were doing. It was as if time stood still.

The first round was birdshot. The light pellets spread out as soon as they left the short barrel and struck several people in a twenty-foot radius in front of Johnny. Although the birdshot wasn't fatal, it caused massive panic. Johnny slid back the slide with his left hand, the spent shell casing was ejected and flew about a meter into the air. He slammed the slide forward engaging a second round. Johnny fired another round. This one sounded even louder than the first because it was not birdshot; it was a slug. The twenty-five grams of solid lead designed for bringing down large game such as a bull moose zoomed across the street and found its target.

Jason Kimberly was too drunk to join in the fight. He stood in the front yard of the blue house, wearing his red soccer jersey, hanging on to the front gate to keep from falling over. The twenty-five-gram solid lead projectile ripped through his chest pushing his heart back and through the huge exit wound that it made in his back. Twenty-three-year-old Jason Kimberly died instantly.

Panic took over on the street. Most people didn't know who was shooting or where the shots were coming from. The Independent Posse gangsters and the soccer team supporters were running in every direction to get away from the shots. Nobody even noticed Jason Kimberly had been shot. Nevertheless, Johnny Johnson was going to fire until empty. He racked the small deadly weapon again and ejected the shell casing, forcing another shell from the magazine into the receiver. He fired a third time into the panicked running crowd. Another flame flashed from the muzzle of the gun and another slug flew out of the short barrel and hit its target. Nineteen-year-old Chelsea Brown was hit in the right upper thigh. The bullet shattered her femur as if it were a matchstick and she fell to the ground in a crumpled heap.

This time Johnny knew what he had hit as he saw the girl fall to the ground. He racked the gun again, BOOM! Another slug flew through the air. Twenty-five-year-old Kyle Healy was hit on the hip. Healy fell to the ground and somersaulted before crashing. He tried to get up but could not. At first, he didn't know what was happening. He thought maybe he had been tripped. He tried to stand again and then the pain hit. He put his hand down to his hip to see what was wrong and felt the warm blood pouring out onto his hand. Seconds later, Kyle passed out.

Neighbours who weren't at either party called 9-9-9 to report the brawl on their front street. Several more called the police again when they heard the roar of the shotgun.

Johnny ejected the spent shell casing from the gun and racked again but the magazine was empty.

He reached into his jeans pocket to reload but Georgy Galvin ran up to him. "Enough for now, let's get the fuck out of here!"

Police cars from all over the city were heading to Manor View Estate. Sirens were screaming through the darkness. The battle was over. All that was left now was panic and the party goers from the blue house and the Langford house running blindly through yards. Mikey Galvin was well aware that the police were on the way. He had no intention of getting picked up for this shooting. Mikey saw his brother talking to Bertie and Eddie Flynn, the two who had started all this chaos.

"Find those shells and pick them up and get out of here!" Mikey yelled at the Flynn brothers and Georgy.

The Flynn's ran over to where Johnny Johnson had been standing and kicked around some snow. Bertie picked up a blue shell casing and Eddie found a red one and Georgy found another red one. The sirens were getting closer and the Flynn boys handed their shells to Georgy and decided to book it!

Mikey Galvin looked towards Trish Langford's house and saw Samantha Brady standing in the yard. Sam was the younger sister of Jeffrey Brady, a high-ranking member of the Independent Posse and a good friend of the Galvin brothers. Jeffrey was currently in Limerick Prison, in Limerick City, doing an eight-year bit for cocaine trafficking.

Sam Brady was a loyal associate of the Independent Posse. She had been in the thick of the brawl and had blood on her shirt and knuckles to prove it. It wasn't her blood.

"Take Johnny inside and clean him up and get him out of here!" Mikey G yelled to Sam.

Johnny Johnson was still standing in the front yard, with the shotgun in his right hand and the muzzle pointed down. He had a glazed look in his eyes but he felt excited and even ecstatic as the adrenaline flowed through his veins.

"Johnny! Get your ass in here," Sam yelled and started to direct some of the older people who were still standing around in the yard, to go back inside the house.

Trish Langford followed Johnny Johnson in through the front door. Trish and Sam took control of the situation inside the house. Johnny's hands were now trembling from the rush. The reality of what he had done was beginning to sink in. Johnny just stood in the small living room still holding the sawed-off shotgun.

"Put that fucking thing down," Sam yelled. She felt like giving Johnny a slap but thought better of it. "Where's Georgy?" she shrieked at nobody in particular.

Trish's mother answered, "He's out back, in the yard."

Sam walked to the back door. She could now see the red and blue lights approaching from less than a block away; the sirens were screeching louder.

Sam beckoned to Georgy Galvin and yelled, "GET YOUR FUCKING ASS IN HERE!"

When he ran into the living room, Georgy saw his wife stripping the clothes off Johnny Johnson and helping him get dressed in Georgy's clean clothes.

Johnny had more than enough room in Georgy's clean jeans and pulled at the waistline. "You're a fat fuck Georgy," he laughed, his unique laugh, with his mouth wide open and his tongue fully out, "Ahhh!"

Now Sam really wanted to slap Johnny as she bundled his clothes into a black garbage bag. She picked up a one-liter bottle of bleach that Trish had provided and poured the foul-smelling liquid into the bag. She knotted the bag and shook it violently to get as much of the bleach on all the clothes. Sam then handed the bag to Georgy; she also gave him the sawed-off shotgun. "Go, quickly! Get the fuck out of here."

Georgy didn't waste anytime. He took off out the back door. He didn't run through the rear lane or the front street; instead he ran through the backyards. He cut through yards and zigzagged across the lane and soon was two blocks away. He saw the familiar green Volkswagen van and stepped out to flag it down. Mikey pulled over, Georgy opened the sliding side door and lay on the ground. "Go, Go, Go," Georgy yelled at his brother as his heart was pounding in his chest. "I have Johnny's clothes and the 'strap,' Go before we're spot-checked."

Mikey calmly drove as far as Kilmore Heights and then headed north until he was at the edge of the city. He turned up Nash's Boreen and turned off the vehicle lights Soon he was on a slushy dirt covered road. Mikey pulled over. There were no houses or traffic around. Nobody was going to disturb them here. Mikey and Georgy were very familiar with this 'off the beaten track' area. They had often brought someone here for a punishment beating and the girls that worked for Georgy would occasionally bring their customers to this quiet area.

Mikey opened the trunk of the van and fished around in all the junk that was back there. He found a meter of plastic hose and an empty cola bottle. Mikey syphoned some gas out of the van. He emptied Johnny's clothes from the bag onto a heap on the frozen ground.

He soaked the clothes in gasoline and was about to strike his lighter, when Georgy yelled, "Check his pockets, fuck! He might have a few euros in there."

Mikey picked up Johnny's jeans and went through the pockets. No cash, but he did find the unfired shotgun shells.

"Good job we didn't burn these," he chuckled and he threw the shells as far as he could into the snow- covered field around them.

Mikey went back to the van and lifted a mat on the floor of the back seat. He tapped the bare floor and it shifted. The Galvins had cut out a hiding place there. He put the deadly shotgun in his hidey hole, started up the van and reversed up the dirt road until he found a place to turn around and headed back into the city.

The brothers were silent for a while until Georgy spoke, "That was a good fucking party!"

"That was good fucking fight!" Mikey answered and the two brothers burst out laughing.

The police were just getting organized at Manor View Estate and attempting to seal off the entire block and corral as many people as they could. The red and blue flashing lights were now lighting up the living room in Trish Langford's house. Sam Brady was just about finished her clean up. She pushed Johnny Johnson into the kitchen and over to the sink. She poured the remainder of the bleach over his hands and told him to disappear. Johnny limped out of the house and into the darkness. He would have no problem getting past the police as long as they didn't have tracker dogs with them.

Sam and Trish turned to the dozen older people who were left in the house with them. "The only people at the party tonight were everyone who is here. Mikey, Georgy, Johnny, Tyson and all those guys showed up for an hour or so but left ages ago. IS THAT CLEAR!" Sam demanded. "We were in here having a New Year's party. We saw a lot of commotion on the street and then heard three or four gunshots. IS THAT CLEAR!"

Her audience nodded.

Minutes later there was a hard knock at the door. It was the police.

ON THE SOUTH SIDE OF the city, at the apartment near The Lough, Kenny Rolland removed his blood-stained jacket and threw it into the large metal garbage bin next to where he had stashed the television. He was somewhat pissed off because it was brand-new and he had it for only a few weeks. "I can't have the cops stopping me and asking me how I got blood all over my coat," he muttered to himself, shaking his head slowly from side to side.

Kenny went back inside the block. He carefully stepped over Julian's dead body at the foot of the stairs and, without a second thought, made his way past the other body and into the kitchen on the second level. Once there he turned on all four rings on the electric stove. The garbage and the papers he had stacked on it earlier started to smoulder. Kenny made his way back down the stairs, stepped over the corpse again and out into the lane.

Kenny jogged gingerly a few streets over to College Road. He stopped at a house half way down the first block and knocked hard at the front door. Kenny continued to hammer the front door until a light went on inside. Kenny saw the drapes move and caught a glimpse of the resident, Ron Glowden.

"Open the fucking door, Ronny, it's freezing out here," Kenny yelled.

Seconds later the bolts and locks on the front door were eased back and the door opened. Rolland stepped into the dark hallway. Ron Glowden was a gaunt looking man in his mid -forties. He was close to six feet tall but his shoulders were hunched over and he always looked like he was gasping for breath. His dark eyes were sunken and his salt and pepper hair stood up on end.

Ron Glowden looked like a street urchin and a down and out drug addict. Indeed, he was all of these, but he was also a highly educated pharmacist. He was a star student in university and graduated at the top of his class. However, Ron Glowden got hooked on cocaine and eventually became unemployable in the main stream of life. Nevertheless, Glowden put his education to work and was one of the best crack cocaine and methamphetamine cooks in all of Ireland. He was smart and kept his recipes to himself and worked for several different gangs. Everybody associated to the drug trade knew Ron Glowden, including the police.

"Kenny Rolland! what the fuck brings you to town? The last I heard; you were banged up in the England."

"I had some work here," Kenny answered. "I need a big favour, Ronny. I got a huge sixty-inch plasma television just up the street here. Can you stash it here for me?"

"I'm not even going to ask where it came from, I don't need to know that but how long do you want me to keep it? I don't want any heat on me."

"I'm heading back out west tomorrow so I'll pick it up sometime before I go. If I can't take that thing with me, can you sell it? You should get five hundred euros for it. You can give half of whatever you get to me mam or Tyson."

"There's is no guarantee I'll get five hundred for it, but whatever I get, I'll give half to your mother. Does she still live down on Sharman Crawford Street?" Glowden asked.

"Yeah, she does. Can you help me carry it here? It's not heavy but it's awkward as fuck!" Kenny replied.

Ron Glowden stripped off his striped housecoat, put on his heavy parka and was tying up his winter boots when his girlfriend showed up at the top of the stairs.

A skinny sick- looking creature with long grey and blonde hair and careworn eyes called out, "RON!"

"Go back to bed, honey, it's just Kenny Rolland dropping in to say hello."

Rolland waved at the woman; she returned the wave and went back to bed.

Kenny and Ron walked in the shadows up Saint Finbarr's Road and along Noonan's Road and turned up on 98 Street towards Bandon Road, until they came to the small apartment block. Glowden looked around when he spotted the extra-large television propped against the fence. He saw the door of the apartment block was slightly ajar. As the two men walked towards the television, they heard a high-pitched intermittent whistle. The smoke alarm had just gone off inside the block.

Glowden walked over to the door and pushed it open even more. The hallway was now full of thick grey smoke. That didn't really disturb him. It was the dead man at the end of the stairs that really caught his eye as he jumped back a step.

"Is he...... you know......dead?" Glowden asked.

"What do you fucking think?" Kenny answered with a hint of annoyance..

"You?" Glowden asked as he nodded his head towards the dead body.

"I told you I was working. Now let's move this fucking television before the cops and the firemen show up."

The two men picked up the large plasma television set and disappeared into the darkness of the lane, carefully picking their steps through the slush and ice. When they arrived back at Glowden's house, Ron kicked the low wrought iron gate open and they trudged through the snow. There was a light on in the kitchen and Ron's girlfriend opened the front door for them.

As the two men walked through the kitchen, the woman started to speak, "Where did...," her voice trailed off as she thought better of asking anything.

The two men placed the television on the floor in the living room. By this time Kenny was freezing. His teeth were chattering and his chest and back were tingling with the cold. He did not have a jacket and all he had for warmth was his grey hoody. Ron Glowden had only one winter coat and he did not want to part with that. Anyway, Kenny Rolland was twice his size so he loaned Kenny a bright yellow hoody. Kenny stripped off his grey hoody, put on the yellow one and then put the hoody over it. He didn't want to stand out in a bright yellow hoody.

As he headed out the back door into the darkness, Kenny turned to Glowden, "I owe you one! I'll probably see you tomorrow but if I don't, you know what to do with that thing. Peace Out!"

Kenny disappeared into the shadows through the lanes and narrow dark streets and headed off to his mother's house. As he jogged in the darkness, he could hear the firetruck heading towards the apartment block.

Ron locked his back door and walked into his living room.

His girlfriend was examining the television. "This is a piece of junk!" she exclaimed. There's a big hole in the back of it and look," as she pointed to the words *North Side Rentals* engraved on the back. "You'll be lucky to get 100 euros for this."

Ron Glowden examined the back of the television and let out a long slow breath, "This is going to be a pain in the ass! Maybe he will pick it up tomorrow, if he's not locked up," and headed back to bed.

Chapter 5

The police cars raced into Manor View Estate with the blue and red lights flashing and reflecting off the windows of the houses and the white snow. If it wasn't so tragic, it would almost look pretty. The different tones of the sirens were wailing in the still of the night. The police sealed off two full blocks of Manor View Estate, keeping vehicular traffic from moving in or out. Patrol cars were dispatched to the scene from all over the city and there were over thirty-five officers in the area.

The first police car to arrive at the scene saw over thirty people on the street. Some were sobbing and hugging each other; others were just staring at the ground. The crew in the police car focused on three small groups of people huddled around what appeared to be bodies.

The two officers jumped out of their car and ran to the first group. One of the officers pushed his way through the crowd telling people to get back and give him room. He found Jason Kimberly lying face up in the snow, now coloured pink and scarlet by the massive blood loss. Jason's eyes were open but his stare was blank. He never knew what hit him. The second officer ran to another group. He also forced his way through the shocked onlookers and found nineteen-year-old Chelsea Brown. Chelsea was alive, sobbing uncontrollably and going into shock.

The officer who stood over Jason Kimberly's lifeless body grabbed the microphone of his portable radio from his shoulder. "November-Three-Zero-Five," the officer called into his microphone.

"Go ahead Three-Oh-Five," the dispatcher answered. There was a quiver in her normally very calm voice. She knew this was a serious call due to the number of 9-9-9 reports they had received from citizens.

"November Three-Zero-Five, we need multiple ambulances at our location. We have at least three people down with multiple gunshot wounds. At least one fatality. There are thirty to forty people running around the streets and lanes here. We have to seal off the area and gather as many witnesses as possible," the officer said with a calmness that did not suit the circumstances.

"Received, there are numerous units in the area now and more heading to assist you. Ambulance has been advised and are en route. Patrol Sergeant Saunders is also on scene and will coordinate the investigation for now," the dispatcher responded.

Within seconds of the radio broadcast, two ambulances arrived at the chaotic scene. Another police car also arrived. The occupants of the second car ran to see what the third small group of people were standing around. The officers discovered Kyle Healy, lying in shallow snow. He was unconscious and barely breathing. The snow around him was also pink but closer to his hip, the snow was a deep dark red. Kyle was losing a lot of blood.

Although feeling overwhelmed by the bedlam around them, the paramedics set about their task and started to triage the three victims. They knew, as soon as they saw him, there was nothing they could do for Jason Kimberly but they checked his vital signs to confirm he was beyond help.

"I think he's gone," the paramedic whispered in the ear of the police officer. "We'll check on the others and come back to him if we can."

"Should I try CPR?" the shocked officer asked.

"Don't even bother. He's got a massive hole in his chest. It would be impossible to survive."

Some of the group standing around Kyle heard this exchange and the crying got louder and soon the entire small group was hysterical.

When the paramedic crew reached Chelsea Brown, she was about to pass out. She was shaking violently and her condition was critical. However, the paramedics knew they had a chance to save her life. Chelsea was placed on a gurney and moved into the back of an ambulance where the paramedics tried desperately to stabilize her. She was hooked up to a saline drip and given oxygen while the paramedics worked to get the bleeding under some form of control. Only torn skin and shredded muscle held Chelsea's right leg in place from above her right knee. Within minutes, the ambulance blared its sirens as it crawled along the street in Manor View, forcing the crowd out of its way. Within ten minutes, Chelsea was in a trauma room at the Cork University Hospital, fighting for her life.

The second crew of paramedics tended to Kyle Healy. Immediately, they knew his condition was grave. Kyle was placed on the gurney and into the back of an ambulance. The paramedic could see fragments of shattered hip bone, sticking out of the massive wound. He also knew that there was substantial organ damage in the wound. Kyle's shallow breaths were getting weaker and his vital signs were deteriorating by the second. There was no time to waste. The paramedic who was driving yelled to the police, "WE HAVE TO GO NOW!"

A uniform police officer jumped into the back of the ambulance and watched in shock as the other paramedic looked like he was performing surgery in the back of the vehicle. The ambulance sped off through the crowd towards Harbour View Road and as soon as it was clear of all the people it began to race towards the colossal hospital complex of Cork University Hospital on the west side of Cork City.

Patrol Sergeant Henry Saunders was now on scene at Manor View. Saunders had been a policeman for over twenty-eight-years and most of it in the hectic north side of Cork City. Normally his demeanor was stoic. However, even Henry Saunders was rattled when he arrived at this scene.

Saunders walked up and down the street and surveyed the scene. The first two ambulances had raced away and the crew from a third ambulance was tending to Jason Kimberly. Saunders took a few deep breaths and then started barking out orders to his troops.

"Round up every single person who is not inside a residence. Find out who they are and put them inside a police car and get them out of this freezing weather. Block off the street, two blocks either side from here. Nothing goes in or out. That includes the back lanes. I want six, no eight cops in each back lane, on foot. Nobody moves back there. The only time I want to see a cop in a car is if there are civilians sheltering in it too. Come On Move!"

The officers heard Saunders' commands and volunteered for the different duties. People from both parties were getting shoved into the back of police cars. Most of the cars were fitted with a 'silent partner,' a plexiglass shield that protected the police in the front seat from prisoners in the back. The 'silent partner' took up a lot of space so the car could usually only hold two average sized people comfortably, three at a push, but on this occasion, most cars had four people jammed into the back seat.

Henry Saunders quickly assessed the situation. The potential "witnesses" in the patrol cars needed to be conveyed to headquarters for interview but he also needed to keep as many officers as possible at the scene. He called the Duty Inspector in the Communication Center. The duty inspector was a senior officer who was ultimately in charge of police operations in the city.

Saunders realized that he had up to forty potential witnesses on the street and each would have to be interviewed in detail by the detectives from the Serious Crimes Unit. He asked the duty inspector to contact Bus Eireann and requested that two city buses be dispatched to the area. This would solve all his problems. He could get all the people into a warm bus and out of the police cars. Saunders explained that next, he would triage the witnesses and put the eye witnesses and those willing to talk into one bus and the more reluctant ones into another bus. Either way, both groups were going to the Garda Headquarters. The inspector took the advice of the experienced street wise cop and made the call.

Some of the first officers that arrived on scene were already asking questions and finding out what had happened.

Garda James McCarthy, a twelve-year veteran, approached Saunders, "It looks like there were two New Year's parties on the street tonight. One in the blue house here and the other over there. That's Georgy Galvin's old lady's house. There was some kind of altercation between a few people from the blue house and the Posse group. That's when all hell broke loose."

"Did anyone see where the shooter was?" Saunders asked.

"Either in Galvin's yard or on the sidewalk in front of their house," McCarthy answered, his lips shivering from the cold wind.

"Take two or three guys over there and find who's inside Galvin's house. Nobody leaves, everyone who is inside is volunteering to come downtown. Got it?" Saunders said as he directed McCarthy to Trish Lanford's house.

"I know what you mean, Boss." McCarthy called his partner and another crew and headed over to Langford's house.

The duty inspector called Saunders back and informed him that the buses were on their way.

"There's one fatality here and two in critical condition. One of those two is circling the drain right now. You may as well call out the Serious Crime Unit and Forensics right away. I'll start triaging the witnesses as soon as the buses get here. It should be about an hour before they start arriving at headquarters. That should give you some time to get things ready down there." Saunders ended the call and spun slowly around surveying the chaos coming under control.

In the Duty Office at Garda Communications on Anglesea Street, Duty Inspector Bob Keating put down his phone, looked at the clock and dialed the all too familiar phone number for Superintendent Paddy Collins.

It was 2:15AM on New Year's Day. Superintendent Collins' cell phone sat on his nightstand next to his bed. The phone lit up and the shrill ringtone sounded through his bedroom. Collins reached for the phone and looked at the call display, "*Duty Inspector.*" He sat on the side of his bed. "Hello," he answered in a low voice. His wife folded her pillow over her head and groaned as she turned away. "Happy New Year, Paddy. I'm sorry I have to call you so early," Bob Keating spoke softly into the phone. "I'll give you a couple of minutes to wake up and get yourself sorted."

Paddy Collins put on a sweatshirt and walked to his kitchen. He sat at the table with a pen and paper. He sighed loudly and spoke wearily, "Hi Bob, what have you got?"

"An absolute nightmare is what we've got. There were two New Year's parties in Manor View Estate. The party goers took offence to each other and there was a huge fucking brawl on the street. Of course, someone produced a shotgun and fired into the crowd. One dead and two critical so far."

"Is there anyone in custody? And are there any witnesses?" Superintendent Collins asked, trying to get a sense of how many investigators he might need for this on a holiday when nobody wanted to work.

"No suspects, Boss. But..." Bob Keating paused, "I had to get two city buses to transport the witnesses to headquarters. About forty people coming down according to Henry Saunders at the scene.

"Are you fucking kidding me, Bob?" the superintendent asked in disbelief. He shook his head, trying to shake the sleep away and ensure he heard correctly. "I'm going to have to call all my squad in and borrow a few teams from the Criminal Investigation Division to try and get through this. I'll call my crew. Can you call around the C-I-D guys and get me as many of them as you can? I'll need four or six people," Collins said, exasperated by the thought of having enough investigators to get through this.

Paddy Collins walked to his kitchen sink, switched on the electric kettle and put a tea bag in a mug. Then he picked up his cell phone again.

At 2:30AM, the phone next to John Cahill's bed rang. He picked it up and crept out of the bedroom trying not to wake Jules. He threw on a housecoat and answered, "Hello," as he walked into the living room.

"Good, you're back from Northern Ireland," was the greeting John got from Paddy Collins. "I hope you had a good time and are nice and refreshed. I need you to come in. All hell has broken loose and the sky is falling," the Kerryman said in his gruff rural accent. "There was a fatal shooting in Manor View and we got about forty witnesses at Anglesea Street, all waiting for you to interview them."

"Jesus Christ, Boss, don't tell me anymore or I'll go back to Northern Ireland," John said, hoping he had misheard. "Did you say forty?"

"That's the word from the scene, two fucking busloads," Paddy Collins confirmed.

John looked in on his wife who had slept through the phone call and the subsequent conversation. John showered and put on one of his suits. He nursed a cup of instant coffee while he loaded his Glock pistol and quickly shined his shoes. The greyhounds were awake in their crates but in no hurry to get up and see him. They were used to him coming and going at all hours of the night and knew that this wasn't their time. John slipped quietly out of his house, into his car and drove the forty minutes to the Anglesea Street Garda Headquarters.

Normally at this hour the streets were quiet. But tonight, after all the New Year's parties and celebrations, there was lots of traffic and groups of pedestrians making their way to the suburbs to sleep off the festivities. John would call his team when he arrived at the Incident Room in Anglesea Street. He found this was beneficial for them and him, as it gave him time to wrap his head around the incident under investigation before the team arrived, and it allowed them to get at least another hour of sleep.

THE ELDERLY LADY WHO lived on the ground floor on the other side of the apartment block near The Lough heard the ear-piercing screech of the smoke alarm from the common area. She detected the faint smell of smoke from the smouldering papers and garbage on the stove in Crystal Mannering's apartment. She then called 9-9-9, gave the operator her address, reported that she was woken up by the smoke alarm next door and thought she could smell smoke.

The first fire engine pulled up and six firefighters jumped out of the truck and ran towards the south side door of the small apartment block. Armed with a pry bar, they were ready to break the door down but found they only had to push it open.

The grey smoke was now quite thick and a cloud of heavy smoke poured out the door as soon as it was opened. Normally the firefighters would barge into the building, regardless of the potential danger, but they stopped suddenly in their tracks when they saw the lifeless body of Julian Hodnett. Two firefighters did what came naturally to them; they leaned over and dragged the body out of the building into the lane. One of them glanced down and almost puked when he saw that the only thing keeping Julian's head attached to his body was a strip of skin and cartilage.

Two more firefighters pulled on their breathing apparatus and headed up the stairs. They found the second body in the living room. They quickly assessed Alvin, checked for a pulse but found none. They knew right away that Alvin had not been overcome by the smoke when they saw the large pool of blood around him. Still the firefighters picked Alvin's body off the floor and carried him down the stairs, laying him on the ground next to his friend.

The firefighters went back up into the apartment, checking for other victims and the source of the smoke. Soon, they saw the four rings on top of the electric stove and, using protective gloves, immediately shut them off. They picked up the smouldering heap of papers, old pizza boxes, plastic bags and cardboard and threw the entire mess into the kitchen sink, turning on the taps and dousing the smoking bundle with water. The garbage that Kenny Rolland had placed on top of the stove didn't start a blaze as Kenny hoped it would; it just smouldered and smoked.

The firefighters opened two windows to let the smoke out, took one more sweep of the suite, and headed back down the stairs.

The fire captain, who had arrived at the apartment block, informed his dispatcher that his crew had discovered two deceased persons at the fire scene and the deaths looked to be 'suspicious in nature.' He requested his dispatcher have the police attend to their scene as soon as possible. The fire dispatcher contacted the police dispatcher and relayed the request. The police dispatcher swore under her breath. How was she going to free up a couple of crews to attend another homicide scene? Almost every crew in the city was tied up at Manor View Estate.

The ambulance arrived at the apartment block. The paramedics looked down at Julian's distorted body and one of them let out a low whistle, "We can't do anything for him, that's an obvious death." A fireman then covered Julian's body with a heavy tarp.

The paramedics quickly moved over to Alvin Pomeroy's body. They leaned down, lifted up his shirt and saw the multiple stab wounds. They placed the heart monitor pads near his ankles and on his chest. Nothing! They checked his neck for a pulse. Nothing! Alvin was stone cold to the touch and he wasn't bleeding anymore. "Was he this cold when you found him?" one of the paramedics asked the fireman.

"He's been out here for seven or eight minutes now. He felt normal when we brought him down, but we couldn't find any vitals on him either," the firefighter said, as he wiped his brow with the sleeve of his coat.

The senior paramedic looked at his partner, "Maybe the cold will help him. Let's take him in."

The paramedics pulled their gurney out of the back of the ambulance, loaded Alvin on to it, and raced the few blocks to the Emergency Department at The Mercy Hospital, situated close to the City Center. They had radioed ahead to say they were bringing in an unresponsive male with multiple stab wounds and possible smoke inhalation so two doctors and two trauma nurses were waiting for them and Alvin was wheeled into the resuscitation room. Alvin's clothes were cut off him and he was hooked up to a ventilator and a monitor.

The young doctors looked at each other, and knew their efforts were hopeless. After ten minutes they stopped; Alvin Pomeroy was pronounced deceased at 2:30AM.

A police car from the Midleton Garda Station pulled up in front of the apartment block. Every cop in the North Side and downtown was tied up at the fight in Manor View Estate or the other calls for service that a busy New Year's celebration usually brought.

Two fresh faced young officers walked casually up to the firefighters who were all standing near the doorway. The cops hadn't taken any notice of the bundle on the ground, covered with the blue tarp.

"Hey guys, busy night?" Garda Mary Duggan greeted the firemen.

"Not as busy as your night is going to get," answered the fire captain, who, in his white helmet stood out from the others.

"Our call history says there was a body found inside. Was it smoke inhalation?"

"Not exactly," the fire captain replied, "We found two bodies. The first one is over here under the tarp."

The young male officer, who looked like he was nineteen years old, was standing with Julian's covered body behind him. On hearing this, he jumped forward. The kid was brand new and only out of recruit class a couple of weeks. This was his first night shift.

"The second body was located on the second floor in the living room. He looks like he has been stabbed up pretty bad. The paramedics carted him off to the Mercy Hospital but he's not going to make it. I think he was dead when we found him but give the paramedics their due, they are making a valiant effort," the fire captain continued.

The female officer walked over to the tarp. She pulled her flashlight off her utility belt and shone it on the tarp, "Is he stabbed too?"

"Oh yeah!" answered the fire captain. "Take a look."

Her recruit stepped over next to her as she pulled the tarp back. What they saw did not look natural. Julian's head was not lined up with the rest of his body. It looked like it had been moved over to the edge of his right shoulder.

"Sweet Jesus!" The recruit ran around the body and over to the fence and puked his guts up. It was the first time he had seen a dead body and to make matters worse, this one was badly mutilated.

The fire captain explained to the officer where the bodies had been located and the cause of the smoke inside the suite.

Although Garda Duggan was shaken by what she had just seen, she managed to hold it together.

She picked the microphone from her portable radio off her left shoulder. "November-Four-Oh-Five," she called into the radio.

"Go ahead Four-Oh-Five," the calm reassuring voice of the dispatcher replied.

"November-Four-Oh-Five, we have two victims here, one is deceased, the other one was taken to The Mercy Hospital by ambulance. Can you get another car to go to The Mercy to check on this victim? Per fire department, this male is unlikely to survive."

"Received," answered the calm but weary dispatcher. "Can you notify the duty inspector right away?" the dispatcher requested.

The patrol officer pulled out her cell phone and called Duty Inspector Bob Keating. She told him the firefighters had found two dead bodies inside the smoke-filled apartment and it looked like someone tried to start a fire by putting a pile of garbage on top of the stove and turning all four rings on.

"Get the names of all the firefighters and find out which of them entered the building first and who found which body. Get good details. I'll notify Forensics and they can get someone to go over there," the duty inspector instructed the officer. "There is no need to take formal statements from the 'bucket-heads' right now. The detectives can do that later."

"There's still one dead body lying in the back lane here. He is obviously deceased... he's almost decapitated and ambulance would not transport him. Can you notify the Medical Examiner's Office and have them attend and take this guy to the morgue?" the female officer asked.

There was a long sigh at the other end of the phone and then, in almost a whisper, Inspector Bob Keating said to nobody in particular, "Happy New fucking Year."

The young officer knew better than to say something. She just stayed on the line.

The inspector went on, "You can call the twenty-four-hour line to the medical examiner. I'll notify Serious Crime. Stay at the scene and I'll try and get you some help as soon as possible."

Garda Mary Duggan found her rookie as white as the snow on the ground. She instructed him to get the names, phone numbers and email addresses of all the firefighters, and then have the fire captain outline the explicit details of how the two bodies were found.

Bob Keating called the dispatch supervisor into his office. "Jane, how many free patrol cars do we have in city right now?"

"I've got one, way out in Bishopstown and it's also covering Ballincollig, that's it!" Jane Lehane answered.

Bob Keating looked at his watch; the day shift didn't start until 7:00AM. "Are there any evening shift cars still working? There's another double homicide at that fire scene near The Lough and we're stretched to the limits."

Jane Lehane was forty-four-years old but had worked in the Communications Center for twenty-five-years. She had faced similar situations and knew exactly what to do to keep the city protected. "I have three evening shift crews. I can hold them over. I can free up a few cars from the shooting scene in Manor View Estate and get them to secure the scene near The Lough and deal with the bodies. We're only going to respond to priority one calls between now and day shift and even then, we'll probably keep half the night shift until noon."

Bob Keating leaned on his elbows on his desk and started to massage his forehead, grumbling, "The overtime bill is going to be through the roof, especially on a stat holiday."

"That's the cost of doing business, Bob." Jane headed back to her desk and started issuing orders to the dispatchers and the patrol cars.

Duty Inspector Bob Keating picked up the phone and dialed the number to the Serious Crime Unit's Incident Room.

Chapter 6

"Cahill, Serious Crime Unit," John Cahill answered the phone.

"Hi Inspector Cahill, do you have a few minutes? It's important," Bob Keating responded.

"I'm pretty busy right now. I'm briefing with a uniform crew from Manor View Estate. What's up?"

"I'm sorry about this but I'm going to have to interrupt you. We got two more dead bodies across town, in a separate incident," Keating replied.

"You're kidding me, right? Hang on, give me two minutes to finish this up."

John was debriefing with four uniform officers who were reporting on what they had learned at the scene in Manor View Estate. After putting down the phone, John looked at his investigative summary on his computer screen.

He typed a few more words and then spoke to the officers seated in front of him, "Sorry guys, I need the room. We'll pick this up in ten minutes. The duty inspector is on the phone and I MUST take this call now." The four officers closed their notebooks and stepped out of the office.

John took a deep breath, let it out slowly and picked up the phone. Bob Keating told him what he knew about the scene at the apartment near The Lough. John jotted down some notes in his notebook, *'Two young adult males deceased, one at Mercy Hospital... one still at the scene. Fire set inside the suite to destroy evidence. Firefighters extinguished the fire before it took hold. No witnesses.'*

Before ending the call, John asked the duty inspector to call a team from C-I-D to assist. He specifically asked for Detectives Travis Dawson and Larry Vickers. These two detectives were his go-to team when he needed reinforcements. They had worked for him in the past and, although not the fastest to complete their tasks, they were somewhat reliable.

"What the fuck is wrong with this city?" John asked even though there was no one else in the Incident Room to answer him. He shook his head, walked to the door and called the four uniform officers back to complete their debriefing. After ten minutes, John formed a picture in his mind of what was likely to have occurred in Manor View Estate.

A few moments later, Detective Pete Sandhu walked into the Incident Room. Pete was one of the few non-white officers in the Garda. He had worked for John Cahill when the Integrated Fugitive Squad was formed. Pete impressed his supervisor with his ability to work with computers, video surveillance and telephone records. John had insisted on Pete working for him again in the Serious Crime Unit.

"What have we got, Boss?" Pete asked, with a strong Punjabi accent.

"The angel of death has been busy in Cork tonight, Pete. There were two New Year's parties across the street from each other in Manor View Estate. Things got ugly after midnight and a scrap broke out on the street. Someone produced a shotgun and killed one kid, two are critical. Forty witnesses stashed all over the city,"

"Oh my God, we're going to be here all day again," Pete sighed.

"That's not all, Pete! We have another incident near Bandon Road at The Lough. Two stabbed to death in an apartment. No suspects, no witnesses. You think you are here all day? Good luck, you're here for three days." Now it was John's turn to moan.

John began to prepare two whiteboards, one for each incident. While he was writing on the boards, the rest of his team filtered into the Incident Room. It didn't take long for the six detectives to notice that there were two boards on the go, with a different incident number on each board.

Looking around and seeing that all his team were present, John strolled over and closed the main door to the Incident Room. He returned to the white board and continued writing. Underneath the incident number for the homicide in Manor View Estate, on the top right-hand corner of the board, he wrote the names of the three victims.

On the left-hand side of the board, he wrote the names of fourteen witnesses; some of them had the initials I-P after their names.

Inspector John Cahill started his briefing at 4:15AM. He turned and faced his investigators. "Happy New Year everyone! This is what we know so far. There was a New Year's party at Trish Langford's house in Manor View Estate. If you don't know, Trish Langford is the wife of Georgy Galvin, one of the top men in the Independent Posse. At this point I don't know for sure that this was a gang party so let us not assume anything yet.

There was also a soccer club celebrating New Year's at a party across the street from Trish Langford's. Both parties ended around the same time and both groups got into it, in the middle of the street. Someone produced a shotgun and fired multiple rounds into the middle of the crowd. At this point, it looks like it was one of the Independent Posse people who got the shotgun because we believe the shots were fired from directly in front of Langford's house. We got one dead and two critical," John continued as he scanned his audience.

"How many witnesses do we have altogether?" Detective Sergeant Mike Williams asked his boss.

"Well Mike, I think we have over forty. They came in two buses and they're housed all over the building here, as well as a few scattered in other stations around the city. I'll continue to debrief with the uniform crews that have the witnesses and triage them as best I can. I have a few teams from C-I-D coming in also. They can take some of the peripheral players. Not everyone will be a good witness but everyone must be spoken to."

"How are we going to do this, Boss?" Detective Tim Warren asked.

"I'm glad you asked, Tim. You and I will take the first three names on this list. Williams and Jenkins, you take the next three names, Rafter and Benoit, take the three after that. Come back and brief with me after you have interviewed all three unless someone has something earth shattering, like the identity of the shooter."

"What about us?" Detective Travis Dawson from C-I-D asked the Inspector.

"Travis, Larry, I am going to keep you two out of this for the time being. I need you guys to head up to The Lough. There was a fire in a fourplex apartment block and two males found stabbed to death inside one of the upstairs suites. I don't know anything else at this point. I haven't been briefed by any of the uniform teams. This is all I got from the duty inspector. So I need you guys to go take a look and let me know."

"Who are the victims?" Detective Sergeant Larry Vickers asked.

"I don't know! I don't know anything about this. The only thing I can safely say is the two incidents are not linked in any way. I don't know if that is a good thing or not. If they were linked, it could get very complicated and as it stands right now, it's complicated enough," the detective inspector answered as he turned and looked at the two white boards.

Chapter 7

Four of the Serious Crime Unit detectives started their preliminary interviews with their assigned witnesses. John finished debriefing with the uniform officers who had escorted the witnesses to the station. Then John and Detective Garda Tim Warren interviewed an older lady from Manor View Estate who lived on the street where the shooting occurred. At the time of the brawl, she had been looking out her upstairs window and had a full view of the action, including the shooting. Their second interview was with a nineteen-year-old girl who had been a guest at the party where the soccer club had been celebrating. She had been standing next to Chelsea Brown when the shooting started. Their third interview was a twenty-one-year-old man, an associate of the Independent Posse, who had been in Langford's house for the party. He was a regular worker at the I-P crack shacks and not very informative.

After the first round of three interviews, Mike Williams, Eddie Jenkins, Jeff Rafter and Len Benoit debriefed with DI Cahill.

"I don't know about your interviews, but our I-P guy saw nothing. He didn't even know there was a fight on the street," John told the others.

"That's what we found too," Eddie Jenkins replied and Jeff Rafter agreed.

"Our first witness is seventy-three years old and half blind. She saw the shootings, even saw the shooter, but she can't describe him. She can't say if he was big, small, fat, thin or a fucking gorilla," John sounded frustrated as he shook his head.

The four detectives brought their inspector up to speed and the consensus was that the shooter had come from Trish Langford's house and after firing off his rounds, ran back to the house where a group of people helped him disappear.

"What we need is a couple of eye witnesses to the actual shooting. Someone who can give us at least a description of the shooter. Let's leave all the occupants of Langford's house until last and just concentrate on the residents on the street and the soccer club," John instructed, as he doled out the tasks for the next interviews.

"We need to get inside Langford's house... who knows what we'll find inside there. Pete, can you get working on a search warrant? You should have enough information from the interviews we've done so far."

"Don't worry about that. I have lots to work with. I'll ask to search for the shotgun and the ammunition. That should let us have a thorough look around. Those shotgun shells can get stuffed into any little nook or cranny. Who knows what else we might find in that rat's nest?" Pete answered with his usual good-humored grin.

While John reviewed some of the reports that the patrol officers had written about both incidents, Pete started on his affidavit for a search warrant. The others continued the witness interviews. Tim Warren did a few interviews alone, specifically picking witnesses who looked like they would be easy to talk to, so he would not need a partner in the room. Tim's second witness was a young Filipino man from the soccer club party who saw the first shooting. While the man did not get a good look at the shooter's face, he did well with everything else.

After the interview Tim went to brief with his boss. "I got a decent description of the shooter. You're are going to like this, Boss. Pete, you can add this to your affidavit."

"Let's hear it!" John said, stopping his review of the reports.

"It's a male, mid-thirties, around five-foot-eight, skinny build, long greasy hair in a ponytail. Wearing blue jeans and a lumberjack checked coat or jacket," Tim Warren read from his notes.

"Jesus, Mary and Joseph! That's half the fucking population of the North Side. That's it?" John was frustrated.

"Hang on, Boss," Tim smirked. "This guy had a very noticeable limp. He was favoring his left leg when he ran to reposition himself. My witness saw him run towards the back of Langford's house too, but he is pretty sure the shooter went in the side door."

"That's awesome, Tim. Will the witness commit that story to a video recorded statement?"

"Already done," Tim replied and dropped the CD on the inspector's desk.

"You can add this to the affidavit. There will be no issue having this warrant granted now. Do you want to go for a ride in half an hour? We'll drop off the affidavit at the court house and go and see what Dawson and Vickers are up to at their scene," John asked Tim and Pete.

"Count me in. Maybe we can pick up some food too. I'm starved. The boss is a slave driver, he says there's no time to eat," Tim joked to Pete, knowing the boss could hear them.

It was shortly after 11:00AM when John, Tim and Pete headed off to the court house to deliver the affidavit for the search warrant to the on-call judge. They had already put in a full day's work and they all knew they were no where near finished. This looked like it would be one of the longest days they had ever worked. They had barely made a dent in the witness interviews and the most important ones hadn't even started.

At the court house the on-call judge took the affidavit from Pete and asked him to wait in a hallway while she read it. Twenty minutes later, she returned and handed him the signed warrant.

"What do you want to eat?" John asked his colleagues.

"There isn't a lot of choice. It's New Year's Day and we'll be lucky if we find a fast-food joint," Tim complained.

"Let's stop by Dawson and Vickers's scene. There's an excellent take away, fried chicken and fish and chips place on the Bandon Road, next to that scene. Here's hoping it's open. That's probably all we're going to get," John suggested, not really looking forward to another fast-food meal.

When they pulled up near The Lough, the medical examiner's investigator had just arrived. Katie Lynch was a registered nurse who chose to work as an investigator for the Office of the Chief Medical Examiner. She was used to attending all sorts of death scenes at different times of the day and night but she never quite got used to homicide scenes. She was speaking with Travis Dawson and standing over the body, still covered by the heavy tarp.

"Detective Inspector Cahill, how are you? How was your Christmas break?" Katie asked when she saw John, Tim and Pete step out of their car.

"It was okay. I spent Christmas in Northern Ireland. Just got back a couple of days ago."

"Oh, how was that?" Katie asked.

"It was alright, pissed rain and sleet every day. But I got to visit with some old friends. I had some mandatory training and some meetings, but it was better that this!" John told her as he pointed, kicked the snow on the ground and nodded towards the dead body.

Larry Vickers was clapping his gloved hands together and stomping his feet to try to keep the circulation going in the bitter cold. He commented, "Let's take a look at this guy, Katie. The firemen said that he was found at the foot of the stairs just inside the door. His head was at the foot of the stairs and his legs were partially up the stairs. He had to have come from the upstairs suite."

"Oh my God! What happened to you?" Katie Lynch asked the corpse in a low, gentle voice, as she pulled the tarp back. Julian

Hodnett's head was barely attached to his body. The blood had now completely drained away from his face and the waxy skin resembled a macabre mask. Katie Lynch looked at her watch and officially pronounced Julian dead. "Time of death, 12:20 PM. I'll call the mortuary service and have this poor fella picked up and taken to the morgue. I must go and see the other one at the Mercy Hospital after this. Do you know what happened?" she asked Larry Vickers as she went through Julian's pockets and found a wallet.

"Not really," Larry Vickers answered. "Maybe they killed each other. That would be the easiest. The other fella was found in the kitchen in the suite upstairs."

John looked at his colleague to see if he was actually serious. Larry Vickers wasn't the sharpest knife in the drawer and would, if he could, take the easy way out. John saw that Larry wasn't smiling when he made that comment.

"That's hardly likely," John butted in. "This guy did not get his head cut off on the top floor and run down the stairs. Someone had to stab the fellow on the second floor too. Did you find a knife?"

"No, not yet but the forensic team will probably find one or two," Larry Vickers offered.

"Let's talk this through for a moment," John said. "The fella in the Mercy Hospital's morgue... he was found on the second floor. He has at least ten or twelve stab wounds. So, this fella under the tarp stabs the other fella a dozen times, then gets his head cut off, runs downstairs and dies at the bottom of the stairs. Who lit the fucking fire?"

Vickers shrugged his shoulders and walked away.

"Who lives here?" Tim Warren asked.

"We're working on it," Travis Dawson replied, slightly embarrassed by his partner's analysis of the scene.

John looked at the two C-I-D detectives. "If you want to bring that theory to the superintendent, knock yourself out. But he's in a foul humor trying to figure out how to get a bigger budget because we are going to go through the whole year's budget in the first couple of days of the year."

John, Tim and Pete walked to the take-out on Bandon Road and. returned to the Incident Room on Anglesea Street to eat lunch. "Those two are just fucking the dog, rather than getting stuck doing thirty or forty witness interviews at the station," Pete said shaking his head as he ate the tasty deep- fried chicken.

Just as they finished wolfing back the food, Sergeant Jennifer Martens from the Forensic Identification Unit walked into the Incident Room. She looked at the empty food containers and wrapping paper on the table.

"Sorry, Jen, you just missed lunch," John apologized as he handed her a copy of the search warrant for Trish Langford's house.

Jen Martens looked exhausted. She had also been to a New Year's party and had just returned home when she was called out to work. She grabbed the search warrant and sat on the chair in front of the inspector's desk. She had spent most of the morning with her team, in the bitter cold, on the street at Manor View Estate, processing the scene.

"We found one spent shotgun-shell casing on the street, right outside Langford's garden. Someone must have scrambled to pick the others up before we got there," Jen told the inspector. "Typical gang bangers, trying to clean up and not leave any evidence behind them."

"Can you tell where the shooter was standing when he fired?"

"Judging by where the victims fell, I would say he moved between some of the shots, maybe six to eight feet to the west. I won't be able to tell for sure until I set up the 3D scanner and get an overall look at the scene," Sergeant Martens replied. "There are foot prints everywhere. It would be impossible to say one set of footwear impressions is the shooter's unless it was extremely distinctive."

"Moving between his shots. Hmm, he wanted to maximise his strikes on his targets. This is someone who is familiar with shooting," John said thoughtfully. "Well Jen, now that you're getting all caught up here, what about our other scene at the apartment block near The Lough?" "That is an inside scene. I sent one of my crew down there and she just called me back. It looks like everything happened between the front door and the suite on the top floor on the south side of the block. The fire is out so there is no danger. I would like to close it down, leaving a scene guard on it and not touching it for at least a day or two. We just don't have the manpower! Or I could call up to Dublin and see if they can send someone down. It's your call."

"That sounds like a gang thing anyway. Two Independent Posse guys living in the heart of Central Area. Probably Mahon Warlords or one of the African gangs took them out," Tim Warren suggested.

"We don't get to pick our victims, Tim," John sighed. "I would prefer to leave the scene for you and your team, Jen. I don't want someone I don't know coming down from Dublin and rushing through it so he can go back home as quick as possible."

Sergeant Jen Martens smiled at the inspector. She took the search warrant, hauled herself out of the chair and headed back to the scene in Manor View Estate. As she walked out, Superintendent Paddy Collins walked into the Incident Room. John described the scene at The Lough to him.

"What about the other two dog-fuckers! Are they coming back to do some work?" the superintendent asked.

"Eventually," John commented as he headed back out on his next task, meeting with Jason Kimberly's family.

JOHN HEADED TO THE North Side and found Jason's family home near Jerry O'Sullivan Park in Churchfield. The home was a former council house that had been sold to the Kimberlys' several years earlier. It was the second house in a row of four, with a pleasant dark pebble dash exterior, a well-kept hedge around the front yard and a black wrought iron gate. John walked down the steps to the front door. He rang the doorbell and within a few seconds the door was opened by a young girl, who looked to be around fourteen years old. The girl's eyes and nose were red from crying and she looked terribly distressed.

John immediately knew that the Kimberly family had learned that Jason had been killed before he delivered the terrible news. He identified himself to the young girl and asked to speak with her parents. She showed John into a neat sitting room at the front of the house. Moments later two older women, who also looked like they had been crying, entered the room and were introduced as Jason's mother and his grandmother. Jason's mother asked if it was true that her son had been killed at a party in Manor View.

"Jason was at a party at a house in Manor View Estate. When that party was over, some people who were at the same party as Jason got in a fight with a few other people who were at a different party across the street. As far as I know, Jason wasn't involved in the fight," John explained and paused to ensure that the two women understood what he said.

"Jason wouldn't be in a fight. He isn't that kind of person," the grandmother said. challenging the policeman to contradict her while she was squeezing a tissue in her hands.

John took a deep breath and let it out slowly. "I don't think he was involved in the fight," he said, trying to reassure the grandmother. "There were quite a few people fighting on the street and someone fired a gun into the crowd. Unfortunately, Jason was one of the people who was shot. He died on the street. I am very, very sorry for your loss."

The two women started to cry again, and held each other's hands as they sobbed uncontrollably. Jason's mother's body shook from head to toe, as she cried so hard. John sat there and let them cry. He knew that soon they would have questions. Minutes that felt like hours passed and Jason's mother spoke for the first time.

"Who killed him? Who shot my son?" the woman sobbed but with anger in her eyes.

"At this time, I don't know. We are doing everything we can to identify the people responsible. When we do that we will arrest them and send them to prison for a very long time."

"It won't bring my boy back," and both women started to cry again.

Before he left the home in Churchfield, John learned that the Kimberly family had heard about Jason's death in a phone call from one of the witnesses who was brought to Anglesea Street Station on the bus. Not the most ideal way to learn of this tragedy but it was out of the control of the police.

John returned to the station to work through the endless number of witnesses still in the station.

BY 11:00PM A REASONABLY clear picture had developed from all the interviews. The only interviews left were some of the occupants of the Langford home. John called a briefing with the detectives to ensure that they were all up to date. Even Dawson and Vickers had returned and completed a few witness interviews.

"Good, everybody is here. Nice of you to join us, Larry, Travis. Got everything wrapped up on the South Side?" John started off sarcastically.

Larry Vickers and Travis Dawson looked a little sheepish but everyone in the room knew they were no balls of fire.

"We have had forty-seven people in here today. That has got to be a record! We've taken thirty-two video statements. Only seven weren't worth recording. We still have eight interviews to go. These are all the people who were found inside Trish Langford's house. So, this is what we know:

- There was a large party at Trish Langford's house. We think there were a lot of Independent Posse members there, including Mikey and Georgy Galvin and some other key players. Hopefully we can identify more of them after we get into the last eight interviews.
- We also know there was another New Year's party across the street. This looks innocent enough. All the party-goers here were supporters of the Churchfield Red's Soccer Club.
- Sometime after the New Year was rung in, some of the Red supporters were leaving and walking up the street towards their car. A few I-P thugs took offence to the soccer people wearing 'the color RED' on their turf.
- A fight broke out and it looks like the sports fans started to get the upper hand on the gang-bangers, until the gang-bangers upped the ante and someone brought a shotgun to a fist fight.
- The shooter came from the side of Langford's house, fired several shots into the soccer crowd and then retreated, but definitely went inside Langford's house.
- The shooter is a male, mid-thirties, five-feet-eight, skinny build, long greasy hair, tied in a pony-tail, pock marked face and walks with a definite limp favoring his left leg.

The last eight interviews are crucial. They know who the shooter is or one of them is the shooter. Let's get some answers here."

"Wow, thirty-two interviews broken down to six points on a white board," Mike Williams commented philosophically. "This would be way easier if it were two gangs fighting each other. At least they would know each other and we could put some pressure of one side or another. These soccer kids haven't a clue what they got themselves into here."

"These eight people are not all gang members but they are close associates. They are going to be tough interviews. Some of these people are harder to talk to than the gang members themselves. Have a short break, get a coffee and a snack and then get to it. We have another long night ahead of us. Here's the starting lineup," John announced as Pete Sandhu recorded the meeting and the tasks in his notebook.

"Tim, you and I will take Trish Lanford."

"Thanks a lot," Tim Warren muttered under his breath.

"William and Jenkins, you're getting Sam Brady."

"Thanks, Boss, she's tougher than any one of us in this room," Mike Williams joked.

"Rafter and Benoit, you get Tom Ellice. He seems to be the nervous type."

"Copy that, Boss," Jeff Rafter said.

"Vickers and Dawson, Jane Langford is yours. Technically, it's her house, everybody else just seems to live there."

Larry Vickers nodded his head and wrote the assignment in his notebook.

John wandered over to his desk and stared at his computer screen. He took a few deep breaths and hoped that they would get a break with the last few interviews. So far, he knew he had done everything right. He had no suspects starting off this investigation. He had gleaned as much information as he could from the cooperative and semi-cooperative witnesses. Now it was down to the wire and time to turn up the heat on the remaining eight. He knew some or all of the eight people had something to offer. He hoped at least one of them would slip up and give them something. He could hear his team talking among themselves in the outer office. He had faith in their ability but knew their task was difficult.

John picked up the phone and called the Intensive Care Unit at the Cork University Hospital to enquire on the condition of Chelsea Brown and Kyle Healy.

"They're both stable for now," the charge nurse told him. "We are going to move Chelsea to the Step-Down-Unit but she'll require more surgery. I shouldn't say this but to be honest, I think she will lose her right leg. Kyle is stable for now but he's is in bad shape. He is going to need more surgeries too."

"Surgeries! Plural, that doesn't sound too good. Thank you. I'll call back in the morning, if that's okay."

"That will be fine. And, if either takes a turn for the worse, we will let you know. We have your number here. Happy New Year," the nurse said as she hung up.

John shook his head, looked at the clock on the wall and thought, "This day is never going to end." He gathered his composure and decided what needed to be done to move this investigation further.

He called Jules and told her that they were up to their necks in witnesses and had two separate investigations with three deceased victims. Jules told him to take it one step at a time and try to get some rest.

When she hung up, she looked at the two dogs and whispered, "He can't keep this up. It's not humanly possible,"

The dogs just wagged their tails.

A few minutes later, John and Tim Warren walked into the interview room that housed Trish Langford. This was not the first time that Trish had been questioned by the police and she was not intimidated or the least bit respectful. John offered her a cup of tea or coffee.

"Tea, two sugars and a drop of milk," she barked, without a please or thank you.

John left the interview room to get her tea and ran into Superintendent Collins. "How are you getting on with the lovely Trish Langford?" the superintendent asked, trying hard to hold back the smile.

"She's a C-U-Next-Tuesday! With a capital C!" John answered as he looked through some of his notes. "She is a hard-core gangster. This is not going to be a quick interview. You may as well have a snooze, Boss, or go home. I'll call you if there is any breakthrough. We will not be out of there for a few hours. Tim is trying to schmooze her but I think she'll eat him without salt if I don't get back there."

John headed back to the interview room. Although he loved to get a quick result and keep chipping away at an investigation, part of him loved the challenge of a real tough interview.

Two hours later, after trying to figure out what made Trish Langford tick, John and Tim were losing patience. Trish was not consistent with her recall of who was at her house all night. John knew she was holding something back. At first, she tried to make it look like the gangsters, including her husband and brother-in-law, only showed up for half an hour earlier in the night. However, she slipped up a few times and the detectives suspected the gangsters were there all night.

John had one last card to play. He did not like playing it because it could blow up in his face in court later on, but he had to press forward. "FUCK YOU TRISH!" John slammed his open hand on the steel table and yelled across at Trish Langford.

Trish's eyes opened wide and she sat up with a jolt.

He knew he had her attention. "YOU'RE A GROWN WOMAN WITH THREE BABIES AT HOME. STOP ACTING THE CUNT AND BE A RESPONSIBLE PARENT FOR ONCE IN YOUR FUCKING LIFE!" Even Tim sat up and got a bit of a shock when his partner slammed his hand on the table.

"Don't..." Trish tried to interject.

"SHUT THE FUCK UP! IF YOU WANT TO GO HOME TO YOUR CHILDREN YOU ARE GOING TO HAVE TO SMARTEN THE FUCK UP AND TAKE RESPONSIBILITY," John yelled. He took a deep breath. "When I leave this room, if you haven't told me the truth about what happened last night, the first thing I'm doing is calling CFS. And I will tell Child and Family Services that you are a gang member. You have gang members in your house all the time. They sell drugs out of there and store weapons there and your children would be much safer in foster care," John paused and looked directly into Langford's eyes. He knew he had hit a nerve. "Do you think I won't do that? Go ahead, fucking try me!"

Trish looked down at her feet. She knew she was between a rock and a hard place. She had to tell them something but she could not give up Johnny Johnson. That would get her and probably her mother killed by Mikey Galvin. "Okay," she said and blew out a short breath. "Georgy and Mikey decided to have a New Year's party at my place," she sighed and looked really irritated.

Trish went on to say that the Georgy and Mikey came over earlier in the day and brought all the booze and food. She named all the gang members who were there and said they stayed all evening. She did not know how the fight started on the street, all true and easy for her to say. But it was here that she deviated from the truth. Trish claimed she stayed in the house during the entire fight. Most of the gang-bangers left when the fight started and she didn't look out, so she didn't know who was fighting. She heard a couple of shots but was too scared to look out and nobody came back inside after the fight broke up.

John and Tim knew she wasn't giving them one hundred percent of the truth but it was probably all they would get. They left her alone in the interview room and headed back to the office to see what their colleagues had learned in the other interviews.

"Jesus, Boss, you scared the crap out of me when you slammed your hand on the table in there. I was just starting to zone out listening to her bullshit when you slapped the table and started yelling at her," Tim laughed.

"I had to do something to wake myself up. Did you see her jump? We could have saved ourselves a couple of hours and done that off the bat."

The first crew they met were Mike Williams and Eddie Jenkins. "It was getting a little loud in your room, Boss," Mike said with a smile. "How did you guys do?"

"Trish is committed to some kind of a story. She puts all the I-P hierarchy at her house all night. She names a bunch of them, Mikey G, Georgy G, Tyson Rolland, Darrell Lyons and Johnny Johnson. She threw out a few other names of people I didn't recognize. But she says she doesn't know how the fight started. Someone just yelled there was a fight on the street. All the guys ran out. She didn't look out, she didn't go out, and she heard the shots and then the police came. Nobody came back inside her house," John read from his notes.

"You got more than we did. Sam Brady is one tough cookie. I would say she could beat the shit out of the two of us in a heartbeat if she started." Eddie Jenkins grinned. "She was in the house all night drinking. She was too drunk to remember who else was there and doesn't even know how she ended up in the police station. She doesn't know anything about a fight or a shooting. She heard or saw nothing or nobody."

"We'd have to torture her to get anymore and even then, we wouldn't get the truth," Mike Williams added.

At that moment Vickers and Dawson came into the Incident Room after interviewing Trish Langford's mother, Jane.

"Jane's a tough old bird," Larry Dawson announced. "She knows what's happened but she isn't going to say anything. She told us that she is terrified of Mikey G. Not so much Georgy, she can handle him, but Mikey is a psycho she said. There is no way she is going to roll on Mikey."

"Is there anything we can offer her? What about relocation, witness protection?" John asked hopefully.

"All she knows is Cork and the North Side. She couldn't leave it." Travis Dawson answered.

Moments later, Jeff Rafter and Len Benoit came into the office after interviewing Tom Ellice. Ellice was an older man; his wife was a friend of Jane Langford. Tom had no ties to any of the gangsters and, for most of his adult life, worked in bakery on Shandon Street.

"What does Mr. Ellice have to say for himself?" John asked, sounding defeated.

"Tom Ellice actually has a good story. It's a pity he was hammered and doesn't know anyone's name but he knows what he saw," Jeff Rafter answered.

"Let's hear it," John requested.

"Tom and his wife were invited to the party the day before New Year's Eve by Jane Langford. Jane and Tom's wife play bingo together a couple of times a week."

John could feel his eyes burning in his head with exhaustion. All he could think was "Who fucking cares about bingo? Get to the fucking point," but he managed not to say it out loud.

"Tom and his old lady got to Langford's around 7:30PM and at that time it was an older crowd, mostly friends of Jane. He recognized one or two people but did not know any of their names. That didn't matter to Tom. The booze was flowing freely and he got stuck right into it." Rafter paused for effect, looked around the room at his dog-tired audience, took a deep breath and continued.

By about 10:00PM a much younger crowd started to arrive. They were nearly all men, only a few girls with them. They were fairly rowdy and looked rough. He did not speak to anyone; he just stayed in the corner drinking on his own. His old lady was chatting with another bunch of her friends.

Pretty soon, there were at least forty people in that small house. Nobody bothered Tom and Tom didn't bother anyone. At midnight there was a big cheer and everyone was shaking hands and patting each other on the back, the usual celebrations. Not long after that, Tom's wife told him it was time to go home. He told her to go ahead and he would follow her. He just wanted to finish his drink, but when she left, he had about four more cans.

Tom was sitting in a corner, all on his own, when something happened. All the men ran out of the room. There was something going on. Tom heard a couple of loud bangs out on the street. He didn't know what they were. A few minutes later a fella came in with a few of the girls. The fella had a sawed-off rifle in his hand. The girls and the women formed a circle around him and he started taking off his clothes and they put them into a black garbage bag. Then they gave him clean clothes and he took off. One of the women took the bag out of the room."

"Does he know who this fella is?" John asked anxiously.

"He hasn't a fucking clue," Jeff Rafter answered. "And I believe him. He doesn't know any of these gang-bangers. However, he has a decent description of the guy with the gun. He's about thirty years old, average height and skinny build. Long greasy black hair, pock marks on his face and had a bad limp. Tom noticed him a few times during the night and remarked that he looked like a scary character."

"Okay, John said. "We need to find an Independent Posse gangster with a limp. Let's get the last few interviews done and we'll shut it down for a few hours and get some sleep. We have a lot of work ahead of us."

The detectives went back to interview rooms and interviewed the last few stragglers. They did not advance the investigation any further than it had been.

It was 5:30AM, on January 2nd when John walked down the steps of Garda Headquarters on Anglesea Street, on his way to his car. It was twenty-seven hours since he first got the call to come to work. He had well and truly earned his pay-check, after over forty witnesses were interviewed. Before leaving, John told his team that he wanted them back by1:00PM that afternoon to continue both investigations.

Chapter 8

John sat in his car that felt like an ice-box. He turned the key, hoping the engine would start. The starter turned slowly and then the engine chugged to life. He left the engine running for less than a minute before driving off, hardly long enough to warm the oil but he couldn't wait any longer. He reversed out of his parking spot and drove home.

Because there was almost no traffic and no icy patches on the road to West Cork, it was just after 6:AM when John drove along the causeway on to Inchydoney Island. The sky was pitch black and not a single star could be seen in the sky. He drove along the coast to the beach road; the tide was in and the wind was blowing the occasional wave over the wall, splashing water onto the road. John drove up the hill above the beach and into his driveway.

"It will be at least two hours before it's daylight," he thought as he locked the car and ran inside to the warm house.

The greyhounds lifted their sleepy heads from their cozy slumber in their crates. They sat up and wagged their tails, happy to see their master return. John took them out to the back paddock so they could relieve themselves. They sniffed around in the snow for a few minutes too long and started hopping on three legs. It was too cold to keep all four paws on the frozen ground. Soon they were racing to the back door to get back inside.

John tiptoed around like a burglar, desperately trying not to wake Jules, who was still on holidays from the school where she worked. He headed to the bathroom, peeled off his stale clothes and stepped into the shower. The steaming hot water felt so good as it washed away the grime of the last twenty-seven hours. A few minutes later he was sliding into bed next to his sleeping wife. He put his arm around her waist and felt himself drift off. It was like falling into a deep, deep pit in slow motion. He spiraled downwards but never hit the bottom... he just slept. Jules held his hand as he slept, happy that he was finally getting some rest and sad, knowing that in a few short hours, he would have to return to the front line and face the horrors that he dealt with on a regular basis.

Five hours later John's cellphone alarm started to chime. He reached for it and shut the annoying noise off. He felt awful. His head felt empty and his throat was dry. Jules, already in the kitchen, heard the chime and poured a cup of coffee and brought it to her husband.

"Why are you getting up so soon?" Her tone was sharp.

John struggled for a second to come up with a reasonable answer and then managed, "I got to be back for one o clock. We are nowhere near finished and haven't even started the second investigation yet."

Jules placed the coffee on the bedside table. "This can't be good for you. Why do you have to go in so early? Those victims are not going to get any deader." She didn't know whether to be annoyed or concerned.

"Because we haven't a hot clue who killed any of them," he answered, slightly more alert as the hot coffee started to work on him.

Shortly after 1:00PM John walked into the office of The Serious Crime Unit, wearing a fresh suit. Within a few minutes all the other detectives arrived. To look at them in their spiffy suits, one would think they had shown up at an accountant's office after a weekend off, instead of getting five hours sleep after a twenty-seven-hour marathon investigation.

John was usually present at least half an hour before his squad, but today he arrived at almost the same time. However, he had been working on a plan long before he returned to the Incident Room.

Within half an hour, Inspector Cahill was starting his briefing.

FLASHBACK TO JANUARY 1ˢᵗ.

On New Year's Day, Mikey Galvin didn't sleep very well. He had gone to Tess Rutherford's house to crash after the party and the brawl. Tess was the mother of his two children, a seven-year-old boy and a four-year-old girl. Tess was aware that something had gone wrong but knew better than to ask Mikey about it. He had a short fuse when he was around her and she was not about to ignite it.

At about 2:30PM on New Year's Day, Mikey received a text from his brother.

Are you awake?" Georgy texted.

Mikey answered quickly, "*Get Tyson and Darryl and meet me at Dan's Bar in half an hour.*"

"*What about J?*" Georgy texted back.

"*NO - HEAT BAG*" Mikey answered, stressing the capital letters. He did not want to be around Johnny Johnson at the moment.

KEN ROLLAND WOKE UP in his mother's spare room on Sharman Crawford Street in the early afternoon on New Year's Day.

He checked the time. "One-thirty and no cops kicking in the door. I'd say I'm in the clear," he thought to himself.

Ken dragged his ass out of bed and walked to the kitchen. His mother was sitting by the table, watching something on the television. She was smoking a cigarette and nursing a glass of dark rum.

"Do you have any coffee, Mam?" Kenny asked.

Cecilia Rolland looked at her son and was about to speak but instead she started to cough and splutter. She spat phlegm into a piece of paper towel that she pulled from the pocket of her filthy housecoat. When she caught her breath, she managed "I think there's some instant in one of those cupboards."

Kenny spooned two heaped teaspoons of instant coffee into a discoloured chipped mug. He couldn't find a kettle so he boiled water in a saucepan. He sipped the steaming coffee and took one of his mother's cigarettes from the open box on the table.

"You could at least ask!" she barked at him in her hoarse voice.

Kenny grunted and walked back to the bedroom.

He picked up his cell phone and texted his brother, Tyson, "*Are you moving yet Bro.*"

"*We got to talk,*" was the reply from Tyson Rolland.

"*No time for talk, just gimme what's owed and I'm outta here,*" Kenny fired back.

"*KK Half an hour at the Grotto.*"

"*KK,*" Kenny agreed.

Kenny didn't have a jacket as he had dumped his blood-soaked one in a garbage bin behind the apartment block so he called a cab to take him to the Grotto. Kenny didn't want to drive and risk getting pulled over by the cops for something stupid. The Grotto was a religious statue situated at the foot of Dublin Hill at the junction of Old Mallow Road in the heart of Independent Posse territory. It was also a short distance to Dan's Bar on Thomas Davis Street near Blackpool Bridge, where Mikey G had called a meeting.

The cab pulled up at the foot of Dublin Hill and Kenny saw Tyson standing near the Grotto. He trudged through the slush to meet him.

"No coat, Bro?" Tyson asked with a slick smile on his face.

"It got ruined during last night's fun and games. I had to dump it," Kenny muttered.

Tyson handed his brother a small package. "Here, you should be able to buy a new one once you cut this up. It's all there, all seven ounces, maybe even a little bit more as a bonus for a job well done."

Kenny took the package and laid it flat on the palm of his hand as he judged the weight. He put the package in the pocket of his hoody. "Nice clean job. I took them out drinking at the Mirage. We had to walk back, couldn't get a cab. Then I surprised them both and stuck them real good. I set a fire in the place afterwards. It was nice and easy."

"Nice, Bro. We had a bit of unplanned excitement ourselves last night. A bunch of haters started a fight but we ended it," Tyson said with a slick smile.

Kenny didn't ask anything about the "excitement." He knew better and really, he didn't care or want to know. "I'm heading back up west later today. If you need me for something like this again, just call. Hey, those two ass-clowns had a sweet sixty-inch Sanyo plasma. I helped myself to that as a bonus."

The Rolland brothers mimicked some lame East L.A. handshake, awkwardly hugged each other and parted company. Kenny headed to the shopping center around the corner from the Grotto and Tyson walked towards Blackpool Bridge.

Later in the afternoon, when Kenny returned to his mother's house, she was nursing a fresh glass of rum and smoking another cigarette. He went into the spare bedroom, threw his things into his bag and walked out to the kitchen.

"Hey Mam, I'm heading back to Galway. Do you know Ron Glowden on College Road? He'll give you some cash in a few days. He's got to move something for me."

Cecilia Rolland didn't break her stare from the television. She put her glass on the table, lifted her arm and waved Kenny away.

"Drive safely," was all she managed to say. However, when she heard the door slam, the tears welled up in her eyes.

A MARKED POLICE CAR sat parked in front of the small apartment block near The Lough. Another police car was parked at the rear of the block. The occupants of each vehicle had a clear view of the entrance to the common hallway and the stairs that led to the crime scene. The forensic team had been and gone and the scene guards would hold the gruesome site until dismissed by the inspector of the Serious Crime Unit. Nobody had come or gone all New Year's Day except when it was shift- change and the scene guards were relieved.

AT 3PM, ON NEW YEAR'S Day, the Galvin brothers parked the Volkswagen passenger van on The Commons Road and walked around the corner to Dan's Bar on Thomas Davis Street. Seconds later Darryl Lyons drove up in a red Seat Tarraco and Tyson Rolland arrived on foot. The four gangsters walked in the front door of Dan's Bar.

Dan's Bar was a traditional pub in the heart of old Blackpool. For generations it had been frequented by hardworking men who stopped off for a pint on their way home from work, but in recent years it became a hangout for the Independent Posse gangsters. Now the bar had lost its traditional charm; it was dark and musty and stank of a mixture of stale beer, puke, piss and blood. Nevertheless, the gangsters felt secure here.

The four men sat in a booth in the dark snug, off to the right of the main bar.

Mikey G took charge of the meeting. "Is everything taken care of with our two renegades?" Mikey directed the question to Tyson and Darryl.

"Ya man. It's all cool. My bro Kenny took care of everything. He's split town and is on his way back to his crib, as we speak," Tyson answered, in a weird North Side Cork accent, in his attempt to sound American.

"Why are you grinning?" Georgy asked.

"Kenny took those two out drinking at the Mirage for New Year's. He got them hammered, took them home and went postal on them. Then he set fire to the place. You got to hand it to our Kenny. He knows how to get a dirty job done," Tyson said as he beamed.

"No loose ends?" Mikey asked.

Tyson shook his head.

"Our New Year's party didn't quite work out," Mikey said, looking down the neck of his beer bottle.

"We probably need an *alibi for our alibi*, aghh!" Georgy laughed with his tongue fully out of his mouth.

Mikey turned his head to look at his brother. He didn't crack a smile and he did not say anything.

Georgy knew immediately that his brother didn't think it was funny. Georgy stopped laughing, put his head down and muttered, "Sorry."

"The cops brought a load of people in on a fucking bus," Darryl Lyons spoke for the first time.

"My old lady and her mother aren't home yet," Georgy added.

"Find out every single person that was on that bus and everyone that was at our party and who lives on that street and find out what they told the cops. We 're gonna have to do some damage control!" Mikey said and then lifted his beer bottle and drained it. "What started all that bullshit, anyway?"

"Big Eddie Flynn started it. His brother Bertie told me that Eddie called out a couple of guys wearing red shirts from that house across from Trish's," Tyson answered.

"Eddie fucking Flynn. He's a fucking liability," Mikey said shaking his head. "Back here tomorrow at seven o clock, no chatter on the phones. Get the word out. No chatter!"

Mikey stood up and walked out of the bar followed by his brother.

When they were sitting in the green Volkswagen van, Georgy asked about his buddy, "What about Johnny? You didn't mention anything about him in there."

"Johnny's a heat bag right now. I'm not worried about him. He's solid. Even if the cops grab him, he is going to dummy up. We'll find out more tomorrow," Mikey answered.

Chapter 9

I t was now close to 1:30PM on the afternoon of January 2nd and Detective Inspector John Cahill was ready to start his briefing. He walked across the Incident Room and closed the main door. He stood in front of his squad; immediately they stopped what they were doing, sat up and paid attention to him.

The inspector began, "We got two separate investigations to work on so make sure you have started two new notebooks. It's not ideal but you are all going to have to work on both of these at the same time. I'm going to start with the double homicide near The Lough. Both victims have been positively identified by their fingerprints.

- Julian Hodnett age 24
- Alvin Pomeroy age 22"

ACCORDING TO OUR DATABASE both are associated with the Independent Posse and are low-level drug dealers. It doesn't make sense that they would be living in the South Side, as they usually stick to the North Side. The cause of death is multiple stab wounds for both. Hodnett was found at the foot of the stairs near the south entrance of the block. Pomeroy was found upstairs, half in the kitchen and half in the living room

Pete and Tim! Chase down the property management company for the block and find out who lives in the upstairs suite, it's Suite C. Then track down the tenant. Tim, you and I will interview the tenant once you have identification. Maybe it will be that easy. The tenant did it and that one will be wrapped up right away. Don't go anywhere yet. Jen Martens from Ident is coming over in a few minutes to give us some more on this and the Manor View Estate shooting.

Okay, switching gears for now to the Manor View Estate shooting. Jeff and Len, Travis and Larry, head back to Manor View Estate and do a complete canvass again, make sure the uniforms didn't miss anything. Mike and Eddie, go to the hospital and check on the two injured people. If possible, have a word with them but I don't think that they'll be ready to talk yet. After that, check the data base for a male with long black greasy hair who walks with a limp. Pete has started that but he could use the help."

There was a knock at the office door and John walked over and opened it.

Mike Williams looked at Pete Sandhu and smiled, "That's just about every second male in the North Side."

Sergeant Jennifer Martens from the Forensic Identification Section handed John a selection of photographs from both scenes. She addressed the inspector but spoke loud enough for the other investigators to hear.

"We finished processing both scenes. But I want to hang on to the scene at the apartment block near The Lough, at least until after the autopsies. The scene in Manor View Estate is a disaster. There are thousands of sets of footprints in the snow and three areas where there's a great deal of blood. It's pretty obvious where the shots were fired from based on the shell casing we found. We did not find all the casings. Somebody picked them up."

"Is there anything remarkable about the scene of the double homicide at the apartment block?" Cahill asked.

"There are several sets of fingerprints in there. Lots from the two deceased and we are running the others through AFIS still. It wasn't much of a fire inside the suite. It didn't cause any real damage, just some smoke damage. Somebody piled a bunch of garbage and papers on top of the stove and turned all four rings on. It just smouldered and smoked instead of blazing which I reckon is what the suspect wanted."

"Any murder weapon there?" Warren asked.

"There's knives on a block in the kitchen, but none with blood and no knife found on the floor," Jen Martens answered.

"How many times were they stabbed? Mike Williams asked.

"Lots. We won't know for sure until after the autopsy tomorrow, but whoever killed these guys wanted to make sure they were dead. I would say Hodnett made a run for it after Pomeroy got killed but he didn't make it very far. He got it on the stairs."

"Anything else inside the suite?" Cahill enquired.

"There were four long black hairs on the ground about an inch from Alvin Pomeroy's right hand. According to the firefighters who found him, his arm was outstretched on the floor and the hairs were lying next to where his fingers would have been."

"You seized them I hope?" John questioned.

Jen Martens didn't even bother to answer that. She turned her head to the inspector and gave him a look that would scare an ordinary man. Then she continued, "It looks like a television may have been stolen. You know the wire that goes from the antenna socket in the wall to the back of a television? Well, the wire is there, plugged into the wall and the antenna plug from the back of a television is still attached to the end of the wire. It appears that it was wrenched out of the back of a television set."

"Maybe a robbery then," Tim Warren added.

"The rest of the suite is relatively tidy and certainly hasn't been ransacked. Whoever lives there has kids. There are kids' clothes and toys in the suite. There was also some mail in the name of Crystal Mannering."

Pete Sandhu didn't waste a second and immediately turned to his computer and entered the name 'Crystal Mannering' into the police database. Within seconds he got a hit, but it wasn't the smoking gun he hoped for. All he found was Crystal Mannering had a valid driver's license, was twenty-three years old and the address on her driver's license showed a residence in the town of Mitchelstown.

Jen Martens continued her briefing. "This could be some type of home invasion, maybe a drug rip or something along those lines." The detectives were paying attention and listening to her every word. "The front door had been forced open. I didn't see any boot prints on it, but it definitely had been broken open. The deadbolt is still in the locked position, the door frame is cracked and shattered and there are wood splinters from the frame all over the floor inside the hallway. If I were to guess, I would say bodily force was used to break the door down."

"That front door only leads into a common hallway, from what I remember. Is that correct Jen?" John asked.

"Yes, that door leads to a common hallway. The downstairs suite, on that side of the building, appears to be unoccupied."

"What about the door to the upstairs suite? Is that forced too? Or is it unlocked?"

"I was about to get to that, Inspector!" Jen Martens snapped. "The door to the scene is at the top of a stairwell and it was open. It had not been forced."

"Could the 'hose jockeys' have smashed the front door?" Mike Williams asked.

"No, the firemen found Hodnett at the end of the stairs and part of his body was in the open doorway," Jen answered as she checked her notebook to make sure she had named the correct deceased person at the foot of the stairs.

"Alright, that's all for now. Get out there and get some answers!" John dismissed his detectives.

"What about next of kin notifications?" Tim Warren asked, as the investigators grabbed their coats and made their way to the door.

"Hang on!" John said called out He let out a slow breath. "I forgot about that. We have two families who have lost their sons. Tim, you and I can track down the families for Hodnett. Mike and Eddie, check in with Pomeroy's family and I presume the hospital would have contacted the families for Chelsea Brown and Kyle Healy, but please, if you can, touch base with them too."

Pete Sandhu was left behind to man the phones and search data bases for gang members and other criminals with a limp and the four teams of detectives headed to their police cars. There wasn't much conversation. Nobody liked the task of dealing with the families of homicide victims; there were always more questions than answers. Even when the detectives knew the answers, they were always slow to provide them as that knowledge could sometimes interfere with the investigation.

John and Tim found their dark red Ford Mondeo parked in the basement of the Anglesea Street Station. Tim automatically sat in the driver's seat and his partner started scanning his notes as they headed to the scene at The Lough. Hopefully they could easily identify the property management company and track down Crystal Mannering, without having to make the drive to Mitchelstown.

It only took several minutes to drive from Anglesea Street to the scene at The Lough. On arrival, the detectives found the uniform officers sitting in their patrol cars ensuring nobody entered the scene. Blue and white police tape blocked off the yard and the doorway. Tim parked on Bandon Road, near 98 Street and John stepped out of the Mondeo and tied up his heavy overcoat. He walked a hundred meters to the patrol car; the occupant let the window down.

"Anyone of interest show up here?" John asked.

"Only some photographer from one of the local papers came by about an hour ago. Nobody else has even noticed that we're sitting here," the young, bored officer replied.

At that moment a small blue sedan drove into the lane and the driver pulled into a parking stall and got out of the vehicle. She opened one of the rear doors and helped two young children out of their car seats. Crystal Mannering walked towards the police tape looking very concerned.

The uniformed police officer stepped out of his warm car as Crystal stopped at the police tape and her son ran under it.

"No Zack, come back here, wait!" she yelled. The young boy stopped and returned to his mother.

"You can't come in here, ma'am" the young officer informed her.

"But I live here. Did something happen?" Crystal's anxiety level was rising.

John, who observed what was happening, lifted the blue and white tape and walked across the yard, to the broken- down door at the side of the apartment block. Crystal had already picked up her daughter, Ellen, and was holding on tight to Zack's hand. She saw the man walking towards her and knew he was a detective. Nobody else would be wearing a suit and an overcoat in this neighborhood.

"Hi," John called out to the worried young woman as he raised the tape. "I'm Detective Inspector John Cahill. Did you say you lived here?" as he pointed to the small apartment block.

"Yes," she answered shakily.

"Which suite?" John asked, "Upstairs or downstairs?"

"Upstairs," Crystal paused. "On this side." Crystal nodded towards the door.

"Are you Crystal?" John asked.

"Yes," she managed in a whisper. "What's happened? What's wrong?"

Tears were now rolling down her cheeks. Crystal knew something bad had happened.

From her reaction, John immediately knew that Crystal was not his suspect but he still had a few questions to ask the young woman. "Where are you coming from?"

"I was at my mom's place in Mitchelstown. Please, what's happened? Where's Julian?" Crystal begged for information.

Ignoring Crystal's questions, John calmly asked, "When did you go to Mitchelstown, Crystal?"

"On New Year's Eve," she blurted out through her tears.

"Crystal, I need to talk to you but we need to talk at the station. Not here, it's too cold to stand around here. Is there anyone who can take the kids for an hour or two?" As John was speaking with her, Tim Warren walked over to join them. "Crystal, this is Tim. Crystal and the kids just got back from Mitchelstown. They went out there on New Year's Eve. She's going to come down to the station with us and we can fill her in on what has happened here. What about the children? Is there someone who can watch them?"

"No, nobody." Crystal whispered.

"That's okay, we can all go together. Tim, bring our car around here. Do you need to get anything out of your car for the children?" John asked.

Seconds later, Tim pulled up next to Crystal's car and Crystal, Zack and Ellen got in the back seat and she buckled her children in as there were no child seats. John sat in the front and they set off in silence to Anglesea Street Garda Station. Crystal was terrified; she was afraid to ask anything because she did not want to hear bad news.

When they arrived at the station, they made their way to the second floor. Crystal looked at the sign on the door, Serious Crime Unit and let out a sob. "What's wrong, Mommy?" Zack asked as he gripped his mother's hand.

John flinched as he looked at the scared young girl with two babies. He felt a lump in his throat as he showed Crystal and her children into the C-I-D boardroom. He was not about to subject this girl to one of their filthy interview rooms, especially with what he was about to tell her. The boardroom wasn't plush by any means, but it looked somewhat professional. There was a long table with eight office chairs, a large television on a portable shelving unit and two whiteboards along the wall.

"Please wait here for two minutes, Crystal. We're just going to take our coats off and we'll be right back," Tim said.

John and Tim went to their office, John took off his heavy overcoat, un-holstered his pistol and put the gun in his desk drawer. He walked across to the Incident Room, where Pete Sandhu looked up from his computer.

"We found Crystal; she's got two little kids with her. She showed up at the block when we were there. It looks like she just got back from Mitchelstown. She went out there on New Year's Eve. She hasn't a fucking clue what's happened at her apartment."

"That would have been too easy, wouldn't it?" Pete replied.

"Can you call up to the Uniform Division and see if there is somebody there that can take these two little kids for half an hour while we talk to Crystal? I think this is going to get ugly."

The Uniform Division at Anglesea Street patrolled the area around City Hall, the docks and the South Mall, Cork's Financial District. Pete made the call to the sergeant in the uniform patrol division and within a few minutes, two young female officers arrived at the door, ready to take the two children on a tour of the police station.

"I'm going to get her to commit to her story in a statement, just in case something goes south down the road. I really think she's being truthful and her alibi for New Year's will be easy enough to check," John said to Tim as he prepared to return to the boardroom.

His plan was to get as much information from Crystal Mannering as possible before having to tell her that her boyfriend was dead. This was a necessary tactic that he hated himself for using. However, he knew that she would go to pieces when she heard the devastating news and most likely be unable to continue with the interview.

After Tim instructed the two uniform officers to keep the kids occupied, he looked over at his partner, "There is no way that young girl with two little kids stabbed those two and then tried to burn the place down."

"I agree but stranger things have happened!" John answered.

John didn't waste any time and started his interview with Crystal in his calm soft Cork accent. "The kids will be fine Crystal. Those ladies will take great care of them, show them all the cool things in the station and give them some treats. Who was living at your apartment with you? There was you and the two children, and…"

"Julian and his friend Alvin have been staying there for a couple of months. Is Julian okay?"

"Before we talk about that, tell me about Julian and Alvin and why they're living on the South Side with you?"

Crystal's voice trembled as she replied, "They are both tied into the Independent Posse in the North Side. Julian is trying to get out of that life and he wants Alvin to do the same. When I hooked up with Julian a few months ago he asked if he could move in because it kept him away from the North Side. Alvin is his best friend. They've known each other since they were babies. They both grew up in care. Julian has no family and Alvin has nothing to do with his family. So when Alvin showed up about two weeks after Julian moved in he kinda stayed too. They're really good with my children. Julian bought us a huge television just before Christmas and Alvin has his PlayStation and they even have games for Zack and Ellen."

John was curious where the men got the money for a huge television but he didn't want to sound judgmental, so he decided to guide her to answer his question without having to ask it. "How big is a huge television?" he asked.

Crystal smiled. "It's a sixty- inch flat screen, plasma. I know what you're thinking. Where did he get the money for that ...it's got to cost over two thousand euros? Well, it's not new. He bought it from North Side Rentals for seven hundred and fifty euros. Julian got a good deal on it. I have the receipt at home for it!" She sounded defensive.

"Good for him, he is taking care of his family. That is what he should be doing. Is he managing to keep away from the gang life?"

Crystal sighed. She knew Julian had not made a complete break from the Independent Posse and she was not about to lie to the police for him. "They still go to the North Side a few times a week. He can't make a clean break like that. Is Julian okay? Please tell me. Why is my place all taped off?"

John ignored her pleas. "Tell me about New Year's. When did you head out to Mitchelstown? Where did you stay and what did you do?"

Crystal composed herself and answered, "We went out there on New Year's Eve. I didn't get there until after supper. We were late leaving and the roads were awful—-blowing snow and black ice the entire trip. I was afraid the highway would be closed."

"Who went? Who is we?" John asked calmly.

"Me, Zack and Ellen!" Crystal answered like it was the most ridiculous question she ever heard.

"And everything was fine when you left?" John kept prodding gently. "Were the guys at home? Did they have any big plans for New Year's or anything like that?"

"Everything was fine. Julian and Alvin were playing video games when I left. They said they might go to a club for New Year's with their buddy, Ken. Ken came around just as I was leaving."

John was interested about hearing more about this Ken. "Is Ken one of their buddies from the Posse?"

"I don't think so. He seems nice but he looks very scary. I think he's from Galway or Limerick or somewhere out west. He said he was visiting his mother. He came around to our place a couple of times. He bought us supper one night."

"Do you know his last name?" John was trying his best to sound casual, despite being excited about getting another person who may have some information.

"Ronald... or no, Rolland! I think that's it. Ken Rolland!"

John tried not to smile but recognized the last name Rolland and wondered if he was a relation to Tyson Rolland, one of the top men in the Independent Posse.

"What does Ken look like?"

"He's tall and he's big. Not fat. Kind of chubby but muscular. He has very long black hair. I think it's longer than mine." Crystal stroked her own long black hair that fell down her back.

"Did you hear from Julian again during the night?"

"He texted me at midnight to wish me a Happy New Year. He said 'they' were at the Mirage."

"Ken Rolland was definitely there when you were leaving."

"Yes, I opened the door to walk out with the two kids and he was right there. He went in and up the stairs. I told him Julian and Alvin were up there."

"Did he look okay? Was there anything strange about him?"

"He was fine. He told me to drive carefully. What happened? Is Julian okay? Did Ken do something?" Crystal's voice rose an octave. She was starting to panic.

Tim Warren looked across the table at his partner. It was a look that meant it was time to tell the poor girl the truth. John caught Tim's glance and knew he had to break the terrible news to the young mother.

He took a deep breath, "Crystal, there is no easy way to tell you this. In the early hours of New Year's Day, Julian and Alvin were found dead inside your apartment. Somebody killed them. This wasn't an accident. They have been killed." It was brutal and very much to the point. John knew that she had to hear the news this way. As savage as it sounded, she needed to know that her boyfriend and his friend were dead. He let his words sink in and allowed the young girl to process them while he held her gaze

The next ten seconds felt like an hour and then Crystal's eyes filled with tears. She tried to say something but when she opened her mouth to speak, all she could manage was a high-pitched wail followed by the deep sobs of someone who was genuinely and deeply upset. Crystal tried to speak, "What," several more-deep sobs and she took a deep breath, "happened?"

"We're not quite sure yet. We found Julian near the front door. The front door had been forced open. Maybe someone knocked on the door and he went to see who was there. The door may have been kicked in and he was overpowered. Alvin was found dead upstairs in the living room." John was trying to make sense of the scene, both for himself and for Crystal.

"How did he die?" Crystal managed between deep sobs.

John thought about this before answering. She would find out from the funeral home. "They were both stabbed. It would have happened fast and neither of them suffered," John added, trying to make this a little more bearable.

"WHO?" Crystal blurted.

"We don't know yet. But we will do our very best to find out who did this to you and your family."

Tim arranged for the two officers who were babysitting the children to take Crystal and the kids back to Mitchelstown, about a forty minutes drive from Cork. He instructed them to confirm Crystal's alibi. He did not think she was lying but he had to be sure.

When Tim returned to the Incident Room, John had retrieved a photograph of Ken Rolland along with his criminal record. "Tyson Rolland's half brother. He was recently released from Strangeways in Manchester. According to this, he is living in Galway." He waved the record in the air.

Superintendent Collins came into the Incident Room, looking for an update. John told him what Crystal said, especially the part about Ken Rolland. John also mentioned his theory of the broken-down door and Julian being found in the doorway.

"That makes sense, that he went to open the door and it got broken down on top of him. How do you want to treat this Ken Rolland character? It looks like they were pals and going out for the night, according to Crystal. Why didn't he get stabbed up?" the superintendent asked.

"Maybe Rolland left or didn't go back there with them. Hopefully the Mirage has video and we can see if they were actually there. Right now, he is a 'Person of Interest,' John surmised.

"It can wait until tomorrow. Go home and get some rest," the superintendent ordered.

"I'll send Tim and Pete home and as soon as the others get in we'll all head home. Right now, we're no further ahead on the Manor View Estate shooting either."

Tim Warren and Pete Sandhu didn't argue with their boss and took the first opportunity to go home. John was exhausted after dealing with Crystal. It was the worst part of the job, telling someone that a loved one had been savagely killed and you didn't have any 'answers.' John texted Jules to tell her that he would be home soon. and within the hour, the other teams had also returned to base.

Shortly after seven John walked into his house at Inchydoney Beach. The two greyhounds were first to greet him. Lucy, the big red girl came right over to nuzzle him while he undid his shoes. Molly, the smaller brindle, was equally happy but a little shyer as she peeked around the corner with her long tail wagging furiously.

"You're home early," Jules greeted him with smile. "That can only mean you haven't made much progress. What happened?" Jules knew that if arrests had been made it would be another all-night process.

John filled her in on some of the details. He knew she would not breathe a word about the investigations to anyone and she often came up with really good ideas about how they should proceed.

After supper, they took the dogs for a walk along the West Beach. Although it was calm, it was still bitterly cold. The sky was lit with stars and a bright half moon. The tide was out and the moon reflected off the top of the calm ocean. John told Jules how terrible he felt interviewing Crystal Mannering before he told her that her boyfriend had been killed in her apartment.

"You didn't do it to be cruel," she said as she squeezed his hand.

Chapter 10

On January 3rd, morning came quickly and at 7AM the detectives were at their desks in the Incident Room, awaiting their tasks for the day. Mike Williams and Eddie Jenkins were assigned to review the recorded statements of the witnesses from the Manor View Estate homicide in case anything was missed. The others were sent to The Lough to canvass the apartment blocks and homes in the area. John and Tim headed to the Mirage to check for video and with the local cab companies to see if any drivers remembered picking up the three men after midnight.

The detectives were led in through the staff entrance by the club manager. At this time of the day there were no flashing, colored lights and no loud music. "This might be one of the fancier night clubs in town, but in daylight it's a bit of a kip," John thought as he looked around.

The club manager pointed out the thirty-five high-definition surveillance cameras strategically placed throughout the club. He was quite proud of the setup. "New Year's celebrations went off without a hitch. Everyone's identification is scanned at the door and customers walk through a metal detector before entry to the club. On a night like New Year's, I have eighteen security staff working. We had only three or four minor incidents during the night." "What's classed as a minor incident?" Tim Warren asked.

"It's usually some type of physical altercation."

"Like a fight?" Tim clarified.

The manager smiled, "Yes. We usually intervene before things get too out of hand. Most of the time it's just some drunk getting annoyed because he thought somebody was paying too much attention to his lady. We toss out the instigator and that usually settles things down."

"Do you ever have any gang problems?" John asked.

"We've had a few issues from time to time when rival gang-bangers start mean-mugging each other. But most of the time they know that they can't conduct gang business here. I'll call the cops in a heartbeat." The manager was trying to sound like a law-abiding pillar of the community but the detectives knew he turned a blind eye to the sale of recreational drugs on the premises and probably got a cut of the profits.

The manager transferred all the video, including the patrons' scanned identification onto a portable hard-drive and the detectives walked back out to the freezing cold street.

"If you were going to walk back to Barrack Street, which way would you go?" John asked his partner.

Tim looked around. "Head to Washington Street and then to the South Main Street! It's a straight line then if you're walking. You can't drive it because of a few one-way streets but it's a direct route to walk. Do you want to walk? I don't. Let's start at the other end and drive back here. We'll be extra vigilant for surveillance cameras along the way."

They found one surveillance camera on a store on South Main Street near Hanover Street. The store owner provided them with a copy of the video from New Year's Eve and the early hours of January 1st.

When they returned to the Incident Room, Tim and Pete Sandhu began to review the video from the nightclub, starting with the scanned identification.

DETECTIVE GARDA JEFF Rafter's cell phone rang and vibrated in his pant pocket. He looked at the call display but did not recognize the number. "Rafter, Serious Crime," he answered the call.

"Hi Jeff! Happy New Year buddy. How's it going?" a male voice greeted him. "It's your old pal, Gerry Campbell."

Gerry Campbell was an independent drug dealer, originally from Belfast, but now based in Limerick. When Gerry was a naïve seventeen-years-old in high school, he was involved in a homicide. Gerry approached Jules Cahill, a teacher's aid in his school and asked to speak with her husband. Gerry met with Detective John Cahill and confessed to his role in the homicide. Campbell testified against his co-accused and pleaded guilty to a lesser offence. Gerry served prison time as a young offender where he discovered his future was in selling drugs.

Upon his release from custody, Gerry was assisted by the Witness Assistance Program to move to Limerick where nobody knew him. He left the government assisted program and now ran a lucrative cocaine and crystal meth distribution empire. He knew all the major gang players but didn't step on anyone's toes. He even paid taxes to the gangs when working close to their territory to keep in good standing with them. Garda Jeff Rafter had cultivated Gerry Campbell as a confidential informant. He was reintroduced to Detective Inspector John Cahill a couple of years earlier when he identified a member of the Independent Posse in another homicide investigation.

"Happy New Year, Gerry. Is this a social call and you just want to wish me well and hope my holiday season was wonderful? Or are you in trouble and hope I can help you out?" Jeff Rafter asked.

"How could I be in trouble? I never break the law. Are you working on that latest murder?" Gerry sniggered.

"Which one? I'm working on three right now and cleaning up a few old ones. Be more specific. I'm a very busy man."

"The shooting in Manor View Estate on New Year's. I might have something for you."

"Did YOU do it?" Jeff asked casually.

"Fool me once, shame on you. Fool me twice, shame on me! That reminds me, how is your boss doing? Is the PSNI man still here?" Gerry was in good form, but he was reminding the policeman that he would never confess to something like a murder again.

"He's still here, Gerry. I'll tell him you said hello and want to confess to another murder, shall I?" Jeff said, giving the informant as good as he got.

"I have a little side business where I three-way phone calls for guys inside."

In Limerick Prison, most prisoners have telephone access to only a limited number of people and must enter a personal identification number before dialing one of their designated numbers. However, prisoner ingenuity found a way around this by calling someone on their list who three-ways the call to a third party not on their contact list.

"You never cease to amaze me, Gerry. Can you get to the point?" Jeff scolded himself for sounding a bit too impatient.

"Jeffrey Brady called last night from the pen. He wanted to speak to his sister Sam. I called up Sam and put them together."

"How come Sam isn't on his contact list?"

"She's a gang-banger and he's not allowed contact with gang-bangers. Normally I just put them together and walk away but I was bored and listened in."

Jeff Rafter was hooked now. Gerry Campbell had his full attention. "Thank God for boredom Gerry, what happened?"

"She's running his drug lines for him while he's banged up. But she said she was at a party at Georgy Galvin's house on New Year's and there was a huge brawl. Sam said Johnny Johnson ended the brawl when he lit the place up. Jeffrey shut her down and told her to shut her mouth. Then they started talking about her car.

"And they never went back to talk about it again?" Jeff asked eagerly.

"Not a word."

"Why are you telling me this?"

"Because I'm a nice guy. I thought this might be worth a couple of hundred euros or maybe one day I'll need a favor from you. I know Johnny Johnson. He's an old-style gangster and a tough guy. Johnny won't say a word to you if you bring him in for questioning."

They ended the call and Jeff Rafter approached his boss in the Incident Room. Jeff revealed what he had learned from Gerry Campbell. Glad of any information, John looked up Johnny Johnson on the police data base. He was the right height and build. He had long black hair but what John liked most of all was that Johnson walked with a noticeable limp.

"So, you're the killer," John said, pointing at the photograph of Johnson on his computer screen.

At the same time, Pete Sandhu had found what he was looking for on the surveillance video. He pinpointed the exact time that Julian Hodnett, Alvin Pomeroy and Ken Rolland arrived at the Mirage. The next task was to follow them around inside the club to determine if there were any problems and see what time they left. Pete called his boss over to look at the three men paying the cover charge at the entrance and scanning their identification.

"Go back! Go back!" John was excited. "Freeze on Rolland. Isn't that the blood-stained jacket that Ident found in the bin behind the apartment block at The Lough? Hang on. I'll pull up the crime scene photos."

John compared the photographs of the bloodstained lumberjack plaid jacket that the crime scene investigators found to the one that Ken Rolland was wearing in the video. The lighting inside the nightclub was not ideal but John was certain it was the same one. Tim Warren and Pete Sandhu were not convinced.

"I don't know, Boss. The jacket in the nightclub looks darker and older. The one in the bin looked very new except for the liter of blood splashed all over it."

"We're going to get Ken Rolland's D.N.A. on that jacket. Wait and see," John pointed to the crime scene photo of the plaid jacket. "I think we've identified the Manor View Estate killer too." John switched screens and pulled up a picture of Johnny Johnson. He told the rest of his crew about the phone call Jeff Rafter had received from his confidential informant.

"Have you ever dealt with this guy?" Tim asked, pointing at the picture of Johnny Johnson on his computer screen.. "I have. Johnny Johnson is as tough as nails. We'll get nothing out of him in an interview. No wonder none of the witnesses said they saw the shooter. This guy is crazy. They're all scared shitless to say anything. Between him and Mikey 'G,' we're going to have a hard time breaking the witnesses down," Tim shook his head in frustration.

When Pete had completed his search of the nightclub video, John summoned his entire team for a briefing, including the team he had borrowed from C-I-D. He also asked Superintendent Paddy Collins to sit in, so he didn't have to repeat it later. He started with the double homicide near The Lough.

"We all know that the victims were planning on going to a club for New Year's with Kenny Rolland. Well, now we know they went to the Mirage. We have all three of them walking into the club together." On an overhead projector, Pete Sandhu showed a still photo of the three men walking in. "Look at the jacket Rolland is wearing. It's similar to the one that was found in the dumpster at the back of the crime scene," John continued.

The team were split. Some said it was exactly the same; others did not agree.

"Tim and Pete found the three of them wandering around the Mirage during the night. They were putting away a lot of booze and a little after 12:30 AM, all three of them left together. So we know for certain that Ken Rolland left the club with them. We have another video from a store on South Main Street. Tim found the three of them strolling along towards Barrack Street on that video. The question is did Ken Rolland go back to their apartment with them and was he there when the stabbing occurred?" John left the question hanging.

"Moving forward! Jeff Rafter had one of his old friends from his drug squad days call him up. The C.I. was three-waying a call from Limerick Prison. The call was from Jeffrey Brady to Mike William's good friend, Jeffrey's sister, Sam Brady. Sam told her big brother about the brawl and she said that Johnny Johnson ended it when he lit the place up! Jeffrey shut her down and they did not speak about it again. So, there we have it! Two possible suspects in three homicides. Now, what the fuck do we do?" John shrugged his shoulders and walked away to his desk.

During the briefing, John was careful not to identify the confidential informant to the rest of the team. The identity of a CI was sacred and had to be protected at all cost. Rafter had only told his boss who the caller was because the Inspector was the secondary handler for this CI.

Everyone in the Incident Room was relieved that at least they had identified suspects. John dismissed his crew and asked them to think about a plan of action to move both investigations forward.

Superintendent Collins waited until they had all left and theorized, "Manor View Estate is going to be a tough one to crack. Those gang-bangers have a code. I can't see anyone rolling on them unless it's to save their own ass! And even then, it would have to be life or death. Do you want me to turn this over to the National Bureau of Criminal Investigation?"

Most homicide investigations in Ireland are overseen by the National Bureau of Criminal Investigation which operates from Garda National Headquarters in Dublin. Two years earlier, Superintendent Collins had created a Serious Crime Unit in Cork to investigate homicides in the southern region. Collins had made a bold move and appointed Detective Inspector John Cahill, who was seconded from the Police Service of Northern Ireland, to head up the new unit.

"That's your call, Boss. It will crush the guys in my unit if you and the bosses here think it is too much for them. And, do you want to go cap in hand to your counterpart in Dublin and ask him for help?" John replied cheekily.

"I suppose you're right! Sure, they are up the walls there with the cartels killing each other every other day," the superintendent conceded.

Chapter 11

S *till January 3rd.*
   Once John arrived home, he and Jules took the greyhounds for their nightly walk on the twin beaches of Inchydoney. The wind was up and the waves were breaking hard on the shore and rolling up the sandy beaches. The cold wet spray from the waves was blowing across the sand almost as far as the dunes. As usual, John told Jules how the day had developed.

"I'm pretty confident that we will find Ken Rolland's D.N.A. on the blood-stained coat. With the photos of him at the club with the two victims and Crystal saying she saw them together, that should be enough to charge him." He also told her about the phone call from Gerry Campbell.

"I don't like that fella," Jules said with a serious, almost worried tone. "He had so much potential as a kid. He got a second chance after he was involved in that murder in Belfast. He should have stayed in school. He could have picked a different path in life when he got out but he chose this life. I think he's very dangerous. Did he ask to speak with you?"

"No, he didn't. Don't worry, I can handle Gerry... "It's this Johnson guy I'm worried about. This is going to be a tough one to prove. Tim says he's a real hard-case and will not speak to the cops, ever! Between him and the Galvins, I bet all the witnesses are intimidated."

Jules gave her standard answer and grinned, "Bring him in and beat it out of him!"

"You know, he would probably fold like a deck of cards. He definitely needs a good beating but unfortunately, we can't be the ones to deliver it. Our confession would be thrown out and he would get away with murder. But at least we would have the satisfaction of slapping the shit out of him! One can only dream. I am so sick and tired of these gang-bangers," he said as he laughed.

"What about the other case?"

"Ken Rolland is another tough nut and it's probably a waste of time bringing him in under arrest, sticking him in the interview box and hoping he'll cave in and give it up. I think I'm going to wait for the D.N.A. testing on that plaid jacket. When the D.N.A. comes back a match to him, I won't be relying on a confession."

The next morning at the briefing, John announced that they would wait for the D.N.A. results to come back on the jacket before approaching Ken Rolland.

"I'll ask the Anti-Crime Unit to try to track him down and keep tabs on him. It's pointless bringing him in without something more solid to go on. Now, what do we do about Mr. Johnson? Does anybody think it's worth taking a run at him and bringing him in for an interview?"

The rest of the squad grumbled. The consensus was that it wasn't worth their time. Johnson would get a lawyer on board immediately, not commit to anything and stick with 'No Comment.' An experienced criminal like Johnson would also use the police interview to learn what evidence the police had against him.

Mike Williams spoke up, "There isn't much point in going back to the witnesses while Johnson is on the street. They'll all be too scared to talk to us again, let alone identify him."

"What about a one- party consent?" John asked the group.

"What exactly is one- party consent?" Mike Williams asked.

"A one- party consent is when a court order is granted to record a conversation between two or more people as long as one of the party consents to be recorded. It is seen by the courts as being less intrusive that a wiretap. Remember when we used the undercover operator in the cell sit a couple of years ago in the Erin McGill homicide? The UC consented to being recorded."

"Are you thinking of using a UC on Johnny Johnson?" Eddie Jenkins questioned.

"I was thinking of using an agent!" John said as he looked at the puzzled faces in front of him. Jeff's CI knows all the Independent Posse guys and he is also tight with Mikey G. Does anyone else have a confidential informant that could get Johnny Johnson talking?"

"Just so I'm straight on what an agent is, it's a CI who is willing to collect evidence for the police and testify later if required?" Mike Williams asked. "I've heard that the National Bureau of Criminal Investigation used them in the cartel investigations in Dublin, but as far as I know, we've never gone down that route in Cork. To the best of my knowledge, we don't usually use agents in the Garda."

"In a nutshell, you're correct, Mike. An agent is often some dirtbag that gets paid for his services. We use them in Northern Ireland quite a bit in serious investigations. They used to be employed much more during the RUC days but that blew up in the government's face more than once. I ask again, does anyone else besides Jeff have a CI close to the Independent Posse?" John looked at his team shaking their heads.

"How much can we pay an agent?" Jeff Rafter wondered. John laughed. "The PSNI would pay twenty or thirty-grand! I was thinking along the lines of fifteen hundred."

"Fuck! We are so cheap. You couldn't get someone on Death Row to do it for that! I'll sound my guy out and see if he's up for it. We'll talk about money later. In the meantime, why don't we have a whip around and see if we can bring it up to two thousand?" Jeff joked. "Maybe we could get the CI to introduce an undercover to Johnny!"

INSPECTOR SEAN HARRINGTON and Detective Sergeant Percy Jones ran the Anti-Crime Unit, a semi-covert unit that would take on just about any job. Primarily the Anti-Crime Unit was established to investigate serious property crimes. However, because of their expertise in mobile surveillance, the Anti-Crime Unit was in high demand by other investigative units, especially the Serious Crimes Unit. Prior to being transferred to the Serious Crimes Unit, Inspector John Cahill worked in the Fugitive Squad at the same remote building that the Anti-Crime Unit was located.

John walked the few blocks from Garda Headquarters on Anglesea Street to the offices of the Anti-Crime Unit on Stable Lane. The building on Stable Lane did not look like a police station. In fact, from the outside, it resembled an old abandoned warehouse. The inside wasn't much better and if the building wasn't owned by the government, it would probably be condemned. Despite its appearance, the building was extremely secure because it housed millions of euros' worth of specialized equipment. The Anti-Crime Unit shared the building with the Technical Surveillance Unit that specialized in high-tech electronic surveillance. John was going to request assistance from Sean Harrington and Percy Jones to locate and gather intelligence on Ken Rolland.

Harrington was an expert in covert surveillance and trained his team to be equally as proficient. The only time targets ever saw a member of Anti-Crime watching them was because within seconds they were about to be arrested. Although swamped with his own work, Sean Harrington agreed to assist the Serious Crimes Unit and attempt to locate Ken Rolland.

Harrington's team set up on various locations trying to find Ken Rolland, including his mother's house, his half-brother's house and a few of the known gang bars in the North Side of the city. After a few days, Inspector Harrington reported to John Cahill that Rolland had gone to ground and was nowhere to be found. On that same day, the D.N.A. results came back from the bloodstained plaid lumberjack jacket found in the dumpster.

"I got bad news and more bad news," John announced to his team during a briefing.

"Give us the best of the bad news first," Mike Williams said with a cheeky grin.

"Anti-Crime couldn't find Ken Rolland anywhere in the city. He must have left town. That's the best of the bad news. Unfortunately, the National Lab did not get a D.N.A. hit on the bloody jacket We are S-O-L on both fronts."

"What does S-O-L mean?" Tim Warren whispered to Pete Sandhu.

"Shit outta luck!" Pete whispered back smiling.

"They tested the usual places for D.N.A., the cuffs, the collar, under the arms, all the places that have contact with the skin or sweat, but the reports says this appears to be a new jacket and has not had a chance to collect human skin cells yet." John read from the lab report, "The blood stains on the front are from our two victims, Hodnett and Pomeroy.

"We got to find Ken Rolland and either rule him in or rule him out." John threw down the report on his desk with frustration.

"The science should have advanced the investigation. This was such a violent scene. It was an absolute blood bath. How could there be nothing left behind by the killer?" Pete Sandhu said, picking up the lab report and reading it.

"It happens. Remember Stuart Killen. That was a bloodbath and Pierce Alfonso left nothing behind and he wasn't even trying to cover his tracks," Mike Williams added as he shook his head in frustration.

"I will put a Be on the Look Out Notice out for Ken Rolland and ensure it goes out nationally, in case another region runs into him. They can notify us of his whereabouts. People always look at the BOLO's. Now any luck with your CI?" John asked Jeff Rafter, desperate to keep at least one of the investigations moving forward.

"He hasn't called me back yet. I'm sure he will. I've called the only number I have for him. I've also called his grandmother. He's fairly tight with her. She knows who I am and said she'll get the message to him."

John dismissed his crew and headed home after the briefing. It was almost completely dark as he drove along the seafront in Inchydoney but there was a red glow still on the horizon after the sun had set. When he arrived home, the two large greyhounds came running to greet him. He let them in the back paddock for a few minutes but they were more interested in sniffing the corners of the paddock than getting down to business. John whistled to summon the two large hounds. Molly came immediately while Lucy gave him a look as if to say, "I'll be with you when I'm ready." He whistled twice more and the big red hound sauntered over to the back door.

The rain had held off most of the day and after supper John and Jules headed to the beach with the dogs. The sky had clouded over and the only light was from a few houses along the hillside and the two street lights on the road. John told his wife about the lack of forensic evidence and the missing person of interest.

"I can't believe there is no D.N.A. On all those CSI shows they find D.N.A. and skin particles on everything," she groaned.

"The reality is the conditions must be near perfect for that to happen. In winter time, in this climate, you don't sweat as much as in summer and if you keep far enough away from your victims, they won't be able to grab hold of you. That gives me an idea though. There were a few strands of hair on the ground next to Alvin Pomeroy's hand. Jen Martens said she didn't think they were suitable for D.N.A. but I think there is another test that can be done. It's a lot more work and we may have to get a private lab to do it but it may be worth it. I'll have to find out more about it."

"What about the zipper? You said they only tested the cuffs and the collar, but if there is a zipper on the jacket, maybe you would get D.N.A. from that?" Jules suggested.

"That's a great idea, I'll suggest they go over the entire jacket inch by inch and see what they find! I hate it when some scientist is deciding what should and should not be tested," John said as he stumbled through the sand dunes on their way home. Jules enjoyed these chats about his cases but she wished that work wasn't constantly on his mind.

January 5th

When John returned to work the following day, he spoke with the supervisor of the Forensic Unit. "Jen, can we send that blood-stained jacket from the dumpster back to the lab? Ask them to go over it, inch by inch, inside and outside and pay special attention to the zipper. There must be something that was left behind."

"That's the problem with using the National Lab! They are so busy, they pick the easy, usual places that they find D.N.A. and if it's not there, they stop looking. I'll call them back and ask them to do a thorough search of the jacket. We might get lucky with the zipper, you never know."

A short time later, John was catching up on reading reports when his cell phone rang. The number was blocked but he answered it anyway. "Cahill, Serious Crime."

"DI Cahill, why are you trying to track me down? It's bad for business and my grandma thinks I'm in trouble with the law." It was Gerry Campbell calling in.

"Maybe you are in trouble with the law! I know you're up to no good most of the time. Why are you calling me, not Jeff?" John asked, a little annoyed that Campbell had called him and not his primary handler, Jeff Rafter.

"I tried his number twice, he didn't answer. I wanted to get hold of one of you so you didn't keep asking people where I am," Campbell whined, while defending himself.

"We need to meet up. We have a proposition for you," John replied not wanting to waste anymore time speaking with the CI.

"I'm intrigued. I'm in Cork today. How about the coffee shop in Blarney? We met there before. I can be there in an hour. Does that work for you?" Gerry suggested.

"Why so far away?" John said, thinking about fighting the heavy traffic in the narrow streets of Blackpool on the way to Blarney.

"Nobody will recognize either of us there, so nobody will see me talking to the cops. And it's on my way back to Limerick."

"See you then," John answered anxious to end the call.

John found Jeff Rafter and his partner Len Dawson in the lunch room, nursing a cup of tea and watching a soccer game on the television.

"The CI called and said he was trying to get hold of you," John said, a little annoyed, giving Rafter a scolding look.

Rafter patted his suit jacket pockets, "Shit! I must have left my phone at my desk, sorry, Boss."

"No worries we're going to meet with him in an hour at that café in Blarney. Len, you ride with Tim and park outside. Make sure nothing goes sideways and this clown isn't setting us up," John ordered as he smiled, letting Jeff Rafter off the hook about missing the call.

The four officers strapped on their guns and headed to meet the drug dealer. Although John had once had a good relationship with Gerry Campbell, he knew that now he was an out and out criminal at heart and could not be trusted. Long gone were the days of the innocent high school kid.

They pulled into the parking lot of the coffee shop and seconds later, Gerry Campbell drove up in his cream-colored Range Rover.

"Business must be good." Tim Warren said to Len, as he gazed at the expensive luxury vehicle.

Gerry Campbell was visibly uncomfortable talking to the policemen in the café. He took a table where he could see the door and out the window to the parking lot.

John broke the ice. "That bit of info about Johnson was a big help. Thanks."

"I thought you might find that useful," Campbell replied.

"How well do you know Johnny Johnson?"

"Very well. We were on the same range in Wheatfield Prison a couple of years ago, when I was banged up for six months. There were no other I-P guys on that range and I had his back."

"So Johnny trusts you? Would it be unusual for you to call him up or meet him out of the blue?" John asked, getting straight to the point.

"Mmm, we don't socialize but we may have done business together once or twice, if you know what I mean! Some of those I-P guys act independently if a deal comes their way. Mikey G doesn't care as long as they pay him a tax. WHY?"

John had to beat around the bush a bit with his sales pitch to Gerry Campbell. "Would you be interested in making a few euros on the side? I may be able to slide a couple of grand your way. But I need you to help me out."

"This sounds really shady! What do you want me to do?" Campbell answered with a glint in his eye and a grin on his face.

"Would you be willing to introduce someone to Johnny so they could get close to him and maybe get a confession about the shooting?"

"Johnny's no dummy. If I introduce an undercover to him and he gets pinched. he'll know it was me who set him up. That wouldn't be good for business." Gerry's mind was racing as he liked the idea of money from the cops, but he didn't want to damage his reputation in the underworld.

"Well, you could play stupid! You are pretty damn good at that!" John said, keeping a straight face but shooting Jeff Rafter a glance. "We could arrest you too for trafficking and get you out in few days. That would probably help your reputation."

"How much?"

"For an introduction," John paused and looked up as if he was doing a calculation in his head, "fifteen hundred. That sounds about right."

Gerry Campbell burst out laughing. "You got to do better than that. I'll get back to you but the price has to come up." Campbell drained his coffee, stood up and walked out the door.

"Where the fuck is the superintendent going to get with his fifteen hundred!" Jeff Rafter asked his boss.

John laughed, "Gerry will do it but it will cost us about five grand. The super knows that. He's just being cheap."

The detectives headed back to their station. John went to the superintendent's office.

"He didn't shut us down, Boss. I think he'll come around but you're going to have to dig a little deeper into the wallet before he joins our team. Let's be fair here, we got to go to five thousand. I'll try and keep it under that but come on! Fifteen hundred wouldn't buy an ounce of cocaine."

"Can't blame a guy for trying," Paddy Collins laughed.

JANUARY 7th

Two days later, both cases continued to progress slowly. John received a phone call from the Garda in Galway. Ken Rolland had been checked during a traffic stop in Galway City by uniform officers. They had seen the BOLO on the computer system and obtained a reliable address for him.

Gerry Campbell called Jeff Rafter back and was ready to negotiate. "I'll make the introduction for you, but I can tell you now that Johnny Johnson will not deal with someone he just met. And, it will cost you three thousand!"

Rafter told Campbell that he would call him back and went to speak with his inspector. They came up with a plan and Rafter called Campbell back on speaker phone.

"Hmm, I was thinking about that. What if you sat in on the meeting and helped steer the conversation towards the shooting? I would pay you five G's for that," Jeff countered.

Gerry Campbell was enjoying bartering with the policeman. "I like the sound of that. How about if I get a confession, you give me another three?"

Jeff Rafter looked at John for direction and John gave him a thumbs up

"Done! I'll get a legal contract drawn up," Jeff said.

"Whoa Whoa! What do you mean a legal contract?" Campbell sounded a little panicked.

"We're a public agency Gerry. We can't just throw money around the place. We have to account for every penny we spend. But this is good for you too... after all, if it's a contract, I can't rip you off."

"Yeah, I guess. Give me a call when you're ready to do this." Campbell hung up.

John walked back to Superintendent Collins' office to ask for more money. Paddy Collins looked up from a stack of papers on his desk.

"How are you getting on?" John asked in his North Side Cork accent.

"Why do I get the feeling you're going to ask me for something,?" Collins replied, looking sceptical.

"I got some good news," John said, trying to soften the ask. "I got a call from Galway. They spot checked Ken Rolland there and they have a solid address for him. I'll arrange to send a team up there to interview him."

"That is good news.

"All good news today, Boss. We just got off the phone with Rafter's CI. He's in, but we need to talk finances. Is this a good time?"

Paddy Collins smiled and shook his head, "Why not? It's only January and by March we will have blown the budget for the entire year. How much do you need?"

"Between five and eight!" John said it quickly so it wouldn't sound so bad.

"Jesus Christ! He better give us the whole JFK conspiracy for that kind of money."

"Five and he'll introduce an undercover operator and three thousand euro bonus for a confession."

Paddy Collins knew this was a bargain, but he was cheap! And he had to make it look to the inspector that he was going to his bosses, cap in hand, to get this money to solve the murder.

"Okay, set it in motion. Who do you want to use as a UC?"

"Malik Hussain. He's the best and he loves doing this stuff. I will talk to him and see if he's up for it and make sure he has no conflicts with any of his other work," John answered with excitement.

Malik Hussain came to Ireland as a refugee, originally from Libya. He joined the Garda after eventually getting Irish citizenship, having arrived there from North Africa. Like John Cahill, Malik was older than most recruits when he became a police officer. He was the perfect undercover operator. Nobody would ever suspect him as being a cop because he had the look of a street thug who would cut your throat as quick as look at you.

"Who are you going to send to Galway to interview Rolland?" the superintendent asked.

Superintendent Collins was hoping John and Tim Warren would go but he also knew that John was needed to run the undercover operation.

"Williams and Jenkins, I think," John sighed, hoping for a quick solution to both cases.

Chapter 12

January 8th

Mike Williams and Eddie Jenkins drove the two hundred kilometers from Cork to Galway. Between traffic and road repairs, the journey took almost three hours. Mike plugged the address of their hotel near the Spanish Arch into the GPS. As they drove down Mill Street towards the hotel, they passed by the prominent Galway Garda Headquarters. The building was an impressive three-storey grey limestone building that looked exactly like a police station.

"Let's introduce ourselves to the local Garda before we head to our hotel. Hopefully they assign someone to show us around town and where we can find Mr. Rolland," Mike said, pointing at the striking building.

"We may as well, we're right here," Eddie answered. "I've never been to Galway before. My first impression is that it looks like a cross between a holiday town and a redneck town"

Mike pulled into the parking lot of the Garda Station and found a spot along the wrought iron railings by the roadside. The two detectives walked in the main door of the station. Although the building looked like it was from the early 1900's, it was actually a relatively new build, from the end of the century.

"Wow, that's impressive!" Mike looked around in awe at the large modern foyer.

"That's what a healthy budget gets you. There's lots of money in this town. Good to see they are spending it on public safety," Eddie replied equally amazed.

The two Cork cops walked up to the counter in the foyer. An older woman sat behind a Perspex shield with a grate in the middle to speak into. She was tapping away on a keyboard and did not look up or even acknowledge their existence. About thirty seconds passed and although she had to be aware of their presence, she still ignored them. Eddie tapped Mike's ankle with his foot. Mike looked over and Eddie and coughed. Still nothing from the woman behind the Perspex shield.

"Excuse me," Mike tried.

"I'll be with you in a moment!" she barked, without raising her head and still tapping away at the keyboard. Mike jumped half a step backwards, overreacting to her bark! Suddenly the tapping stopped, the lady looked up looking bored. She sighed and then spoke, "Yes! Can I help you?"

Mike showed her his Garda identification, "I hope so. Can we see the sergeant in charge of the Criminal Investigation Department, please?"

The lady blushed ever so slightly and realized that these two were not the usual members of the public that she regularly had to deal with. "I'll see if I can get hold of him," she stammered as she picked up the phone. "Where did you say you are from?"

"We're with the Cork City Serious Crime Unit." Eddie said.

"Somebody will be with you in a moment. You may have a seat over there," and she pointed to a waiting area.

"She's some fucking battle axe, isn't she?" Mike said quietly in a low voice, as he sat on a wooden bench by the wall.

Two minutes later, a young well-dressed man came from behind the counter and walked up to the two Cork Detectives. He held out his hand, and introduced himself. "Joe McGrath, I'm the Sergeant in C-I-D, I hope you guys had a good trip."

Mike and Eddie shook Joe's hand and followed him into the investigative offices. "I see you met Sandra," Joe said with an infectious smile. "She is Galway's idea of 'Crime Reduction.' You take your life in your hands reporting a crime to her. She is probably the rudest person that I have ever met and that includes all the assholes we deal with." Joe laughed, while directing his guests to sit at his desk.

"Yeah, we kind of got that impression from her," Mike laughed.

Mike and Eddie explained their mission to Joe McGrath. Joe had notified DI John Cahill that Kenny Rolland was in Galway and he was only too happy to help the visiting cops especially if it meant getting the likes of Ken Rolland out of his town.

"Do you think he's your killer?" Joe asked.

"It's hard to say, Joe. He was with them all night and he was hanging out with them a few days before New Year's. We have video from the nightclub on New Year's Eve and they all look like they are getting along just fine unless something went terribly wrong when they got back to the apartment. I don't know if he is the killer." Mike answered, sounding sceptical.

"Well, if he is your killer, we'll be glad to see the back of him in this town. We got enough of our own troublemakers without getting an influx from Cork." Joe laughed.

Joe showed Mike and Eddie around the police station and offered them the use of his interview rooms and anything else that he could do to assist. He provided the address they had recorded for Ken Rolland. "I'll drive by and show it to you. It's a dodgy part of town where most of our problems come from," Joe offered.

Twenty minutes later, Mike and Eddie followed Joe into a small square with local government-built townhouses all around it. The area looked a little run down and at first glance it appeared to be a low-income area.

"This is their hotspot!" Eddie said to Mike with a grin as Joe McGrath walked towards their car.

"These guys would crap their pants if they had to spend a few weeks in Cork's North Side," Mike answered as he opened his car door.

"It's at the corner, over there." Joe pointed to a house that had a battered front door and broken Venetian blinds in the downstairs window. There was a Confederate flag hanging in one of the upstairs windows.

"Charming," Mike mocked.

"Like I said, this is our dodgy area, I can stick around if you want," Joe suggested.

"I think we'll be okay," Mike answered as he and Eddie started to walk towards the house. "Thanks for getting us here, though. I'll call you to let you know if he'll come in for an interview."

Mike Williams kicked the bottom of the door four times with the toe of his shoe. It was louder than knocking and would probably alert any occupants that it was most likely the police at the door.

"I can hear some shuffling around in there. It's probably rats!" Eddie said as he instinctively stood to the side of the door.

A couple of minutes later and more persisting banging on the door brought a semi-stoned looking girl in her mid-twenties to answer the door. "WHAT!" she yelled, as she swung the door open.

"Oh, I am really sorry for disturbing you, Miss. But we are the police!" Mike said sarcastically.

"What do you want?" the girl said as she rubbed the sleep out of her eyes and shaded them from the brightness of daylight.

"Where's Kenny Rolland?" Mike asked sternly.

"He's upstairs sleeping."

"Well, get him up, we'll wait in here." Mike and Eddie stepped into the dark grungy hallway as the girl stepped back.

The girl walked halfway up the stairs and yelled, "KENNY! The cops are here for you. What the fuck did you do now?"

"He didn't do anything," Mike answered loud enough for Kenny to hear, in case Ken panicked and jumped out the window, trying to make a run for it.

A few minutes later a dozy barefooted Kenny Rolland came down the stairs, wearing only a pair of jeans. He looked at the two cops standing in his kitchen and walked straight over to the fridge. He took out a two-liter carton of milk, pinched the carton open and drank straight from it. After a considerable slug, he put the milk back and rubbed his bare stomach in a circular motion with the palm of his left hand.

He looked again at the two cops. "How's it going?"

"Not too bad, Kenny. How's it going with you?" Mike answered.

"What do you want?"

"We're Cork Garda. We have come all this way just to talk to you Ken. Can you come down to the Garda Station on Mill Street? We need to talk to you."

Kenny Rolland's stomach gave a slight twist and his heart rate quickened but his face showed absolutely no emotion. "What about?"

"The guys you were with on New Year's. They're both dead," Mike answered.

Again, Kenny's facial expression didn't change; he would have made a great poker player. "What happened to them?"

"Somebody killed them."

"Let's go down to the police station and talk about it We'll fill in the blanks together."

"They were fine the last time I saw them. Pretty fucking drunk, but still breathing. Can I make something to eat first?" Kenny was stalling.

"How about we get you a coffee and a sandwich on the way? The sooner we get this over with the sooner we can get out of town and back to Cork," Eddie answered.

"Okay, I got to throw on some clothes."

"That would be helpful," Mike grinned.

Ken walked back up the stairs and the girl stood by the sink drinking a cup of coffee.

"What do you have going on for the rest of the day?" Mike asked, trying to break the awkward silence.

"I'm going back to bed for a couple of hours."

"Late night last night?" Eddie asked.

The girl did not answer, just turned around, emptied the contents of her cup and walked out of the kitchen and up the stairs.

"Friendly kind of girl," Mike said to his partner as he stepped into the hall to try to listen to see if Ken and the girl were talking. But he couldn't hear anything.

Ken came down the stairs wearing a black shirt and the same jeans. He found a dark blue hoody on a chair and put it on. He tossed his long hair, grabbed it and put a rubber band on the clump to form a messy ponytail. "You're bringing me back here?" Kenny asked Mike.

"That's the plan," Mike answered as the three men walked out of the house to their waiting car.

On the way to the Garda station, they stopped at a McDonalds drive-through and Kenny ordered two sandwiches and an extra-large coffee. Why not? The cops were paying.

At the station's interview room, Mike and Eddie started their interview with easy questions about Kenny Rolland's background. Kenny was easy to talk to and did not appear to be holding anything back. He seemed very relaxed, sitting back in the chair, his legs stretched out in front of him and his arms open, not folded like a shield. Kenny happily told the detectives about his stint in the British prison and how it was so much better than doing time in Ireland. He didn't share much information about his half-brother, Tyson, except to confirm that they were related. Although Kenny spoke freely with the cops, he did not discuss any criminal activity such as his drug trafficking and gang affiliation.

"Kenny, tell us about your trip to Cork over New Year's, Mike asked casually.

"I had to go visit me mam. She called me a bunch of times when I got back to Ireland and I told her I would visit over Christmas. I drove down there, spent a few days, did my duty, dropped her a couple of euros and drove back here."

"Aren't you the good son! What about New Year's Eve and the two guys you were with?" Mike enquired.

"Yeah, Julian and Alvin. I ran into them the first day I got to Cork." Kenny wasn't giving away any answers to questions he had not been asked.

"Do you know their last names?" Eddie asked.

"Sure, Alvin Pomeroy and Julian Hodnett."

"This is going to be like pulling teeth!" Mike thought to himself. "Did you know these guys before you came back to Cork?"

"No. I went to the take-away on Bandon Road to get something to eat. They were in the line ahead of me and they recognized me because they knew my brother." Kenny knew this was not a complete lie and he was very confident and comfortable telling the cops about his first meeting with the two dead drug dealers. "I got talking to them, I didn't want to spend any time in the North Side, while I was in Cork and they were keeping out of there too, so I hung out with them a couple of times."

"Tell us about New Year's Eve," Mike prodded.

"I don't know who fucking killed them but I'll tell you what I know about the night."

Kenny Rolland was an accomplished liar and had been arrested many times. He knew how to tell a story by sticking to the truth as much as possible. It was the easiest way to keep his story consistent.

"I was staying with my mother on Sharman Crawford Street. I didn't want to ring in the new year with her. She was probably passed out by ten o clock anyways. So, I arranged to go to the Mirage with Julian and Alvin. Julian's old lady was going out of town with the kids and they were looking for somewhere to go too."

"Why the Mirage?" Eddie asked.

"I know all the doormen there and I knew we could get in no matter how busy it was. When I went over to their place, Julian's old lady was just leaving. She was late and trying to get to Mitchelstown before the weather got worse. I had a few drinks with the guys, ate some pizza and we took a cab to the Mirage. Julian and Alvin got shit-faced there. I didn't think they would be able to walk home, but we couldn't find a cab so we walked back to their place. It took forever."

"Did you stop anywhere on the way?"

Ken thought about that for a second. He knew the smart cops rarely asked a question that they didn't know the answer to. "Julian took a leak in a lane off South Main Street, Hanover Street, I think it was. Julian pissed all over his leg." Kenny said and he chuckled, thinking about it. "We eventually got to their place."

"Did you go in with them?" Mike asked.

"No. I just made sure they got home safely and didn't pass out in the snow on the way."

"Aren't you the nice guy!" Eddie added sarcastically.

"Well, Julian couldn't get the door opened, so he booted it in. I didn't want to be around if someone called the cops, so I headed to my mam's place."

Mike glanced at his partner and they held each other's gaze for a brief moment. "So, they hadn't been home invaded," Mike thought to himself.

"Tell me about that again," Mike said.

"What? The kicking in the door part! Julian couldn't get the key in the lock. He was shaking so much from the cold and he was pissed as a newt. Alvin wanted to try but he was just as drunk and Julian was getting mad at him. Then Julian said 'FUCK IT' and booted in the door. Actually, I think he used his shoulder to force it, not a kick. He ripped the frame off and the door was hanging on, on one hinge."

"What did you do then?" Eddie asked.

"We busted out laughing. Julian said something like, 'I'm going to be in shit for that tomorrow.' And that was even funnier. They climbed over the broken door and went upstairs. They wanted me to go with them but I had enough, so I fucked off home."

Mike and Eddie had Ken repeat his explanation of New Year' Eve a couple of times and his story never wavered. In the end, the detectives were satisfied that Ken Rolland was telling the truth. They drove him home and called Inspector Cahill to report.

Mike Williams and Eddie Jenkins got back to their office in Cork City, late in the afternoon of January 10th. John was eager to talk to them about their interview. John was surprised by the report he received over the phone the previous evening and now he wanted to dissect the interview with Mike and Eddie.

When the two detectives walked into the Incident Room in Anglesea Street station, they were weary from the day's travelling and also because they had a few drinks the night before with the Galway cops. John barely let them catch their breath.

"Do you really think Ken Rolland is telling the truth? Can you write him out of this one hundred percent?" John asked, looking up from his desk.

Mike Williams sighed. "Boss, you can write Ken Rolland out of this one, one hundred percent. I have been fooled before and I know I'll be fooled again but I'll tell you this for sure. I don't know who killed Pomeroy and Hodnett but I guarantee you, Ken Rolland didn't do it."

"That's a mighty strong statement, Mike," John said, not wanting want to push the issue any further at this point. "Write your report and put the recorded interview on the database."

John would read their reports later and watch the video recording of the interview with Ken Rolland to see if he could find any discrepancies. "I hope you don't regret that guarantee, Mike," he thought to himself, giving his head a shake.

John switched screens on his computer and opened up the autopsy report. Julian Hodnett had significant bruising to his right shoulder. John hadn't given this a second thought earlier and neither had the forensic sergeant as they both assumed the bruising was caused by falling down the stairs. Now, it was possible that the bruising had been caused by Julian forcing the door.

On the drive home to Inchydoney, John started to second guess himself. How could he have been wrong about Ken Rolland? After dinner, John and Jules took the greyhounds to the beach. The major topic of discussion was the Galway trip.

"Is there any chance that Rolland could have fooled those two?" she asked, as they stumbled through the sand dunes. Jules knew John's instincts were keen.

"It's not impossible, we all get lied to every day. Some liars are better than others. But he had the story right, according to Mike. He confirmed everything they knew going out there. What we didn't know is that Julian Hodnett broke his own door in, not some home invasion. I'm going to go over all the Ident reports and look at the photos of the door and frame in the morning."

"Shouldn't Jen Martin do that?" Jules asked.

"I would prefer to do it myself and if anything stands out, I can ask her about it. They have enough going on in her office."

"Don't doubt yourself too much. Your initial instincts are usually the best," Jules reassured him.

As the Cahills and their dogs walked up the steps to the rocky headland between the East and West Beaches, the wind started to pick up. John barely heard the dreaded ringtone from his cell phone. He pulled the device from his coat pocket and looked at the call display.

Jules rolled her eyes and sighed, "Who's that now?"

John let out a groan, "For fuck sakes," he whispered under his breath. "It's Gerry. I'll make it quick," he muttered as his wife glared at him, letting him know she was not impressed.

He jogged towards the entrance of the hotel, to keep out of the wind so he could hear what Gerry Campbell had to say. "Can I call you back in ten minutes? I'm out and about! And, why haven't you called Rafter?" John said, snapping impatiently without even saying hello as he huddled in the doorway of the hotel.

"Can't get hold of him. Anyway, he'll have to ask you first."

"Jesus, Gerry, I rarely get home at a decent time. I'm walking my dogs, give me ten fucking minutes and I'll call you back, okay?"

"No-can-do, I got to meet some people right away. But I can meet with our friend in a couple of days. I'll need a hotel suite at the casino to make it look legit."

John sighed and then countered, "I can make that work but I want my man in there with you."

"That wasn't part of the plan. Our friend won't know your man and won't want to do business with a stranger," Gerry said, determined to get his way.

"It's my way or no way, Gerry. We'll talk tomorrow."

"Fair enough, it's your money," Gerry conceded and the call ended.

John stepped out of the doorway and caught up with Jules who had both dogs on their leads. Jules handed him the lead for Lucy.

"So much for a quiet walk together," she said, as she kept her eyes looking straight ahead.

"I'm sorry. That was Gerry, he couldn't talk later. I had to deal with it now."

"Oh well, at least you have your priorities right. You'd rather talk to some rat than with me." Jules quickened her pace and walked away.

After a hundred meters, she slowed down, waiting for him to catch up and they talked as if nothing had happened. John knew her patience was running thin with this job. He kept telling her it wouldn't be forever, but right now, it felt like it would.

Chapter 13

January 11th

At 1:30 AM, the Cahills were sound asleep when the cell phone lit up and the hushed ring tone woke John. Jules stirred but unlike her husband, she wasn't always expecting the phone to ring and this time she slept through it. John picked up the phone, and saw it was Superintendent Paddy Collins.

He whispered, "Hang on a second," as he walked out of the bedroom, picked up his housecoat and went into the spare bedroom. He closed the door, picked up a notepad and pen that were at the ready. "Hello," was all he could manage at that moment.

"Hi John, Paddy Collins here. I just got a call from the duty inspector. We got new business. A seventeen-year-old gang-banger was stabbed in a park in Ballincollig. He was pronounced deceased half an hour ago. A few witnesses but no eye witness as far as I know."

"Okay, thanks. I'll be in within the hour." John ended the call and sighed. He walked into the kitchen, switched on the electric kettle and made himself a cup of instant coffee. The greyhounds barely lifted their heads. They were all too used to this routine.

A little over two hours later the Serious Crime Incident Room was as busy as it would be at noon. John had briefed with the uniform officers who were first on scene at the Ballincollig stabbing and he was now starting his briefing with his investigators.

"Our deceased is Chris Shorting, seventeen years old. He is an associate of the Mahon Warlords. He was stabbed four times while in a park in one of the estates at the west end of Ballincollig. He managed to alert some people who were in the area. Ambulance attended and the victim was transported to hospital. He succumbed to his injuries and was pronounced deceased at 1:10 AM. He told the paramedic that he knew his attacker but did not know him by name. Hopefully, somebody knew who he was with last night."

"Not another fucking gang murder," Tim Warren said to Pete Sandhu. "Why can't we get a good old fashioned domestic slaughter?" he joked quietly.

John heard Tim's comment and shot him a sharp glance but continued with his briefing. "Mike and Eddie, go find the next of kin and let them know their son is deceased. Hopefully they know who he was with. Jeff and Len, go to the hospital and see if anyone has shown up there, then head to the scene. Interview the people who found Mr. Shorting after he was stabbed and get a canvass going. Pete, one of the uniform crews brought in some CCTV video from the gas station near the entrance to the estate. Go through it and see what you can find. Tim, you're with me. Let's get this wrapped up."

The detectives set off to start their tasks. Mike Williams and Eddie Jenkins walked up the frost covered path to a small house in Bishopstown. The house was in darkness, as could be expected at 5:00AM.

"It looks like it's in relatively good shape." Mike said to Eddie, as they stood in front of the door, looking at the well kept exterior.

Eddie rang the door bell. Not a stir from within the house. He rang the bell again and this time knocked hard on the door. Still nothing.

"I'll go around the back," Mike said, just as a light came on, in what was probably the living room.

"Who's there?" a male voice questioned.

"Cork City Garda," Eddie answered.

There was a fumbling of a lock, chain and a bolt and then a bleary-eyed grey-haired man opened the door and peeked out.

The detectives showed their identification and Eddie spoke, "Mr. Shorting?"

"Yeah," the man answered. "What has he done now?" The man stood back, holding the door open and invited the detectives in out of the cold morning. A tall thin woman, with her hair tied up in a bun, came into the living room, wrapping a pink terry towel housecoat around herself.

"What's wrong?" the woman asked. "Is it Chris?"

"Please sit down, folks. I am afraid I have some terrible news to give you," Mike Williams said, his voice was low, but strong, however, he avoided eye contact with the couple.

The man and the woman sat together on a sofa. Eddie wrote down their names and their contact information in his notebook and then Mike Williams broke the devastating news.

"I'm afraid Chris was involved in some sort of an altercation last night. He was stabbed in a small park in an estate in Ballincollig. I am terribly sorry but he didn't make it. Chris is dead." At this point Mike stopped talking and just looked at the couple across from him.

It took a few seconds for the words to sink in and then the woman stood up and let out an eerie, high-pitched scream as she stood up, held her hands to her face and started to tear at her hair. Her husband stood to hold her but he wasn't taking the bad news any better.

"What happened?" the man finally managed to ask.

"We don't know yet. We're trying to piece it together. Where was he supposed to be last night? Do you know who he was with?" Mike Williams was desperately trying to get something, anything, that could help move this investigation forward.

The woman tried to speak but all she could manage was one word, "Girl" and she sobbed as if her life was over.

"He was probably with his girlfriend, Kyla Hartnett. She lives in Ballincollig," her husband managed to say. "He's been spending more and more time with her and keeping away from his old friends who always got him in trouble."

Eddie Jenkins excused himself and stood in the small narrow hallway at the front door. He called DI Cahill, "The kid was supposed to be with his girlfriend, Kyla Hartnett. She lives somewhere in Ballincollig. I bet it's near that park where he was stabbed."

At that moment Jeff Rafter called on another line. John ended the call with Eddie Jenkins and answered Rafter's call.

"Nothing at the hospital, Boss. Those people who called the ambulance didn't witness anything. All they saw was the kid come running through the park and collapsing. They didn't see anybody else. We're going to take their statements here and cut them loose."

"Thanks Jeff. There's a lot of houses around that park. Get going on the canvass. Look for CCTV everywhere," John instructed.

John did not waste any time and called out to Tim Warren. "The victim was with his girlfriend in Ballincollig. Her name is Kyla Hartnett. Get an address for her and we'll go and find out what she knows."

Tim ran a quick computer check on Hartnett and found that she was eighteen years old and held a valid driver's license. Kyla Hartnett lived in a semi-detached two-storey house in the same estate that the stabbing occurred. Tim drove his boss there in record time.

"I guess she lives with Mom and Pop," John remarked as they pulled up outside a well-maintained two-storey house, with a tidy garden, a teak front door and two cars parked in the driveway.

It was now after 6AM, the time of the morning when it felt colder and darker than the rest of the night. The detectives' knock to the door was answered relatively quickly by a middle-aged man, dressed in grey sweat pants and a blue tee-shirt. He was wearing plaid slippers and holding a newspaper.

"Mr. Hartnett?" John enquired as the man looked at the two men wearing business suits and overcoats. John showed his badge and warrant card to the man, who immediately looked panicked. It was the usual reaction when police showed up at the door, especially detectives.

"Mr. Hartnett, I don't want to alarm you. There is nothing wrong with anyone in your family." John tried to put him at ease right away. "We need to speak to Kyla. She may have some information about her boyfriend."

"Oh, what the fuck did he do now? I don't like that boy!" Mr. Hartnett groaned and blew out a long sharp breath. He invited the officers in, "I wish I could get her to dump him, but the more I say, the more she's besotted with him," Hartnett sighed as he showed his visitors into the dining room.

John looked around and seeing that they were alone, took the opportunity to test the waters with Kyla's father. "She is going to need some support from you right now, Mr. Hartnett. Chris has been in an altercation with someone. He has been killed."

"Oh Jesus Christ! And you think Kyla knows something about this? Or had something to do with this?" Hartnett replied shocked.

John shook his head and tried to put him at ease, "No, but she might know who he was with or where he was going. Can we please speak with her?"

Hartnett walked down the hall and soon brought his daughter to the dining room. She looked like she had been crying and hadn't slept very much. Kyla's mother also came out of a bedroom. Her husband walked her back into the bedroom and filled her in on what he knew so far. A few minutes later she came out and sat next to Kyla while John was asking the girl some background questions.

"Kyla, you look upset. Can you tell me what's the matter?" John asked, putting the girl at ease with his soft familiar Cork accent.

"Something bad happened last night," Kyla said and it looked like she was about to break down.

"Yeah, we know that. That's why we are here. Can you tell us about it? It is very important we find out what you know," John asked softly and calmly.

"Is Chris okay?" Kyla whispered. At the same time her mother tightened the grip on Kyla's hand.

John quickly glanced across at Tim Warren. It was obvious that Kyla wasn't going to be an eye-witness. The glance was also a signal to Tim to jump into the conversation.

"We'll talk about that in a moment, Kyla. But you know something bad happened and we must find out what you know first. Tell the inspector what you know and we'll give you all the answers we can."

"Chris and I were over at my friend Sharon's place. We hang out there all the time cos Sharon has her own place," Kyla glanced at her dad after she said that.

"What's Sharon's last name and where does she live?" John didn't like to interrupt but he suspected this interview would end in hysterics so he had to ask the relevant questions now.

"There's a small apartment block next to Tesco, in Ballincollig. She has a suite on the ground floor. Malone is her last name."

"Okay," John said, encouraging her to continue.

"Sharon has this new boyfriend. He came over while we were hanging out. He's an asshole. He has Independent Posse tattoos on his arms," Kyla responded between sobs. Her mother now put her arm around her and squeezed her reassuringly.

"Chris runs with the Mahon Warlords, doesn't he?" John suggested, trying not to sound accusatory.

"He used to but he doesn't see much of those guys anymore. He wants to make a clean break." Kyla fidgeted with her fingers and was looking at her feet on the floor.

"Hummph" her father growled under his breath.

Cahill looked across at him and asked another question before a family argument blew up. "Do you know this guy's name?"

"Tony Connolly or Collins, something like that."

"Did Chris and Tony get into it? Was there some sort of altercation?" Now we're getting places, John thought.

"Yeah, but nothing too serious. Tony hates M-W cos he was beaten up by a few of them a couple of months ago, so he was talking trash about them and Chris was standing up for them." Kyla was tearing up again.

"So what happened?"

"Tony said 'Let's see how tough you are, let's do a score together.' Chris wouldn't back down and he agreed to go with him. I know he didn't want to but he felt pressured." Kyla gasped for a breath and was really struggling with these questions.

"What kind of score were they going to do? Just jack someone or hold up a convenience store or the gas station?" John asked as he noticed the look of sheer horror on the parents' faces. However, he was very impressed that they were not interfering in the interview.

"The convenience store in the gas station. It's at the corner by the traffic lights at Muskerry Estate."

John nodded. He knew where she was talking about.

"Then Tony came back about twenty minutes later and he said he stabbed Chris," Kyla blurted out and started to wail. She put her head on her mother's shoulder and sobbed uncontrollably.

John let her cry and when she finally started to slow down and take some deep breaths he began again. "Tell me about those few minutes. It's very, very important."

"He had this knife. It's like a big butcher knife, and all I could see was blood on it."

John waited another minute before continuing. "Do you remember exactly what he said?"

"He said 'That fucking slob was going to chicken out so I shanked him,'" Kyla wailed, gasped for breath and then asked, "What's happened to Chris?"

Ignoring her question, John continued. "What happened then?"

"Sharon and me both asked where was Chris now. Tony said Chris ran off through the park. He said he didn't know where he was but he was fine, he was able to run away. Sharon said we should go look for him so we got into Sharon's car and drove around Muskerry Estate. We didn't see anyone. Then Sharon went by her mother's place. She went inside for a few minutes and I stayed in the car with Tony. Tony said he was going to get Sharon to drive him to Dublin so he could lie low for a while. Sharon came back out and she drove me home."

"Did Sharon say she was going to drive him to Dublin?" John asked.

"He asked her but all she said was how far away is Dublin? He didn't know how far it was." Kyla was still crying but not as hysterically.

"What kind of car does Sharon have?" John knew he wasn't going to get much more and this girl was only seconds away from completely going to pieces.

"It's a really small Ford, a Ka, dark green," Kyla answered, with tears streaming down her cheeks.

Cahill glanced again at Tim, "Kyla, I have some awful news for you. Chris did run away after he was stabbed but he lost a lot of blood. I am sorry, Kyla, but Chris died after being stabbed."

"Noooo No Nooo, he can't be! Nooo. Mammy!" Kyla sobbed loudly into her mother's shoulder. It was like her world had ended.

John left the table and walked to the hallway. Kyla's father went to follow him but he put up his hand to stop him and pointed towards his wife and daughter. "You should stay with them. I have to make a quick call and I will come back and talk to you."

John called Pete Sandhu in the Incident Room. "We are looking for a Tony Connolly or Collins. He's an I-P. He confessed to stabbing our victim to two girls, right after it happened. We're with one of them now. He's with the other one, his girlfriend, Sharon Malone. She's driving her own car, a green Ka. They might be headed to Dublin in the car. I'll fill you in on the rest later but that's enough to get you started. Get the right name for Tony and put out a BOLO for him and Sharon and the Ford Ka."

John terminated the call and called Kyla's father out to the hallway. "I know this is very difficult for all of you, especially Kyla. But I'm going to have to get her to come down to the Anglesea Street Station to give us a proper recorded statement and look at some photographs so we can identify this Tony clown!"

"I understand, Officer. Oh my God, how will she ever get over this? Is it okay if we bring her down?"

"Of course. The sooner we get through this, the sooner it's over with and we can go about picking this fellow up and you can get Kyla the help she needs to get through this."

John and Kyla's father walked back into the living room. "Kyla, your mom and dad are going to bring you downtown to the Garda Station now so we can finish this and concentrate on catching Tony and putting him in prison where he belongs." John didn't give Kyla or her parents an opportunity to change their minds or make alternative arrangements.

By the time they arrived at Anglesea Street Garda Station, Pete Sandhu had identified not only the license plate number of Sharon's vehicle but also Tony Connolly, a low lever Independent Posse hanger-on.

Kyla was a superstar witness; she gave a detailed recorded statement and picked Tony Connolly out of an array of ten photographs. Now the hunt for the killer was well and truly on.

Pete Sandhu sent a BOLO, to all the patrol cars and beat officers with the particulars of Sharon Malone's car and also a police file photograph of Tony Connolly. It was a shot in the dark but sometimes it paid off.

And this time it did. The uniform day shift started at 7:00AM and the fresh officers, having heard about the BOLO at their morning briefing, were anxious to assist the Serious Crime Unit. A patrol car driving through the parking lot of a flea-bag motel near the Lower Glanmire Road spotted the green Ford Ka parked near the office entrance. The young officer immediately called John Cahill.

"Inspector Cahill, it's Garda Clifford in Delta 2-Zero-1. We found the green Ford Ka you were looking for. Is it related to the homicide last night?"

"Outstanding, Garda Clifford. Yes, it is related to the homicide. Is it occupied or parked somewhere?"

"There is nobody in it at this moment but it's parked outside the office at the Lodge Motel on the Lower Glanmire Road. What do you want us to do?" the excited young Garda asked.

"Try and park somewhere out of sight but keep a close eye on that vehicle. If someone comes and gets into it, take it down. Do NOT allow that vehicle out of the parking lot. I'll send a couple of teams there right away."

"Gottcha! It will not get away from us," Garda Clifford said with eagerness and enthusiasm

John looked around the Incident Room. He yelled out to the first team he saw, "Mike, Eddie! A dayshift uniform car just found the green Ka parked at the Lodge Motel on the Lower Glanmire Road, near the railway station. Let's get over there quick and find out if our two desperados are staying there. Tim, with me!"

The four detectives did not waste a moment. They holstered up, grabbed their coats and ran to their cars. They drove through the city center with their emergency lights flashing and their sirens wailing until they were passing Saint Patrick's Church, about half a kilometer from the motel. Then they shut off the emergency equipment so they wouldn't alert their quarry as they approached.

When they arrived in the motel parking lot Mike Williams instructed the uniform crew to move closer to the suspects' vehicle and ensure it did not move.

John approached the motel clerk in the lobby, "We're looking for a girl around twenty and a guy maybe the same age. They would have come in here in the last couple of hours."

John went on to describe Tony Connolly. The clerk told him they were in a room just down the hall from the office. The girl had paid cash for the room and they arrived about two hours earlier.

As the four detectives walked towards the door, Sharon Malone stepped out of the room, holding an ice bucket. She looked up and saw the four plain clothes cops. She knew exactly who they were. Sharon dropped the ice bucket and turned to run back to the room. She wasn't fast enough for Tim Warren. He grabbed Sharon by the shoulders and pushed her to the wall. Sharon squealed and swore at Tim. On hearing the commotion, Tony Connolly opened the door. He too saw the cops and went to slam the door shut. John booted the door open before it was fully closed. The door swung back and hit Connolly square in the face, sending him flying across the small dingy room. Connolly looked up and saw three Glocks pointed at his head.

"You're under arrest for murder or some similar offence, Tony. Don't make it worse than it is," John warned their prisoner.

Tony Connolly's eyes were wide open; they filled with tears and all he could muster was a squeaky "Okay," as he raised his hands above his head. Eddie Jenkins was on him in an instant and placed the handcuffs on him.

"Nice kung-foo kick, Boss! You got him right on the noggin and he went flying," Tim Warren jeered as he handcuffed Sharon Malone.

Connolly and Malone were taken back to the Anglesea Street Station. The motel room was secured until a search warrant was obtained so they could search for evidence. The green Ford Ka was towed to the Major Crime Forensic Bay at the Garda Station, where it would be searched for evidence under the authority of a search warrant.

"Thank Christ we'll get this wrapped up in one day," John said to Tim. He was elated and relieved.

After a couple of hours of questioning, Tony Connolly made a full confession to stabbing Chris Shorting, but like most killers, tried to blame his victim. He said Chris had picked a fight with him. Sharon Malone provided a statement where she repeated to the detectives everything Tony had told her about what happened and how they planned to leave town.

The forensic team found the murder weapon in the motel room as well as Connolly's blood-stained shoes. They also found some of Chris Shorting's castoff blood from the knife on the floor of the passenger seat of the Ford Ka.

Chris Shorting's parents and Kyla Hartnett were relieved that the killer had been caught but they soon realized that their loved one was never coming back.

Chapter 14

A t 12:30 AM, twenty-three hours after the duty inspector called him out to work, John walked back into his house. The greyhounds were in their crates in the living room. They both opened their eyes and looked at him. They knew that he was not going to take them out at this strange hour. Molly, the smaller of the two, wagged her tail in her usual up and down motion as she lay in the crate.

"Hi girls, go back to sleep," he whispered to them.

John crept downstairs and stepped into the shower to wash away the grime of the long workday. He tiptoed back up the stairs and slid into bed, next to his wife, hoping not to disturb her.

"What time is it?" Jules asked groggily.

"Shhh. It's just gone one. Go back to sleep, sorry for waking you."

"Is it solved?"

"Yeah, the bad guy is in prison now. It's all wrapped up in a nice tight package. We got some lucky breaks on this one. Now we can focus on the New Year's murders again."

Jules turned to him and wrapped her arm around his chest. "Good, we have to go to my mother's for dinner tomorrow night," and they both fell into a deep sleep.

Several hours later, after allowing his team a late start, John returned to the Incident Room just before 9:30AM. The Incident Room was dark, but a stale smell from the detectives' previous evening's takeout food lingered. John opened the door wide and turned on a fan to freshen the place. He made his way to his desk and began to prepare the disclosure material, related to the Tony

Connolly arrest for the Office of The Director of Public Prosecutions.

Superintendent Paddy Collins came into the office. "Nice job on wrapping up yesterday's incident. Was there much to it?"

"We got off to a good start and got some good information early on. We were lucky when a couple of tuned in uniform officers found our suspect's car on the Lower Glanmire Road." John hoped the superintendent was happy with the update because he decided to bring up the other project. "I'm going to try to get hold of Jeff Rafter's CI and have him set up the meeting with Johnny Johnson as soon as possible."

"Do it!" the superintendent said as he smiled, turned around and walked out of the office.

Within the hour, the rest of the Serious Crime Unit detectives were in the office, catching up on their notes and reports from the day before. Jeff Rafter called his informant. Gerry Campbell was already up and about. He agreed to set up a meeting the next evening in a room at the Casino Hotel. Campbell wasn't crazy about introducing the UC but he was confident that between them they would get a confession out of Johnny Johnson. John contacted the security manager at the Casino, who just happened to be a retired cop, and was happy to help out. He knew the police were operating some type of covert operation but he also knew better than to ask about it. John booked two rooms.

John walked over to the run-down building on Stable Lane and met with Sergeant Colin Spence, the officer in charge of the Technical Surveillance Unit. Spence sent a team of technicians to the hotel where they installed listening devices and cameras in places that would never be found in one of the rented rooms. They set up an observation post in the room next door.

John allowed the team to take it easy for the rest of the day and dismissed them at 3:00PM. He met Jules at 4:30 outside the station and they walked across Parnell Bridge up to Oliver Plunket Street where the sidewalks were so narrow you could barely walk two abreast. However, that was impossible because there were hundreds of people out walking and traffic was crawling along the narrow two-lane road.

They wandered up the pedestrianized Princess Street and into the English Market. This Market is a unique shopping experience. It is a covered area with close to sixty stalls, storefronts and cafes and an ancient stone fountain at its centre. There are butchers, bakers, fish mongers, florists and fruit and vegetable stalls, cafes and restaurants... all in this enclosed area of about half a city block.

The atmosphere in the English Market, was nothing short of electric! The smell of sawdust and salted blood near the butchers' stalls and fresh fish from the fish mongers filled the air. The banter among the vendors and the customers and the different competing vendors is like a comedy act and at any given time, visitors would think they had just walked onto a stage in the middle of some theatrical skit.

Jules bought a few salmon fillets for supper and then they headed over to visit with Jules' mother, Elizabeth, who lived in the residential suburb of Bishopstown in the west side of the city.

Although now in her eighties, Elizabeth was a very controlling and demanding woman with a tongue so sharp that it could clip a hedge. She was widowed in the 1970's, when Jules was twelve years old. Elizabeth had never really dealt with the death of her husband. In fact, she was angry with him for dying on her. Jules, who was the eldest of three, had to step up and take on far more responsibility in the household than a normal twelve-year-old would. Elizabeth was not happy when Jules and John fell in love and decided to marry. She told her daughter it wouldn't last. She was doubly furious when the couple told her they were moving to Northern Ireland. Jules often thought that if she did not have her Aunt Nan as an ally, she would have gone off the deep end a long time ago.

John and Jules drove into the small cul-de-sac where Elizabeth lived. John took a deep breath, let it out slowly and said, "It's like kicking in a door in a search warrant. You just never know what's going to be on the other side."

Jules smiled, "Lets get it over with."

For the next two hours they listened to Elizabeth complain about the weather, the economy, the government, interest rates, the police, the traffic and everything except the clergy. Then she turned her attention to Northern Ireland and complained about that too. "What are you working at now, John? I suppose they'll send you back to that oul place in the North soon."

"No Mom, I would have told you if there were any changes. John is the detective inspector in charge of the Serious Crime Unit in Anglesea Street," Jules answered proudly defending her husband.

"An inspector, huh, you should have joined the Garda instead of down there by that oul beach playing with horses. You would probably be a chief superintendent or higher by now," Elizabeth shot back in her usual manner.

John and Jules didn't even engage but just changed the subject.

JANUARY 13th

At 2:00PM the following day, John held a briefing with his team. "Alright! It's showtime! Tonight, hopefully the informant will lure Johnny Johnson to a room at the Casino Hotel to sell him some illicit product. The informant will introduce our undercover operator to Johnny and the UCO will befriend him. During their time together, the informant will steer the conversation to the New Year's Eve party. Hopefully between them, they will extract a confession from Mr. Johnson about him killing Jason Kimberly and maiming the other two victims after the party. It all sounds very simple. What could possibly go wrong?" John said as he laughed nervously. He knew there were a million things could go wrong in such a scenario.

Malik Hussain, the undercover police officer knocked at the office door. John let him in. Because of the rule of law in place, to prevent claims of entrapment, Malik could not be privy to the entire investigation. In fact, he could not even know the role Johnny Johnson played in the murder.

All the other detectives knew Malik. He was already prepared for his role; he did not look like a policeman. Malik was not a tall man, standing at five foot six inches, but he was built like a weight-lifter. He had long greasy salt and pepper hair and a dark olive complexion. He spoke with a Middle Eastern accent and looked the part of a terrorist.

The meeting was set for 7:30PM and the investigators arrived at the hotel for 4:00PM. They made their way to the two rooms in a quiet wing on the ground floor of the hotel. A member of the Technical Squad was waiting for them. They went into the observation room set up with monitors and several sets of headphones. The monitors were showing an identical hotel room next door. The rooms were spacious and very comfortable with a little office/work space area separate from the sleeping area. Three armchairs had been set up around a coffee table. There was also a small fridge stocked with a bottle of vodka and a bottle of whisky. The cameras were high-definition and the microphones were super-sensitive. Nothing was going unrecorded here, not even the lowest whisper.

Gerry Campbell texted Jeff Rafter and John to tell them he had arrived at the casino. John and Malik walked towards the playing area.

Malik, smiling broadly, walked up to Gerry, shook his hand and slapped him on the back. "Gerry, it's great to see you again."

Gerry Campbell looked quizzically at this Arab looking man.

"DI Cahill sent me over to meet you. I'll be working with you tonight," Malik whispered and nodded in the direction of the inspector, who made eye contact with Gerry Campbell and nodded.

Gerry nodded back in recognition.

Gerry and Malik went to their hotel room. John texted Malik with the ideal seating arrangements, so the cover team could get the best view of everyone. A few minutes before 7:00PM, Gerry received a text from Johnny Johnson; he was there and ready to do business. Gerry and Malik walked to the casino. Johnny wasn't hard to find as he looked completely out of place there. His idea of dressing up was wearing a denim suit and work boots instead of runners. Johnny was uncomfortable meeting Malik. He did not know him so he didn't trust him.

Malik played it cool and let Gerry do the talking for now. "This is Mohammad, we call him Mo. This guy has a never- ending supply of fentanyl. I can't handle it all, it's too much for me. Mikey G doesn't want to diversify right now and you and I have done a few deals in the past so I'm giving you the option."

"Why do I have to meet this guy?" Johnny asked, pointing to Malik by sticking his chin out.

"He needs to know he can trust you, so that nothing comes back to bite him. Come to his room, we'll talk business."

The three men walked down the quiet hallway and into the 'recording studio' that the police had set up. Although Malik's heart was racing he easily took on the persona of a drug dealer and all out thug. He didn't try to befriend Johnny Johnson; he was quite cool and spoke to him through Gerry.

After a few minutes of this, Johnny snapped, "You can talk directly to me, you know. I don't need Gerry to explain shit to me!" Malik goal was to make Johnny want to feel important.

"Fair enough, Johnny, but I need to know I can trust you. I 've never met you before and I know nothing about you. Only what Gerry tells me and you know Gerry as well as I do, he talks through his ass sometimes." Malik cracked the slightest of smiles.

"I don't know you either, Mo. You could be anyone," Johnny answered.

"I'll tell you who I am. I am the fucking guy taking all the risk by meeting up with you. How do I know you're not wearing a wire?" Malik could earn an Oscar for this performance.

In the suite next door, while watching the show play out on the monitor, John looked across at Jeff Rafter, Len Benoit and Tim Warren and gave them the thumbs up signal. Malik was taking control and playing it real cool.

"Well, I'm taking a risk with my money if I do a deal with you." Johnny sounded flustered. He didn't like the comment about him wearing a wire.

"Relax Johnny. Let's have a drink." Malik poured a few drinks and handed them to Gerry and Johnny. He handed Johnny the room service menu. "I'm fucking starving Johnny. I'm going to order pizza and chicken wings. Do you want something?"

Johnny took the menu and looked through it. "I'll have a steak sandwich and fries."

"Of course, you fucking will!" John muttered in the room next door. "Why don't you order champagne too, you fucking savage." The others laughed, "Well he ordered the most expensive thing on the menu," John said sourly, but then broke into a smile.

Malik called down to order the food and while they were waiting, Johnny started to open up a bit about his involvement in the Independent Posse. He made himself sound far more important than he was. By the time the food arrived Johnny had become much more comfortable speaking with Malik.

Malik provided Johnny with a baggy containing three fentanyl pills. He then showed Johnny a photograph of thousands of pills, on his phone. "I got the really good stuff too," Malik said.

"What good stuff?" Johnny asked.

"Carfentanyl! The strongest opioid out there. You can cut one pill five thousand times." Malik produced another photograph. "I'm importing direct from China. I got connections with the Triads."

Johnny Johnson was impressed. Malik knew he had him hooked. All he needed to do was reel him in. The three men ate their food and had a few more drinks.

"Before we talk money, Johnny, I need to know more about you. I need to trust you. Do you have the finances to back up an order? That sort of thing," Malik said, while the mood in the room was relaxed.

"You can trust me," Johnny replied.

"Tell me more about what you do with this Independent Posse," Malik asked as he sat back and put his glass down.

"I'm like you and Gerry. I'm a business man, I just make money for me and my gang," Johnny boasted, sitting up straight, showing off.

"If you're like us, you'll have done some crazy shit. Isn't that right Gerry?" Malik fished for information.

"You may as well tell him something, Johnny, or this deal will go south very quickly." Gerry sounded bored as he finished off another drink and refilled his glass. "Tell him about New Year's Eve!"

"Take it easy, Gerry, that's too direct," John said as he shuddered in the observation room.

After that comment, Johnny glared across at Gerry but directed his answer to Malik, "I collect some debts sometimes. Occasionally you must lean on someone who doesn't want to pay up. But nothing serious. Like I said, I'm a business man."

Gerry was getting impatient and the booze was starting to affect him. "Bullshit! I heard you went all Rambo at some party at the start of the year."

"Where did you hear that?" Johnny shot back.

"Everybody is talking about it. Mikey G and Georgy. Nobody can believe you did that," Gerry spoke loudly as the drink was taking effect.

"You're full of shit Gerry. I don't know what you're talking about." Johnny looked very uncomfortable and was about to stand up.

"FUCK YOU JOHNNY!" Gerry yelled. "DO YOU THINK I'M A FUCKING COP OR SOMETHING? IS THAT WHAT YOU THINK? TELL ME WHAT YOU DID!"

"Sit down Gerry," Malik ordered as he tried to gain some control of the situation. But Gerry was not finished yet.

"Mikey G would never speak out of turn about that," Johnny said defensively.

Gerry picked up a knife that came with the food, "TELL ME WHAT YOU DID OR I'LL FUCKING STAB YOU!" as he toppled the coffee table. The food and the drinks went flying across the room.

"Shit! Shit! Shit!" John yelled as he and the others leapt out of their chairs and ran to the door of the room next door.

John hammered on the door. "HOTEL SECURITY! OPEN THE DOOR."

Malik opened the door instantly and everything cooled down inside the suite.

Malik went along with the ruse and explained that he and his friends had a disagreement and things got out of hand. He would pay for any damage.

John knew that no matter what Johnny Johnson said now would never stand up in court, so he continued to play the role of security guard and threw Gerry and Johnny out of the hotel.

After the two had been put in separate taxis, Malik poured himself a drink, sat down and sighed loudly. "I think we were close, Boss, real close, if it wasn't for that moron,"

With the mission in tatters, the detectives went home for what was left of the evening. The next morning, John listened several times to the recordings from the meeting. He hoped there was something he could salvage and there was. Just before Gerry Campbell went bat-shit crazy, overturned the table and threatened to stab the suspect, Johnny Johnson made a comment, "MIKEY G WOULD NEVER SPEAK OUT OF TURN ABOUT THAT!"

It wasn't much but it was enough to tell the detectives they had the right man. John knew there was enough there for them to get a wiretap for the main players in the Independent Posse. Those ten words would be enough to convince a judge to sign an order authorizing the interception of private communications. Before John started working on the affidavit, he called up Superintendent Collins and convinced him that this was the only way to advance this investigation. It was now up to the superintendent to get the assistant commissioner to approve it.

That evening, while on the way home from work, Gerry Campbell called John.

"I'm surprised you have the balls to call me. You really fucked up last night! What do you want now?" John barked down the phone.

"Sorry man. It wasn't that bad, was it?" Gerry replied sheepishly.

"You couldn't keep your trap shut, could you? What were you thinking?"

"I was trying to get your confession so I could get paid."

"Well, it kills me but I have to pay you anyway, but only because when I eventually arrest Johnny Johnson, you might still have to testify in court," John told him and hit the call end button, leaving Gerry hanging.

When John arrived home, the wind was blowing in hard from the Atlantic Ocean and the rain was hopping off the car windshield. The waves were breaking high over the rocks of the bank between the twin beaches. The dogs met him at the door but even they didn't want to be out on such a wet and windy night. Over a late supper, John brought Jules up to speed on the meeting at the hotel since they hadn't seen each other in nearly two days.

"How do you feel about another wire tap project?" Jules asked.

"I'm not looking forward to it. It's a ton of work and the targets are all drug dealers, so it's going to be really hard to focus on the murder investigation. I'm sure we'll hear lots of drug deals and drug talk," he sighed.

"Are you going to act on illegal drug deals when you hear about them? They'll all be breaking the law," Jules asked, forcing her husband to consider another dilemma.

John thought about this for a moment, letting out a long breath. "Not necessarily, we'll gather the intelligence and pass it on to the Drug Squad, but if it's something massive or dangerous to the public, we'll have to make a quick decision on how to react." John said, not looking forward to the prospect of hearing thousands of drug related phone calls.

Chapter 15

In his affidavit to obtain judicial authorization for the wiretap, John was trying to mitigate the bizarre meeting between the undercover cop, the informant/agent and the suspect in the hotel room. He needed to explain to the reviewing judge how they obtained the comment made by Johnny Johnson.

While he was deep in thought, Jen Martens, the forensic supervisor, walked into the Incident Room and went straight to John's desk. "I got news on the bloody jacket from the double homicide scene," Jen said, grinning broadly.

"Good news or bad news?" John asked, looking up from his computer screen.

"I really don't know. You tell me? I told the lab to go over every inch of that jacket and test it. They did and they found a hair on top of the left shoulder by the collar."

Jen Martens now had the inspector's attention.

"Did they test that hair?"

"Of course, I asked them to do that, but I haven't got the full results yet. I called the lab again, before I came over here. All they could tell me is that the single hair came from a female. They haven't run it through the data base yet." Jen seemed disappointed.

"That's odd. It probably belongs to Crystal Mannering. I'm thinking the hairs on the ground could be hers too," John said while pondering his thoughts. "What about those hairs we found near Alvin Pomeroy's hand?"

"I looked at them under the microscope and they aren't suitable for D.N.A. analysis. There are no follicles attached but I still have the hairs in storage," she answered.

"What can we do? There must be something we can do. We need a break here. There is another test. It has been used in the UK but it has to be carried out in a private lab. Do you know what that test is?"

Jen Martens peered over her glasses at the detective inspector and started into her long-winded explanation. "There are two main types of D.N.A., nuclear D.N.A. and mitochondrial D.N.A. Actually, there is a third, Y-STR, but that doesn't apply to this case. Now let me explain the difference."

"Jesus Christ, Jen. I don't have time for a biology lesson. Can you give it to me in twenty words or less?" John said with a smile.

Jen removed her glasses, sighed and shook her head. "I'm amazed that you detectives get anything accomplished. "Nuclear D.N.A. is unique to everyone except identical twins and that's because..."

"Just tell me about the other one, the mito whatever one," John urged, cutting her off.

"Everyone has mitochondrial D.N.A. We get it from our mothers. So, if I had two brothers and two sisters, we would all have the same mitochondrial D.N.A. But my children would get their mitochondrial D.N.A. from me and my brothers' children would get their mitochondrial D.N.A. from their own mothers."

"Mmmm, clear as mud Jen, thanks. Would we have to wait long to get results from those hairs?"

"Not as long as we wait for results from the national lab. I'll have to go to a private facility for the mitochondrial test. We would possibly get the results in a few days. However, the negative side to this is that it's going to be expensive," Jen answered.

"How much?"

"About four or five thousand per exhibit and we have four hairs."

"Fuck it! Let's do it. Can you arrange to send them to the private lab and I'll work on the authorization to pay for it?" John said with the enthusiasm of a man waiting for a colonoscopy.

Jen Martens smiled; both she and the homicide detective loved trying different investigative techniques and she didn't have to worry about the funding.

John switched screens on his computer and crafted a memo regarding the mitochondrial D.N.A. test and sent it off in an email to Superintendent Collins for approval.

Half an hour later, the superintendent opened the door to the Incident Room, "What kind of voodoo are you trying now?" he yelled from the doorway. He had obviously read the memo.

"We have to test the hairs that were found next to Alvin Pomeroy's hand on the floor. If the result of the test showed that the hairs came from Ken Rolland or one of his siblings it is strong circumstantial evidence. If the hairs come from Crystal Mannering, at least we know they are hers. But if we don't bother to test the hairs because the cost is prohibitive, even the stupidest defence lawyer could say the hairs belong to an unknown killer." John looked at his boss, to see if he was grasping the explanation.

"What you're telling me is that this type of D.N.A. test will not be enough to convict our suspect but if we don't do it, he'll get off?" Paddy Collins responded, appearing quite confused.

"We must try to identify whose hairs these are. It can't be our two dead guys. They both had short hair. If it is Crystal's hair, well that is easily explained, she lived there. The best case scenario is it's Ken Rolland's hair. It definitely puts him in the suite. It's strong circumstantial evidence and well worth the cost," John said, trying not to sound like he was begging.

"I suppose we are not in business to turn a profit! Go on, get it done," the superintendent nodded, confident in his inspector.

Almost four weeks after New Year's day, nothing much was getting accomplished with either of the investigations. This was not good; the first three murders of the year were getting colder by the day and the consensus in the Incident Room was that they would remain unsolved. Cops in general did not like unsolved murders. Somebody was getting away with the most serious offence in the Criminal Code and it made the investigators look incompetent.

Four days after submitting the hairs from the floor for mitochondrial D.N.A. testing, Jen Martens found two messages marked urgent on her email. One was from the national laboratory and the other from the private lab. "Mmm, which shall I open first?" Jen thought.

She opened the email from the national lab first. It was regarding the second examination of the hair found near the left shoulder of the blood-stained coat. Jen quickly read through the first two pages of 'scientific bullshit' as she called it, and got to the main results. She was confused by what the report said.

"On initial testing, a single profile from a female was developed from the exhibit JK6. The single profile was entered into the National D.N.A. Data Bank and matched a profile of a registered offender, 793541B, Cecilia Bridgit ROLLAND. The instance of another profile matching this profile is 16.253 billion."

"Cecilia Rolland!" Jen said aloud. She pulled up Cecilia Rolland's profile on the police data base. "That doesn't make any sense; she's fifty-two years old and looks like she's seventy-two." Jen checked Cecilia's record, "She certainly has the pedigree for it and has a few convictions for violent offences racked up," Jen was puzzled.

Jen Martens opened the other email from the private laboratory. Again, she skipped through the first couple of pages and got to the main results.

"The four hairs received for mitochondrial D.N.A. testing were marked AP10, AP11, AP12 and AP13. Exhibits AP10, AP11 and AP12 all contain the same mitochondrial D.N.A. AP13 was unsuitable for testing.

Should you have a control sample or a suspect sample to compare to the mitochondrial D.N.A. profile that was developed, please contact us regarding further comparison testing."

Jen picked up her phone and called the Incident Room. She asked Inspector Cahill to come over to her office. When he arrived, she handed him printed copies of the emails. He read the one from the national laboratory.

"What the fuck? Ken Rolland brought his mother along to help him kill two drug dealers!" John said, frustrated and exasperated.

Jen Martens could not help laughing as the image formed in her mind. "Stranger things have happened."

John scanned through the second email. "Am I reading this right? The three hairs are from the same person or from three people who had the same mother. Is that accurate?"

"That's correct," Jen Martens answered him.

John's mind was racing as he was understanding the content of the mail. "Well, they can't be from the victims; they were not brothers. It could be Crystal Mannering and it could also be Kenny Rolland.! If I get a D.N.A. swab from Crystal, and we can get Kenny Rolland's profile from the National D.N.A. Data Bank, can they rule one of them in or out?"

"Yes, they can. They'll probably charge us another few thousand euros, but that's your problem, not mine," Jen said mischievously.

"Make the arrangements to get Ken Rolland's D.N.A. from the National D.N.A. Data Bank and I'll get a swab from Crystal by tomorrow. Then we'll finally get an answer." John was excited as he stood up to head back to his own office.

Back in the Incident Room, Tim Warren was busy typing up the report from the Chris Shorting homicide. John explained what he had learned from Jen Martens and Tim immediately called up Crystal Mannering to arrange to get a D.N.A. swab.

John's phone rang. He looked at the call display and recognized the number. It was the Judges' Chambers at the Law Courts. A little bit of anxiety crept into his voice as he answered the phone. This call would let him know if his wiretap for the Galvin Brothers, Johnny Johnson and Trish Langford had been granted. Good News! The order had been signed by the chief judge himself and was ready for pickup. John was elated. Both investigations were moving forward again, even if it was at a snail's pace. Now it was just a matter of playing the game of finding out all the phone numbers and trying to get a listening device into Georgy Galvin's old green van and Trish Langford's house.

Gerry Campbell had provided a cell phone number for Johnny Johnson, so that was easy. He would be hooked up within a day. Then they would have to monitor all of Johnny's calls to see if he called Mikey G or Georgy. They would have to resort to those numbers. The van and the house were going to be another problem.

With the intercept court order in hand, John headed off to see Sergeant Colin Spence at the Technical Surveillance Unit on Stable Lane. They went over the conditions that the judge had recommended on the order. The judge made a specific order that the police could only listen to conversations in Georgy's van and Trish Langford's house, if one of the targets was present during the conversation. If a target wasn't present, the police could not listen in or record.

"How soon can you get Johnson's phone hooked up?" John asked.

"I should have everything in place by noon tomorrow. We will have to have the civilian monitors listen to it live for the first couple of days, just until we establish that Johnny is the primary user of that phone. Do we need to listen to this 24/7 right now?" the sergeant asked.

"No, not at this time. Your monitors do a great job. I'm sure they'll figure out Johnny's voice in no time and hopefully he calls or texts the other two clowns. Trish Langford's phone number should be good too. That is the number she provided us with when she was in on New Year's. I doubt she's changing her phone number too often as she has kids that need to get hold of her."

"What about the house and the van? How are we going to do them?" Colin enquired.

"I have a few ideas. Let's hook up the phones first and I'll talk to you tomorrow about Langford's house and the van. I need to check out the legislation in the Republic and see how far I can push things," John answered.

It did not take the Technical Surveillance Unit long to get the phone service providers on board and set up the connections to intercept the targets' cell phone use. Now it was up to the phone line monitors to listen and identify the voices of Johnny Johnson and Trish Langford. The first week of an intercept was always the most challenging. It was a time for the cell phone numbers to be established, the targets to be confirmed and their voices learned and hopefully the other targets could be identified so their phones could get hooked up too.

That evening John got home at a reasonable hour for dinner.

"Any developments in your two cases?"

John told Jules that Johnny Johnson's and Trish Langford's phones were being intercepted. He then told her his plans for installing the listening devices in Georgy Galvin's old van and Trish Langford's house.

"Won't they suspect?" Jules asked.

"I guess we'll see," he answered with a grin.

Jules and John took the greyhounds for their usual walk along the beaches that evening. It was a typical winter's evening, cool, damp and rain showers that appeared without warning. They had both beaches to themselves. As customary, while they strolled along, they continued to discuss the homicide investigations.

"We identified Rolland's mother's D.N.A. on a hair on the shoulder of the blood-stained jacket that we found behind the apartment block. I'm pretty sure Kenny Rolland was wearing that jacket when he was at the club with the two victims. It's not making any sense to me. How is her D.N.A. on the jacket and not his?" John said quite bewildered.

"Didn't Rolland stay with his mom while he was in town?" Jules asked.

"Yeah, that's what he told us when the guys went up to interview him in Galway. Why?"

"I often put on your coat if I'm running out in the back yard for a few seconds. Especially if your coat is closest. Or maybe his mom hung her coat on top of his. I think it's very easily explained," Jules smiled and gave her husband a knowing look.

John thought about it for a couple of seconds.

"You know what? You're right. It is as simple as that."

Before bed, John turned on his tablet and looked up electronic versions of the criminal statutes surrounding the Interception of Private Communications in the Republic of Ireland. He confirmed that he would not be breaking any laws by implementing his plan to install the listening devices.

When he returned to work the following morning, Sergeant Jen Martens telephoned John and requested he attend her office.

"I was able to pull a few strings and get Ken Rolland's D.N.A. profile to the private lab at lightning speed. The hairs on the floor near Alvin Pomeroy's hand came from Ken Rolland or another one of Cecilia's demon spawn."

"That is awesome, Jen, you're the best!" John said and clapped his hands with excitement. "It can't be Tyson. He always has short hair and has the perfect alibi. He was at the other party across town. I don't know of any other males in that family. We're getting closer by the day on this one."

On his way back to the Incident Room, John stopped in at Superintendent Collins' office and told him the good news on the mitochondrial D.N.A. tests.

In true form, Paddy Collins, barely raised his head and said," It cost enough! It's still not a home run. Ken Rolland spent time in that apartment and he could have been combing his hair."

"Nice one, Boss, way to rain on my parade," John said, turning around and laughing as he walked away from the boss's office.

When he was gone, Paddy Collins smiled and continued working.

John and Tim Warren drove to Cecilia Rolland's house on Sharman Crawford Street. The house, like many on the street, was old and in need of a facelift. The roof looked like it had a bow in it and was sagging in the middle. The upstairs windows were rattling in the breeze. One had a blanket across it as a curtain; the other had a red and white flag with a big green marijuana leaf in the middle of the white field. The two ground floor windows were just plain dirty. The patch of garden in front of the house was overgrown with weeds and grass and large patches of mud in between.

Just as John was about to knock on the front door, he turned to Tim, "Have you ever met the lovely Cecilia?"

"No, I don't think so," Tim answered.

"Alright then, you can talk to her. She's a scary looking woman from her police photo. She reminds me too much of my mother-in-law," John said, shuddering at the thought.

John gave the usual police knock, four hard thumps with the side of his fist. Half a minute later the haggard Cecilia opened the door.

And true to form, she was scary. Her mostly dark hair, with a few grey strands running through it, was standing on end. She reminded Tim of the professor from 'Back to the Future.' She wore a black freezer jacket with a sweater underneath and blue jeans that were at least two sizes too large. To top off this look, she had a cigarette dangling out of the side of her mouth and smoke rose into her eyes.

"WHAT!" Cecilia barked at the two detectives.

Cork Garda Ma'am," said Tim showing her his warrant card and badge.

"I know who you are. You're either Mormons or cops and Mormons don't knock like that. WHAT DO YOU WANT?"

"Can we come in and talk to you for a couple of minutes?" Tim asked.

"Do you have a warrant?"

"No, do we need one?"

Cecilia looked Tim up and down and then she looked across at John.

"You haven't much to say," Cecilia said, challenging the cop.

"To be honest with you, Mrs. Rolland, you scare the crap out of me and I'm afraid to say anything," John answered, smiling.

Cecilia chuckled and it rolled into a chesty cough. "You should be scared. Come on in, don't mind the mess. I was just going to start to tidy the place when you knocked."

Tim looked around and thought, "This place hasn't been tidied since 1975."

"Well?" Cecilia asked.

On the drive to Sharman Crawford Street, John and Tim had decided to ask Cecilia about her children in a roundabout way; they were going to ask her about someone with the same last name, knowing he was not related to her.

"We're trying to track down Brian Rolland. We were hoping he was related to you and you could point us in the right direction," Tim explained.

"I never heard of Brian Rolland. He's not related to me, d'you know that?"

"Well, this fella came in from Galway where Ken is so we assumed they were related, maybe brothers, are they?" John asked.

"No, I don't know him."

"He's not a cousin or a nephew or anything?" Tim asked. "I know Ken and Tyson...we've run into them before, but not this guy. So, he's not one of yours?" Tim pushed the questions again.

"Jesus! I know how many children I had. I wasn't that fucked up."

"Just the two boys, was it. They would have kept you busy anyway, I suppose," Tim chirped in.

"I had a little girl too. She wasn't with us for long. She died when she was six years old." Cecilia's eyes drifted away to some time long ago and they misted over with tears.

"I'm very sorry to hear that, Cecilia. That's a terrible thing for anyone to go through," John said sympathetically. "That's something you can never fully get over. Was she older or younger than the boys?"

"She was the baby. Ken was the oldest. Tyson was two years younger than him and Charlene was a year and a half younger than Tyson." Cecilia's memory was back in a time when she was somewhat happy with three very young children, not knowing what the future held for any of them.

John couldn't help but feel sorry for the woman. He had opened up old wounds to get the answers that he needed. "I am sorry to have bothered you, Cecilia. You don't know this fella that we are on the hunt for. Are you going to be okay? Is there anyone we can call for you?"

"Ah go on! I'm fine." Cecilia smiled at the detective. "What did that fella do, anyway?"

"Terrible things," Tim responded.

"Ha! Sure, you'll probably never find him," Cecilia said taunting them.

"You're probably right, we'll never find him! We're sorry to have bothered you," John said, laughing and walking out the door.

"Sure, it was no bother this time," Cecilia shouted after them as she heard the door close.

John looked at his partner as they sat in the police car. "Do you think she told us the truth?"

"Yeah, I think she was relieved that she didn't have to think of a lie to protect one of the shithead kids she has. I can't help thinking that one day we'll be back here telling her one of them is dead."

"Let's go by the Technical Surveillance Unit. I want to propose something to Colin Spence," John suggested.

The officers drove to what looked like an abandoned warehouse on Stable Lane. Despite holding millions of dollars worth of equipment, there was no money in the budget for decorating and renovating. They walked up to a battered but solid door and rang a discreet doorbell, almost impossible to see. John took a step back from the door and looked up; he knew there was a pinhole camera on the door frame and he was being watched. Seconds later the officers heard a low whirring sound and the door unlocked and they stepped inside.

Closing the door behind them they walked up flights of concrete stairs where they found another locked door. This one had a buzzer and a speaker attached.

John pressed the buzzer and a chirpy female voice answered him. "Hey DI Cahill, what are you doing here?"

"Hi Madge, is Colin in? I need a few minutes of his time."

The door buzzed and John stepped into the reception area where the clerk, Madge Eastwood, sat at her desk. They exchanged pleasantries and the officers walked through the grungy hallway to Colin Spence's office.

John walked into Colin Spence's small office; Tim Warren stood in the doorway.

"I got a plan for putting the listening device in Trish Langford's house. I've checked it out and it's legal," John announced.

"I asked Anti-Crime to sit on that place for a couple of days and they said it's like Grand Central Station, people coming and going all the time and Langford and her mother and the kids all live there. The old lady seems to have hundreds of acquaintances too as they all come and go. That house is never empty. So, I hope you got a good plan, or we'll never get in there," Colin sounded somewhat defeated.

"Do you have a good relationship with the TV cable company?" John asked.

"Yeah, pretty good, their security department is really good. The Dublin guys use them for phone intercepts all the time," Sergeant Spence answered.

"Perfect. We'll get the cable company to shut off Langford's T.V. cable for a few hours. She'll call to get someone to come and fix it. The repairmen will be your Garda installers and they can install the listening devices in the plugs inside her house. Before the installers leave, they can call up the cable company to switch the service on again. It's the perfect plan. She calls and asks us to come into her house. Nobody can live without TV. I know I couldn't!"

Colin Spence looked at the inspector as he gave serious consideration to the plan. Then he smiled, "That's a fucking great plan. It's so simple, why didn't we think of that before?"

"Because you're not devious enough Colin," Tim Warren chimed in.

"I also have a great plan for Georgy Galvin's van," John said, with that glint in his eye that meant his brain was working overtime.

"I can't wait to hear that!" Colin Spence laughed.

"I have to talk to Percy Jones and Sean Harrington in Anti-Crime, but between us, we'll make sure that the van gets towed to a compound and your guys will have a couple of hours to put the listening device into it."

"When this is all over, you have to tell me how you got the van towed to a compound," Spence asked.

"Yeah, sure, maybe!" John replied, rising from his seat.

John and Tim left the Technical Surveillance Unit and walked another two flights of stairs to the top floor of the warehouse. This was the office space for the Anti-Crime Unit. The Anti-Crime Unit was primarily an investigative unit for serious property crimes; however, they had evolved into a "Grey-Op's" unit that could be counted on to do what was needed to get any job done. They walked a very fine line, close to the edge every day, careful not to cross the line and become criminals themselves. John had worked in the building on Stable Lane alongside the Anti-Crime Unit, when he ran the Integrated Fugitive Squad. Detective Inspector Sean Harrington and Detective Sergeant Percy Jones, the officers that ran the unit were two of John's closest friends and confidants.

"Hey Percy! How's it going?" John called out as they walked into the office.

"John Cahill, why are you slumming down here?" Jones answered.

"I thought I recognized that voice," Sean Harrington said as he strode around the corner. Harrington was six foot four and built like a wrestler. He had long wavy hair to his shoulders and a goatee. The big man shook John's hand vigorously.

John told his associates that he needed to get Georgy Galvin's van disabled for a few hours and towed to a 'friendly compound,' so the Technical Surveillance Unit could install a listening device and a tracking device in it.

"What did you have in mind?" Percy Jones asked.

"How about we slowly deflate his tires while he's moving. That way he won't lose control and kill someone and you can arrange to tow him off as soon as he stops," John replied.

"How many tires do you want to puncture?" Percy asked.

"Just the two back ones. That way he won't lose complete control. I was thinking you could 'warthog' them."

"What's a warthog?" Tim asked.

"Don't worry about it, your boss might tell you later," Harrington said as he grinned slyly. John nodded at his partner.

"Sounds like a fun day at the office!" Harrington joked. "Leave it with us for a day or two and we will let you know when it's done. I'll coordinate with Colin Spence."

On the short walk back to the Incident Room at Anglesea Street Station, Tim asked again about the warthog.

"We used the warthog in Northern Ireland all the time, and I used it a few times in the Fugitive Squad here. I introduced it to Anti-Crime; I think they use it a lot. The warthog is a small, three-inch, thin steel hollow tube with a razor-sharp point on one end. The tube stands in a rubber tray and is placed under a tire while a vehicle is parked. When the vehicle drives over the metal tube, the tube pierces the tire and sticks in it. Because the tube is hollow, it allows the air to escape slowly and safely, disabling the vehicle. It's like a miniature spike belt with only one spike," John answered.

Tim looked at him with both shock and bewilderment in his eyes.

Chapter 16

P rogress was slow, but at least things were moving forward, now by the beginning of the second week in February, the Technical Surveillance Unit was busy. Colin Spence had provided the cable company with a copy of the assistance order that had been issued by the judge and they sent a technician out to the junction box in Manor View Estate to disrupt the cable service at Trish Langford's house. All it took was twenty minutes of kids fighting and yelling for Trish to call the cable company and demand that her service be restored immediately. Within half an hour of the call, two policemen, dressed as technicians, arrived at the Langford home.

"Your cable isn't working ma'am?" the cop asked Trish.

"I don't know what happened to it, it just stopped. I asked next door and they said theirs is fine, so I called it in. I don't think it's the television, that's pretty new."

"We'll take a look for you. Can we come in?"

Trish invited the men in and showed them to a cupboard under the stairs where the modem was. The men took out screwdrivers and flashlights and said they would test the input. Trish left them alone. After five minutes the two men came into the living room and went to the television.

"Would you like a cup of coffee or tea? I was just making a cup for myself," Trish offered.

"Coffee would be great," one of the men answered. "Black for me please, same for you Bob, isn't it?"

Trish made the two policemen coffee and chatted with them as they pretended to fix her cable. They installed three tiny listening devices in the outlet plugs and light switch in her living room. Trish had three televisions in different rooms in the small house and the 'technicians' inspected, (and installed) in each one. Once they were finished, the technicians went back to the cupboard under the stairs and called their contact at the cable company who restored the cable service to the Langford household.

Trish was thrilled and thanked the two undercover officers for coming around so quickly as she walked them out the front door. A few minutes later the police monitors in the Technical Surveillance Unit were listening to Trish yell at her kids.

Georgy Galvin had just dropped off a few of his working girls on Penrose Quay, near the deep-water wharf. Georgy drove his old Volkswagen van across Brian Boru Bridge and along Merchants Quay. He pulled into the bus station and parked in a handicapped stall. Georgy jumped out of his van and ran towards the public washroom in the bus station.

An undercover policewoman, a member of the Anti-Crime Unit, walked casually through the parking lot. When she got to the old green Volkswagen van, she bent down to tie her shoelace. As quick as lightning she placed the slick warthog under the rear tire on the driver's side. Before she stood up, she looked around, saw nobody taking any interest in her, went across to the passenger side and placed another tiny device under the other rear tire and walked away. Minutes later, Georgy Galvin came out of the bus station and got into his van. He headed back towards Merchants Quay.

Georgy drove along the Quay, across Saint Patrick's Street and along Lavitt's Quay and made a sharp right to cross the River Lee over the Christy Ring Bridge and back to the North Side. There were two cars in front of him and three behind. What Georgy didn't know was that all the vehicles were Garda surveillance cars driven by undercover cops. In the middle of the Christy Ring Bridge, Georgy's back tires went completely flat. He pulled over, got out and looked at the two flat tires. As Georgy pulled out his cell phone to call for assistance a marked police car 'just happened' to come from the opposite direction. The uniformed officer stopped and put on his blue and red overhead lights.

"What's the holdup here?" the cop asked Georgy.

"I got two punctures. I'm going to call someone for help," Georgy replied, quite aggravated.

On cue, the undercover cops in the vehicles behind Georgy started honking their horns.

"I got to get you off this bridge right away," the uniformed cop said to Georgy. "There's no room to pass. I'll call a tow truck."

The cop got on the radio and in less than five minutes a tow truck miraculously showed up. The cop told Georgy the van would be towed to the local impound lot and he offered to drive Georgy home so he could arrange to get the tires fixed. Georgy declined the offer and said he would walk. Seconds later, his van was spirited away by the tow truck. Instead of the impound lot, the van was towed to the police garage at Anglesea Street Garda Station.

Percy Jones, who was stopped directly behind Georgy on the bridge, called Sean Harrington and told him that the tech guys had about forty-five minutes to install the listening device and get the van to the impound lot.

At the police garage, the technicians installed a listening device and a GPS tracker in Georgy's van while the mechanics removed the steel tubes from the tires with the speed and efficiency of a pit crew in a NASCAR race.

Half an hour later, Georgy's van was waiting for him at the impound lot. When he picked it up, Georgy was told that he did not have to pay for the tow as the police ordered it and covered the cost. Georgy couldn't be happier as he changed the two flats.

Now that the wiretap project was up and running, John had to stimulate the targets to talk about the New Year's murder and put increasing pressure on them to make them slip up.

AFTER THE TWO DETECTIVES left, Cecilia Rolland spoke to her son Tyson on the phone and told him about her visitors. Tyson told her not to worry but he felt uneasy. He knew something just wasn't quite right. Tyson called his brother in Galway and asked him if the cops had been sniffing around since the previous time that he spoke with them. Kenny told him no.

Tyson still felt perturbed and decided the best thing he could do was send the cops off in a different direction. He met with one of his underlings, Des Cotter. Des was one of the Independent Posse's up and coming thugs. He sold drugs, collected debts and was willing to go into battle when called upon by his gang.

"I need you to do something for me," Tyson said as he placed his arm around Des' shoulder.

Des looked at the arm and got a shiver down his spine. For a split second he thought Tyson was going to stab him with his free hand.

Tyson picked up on it. "You look kind of scared. Is there something I should know about?"

"No, no Tyson," Des stammered in a flat North Side accent as he covered his tracks well. "I'm just thrilled you would ask me for a favor,

"I want you to get pinched on your warrants."

"You want me to go to prison? Ah fuck no, Tyson, I hate fucking prison, it's so fucking boring in there," Des whined

"This is important. I was talking about this with Mikey G and he suggested you would be the right guy for the job."

Des Cotter's eyes lit up. Mikey G wanted him to do this job too, not just Tyson. "What do you want me to do, suitcase in some product?"

"No buddy, nothing like that. Do you remember at New Year's when Julian and Alvin were killed?" Tyson asked.

"Yeah, that was brutal, they were our brothers."

"Well, whoever popped them stole their big screen TV too. That TV is in Jimmy O'Connell's sitting room. It's a sixty-inch flat screen Sanyo. When you get pinched, Des, I want you to tell the cops you were in Jimmy's house two days ago and you saw the TV and he told you it came from Julian's place," Tyson said, keeping a tight grip on Des' shoulder and looking directly at him.

"That's all I have to do?" Des asked.

"That's all buddy, can you do that for Mikey and me?"

"What if the cops ask me to describe it?"

"It's a big fucking TV, Des, it has a sixty-inch flat screen and it's made by Sanyo. That's all you got to say. It looks like any other TV, except it has Sanyo on the front. Can you do this, yes or no? I can tell Mikey we have to get someone else." Tyson stated, slowly and loudly as he was getting annoyed talking to this idiot.

"No, ah no Tyson, I can do this. I'll tell the cops I have information and I want bail on my warrants."

"Good lad Des, I knew I could count on you."

A couple of days later, Des Cotter walked into the Gurranbraher Garda Station. He went up to the counter and waited for the cop at the other side to look up.

"What do you want?" the gruff older cop asked.

"I got some warrants and I want to deal with them," Des replied.

"Name?" the old cop said with the enthusiasm of a man going in for a vasectomy.

"Des Cotter."

The cop typed the name into the computer, stared at the screen for a few seconds and then spoke without moving his eyes from the monitor. "Well Des, you do have warrants, two in fact. And you want to turn yourself in, is that it?"

"Yup."

"Have a seat over there," the cop pointed to a row of chairs near a door by the wall. "I'll have someone come in from patrol and take care of this for you."

Des looked at the cop, "Aren't you going to arrest me?"

"Not my job Des, my job is to sit here and talk to people. I'll call a car in off the street and they can deal with you. You're not going to run away, are you?" the cop answered, still staring at his computer screen.

"How long will they be?" Des asked.

"Half an hour, maybe an hour, I don't know."

Des looked puzzled. "I'll wait for a while, maybe I'll take off if it takes too long."

"Suit yourself," the old cop said, as he typed some more on his keyboard.

Twenty minutes later, two young officers walked to the front foyer from the back. They arrested Des and took him to a holding room at the back of the station.

Des told them he was tired of dodging the cops because of a couple of lousy warrants and he decided he wanted to deal with them. But he was hoping he would get bail because he had some information about a homicide.

The two young officers listened to Des and wrote down everything he said. They left the holding room and called Detective Inspector Cahill at home. John was cautiously excited and told the officers to hold onto Cotter until he told them differently. John was careful not to divulge anything about the missing television to the officers, He wouldn't confirm or deny that a television had been stolen or what size or make it was.

John called Sean Harrington who was working an evening shift. Harrington sent a surveillance crew to drive by Jimmy O'Connell's house to check if they could see a television from the front or back windows. An hour later, Harrington called John and confirmed that one of his men could see a large flat screen television from a window at the rear of O'Connell's house. The television looked like it could easily be a sixty-inch television. John then called Pete Sandhu and asked him to go into work and prepare a search warrant for Jimmy O'Connell's house.

A couple of hours later, John and Pete Sandhu were with an entry team half a block from Jimmy O'Connell's. Jimmy was a low-level drug dealer with strong ties to the Mahon Warlords. He lived in a small house near the Mercy Hospital, on the south banks of the River Lee. Jimmy had an unstable history and at times was prone to extreme violence.

After a short briefing, the entry team drove down Sheares Street to the front of O'Connell's house. The team exited their van and ran to the front door as more of their team drove to the back lane at the rear of the house.

Jimmy Cotter's door came down with a crash and Jimmy, quick as a flash, grabbed a couple of freezer bags from a shelf, ran to the upstairs toilet and started to empty the contents of the bags into the water. He was grabbed from behind and dragged out of the toilet as the freezer bags, with their white powdery contents, went flying in the air.

When Jimmy was under control and sitting in handcuffs, John and Pete strolled into the house. John looked at the powder on the floor in the toilet. "Better call someone from Vice to come and deal with this shit," he said to Pete.

John walked down the stairs and straight over to the TV. Sure enough it was a Sanyo. He looked at the back, no hole, where the cable antenna should have been ripped out. He checked the serial number, not a match for the one stolen from Julian Hodnett's place. John called headquarters and had them check the serial number anyway, and of course, it was also a stolen television.

"Tell Vice the television is stolen too," he yelled to Pete. The disheartened inspector drove back to the Incident Room Unit and thought, "What a waste of time. We need a bigger break on this one."

Chapter 17

Georgy Galvin was happy that he got his van back and that the cops had covered the tow charge. The manager at the impound lot told him it must have been an oversight because he should have been liable for the cost.

What Georgy did not know was that the police were monitoring his every move and listening to every conversation. The tech team had installed a GPS tracker under the hood and wired it to his battery so it would never lose charge. They had also installed three tiny listening devices, one in each of the front seat headrests and another in the center of the consul. The sound from inside the vehicle was crystal clear.

The investigators from the Technical Surveillance Unit were able to figure out Mikey and Georgy Galvin's phone numbers too. Trish Langford called Georgy several times a day so that was his phone identified and both Johnny and Georgy called Mikey. So now the phones, the vehicle and one home were all being intercepted.

With everything in place, it was time to turn up the heat and put some pressure on the targets. John had to make sure that his suspects were thinking about the shooting on New Year's Day. He had to ensure that the targets were worried and believed that the police were closing in. All this had to be done without confronting them. First up, was the weaker of the Galvin brothers, Georgy.

John ordered the reinterviewing of some of the guests who were at the New Year's party at Trish Langford's house. He didn't expect that any of their stories would change from their initial interviews but it would probably make Mikey and Georgy Galvin panic a little wondering why the police called in a handful of people.

Trish Langford texted her husband and told him to call her.

"What do you want? I'm kinda busy," Georgy said curtly.

"I bet you are!" Trish shot back. "I thought you and your brother would want to know that the cops are talking to some of the old people who were here on New Year's Eve again."

"What the fuck?" "What are they asking them now?"

"I think it's just the same stuff, who was here? did they see anyone with a gun? did they see any I-P members?"

"Did anyone say anything different?" Georgy was panicked.

"How the fuck do I know? I wasn't there when they spoke with them." Trish was pleased with herself that she had rattled Georgy's cage.

"They better have stuck to the same story!"

The police monitors who were listening to the conversation marked the call on their computer screen as 'Pertinent.' The monitors could identify the interesting conversations that they listened to as 'Pertinent' or 'Urgent.' Pertinent was something that could probably be useful to the investigation. Only John could decide if the conversation should be upgraded to 'Evidentiary' at a later time. A call marked 'Urgent,' would require immediate attention as it may refer to the destruction of evidence or imminent danger to some other individual.

Georgy hung up on his wife and called his brother. "It's me. We got to meet! The bar in half an hour?"

"Okay" is all that Mikey Galvin said and hung up.

Georgy got to the dingy bar on Thomas Davis Street twenty minutes before his brother. He ordered a double rum and swallowed it fast while still standing at the counter. He followed up with a beer and then found a dark booth opposite the entrance.

Mikey G stood at the entrance to the bar and squinted as he adjusted to the dark gloom of the barroom. His eyes watered slightly from the stale stench that rose from the mouldy carpet. Mikey spotted his brother in the booth. Georgy waved his beer bottle, Mikey, as cautious as ever, nodded in recognition as he walked across the bar floor, scanning his surroundings and assessing everything and everyone.

"You want a beer?" Georgy asked.

"Nope. Where's the fire?" Mikey replied impatiently.

"I thought you would want to know. The cops are asking questions about New Year's again."

"Try to say that a bit louder, you fucking hammer! I think the barman didn't hear you," Mikey sneered..

Georgy's face flushed. "Trish called me and said they are bringing in some of the old people for questioning again."

Mikey was staring at the table top. He let out a slow breath and without lifting his head and ordered, "Get hold of Trish's mom. Tell her if her old friends want to get any older, they better not say anything to the cops! I mean it." Mikey looked up and held his brother's gaze. "This is the one and only warning they get!"

Mikey Galvin stood up and walked out of the bar. Georgy walked to the bar and ordered another shot of rum, drank it quickly and headed to the Langford household.

When he walked into the house, Trish took one look at Georgy and knew he had a few drinks. "Are you here to help with your children?" she sarcastically asked.

"Where's your mother?" Georgy asked.

Trish looked towards the kitchen and Georgy walked through. Jane Langford was standing over a sink full of dishes, with her usual lit cigarette hanging out of her mouth. She turned and glanced at Georgy but didn't speak to him. Secretly Jane Langford despised her son- in- law but took his money and the status in the neighborhood that came with it.

"Who are the cops talking to about New Year's?" Georgy asked.

"Just some of my old friends that were here that night," Jane answered without turning.

Georgy raised his voice, "I know they're your friends, but who? Which ones?"

"I'm not telling you. You and those other thugs will go around and scare the crap out of them. They won't say anything about you and your friends. Don't worry. I've spoken to them all."

"They fucking better not. Mikey knows all about this and he's pissed. If one of them puts the cops in our direction, Mikey will make sure everyone pays and that's you too."

"Fuck off Georgy," Jane said quietly and sucked on her cigarette.

The police monitors heard the entire conversation and marked this recording 'Pertinent.'

John went to the Monitor Room on Stable Lane and reviewed the recordings. For now, that would do; they had reinterviewed eight people and got no new information. But in a few days, they would speak with a few more people, this time, some of the low-level gang members. "Divide and conquer!" John smiled to himself.

After letting the Galvin brothers feel unease over the first round of reinterviews, John addressed his team at the morning briefing. He told them about the reaction they got from Georgy and Mikey G. There was no doubt that they had the right crew. All they needed now was evidence to get this before the courts and get a conviction.

"We will now interview a few of the low-level gangsters and maybe someone near the top, just to get them second guessing each other. Do you have anyone in mind?" John asked.

It was decided to bring in Mick Sheldon, Suzanne Langford, Trish's sister, Eddie Flynn and Tyson Rolland's right-hand man, Darrell Lyons.

John and Tim took Eddie Flynn. Eddie was a large man but not very bright. He didn't admit to much but what the detectives did learn from this interview was that Eddie and his brother Bertie were involved in the brawl on New Year's Eve.

Mike Williams and Eddie Jenkins interviewed Mick Sheldon. Sheldon's older brother Walter was tight with the Galvin brothers and particularly with Mikey. Walter was an O-G, an Original Gangster and hard-core to the end. Walter had a penchant for violence and was currently serving time for manslaughter in Cork Prison

Jeff Rafter and Len Benoit interviewed Suzanne Langford. Suzanne was like her sister, mouthy and obnoxious. Suzanne spent the entire interview giving smart Alec answers and just being rude.

Travis Dawson and Larry Vickers interviewed Darrell Lyons. Darrell didn't answer any questions and said 'No Comment" to everything that was put to him.

As soon as Darrell was released from custody, he called Mikey G. "The cops brought me in today and questioned me about that thing."

"Who else did they bring in?" Mikey asked.

"They walked me past all the interview rooms, I could see the names written on the doors. Mick Sheldon, Eddie Flynn and Suzanne, you know? Trish's sister."

"I'm worried about Eddie," Mikey said thoughtfully. "Walter can talk to his little brother Mick."

"Eddie should be solid. He works for me and Tyson. He's as dumb as a post but doesn't know fuck all, so he can't have said anything. I'll suss him out." Darrell said in his tough monotone voice.

The police monitors heard it all while intercepting Mikey Galvin's cell phone. This call was also marked 'Pertinent.'

But Mick Sheldon was much weaker than his older brother and after the interview. The detectives had some success interviewing him. Sheldon said that he was present when the brawl began but didn't hang around. He said he thought Mikey, Georgy and Johnny were all there at the time but he could not be sure. One thing that he said, which didn't make sense, was Mikey ordered all the gang members to remain at the party and not to leave early. No gang members left the party before the fight broke out. Mick Sheldon didn't know why Mikey ordered this. After the interview, Mike Williams felt that he could probably break him and get a statement. Whether Mick Sheldon would testify or not was another issue.

At least once a day, John went to the Monitor Room and reviewed all the recorded intercepted calls, paying special attention to the ones marked 'Pertinent.' John read the synopsis of the calls and then listened to the spoken word. "It's all coming together," he said to no one in particular.

Winter had truly ended; the snow that fell over Christmas and New Year's had completely disappeared. However, spring time in early March brought moist grey weather to the south coast of Cork. Nonetheless, there was a great stretch in the evenings and John and Jules were able to take their greyhounds for a proper walk, provided he got home at a reasonable hour. The skinny dogs no longer required their heavy coats and were happy sniffing their way through the sand dunes and digging holes on the beaches. The hundreds of daffodils in the Cahills' front yard were all blooming and the lemon-colored primroses lined the driveway from the road to the house. When the sun made an occasional break through the clouds, the old homestead looked magical.

On a Sunday afternoon, in between rain showers, walking along both beaches, John brought Jules up to speed on the wiretap investigation and told her how a little bit of pressure had sparked conversation.

"I think I'm going to start putting pressure on Johnny Johnson next. I don't know much about him but I don't think he'll react very well to pressure."

"Are you going to bring him in?" Jules asked. "If he's anything like the rest of them, he'll just call a lawyer and say 'NO COMMENT'!"

"I was thinking of using a newspaper article. Do you remember it worked like a charm the last time that I used one? This time, I'll describe the shooter as Johnson, right down to the limp but not naming him obviously," John replied and Jules could hear his enthusiasm.

"Do they read the papers?" Jules asked.

"They will if they get it for free! I'll arrange free delivery to the entire block for a week before hand. Someone will read it and point it out."

"What about the other investigation? the double homicide?" Jules enquired.

"We badly need a break on that. The D.N.A. from the hair on the coat identifies Ken Rolland's mother. It makes sense that it's his coat and her hair was transferred onto it innocently. But that is so circumstantial, we still need some more."

"Sounds like you need a miracle," Jules laughed.

They reached the end of the East Beach, near the channel when Jules spoke, "I look around the beach and see other couples walking with their kids or their dogs and wonder what they're talking about. Probably their lives and jobs or the what they'll have for dinner tomorrow. Look at us! We talk about gruesome murders and how to catch the killers. If they only knew." Jules sounded philosophical as she glanced around at the others walking along the beach.

The tide was beginning to come in. Soon access to the East Beach would be cut off near the rocky bank between both beaches.

"You're right, we should talk about something else besides work, the kids and the dogs. We live in this beautiful place and there's more to life than work." John nodded in agreement.

"I met my cousin Elaine and her husband Barry, walking on the beach a couple of days ago. You were working late as usual," Jules said with a smile.

"How are they? He's an accountant, isn't he?"

"Oh yeah," Jules giggled. "Well Barry couldn't be anything else but an accountant. He looked so uncomfortable and out of place here."

"Why?"

"He was so overdressed for a walk on the beach... in his dress pants and a shirt and tie and polished shoes. I met them as they were heading to their car and he was desperately trying to shake the sand off his shoes before he got in. I can only imagine you working with figures all day long. What would we talk about then?"

"I suppose we could talk about profit and loss and bankruptcy." John closed his eyes and shook his head. "I couldn't do it. Remember the trouble I had, trying to keep books when we had the stables here." John smiled remembering their old life in Inchydoney.

"You know what? I think we'll stick to talking about murder and mayhem. At least it's interesting and challenging." Jules laughed and whistled for the dogs as they headed for home.

After an early night, John was woken from his deep sleep by the nightmare that usually recurred after he closed a homicide investigation. The victim of every homicide he had investigated lined up outside his bedroom door and down the hall. All the corpses presented in the condition that they were in, when their bodies were discovered. Tonight, the grotesque parade was led by Chris Shorting. As usual, in the dream, John was standing at the foot of his bed. Shorting, followed by all the cadavers stepped forward. Shorting whispered something unintelligible, then turned and disappeared.

The next corpse, Julian Hodnett, did the same thing, and so on and on.

John shot up in the bed and gasped. It wasn't so much the distorted dead bodies that bothered him but the fact that he could not grasp what each one whispered before disappearing.

FINALLY, THE BREAK the Serious Crime Unit was looking for came along. Garda Tom Donegan was well known throughout the police department as a tough no-nonsense old fashioned beat cop. Tom hated drug dealers and did everything he could to make their lives miserable. His cases didn't always make it to court because of his unorthodox methods but he was feared by every drug dealer in town. Tom was also feared by many of his peers because they knew if they were involved in a case with him, they were likely to be named in a complaint.

However, John Cahill liked and trusted Tom Donegan. A few years earlier, Donegan had turned up to help the Integrated Warrant Squad in a sticky situation. And although Tom was rough and unorthodox, he was dedicated and honest to the core.

Tom Donegan walked into the Incident Room and went straight over to the Inspector's desk. "JC- how's my favorite Orangeman? How are you doing little buddy?" Donegan said loudly as he towered over Cahill.

Some of the other investigators looked up warily at Donegan and put their heads down hoping not to get drawn into something with this loose cannon cop.

"Hello Tom, did you come to tell me where you've buried a body?" Cahill joked.

"I'll never tell that," Tom answered smiling roguishly. "Are you working on that double homicide from New Year's? Or are those pricks from Dublin running it?"

"Yup, we kept it here and we need some help with that one. Actually we need a lot of help with that one. Have you got something?"

"Let's talk, buy me a coffee and I'll see if I can help you out."

John grabbed his jacket, took his pistol out of his drawer and put it into his holster.

"I won't be long," he said to Pete Sandhu as he walked out of the office.

John and Tom Donegan found a quiet table in the coffee shop next to City Hall near the police station.

"A guy called me from Cork Prison last night. He said he has some valuable information about that case."

"What does he know and what does he want?" John answered.

"He knows who did it and he has some other proof too. He mentioned something about a fire. He also has a confession from the killer."

John was very interested but he held his poker face. "Do you trust this guy?"

"I wouldn't trust him to hold my wallet but he's never given me bad information. He's not a regular informant but when he has something, he's good." Donegan's tone was serious.

"What's he in for?" John asked.

"Drugs and guns. He's looking at five to six years. He had half a kilo and a 9mm Smith and Wesson with a suppressor.

"Has he done that kind of time before?" John's mind was racing as he processed his options in dealing with this new rat.

"Not that long. Five or six years will kill him and he's in poor health at the best of time," Donegan responded.

"Tell him that I want a witness, not an informant. You know the score. I'll do what I can for him but it depends on the quality of what he has to offer. Can you pass that message on and ask him if he'll meet with me?" John probed.

"I'll do what I can. What about the other murder on New Year's? I heard that was I-P." Donegan was now doing the probing.

"It looks that way, Tom, but I think we'll wrap that one up. We just have to be patient," John said smiling cunningly.

Donegan nodded and knew better than to ask more.

When John returned to his office, Mike Williams asked, "What did Big Tom want?"

"He's got a guy in Cork Prison who might be able to help us with the double," John replied, taking off his jacket and returning his pistol to the drawer.

"Thank God he's on our side," was all Mike Williams said as he walked away.

That evening, Tom Donegan called John at home. "I spoke to my guy. He's willing to meet with you. I told him once that happens, I'm out of it and any dealing he does from there on is between you and him. Is that okay with you?"

"I'd prefer it that way Tom, thanks."

"Good, he'll meet you in the IPSO's office tomorrow or the next day. He gets pulled in by the IPSO regularly so it won't look bad for him. His name is Ron Glowden. Do you know the IPSO there?"

"I know him well. I'll arrange that, thanks Tom."

The Internal Preventative Security Officer, or the IPSO, was the prison's intelligence officer and responsible for keeping the prison relatively safe and rival gangs apart. John called the IPSO at Cork Prison and asked to meet in private with Ron Glowden. John ran a background check on Glowden and found numerous charges for drugs but few convictions, a sure sign of someone who had valuable information to trade.

John and Tim Warren drove across town, up Summer Hill to Saint Luke's and continuing straight ahead to Dillons Cross. They turned onto the Old Youghal Road and down the narrow Rathmore Road to the menacing presence of Cork Prison. The main entrance to the modern prison was part of the old prison, built in the early 1800's. The gallows where unfortunates were strung up by their necks had been inside the main gate, but thankfully that was long gone. John looked at the impressive limestone walls and thought that many of his ancestors had languished behind these walls after the 1916 Rising, when the old prison was used as a detention barracks for suspected Republican insurgents.

"I wonder what they would make of me, wearing the Royal emblem, serving with the PSNI in Northern Ireland," he thought as Tim rolled down the driver's side window and pressed the buzzer to request entry to the prison.

After parking and securing their pistols in the gun boxes, they made their way to the duty office. At the back of the office block was the start of the prison. Here the smell of body odour along with a depressing atmosphere always hung in the air. The detectives went to the main counter in the duty office and asked to see the IPSO. Minutes later the security specialist appeared and took them to his office on the third floor.

"Glowden says he will only meet with DI. Cahill," the IPSO said. "He won't give you any trouble, he's not the troublesome type and his health isn't the best. You can wait out here if you like." He pointed to an outer office as he offered it to Tim.

"That's fine," John said and Tim left feeling disappointed.

The IPSO showed John into his inner office. Sitting in a wooden chair was an older looking, thin man with a dark complexion, sunken eyes and protruding cheek bones He was wearing a grey prison issued track suit at least two sizes too big.

The man looked up at John, "Are you Cahill?"

"Yes, are you Ron?" John asked as he stepped towards him and shook the other man's hand.

"Yes, I am," he answered.

The two men were sizing each other up. John thought Ron Glowden looked like 'death warmed up,' giving the impression he was a man who was always gasping for breath. Glowden thought the cop looked confident and professional, in his light grey suit, clean well pressed shirt and colorful but not too bold tie. Glowden looked down at John's shoes and was fascinated to see they were well polished. The prisoner was impressed.

"Thanks for meeting with me Ron," John began, taking a seat in front of Glowden, but not behind the vacant desk. "What can I do for you?" John decided to let the prisoner make the first move and see what was on offer. He didn't want to look too desperate.

"Perhaps we can help each other out," Glowden answered, in a somewhat refined well-spoken voice.

John was surprised to hear Glowden speak like a well-read scholar, in what North-Siders would call a Montenotte accent as he looked like he had crawled out from under a rock in the gutter with his skinny build and slumped shoulders.

"Maybe we can," John replied. "Let's not beat around the bush. You told Garda Donegan that you have information about a homicide and I want as much information as I can get about homicides that are still open."

"I have information about two murders that were carried out by the same person on New Year's Eve."

And so, the dance began between the detective and the would-be informant. They both wanted as much from the other person as possible but neither wanted to show his hand too much in case the other one walked away from the table.

"Give me a taste of what you got Ron. And I will give you an idea of what I can do, IF it's something that I can use," John said replied, with his best poker face.

Glowden thought it over for a moment, deciding what he should say in order to keep the cop interested but he didn't want to show his entire hand. Glowden sat back in the chair, crossed his arms and put his right fist under his chin. "These two men were killed in an apartment near The Lough. At the time I lived on College Road, less than a block or two away. The person who did this brought me there before the police arrived. I saw the guy at the foot of the stairs. He was just about decapitated. The person who did this also lit a fire inside the apartment to get rid of evidence." Glowden paused, waiting for a reaction.

"That's pretty generic stuff, Ron. I'm not going to say if it's right or wrong but you've been around long enough to know I need more than that. How do I know you were not involved in this? How do I know you didn't do it?"

"The only way I could get the better of two young fellas like that would be to shoot them. Take a look at me. I'm a sick old man." Ron slowly looked down at his body.

John smiled, "You could be a kung fu expert for all I know."

Glowden chuckled. He liked the inspector and decided to give him a bit more and see what he could get out of this deal. "There's someone who can verify my story and vouch for my whereabouts before I went to that place."

"Okay. So why would this person show you his handiwork? It doesn't make sense. If I killed someone, let alone two people, I wouldn't be swanning around the block calling on my buddies to show them what I did," John commented, pushing for clarity.

"That person needed me to help carry something that was heavy and awkward. That item was stored in my place and I sold it later on. It was too awkward for one person to carry down the street," Ron replied confidently.

John immediately knew that Glowden was referencing the television from the apartment. This information was golden. It had been held back from all reports and the media.

"Ron, we should really continue this conversation at the police station where we can formally work out the benefits for each other. Do you want to come with me now?" John asked, eager to get this information.

"No, not now. I've been off my range for too long as it is. Some of the others will be asking me what took so long. If they suspect I've been speaking to police, it may not be pretty for me. Write your number down on a piece of paper and I'll call you in a day or two."

John pulled a business card from his pocket and went to hand it to the prisoner.

"No! write the number on a piece of scrap. If I go back with a cop's card and someone sees it, it's curtains for me." Glowden showed how experienced a prisoner he really was.

John tore a piece off a page in his notebook and wrote down his cell phone number and the letter J and passed it to Glowden. "What do you want out of this Ron?"

Glowden took the paper, looked at it and put it in his pants pocket. "I want to get out of here. I need to get out of here. One of my kids is fourteen and is starting to follow in my footsteps and get into trouble. I want to try and turn him around before it's too late for him too," Ron said sounding philosophical.

John was impressed with Ron Glowden. He didn't know if it was true or not but it was different. A con wanting something for someone else was unusual. "Give me one other thing now that I can bring to my bosses Ron, but I must be perfectly honest with you. I need a witness, not an informant. Do you know the difference?"

Glowden stood up and let out a long sigh. "I know the difference." He stretched out his right arm and the two men shook hands, "It was a plasma television with engraving on the back," Glowden said walking to the door of the office.

"Do you need someone to bring you back?"

Glowden smiled, "I know my way, I won't get lost." He walked out the door and said, "I might call," without looking back.

Seconds later John followed Glowden into the hallway and met Tim Warren who was standing a couple of meters away with the IPSO.

"He said he knew his own way back," John mentioned smiling at the IPSO

"Oh, he does, no need to worry about Ron, he won't go too far astray. It's almost supper time in there," the IPSO replied laughing.

On the drive back to Anglesea Street, John told Tim what had transpired during the meeting. "I guess we wait and see if he calls," Tim said excitedly.

That evening while walking the greyhounds on the West Beach at Inchydoney, John told Jules all about the meeting with Ron Glowden. "He's not what I expected. I knew going up there that he is very well educated but went to the dark side a long time ago. There was something about him. It's as though he's completely lost and knows he can never find his way back."

"What about his family?" Jules asked.

"His parents are long since dead and left him quite a bit of money but it is all held in trust. He has a sister who manages it for him. She's a doctor up in Dublin. I'll find out more if he calls me back."

Chapter 18

A few days passed and there was no call from Ron Glowden. John intended to let it go for a little while and then go back to the prison and see him again. Right now, it was time to rattle the cage of the other gang members and see what he could stir up in their pathetic lives.

John asked Superintendent Paddy Collins to call up his old friend, a journalist, and request a meeting. John and the superintendent met with Doc Watson, the crime reporter for the local newspaper, in the coffee shop near City Hall.

John did the talking. "Doc, I want to appeal to the public for assistance in the New Year's Eve murder at Manor View Estate in the North Side. A young innocent man was killed and two other kids were shot and seriously injured. They're both left with life altering injuries. Do you remember the big fight on the street?"

"What kind of story do you want to do?" the reporter asked, nodding his head.

"Just an appeal for any information. There were about a hundred people involved in that brawl. Someone knows something. I just want to get this back into the news and get people thinking about it. It's been nearly three months and just maybe people aren't so scared anymore. I'm going to give this to all the media outlets too, but you get it first so you can run the big story," John said, trying to pique the journalist's interest.

"When do you want it?" Doc asked.

"At the weekend, if you can. Everyone and his dog in the North Side reads your paper on a Saturday," John answered, trying not to sound desperate.

"I can't promise you front page but I will be able to get page 3. That's the first page everyone reads when they open the cover," Doc Watson responded, smelling a story brewing.

John then gave the reporter specific details that he wanted to appear, knowing that it would shake up his suspects.

After the meeting, John walked to the old warehouse that housed the semi-covert Anti-Crime Unit. He walked in to Sean Harrington's office and found him chatting with Percy Jones.

"Hey buddy, what brings you down here?" Jones asked. "Do you want a coffee?"

"No thanks, I'm all coffeed out and I'm running around like a scalded cat. Do you have time to help me over the next couple of days? I want to stimulate some conversation and put pressure on our suspects."

"Anything for you," Harrington grinned.

"It's time to turn up the heat on Johnny Johnson and the Galvin brothers. I'm running a story in the Saturday paper and doing a press release about the murder that should freak them out. I want Johnny feeling the heat before that."

"Do you want us to pull him over and shake him down?" Harrington asked. "That could backfire if we find something on him and are forced to arrest him."

"I was thinking of a more subtle approach," and John explained his plan to the other two.

THURSDAY CAME AROUND quickly and the surveillance team from the Anti-Crime Unit were split in two. One section was watching Georgy Galvin's van and the other was sitting near Johnny

Johnson's sister's house at Kilmore Heights, in Knocknaheeny. Percy Jones walked casually along the street and placed one of Detective Inspector Cahill's business cards in the mailbox and walked on as if nothing had happened.

A short time later Johnny's sister opened the door and brought in the mail. She went through the bills and picked up the business card. Johnny was sitting at her kitchen table drinking a coffee and smoking a cigarette. "What the fuck is this?" she asked waving the card at Johnny. She handed him the card.

His tanned face turned white when he saw 'Serious Crime Unit' under the name. "Who put that there?"

"How the fuck would I know? I suppose it's for you or your idiot friends," she scoffed as she walked away.

Johnny picked up his cell phone and called Georgy Galvin. "Bro! Pick me up at my sister's," was all he could manage as he gasped for breath while his heart was pounding in his chest.

Half an hour later the rest of the surveillance team followed Georgy Galvin to Johnson's lair and watched as he stepped out the front door, looked up and down the street and ran to the van.

The police monitors and Inspector Cahill were listening to the conversation inside the van.

"Hey Bro! What's up? Looks like you've seen a ghost," Georgy said, joking.

"It's worse than that." Johnny pulled out the business card and showed it to Georgy. "Serious Crime were looking for me."

"What the fuck? Did they come to your sister's place? What did they say?" Georgy quizzed.

"This was in my mailbox. They must have come around when I was out."

"Did you call them?" Georgy asked.

"Fuck no!" Johnny answered shouting with fear.

"Maybe it's not for you." Georgy tried to put his friend at ease.

"Who else is it for? It's not for my fucking sister. We should tell Mikey." Johnny's panic was rising as pulled out his cell phone and started to dial.

"Jesus Christ! Not on the phone. He'll kill us both. I'll set up a meeting." Georgy was starting to panic now too.

John called Sean Harrington, "Okay, this has them freaking out. Let's step it up a bit before they go to see Mikey."

"You're a devious fucker, Cahill, but I like it," Harrington laughed.

As Georgy drove north on Harbour View Road, a marked police car pulled in behind him. Georgy spotted the police car in his rearview mirror. "Cops are behind us."

Johnny spun around in his seat, stared at the police car and whispered, "Shit!"

The surveillance cars pulled back. The marked police car stayed about four car lengths behind Georgy Galvin, who was doing his level best to not break any rules of the road. After what seemed like a lifetime, but was less than two minutes, the passenger in the police car activated the emergency lights and the siren.

"Oh, holy fuck! They're pulling us over!" Johnny cried as he looked back at the police car. "This is it Bro, they're going to bring me in."

"I wasn't speeding or nothing. I'm going to have to pull over," Georgy said, stammering, while a bead of sweat formed on his forehead.

Georgy turned on his turn signal and started to pull over to the curb. The police car slowed behind him and just as Georgy came to a stop, the police car swerved around him and sped off towards the industrial estate and turned off out of sight.

Johnny gasped a breath and looked at Georgy and the two men burst out laughing. "I thought I was done!" Johnny laughed nervously.

"Me too. I thought for sure they were pulling me over. Do you still want to go see Mikey or will I drop you home?" Georgy asked.

"Take me home Bro. I think I have to change my underwear," Johnny said in his North Side accent but trying to sound like he was from East Los Angeles.

Johnny Johnson went back to his sister's house and although he was somewhat relieved that the police car did not pull them over, the Serious Crime Unit business card still worried him. He sat looking out the front window onto Kilmore Heights while drinking a beer. He did not take any notice of the white cube van parked a few doors down. Why would he? It had been there all day long. Johnson had no idea that Percy Jones was in the back of the van, watching him drinking his beer.

"He's been sitting at the front window since he got back. He only gets up to get another beer," Sergeant Jones reported to John.

"Right! Let's have some more fun and scare him again."

Minutes later two marked police sports utility vehicles pulled up in front of Johnson's house. The four cops, wearing the Armed Support Unit uniforms, exited the cars; two of them were carrying carbine rifles and one of them had a sledge hammer. They ran as fast as they could towards the front door. Inside, Johnny's heart stopped. He dropped his beer bottle and it spilled on the table. He watched the scene play out in slow motion and made an unintelligible noise.

As the four cops were about two steps away from Johnny's front door, they peeled away to the left and were out of his view. Johnny gasped. His hands were shaking and his breath was shallow. He leaned up to the window and looked out to see if he could see where the cops went but they were nowhere to be seen. Johnny went to his sister's room, found a bottle of vodka and got drunk.

The next morning, Saturday, Johnny Johnson woke with an awful hangover. Not only did his head hurt but his sister was furious at him for drinking her vodka. He was still shaking after yesterday's close encounters with the police. The fear of getting arrested for the murder was eating away at him; little did he know that the fear was being fueled and driven by the police.

Johnny sat at the kitchen table looking out the window, nursing a cup of steaming hot coffee and smoking his third cigarette. He watched his sister walk up the path to the front door. He scanned the street as best he could from his vantage point to see if the police were nearby.

Johnny's sister slammed the front door behind her, hoping the loud noise would piss him off. "Oh, you're up. Are you still feeling sorry for yourself?" she asked sarcastically.

"Fuck off," Johnny muttered under his breath.

"Here, this will brighten your day. Who do you think they're talking about?" she said as she threw the newspaper on the table.

The front page had a huge colour picture of Manor View Estate from New Year's Day with all the police cars, the blue and white police tape and yellow markers on the ground. "**POLICE NEED ASSISTANCE**" the banner headline read. Johnny could hear his heart beating. He dropped his cigarette onto his lap and fumbled to pick it up before it burned a hole in his jeans. He opened the paper and stared at page 3. A smaller photograph of the crime scene, this time in black and white and taken from another angle. A different headline read: "**SHOOTER WALKED WITH A LIMP.**"

Johnny began to read the article and saw a clear description of himself as the shooter...from his physical description, hair, height and build, right down to his limp when, a few years back, he accidently shot himself in the leg. Johnny took a sip of his coffee, immediately felt it back up in his throat and ran to the bathroom and puked his guts up. A few minutes later he came back to the table and stared at the newspaper.

His phone buzzed. "Unknown Name Unknown Number."

Johnny knew it was Mikey Galvin. Johnny answered the phone with a whisper. "Did you see the paper?"

Mikey G barked, "Be prepared to get picked up. Say nothing!"

"You know I'll never talk," a nervous Johnny Johnson stammered, barely above a whisper. "Someone must have said something. How else would they know all this?"

"There were a hundred people out there and all they had to do was piece it together. Say no more now. We'll meet later." Mikey G hung up.

The police monitors recorded the conversation, marked it 'Pertinent' and called John to report.

An hour later Georgy Galvin surfaced in one of his crack shacks and picked up the paper. He too was worried when he saw the headline on the cover and even more worried when he read through the article on page 3. Georgy filled in all the blanks and was sure that everyone would know that Johnny Johnson was the man with the limp and the people who orchestrated his getaway were the Galvin brothers.

Georgy immediately called his wife, Trish Langford. Trish had been up for a few hours taking care of their kids and running her household.

"Yeah, I saw it and I'd say you, your brother and your half-wit buddy are fucked. Now go away, I've lots to do!" and she hung up.

Georgy had a good mind to go over and yell at her and maybe give her a good slap. But he thought better of it. He just didn't feel like fighting with Trish.

Georgy called his mother. "Hi Mom, how's it going?"

"Hello luv. I'm good. How are you?"

"Did you see that thing in the paper about us this morning? That's us they are talking about. I think we're going to go down for this." Georgy sounded like a little boy.

"That's not ye surely? Is it? Sure, they don't know who it is, that's what the story is about, they are asking for information." Mrs. Galvin tried to comfort her son.

"I'm coming over," Georgy stated and ended the call.

Again, the police monitoring the phone calls reported to John.

"What are you grinning about?" Jules asked him.

"The targets are feeling the heat. Georgy G has gone to see his mammy and told her he is going away for a long time. Johnny doesn't know what he best do. He sounds like he's scared shitless. I wish I thought of putting a listening device in Mammy Galvin's house. I would love to be a fly on the wall for that conversation."

A few hours later the senior monitor called John back with an update. "Have we got a confession?" John asked anxiously.

"Not yet, but we might get one before the day is out," the woman answered. "Mikey just called Johnny. Johnny sounds like he is half cut and depressed."

"I like the sound of that," John laughed.

"Mikey barely asked how he was doing. It appears there is a party at Darryl's house tonight, I suspect that's Darryl Lyons. Anyway, Mikey told Johnny, under no circumstances, was he to go to the party. Mikey called him a 'HEAT BAG' after the newspaper this morning."

"How did Johnny take that?" John asked as his mind raced, to try to figure out the best way to take advantage of this new information.

"Johnny said he wouldn't go but he sounded really down and out. I think he's been drinking all day. He certainly sounds like it," the monitor reported.

During the evening Johnny Johnson received two more phone calls from gang members. They taunted him, laughing at his predicament and calling him "Heat Score" and" Heat Bag." They jeered asking how his limp was. Johnny sounded really drunk and swore at his callers.

The monitors only worked until midnight and after that the lines were recorded and had to be listened to the next day. John guessed that there would be a lot of chatter on the phone lines and on the various listening devices. He didn't want to miss something important in case he had to act on it right away. He decided to sit in the monitor room overnight and listen to his targets.

"You're kidding me! It's bad enough that you must go every time someone gets killed. Now you're going to work all night listening to a bunch of assholes at a party!" Jules was upset at the prospect of another Saturday night alone.

"I'm sorry. You know what these projects are like. They're a living beast and you have to keep up with them." He felt bad and was genuinely apologetic but he wasn't going to change his mind.

John arranged for a patrol car to drive by Darryl Lyons's house a few times during the evening and early hours of the morning. The place was a hive of activity with people coming and going. Again, John wished he had a few listening devices in there but he knew he didn't have the legal grounds to do that.

The building on Stable Lane was empty and the only sounds were the mice scurrying around behind the walls of the old building. John was dozing off in a chair around two in the morning. Then the computer screen showing the GPS tracker on Georgy's van buzzed to life. Georgy Galvin was on the move. John turned up the sound on the listening device inside the vehicle. All he could hear was the sound of the engine as the vehicle was driving through the North Side.

"Hmm, no chatter, he must be alone," John thought.

As the van drove towards the Farranree area, Georgy Galvin's cell phone buzzed to life on another computer screen. John switched it on and made sure it was recording as well as playing live.

"Hi. It's me." The familiar sound of Georgy Galvin's voice came from the speaker in the monitor room.

"Oh hi. What time is it?" a sleepy, groggy female voice answered.

"I'm coming over, okay? I've done something really bad. I'm not going to be around for a really long time and I want to tell you about it before you hear it from someone else. I'll be there in five minutes." Georgy sounded contrite and serious.

"You can't come in; my dad is here. You know what he thinks of you. I'll meet you outside," the female said, stifling a yawn.

John was wide awake now in anticipation of the conversation he might hear. He was frantically checking several data bases to identify the woman by her phone number. She needed to be interviewed and soon. He anxiously checked the vehicle listening device icon on the computer to ensure it was recording. "This is it. He's going to tell her all about it," he thought beaming with expectation. While watching the tracking icon and listening to the engine change gears as it motored along, John almost jumped out of his chair when Georgy called the mysterious girl back.

"I'm outside now," Georgy said.

"Gimme a few minutes. I 'll be right out," the girl replied.

The next few minutes felt like hours. "What the fuck is keeping you? What are you doing?" Georgy muttered.

John was several kilometers away in the Monitor Room in Stable Lane, feeling exactly the same way. "What the fuck is keeping her. Hurry the fuck up!" he shouted at the computer screen.

Then he saw a text from Georgy's phone on the screen. "*I'm coming in.*"

"NOOO wait for her, Georgy, she said she would be right out!" John yelled at the computer screen. Then he heard the car door close and silence in the vehicle.

Georgy's cell phone received a text. "*No, I'm out now.*"

"Get back in the van! Wait for her!" John again screamed at the computer screen,.

Seconds later John heard the sound of muffled voices outside the vehicle and banging on the windows. He couldn't understand what was being said but it was definitely a male and a female voice outside the vehicle. Five minutes later, Georgy's cell phone came to life on the computer screen. He was calling his brother.

"Hey Mikey, I'm at Cathy's. I locked my keys in the van. Can you get someone to pick me up? I have no money on me for a cab," Georgy said sounding pitiful and dejected.

"Do you know what Georgy? You're a fucking waste of space. I'll send one of the boys," Mikey Galvin replied and hung up abruptly.

John continued to hear the muffled voices outside the vehicle. The conversation was mostly one way, with the male doing all the talking. Occasionally the female would say something in a higher pitch. John imagined that she was shocked about what she was being told, but he was only guessing.

Several minutes later, Georgy got a phone call. "That you Georgy? I heard you locked yourself out of your van! Haaaahaa!" the male voice teased.

"Hurry the fuck up. It's freezing here."

"Where are you exactly?" the male voice asked.

Cahill hoped he would give up his location; at least the entire night would not have been a write off.

"I'm on Fair Hill near Mount Agnes."

"Two minutes Boss."

There was no more communication from Georgy Galvin after that.

"Cathy, at Fair Hill and Mount Agnes. Hmm. I think you have been told a great deal tonight. Hopefully you won't be too hard to track down," John thought to himself.

Chapter 19

John got home around 5AM and crept into bed next to his wife. She tossed and groaned, letting him know that she knew he was home. He woke at 11AM to a quiet house. He crawled out of bed and walked to the kitchen. Nobody was home. John made a cup of instant coffee, turned on the television and stared out the window. It was a beautiful morning; the sun was shining and there was barely a cloud in the sky. A light breeze blew in from the ocean and up the cliff towards their home. He was too tired to think about anything. He sipped the steaming hot coffee and as the caffeine streamed through his veins, he eventually began to function. He saw Jules walking up the driveway from the road, with the two large greyhounds on leashes, one on either side of her. John realized he was smiling when he saw them walk towards the house.

Over brunch, John told Jules about the fiasco the previous night when Georgy Galvin locked his keys in his van as he was about to confess to some girl about the murder

"Nothing is easy, is it?" Jules said, sympathizing with him. "It's such a pity. They're not even trying to be clever and their stupidity is helping them stay ahead of you. You'll just have to track her down and hopefully, she tells you what that eejit told her."

In the office on Monday morning, after an uneventful weekend, John held his usual briefing and informed the rest of his team about what happened Friday night. The priority was to find out who Cathy from Fair Hill was. She would definitely have to be interviewed and soon. Pete Sandhu was tasked with identifying her.

During the morning John's cell phone rang. He immediately recognized the number; it was the Internal Preventative Security Office at Cork Prison. He answered the call and got the message that Ron Glowden wanted to see him.

"Tim, with me! Glowden wants to talk," John yelled, pulling his pistol from his desk drawer and grabbing his jacket. Tim leapt from his chair and did likewise and the two detectives headed to their car.

"He has to come in here if he wants to talk. We shouldn't interview him out there on his turf," Tim commented as he drove through the traffic.

"Damn right he's coming in. He reached out to us. If it had been the other way round, I might let him call some of the shots but if he's calling us, he wants to deal."

They arrived at Cork Prison and went through the process of locking up their pistols in the lock boxes and were escorted to the IPSO's office. This time they both went in and Ron Glowden was sitting waiting for them.

"Hi Ron," John said. "This is Tim, he works with me. He was here last week but you didn't want to see him then. But I told him everything you said and he knows all about this."

Glowden nodded to show he understood and shook hands with the detectives.

"Why did you call us today?" John asked.

"I want to get out of here. I want my charges dealt with and I want protection for me and my family," Ron replied calmly.

"You need to come to our office. We can't talk about it here," John agreed with equal calmness.

Glowden let out a long breath. He knew he had to comply if he wanted a deal. "Let's go."

"Sit tight, I'll fix it with the IPSO. I'll be back in a few minutes." John left to track down the IPSO, while Tim remained with Glowden. Tim put the man at ease and they spoke about sports.

Glowden engaged him in conversation as Tim didn't give him time to think about what was happening.

When John returned, he handcuffed Glowden and led him to the front offices where the detectives retrieved their pistols. Glowden was taken to the police car and driven to the Anglesea Street Garda Station. The conversation in the car was somewhat strained but casual. This was not the place to talk about his predicament. Both John and the experienced criminal, Glowden, knew this and neither brought up the reason for this meeting.

They made their way through the C-I-D Office and Glowden was placed in Interview Room # 1, the room closest to the Serious Crime Incident Room. Tim removed the handcuffs and asked Glowden to sit on the only chair in the room, bolted to the ground, next to the graffiti covered steel table, also bolted down. The room was wired for video and audio recording but John wasn't about to turn anything on, just yet.

"We have to put away our guns and hang up our jackets. We'll be right back. Do you want anything? A cup of coffee, a smoke? Tim asked.

"A coffee and a smoke would be great, thanks," Glowden replied settling into the cold, uncomfortable chair.

The detectives left and closed the steel door behind them. Glowden heard the bolt sliding across the door. He walked to the door, stood on his toes and looked out the small wired-glass window near the top of the door. The steel shutter slid home on the outside of the door and Glowden's view was gone.

"What do you think, Boss?" Tim asked as he unloaded his pistol at the unloading station. He dropped the magazine into his free hand and pulled back the slide. The live round jumped out of the chamber and fell into the Kevlar lined bucket. Tim slid the slide back and forth a couple of more times ensuring the gun was unloaded, then reached into the bucket and picked up the live round and stood aside.

John repeated the process with his pistol as if it was second nature. "I think he's going to wrap this case up for us today as long as he isn't expecting too much in return."

The detectives walked back to the interview room. Glowden was pacing but sat as soon as they returned. Tim wheeled in two office chairs and the three men sat around the ugly steel table. Tim handed Glowden a Styrofoam cup with steaming hot coffee. He placed another cup with water in the bottom next to the coffee. Tim then produced a pack of cigarettes from his shirt pocket. He carefully extracted one cigarette and placed it between the cups.

Glowden picked up the cigarette and Tim produced a lighter. "You can use the cup with the water as an ashtray." Tim placed the pack of cigarettes on the table out of Glowden's reach. If Glowden wanted more cigarettes, he would have to earn them.

"Ron, I'm going to be up front with you right from the start," John began from his chair directly across from Glowden. "I don't need an informant for this investigation. I need a witness and that witness must be credible. That means you may have to testify in court and everybody is going to know. It will be public record. Do you understand that?"

Glowden swallowed hard and nodded.

"There are rules that we must follow. They are our rules and they have to be followed by all of us... that means you and us and the prosecution. The rules are easy. Do you want me to go on?"

"I'm listening," Glowden answered, showing intense interest.

"You must tell me everything you know about the homicides we're investigating. You cannot leave anything out. Everything means everything! You cannot lie or make something up or embellish. It must be one hundred percent the truth. If we catch you on one lie, no matter how small it is, No Deal! If ninety nine percent of what you tell us is true and factual and one percent is a lie, No Deal! AND we will use what you told us. Do you know what that means?"

"It means everyone will know I'm a rat and I'm on my own," Glowden said, dropping the cigarette butt in the cup with water. "I'll tell you the truth."

"I know you will Ron," John said, smiling at the man across from him and putting him at ease. "Before we get into what happened that night, what do you want from us for your testimony?"

"I want to get out of prison and my charges to go away. I told you that I got a kid who just turned fourteen and he's going down the wrong path. I got to make sure he doesn't turn out like me.

"Does he live with you?"

"He lives with his mother and she can't control him. But he likes to hang with me and my girlfriend. He's going to get mixed up in street gang shit before long if I don't get him to see sense." Glowden's explanation sounded genuine.

John's brain was working overtime. He was trying to figure out how this would work with witness protection since the kid didn't live with Glowden...and Glowden would need protection! "I'm sure we can work with that. However, there is one last thing you need to know. Only the prosecutor can drop your charges and get you out of prison. In order to do that, he must see your statement first. That means you have to trust me and tell me everything first and then I show it to the prosecutor. He reviews it along with your record and decides if a deal can be made or not. IF, a deal is made you will have to go into witness protection. If a deal isn't made, we will not use your statement."

Glowden drained his coffee cup and looked longingly at the cup with the cigarette butt floating in it. He exhaled slowly, "I trust you. I'll tell you what I know."

"I trust you too Ron but I'll triple check everything you tell me," John grinned. "Do you want another smoke?"

"I would love one, but if I go back to the prison stinking of cigarette smoke, they'll know I was talking to the cops. No, I'm good."

John smiled; he was impressed. Ron Glowden knew how to survive. Not many smokers could resist the chance of one last drag before going back to jail.

"I'm going to turn on the recording equipment and we'll get going," Tim said standing up and leaving the room to engage the video and audio recording equipment.

Once the recording began, Ron Glowden started to tell his story with exact detail as it occurred in the early hours of January 1st. The detectives didn't interrupt as Ron described the bloody scene that he found after Ken Rolland came to his house. Then Ron described how he helped Ken carry the television back to his house. He added a detailed description of the hole in the back of the television where the antenna wire had been ripped out and also the engraving of North Side Rentals.

"This is dynamite!" John thought to himself while Ron was speaking. "Nobody knows about the hole in the back of the TV or the engraving."

When he was finished his account of New Year's Day, the detectives asked Glowden some clarifying questions. John had him speak about his criminal past and his job as a crack cocaine and crystal meth cook. Ron Glowden was not the ordinary criminal and had a fascinating background. He had a science degree and was independently wealthy. His parents had left him over 2 million euros but it was held in trust by his sister, a doctor in Dublin. When he wasn't in prison, she paid Ron a monthly allowance through a lawyer. Ron couldn't access his money; in fact, he couldn't even have a bank card.

As always, Tim asked the difficult questions after John had extracted what they needed. "Where is the television now?"

"I sold it," Ron answered immediately.

"To who?"

"That could be tricky. I don't know if the person has it or not. It probably didn't work because of the hole in the back. I can make a few calls for you and find out if it's still around," Glowden said, obviously hedging.

"No Ron, we need to try and get it back right away. It shows you are being fully cooperative. If you phone around asking about it, whoever has it is going to get worried and get rid of it. It's best you tell us who you sold it to." Tim wasn't going to let it slide.

John sat back in his chair; he wouldn't interfere. He was the good cop in this conversation, Glowden looked to him as the senior officer who was calling the shots. The inspector shrugged his shoulders and held his gaze until Glowden looked down at his shoes.

"The person who bought it has connections to some old-time gangsters. Shelley Langton is her name," Glowden said without looking up.

"I know Shelley. She used to be shacked up with Harry Lawson, a money launderer for the Dublin cartels. There are so many people in and out of Shelley's house all the time. You're the last person she'll think ratted her out," Tim responded.

"We won't charge her anyway. All we want is the television, if she still has it," John added and Glowden looked slightly relieved.

As the interview was about to wrap up, John opened the folder in front of him. He laid out the photograph of ten men all similar in appearance. One of them was Ken Rolland. "Do you recognize anyone in these photographs Ron?"

Glowden picked up photo # 4, "This is Ken Rolland."

"How do you know him?" the inspector asked again.

"He's the person who asked me to help him move the television from the apartment by The Lough, to my house on College Road on New Year's Day. He told me that he killed the two kids inside the house. I saw one of the dead kids at the foot of the stairs." Glowden stared intently at the photograph.

Once the statement was concluded Tim turned the recording equipment off. John told Glowden to wait for a couple of hours as they were going to try to retrieve the television.

"Do you want anything to eat or drink while you sit here?" John asked.

"Can I call my girlfriend?"

John dialed the number and gave Glowden the receiver and left him alone.

Mike Williams and Eddie Jenkins turned off Pouladuff Road on to the street where Shelley Langton lived. Mike pulled up in front of a dishevelled house that was crying out for a coat of paint. There was a broken bike and few dirty plastic children's toys in the front garden. Mike noticed that one of the glass panes in the front door was broken.

"I should have known. We never go to the nicest house on the street, do we?"

Mike and Eddie knocked on the front door. They could hear a woman yelling inside and a young child yelling back. Then the door swung open.

"What?" Shelley Langton stood in the doorway with her hands on her hips. She wore a black tee shirt, tight black leggings and bright pink flip-flops. Her bleached blonde hair was cut in a bob and although she hadn't an easy life, she had a pretty face.

Before Mike could introduce himself and show his identification Shelley sneered, "Let me guess, police. Either that or bible thumpers dressed in cheap suits."

"You got it. Police. Can we come in?"

Shelley turned and walked into the house. "Come on in!"

The detectives followed her into the living room as Shelley picked up a few toys and cushions off the floor. "I was just going to hoover the place."

"Don't do it on our behalf," Eddie answered, thinking the room hadn't been cleaned in years.

Mike looked around the room and focused on the big screen television.

"Your TV there Shelley, I think its stolen. Can I have a look at it?"

"Ah fuck! It could be. I never asked but I got it from an unsavory individual who owed me money."

Eddie Jenkins looked at the back of the television and saw the engraving and the hole where the antenna plug had been ripped out. The new antenna cord was taped in with duct tape. Eddie checked the serial number and it matched. He nodded at his partner and confirmed, "This is it."

Mike told Shelley they would have to take the television as it was evidence in an investigation. She was relieved that she wasn't getting charged with possession of stolen goods and gave the detectives a short statement but didn't identify Ron Glowden as the person she bought the television from. She confirmed that she got it in early January.

Back at Garda Headquarters on Anglesea Street, Tim Warren went to check on Glowden. Glowden still had the phone. He took it away from his ear and asked Tim if his girlfriend could come by and visit for ten minutes before he went back to prison. Tim liked Glowden so told him it was fine.

Ten minutes later Glowden's girlfriend showed up at the station. Tim escorted her up to the second floor. He had a female officer search her and then allowed her to visit with Ron. Twenty minutes later Tim returned and Glowden's girlfriend was escorted from the building. On the drive back to Cork Prison, Tim asked Ron if he had told his girlfriend why he was at the police station.

"We didn't really talk much. She was kinda busy."

"Busy with what?" Tim teased, knowing what the answer would be.

"Busy giving me a blowjob," Glowden laughed and looked out the car window.

John just shook his head and said nothing. He was lost for words.

Upon arrival at the prison, Ron Glowden had to be returned through the regular intake process. The detectives announced their arrival to a guard at the gate to the admissions section. The guard opened the thirty-foot gate that was topped with a few layers of razor wire. They had to remain inside the vehicle until the gates closed behind them. Once the gates were closed, the three men walked up to a grey steel door.

Tim pressed on the intercom and was answered by a tinny voice asking "YES?"

"Cork Garda, bringing one back." Tim spoke into the intercom.

"Come on in, put your weapons in the lock boxes and someone will come and get you," the tinny voice announced as the lock in the grey steel door clicked.

Tim pulled the door open and John entered a narrow hallway first. He unholstered his pistol and placed it in a lock box secured to the wall. He locked the box and placed the key in his pocket. He went outside and stood with Ron Glowden while Tim did the same.

All three men entered the small hallway and closed the door. Seconds later the lock clicked again.

A door off to the side opened and a prison guard stepped through, "Who've you got? Oh, Ron Glowden, bring him through."

The three men stepped through the doorway into a large foyer.

"Put him in there and take your cuffs off him. The guard pointed to a cage about the size of a telephone box.

Tim walked Glowden to the cage and Glowden stepped in, putting his hands through the bars to have the handcuffs removed.

"We'll be in touch in a few days," Tim said quietly as John signed a few papers for the return of the prisoner and then the detectives left the way they had come in.

By the time they returned to the station, everyone else in the Serious Crime Unit had gone home.

Later that evening, while walking the greyhounds on the beach at Inchydoney, John told Jules about the day. The beach was deserted and they let the dogs off leash. The tide was out fully and the red sun was sinking into the ocean on the horizon. With barely any wind, you could hear the small waves lapping on the strand. The dogs started off sniffing in the sand. Molly, the smaller of the two, started her favourite pastime, digging. She had sand flying into the air as she dug a hole over a foot deep in record time. Lucy just kept sniffing the seaweed. Then without any provocation or notice the greyhounds broke into a mighty gallop and took off down the beach towards the channel at close to seventy kilometers per hour. As they reached the softer sand around the channel, they slowed down and ran back to their humans.

"Of course, Tim let Ron's girlfriend visit him for twenty minutes and shut off the recording while she was in the room," John said grinning slyly.

"Is that allowed?" Jules asked.

"Probably not, but it kept Ron happy. He's certainly on board with us."

"Why are you smiling?" Jules enquired.

"Ron got a blowjob in the holding room. He was a content man going back to prison."

"Now, that's definitely not allowed. You knew that was going to happen, didn't you?" Jules asked, trying to sound critical, while hiding her smile.

"Tim didn't ask me and I didn't tell him not to do it. Now, I bet if we checked all the rule books in all the police services in the entire world, we would not find a rule that says do not let your prisoner get a blowjob in the holding room!" John laughed as he broke into a run and the dogs followed after him.

Chapter 20

The focus on Monday morning was on getting Ron Glowden's statement to the Office of the Director of Public Prosecutions and having them approve a deal to use Ron as a witness. Second on the list was to identify Cathy, the girl Georgy Galvin met with when he locked his keys in his van.

Pete Sandhu, the unit analyst, spent hours running background checks on almost all the occupants of every house on the block where Georgy Galvin stopped. Pete was pretty sure he had identified the girl as Cathy Clancy. In an earlier intercept, Georgy Galvin had spoken to Johnny Johnson about a girl called CC. The name had come up only once, but it sounded like Georgy was sweet on her. Cathy Clancy did not have a criminal record but her younger brother had been charged with possession of marijuana a couple of years earlier. Since Cathy was an adult, she had picked him up from the Garda Station and provided her address on Mount Agnes Road, near the intersection with Fair Hill. Mike Williams and Eddie Jenkins were tasked with locating and interviewing Cathy Clancy and one way or another they had to find out if she was the girl who met with Georgy Galvin and if so, what had he told her?

Cathy Clancy was at home with her mother when the detectives knocked on her door. An older lady, probably in her late sixties, opened the door. She wore a navy-blue skirt and a light blue coloured blouse. Her black hair, obviously a cheap dye job, was collar length. This woman wasn't used to the police coming to her house and was a little bit anxious when the detectives introduced themselves and asked for Cathy. Of course, she expected bad news. What else would the police be there for? Mike Williams held his ground and would not tell her why they wanted to speak with Cathy. After a few minutes of trying to pry more information, she conceded and went to fetch her daughter, leaving the detectives waiting at the open front door.

When Cathy Clancy came to the front door, Mike Williams was taken back by her stunning good looks. Cathy had shoulder length black hair and piercing blue eyes; she had high cheek bones and thick lips. Cathy was wearing tight jeans and a tight black shirt that showed off her athletic figure topped with an open light grey hoody.

For a second Mike was caught off guard and almost stammered as he started to speak. However, he gave his head a slight shake. "Cathy? Hi, I'm Mike Williams and this is Eddie Jenkins. We are detectives with the Serious Crime Unit in Anglesea Street. Can we ask you a few questions?"

"What about?" Cathy's reply sounded confident and slightly abrasive.

"About a friend of yours, George Galvin." Mike decided not to ask if she knew Georgy, but let her assume that they knew she did.

This startled Cathy and she looked around to see where her mother was, knowing that she would not be too far away and would have her ears on high alert.

Sensing her discomfort, Mike quickly gave her an out. "We can talk in our car. It will be more private if you would prefer."

"Do I have to talk to you?" Cathy asked sullenly.

Eddie Jenkins stepped in the doorway, ensuring it wasn't slammed in their faces and spoke for the first time. "We are going to talk to you one way or another, Cathy. We can do it here in your house, in front of your mom, or in private in our car. It's really your choice."

"MOM, I'm just stepping out to speak with these guys for a minute. I'll be right back, Okay?" Cathy yelled down the hallway as she stepped by Eddie and walked towards the unmarked police car.

Leaving the door open, Mike and Eddie walked with her. Cathy's mother came to the front door a few seconds later but the trio had entered the police car and closed and locked the doors. The older woman closed the front door and went upstairs. Seconds later, the curtains moved and Cathy's mom was staring out the window.

In the police car, Cathy told the detectives that she was a student at University College Cork, studying Social Work. She still lived at home with her parents but could not wait to get out on her own and start living her own life. She met Georgy Galvin through her younger brother who bought weed and ecstasy from some guys that worked for the Galvins.

"When will you be finished your studies?" Mike casually questioned Cathy trying to find out more about her.

"I have about a year and a half left."

"And then what?"

"I want to help some of the girls I see working the streets, especially some of the girls from Eastern Europe or Africa. Most of them are my age or younger and I feel so bad for them. Sometimes I feel bad about myself for thinking I have it tough, but really, I'm so lucky to have a good supportive family." Cathy was comfortable speaking about her dream to helping Cork's less fortunate female population.

"Obviously you know that George, his brother and all of their friends are gang members." Mike posed this as a statement and not a question. Cathy nodded as she looked down at her hands on her lap. She was now fidgeting with the zipper on her hoody.

"Do you know what else he's into?" Eddie asked softly.

Cathy looked straight into Eddie's eyes with defiance in her glare. "George treats me very well. All we do is talk, we talk and talk and George has lots of problems with his family but he treats me very, very well."

"I know he talks to you. He tells you about some of his problems. He likes the fact that you listen to him. Perhaps he's told you about the other side of his business?" Mike asked.

Cathy shrugged her shoulders and looked puzzled. "I'm not going to ask you anything about George Galvin right now. But will you come for a ride with us for half an hour. I want to show you something. I think it's something you need to see. We'll bring you right back here whenever you want. I promise." Mike said quite sincerely. Before Cathy answered, Mike started the engine of the car and Cathy automatically agreed to go for the ride.

Mike Williams drove the police car down to Leitrim Street near Fever Hospital Hill. This was the area where exploited women were forced to work at all times of the day and night. Most of these girls were in very rough shape and hooked on crystal meth and crack cocaine. The majority of them worked for the Independent Posse and were managed by Georgy Galvin. Those that did not work for the I-P ran the risk of getting beaten off the patch at any given time.

"Are these the people you want to work with and help?" Mike asked as they drove slowly up and down some of the lanes and narrow streets off Leitrim Street.

"Yes," Cathy answered with a lump in her throat. Mike watched her in the rear-view mirror and knew her answer was truthful and sincere. He also knew he had her hooked.

Mike pulled up next to one of the girls and opened his window. "Hi, we're the police!" he announced and showed the girl his badge.

"Hi yourself," the girl answered with a Serbian accent.

"What's your name?"

"Jackie," the girl replied as she bent down and looked in at the other two occupants of the car.

Jackie wore knee high plastic black boots, a very short denim skirt and a tight blouse showing off her cleavage. Her hair was long, past her shoulders and badly needed to be washed. Jackie had the typical signs of crystal meth abuse ... burns on her lips from smoking plastic crack and meth pipes, scabs on her face and bad rotting teeth.

"How long have you been out today?" Mike enquired.

"A few hours." Jackie answered.

"Has it been busy?"

"No. It's fucking dead, just a few losers. And you're not helping driving around. Everyone knows you're the heat!"

Mike handed the girl a five-euro bill and she pocketed it as quick as lightning. "Do you know this girl?" Mike asked, pointing to Cathy in the back seat with his thumb.

Jackie stooped down again and looked in the open window. "No, she's not from down here."

"Do you work for yourself or do you work for the Posse?" Eddie asked casually.

"I-P," Jackie sounded defeated as she responded.

"Are you one of the boss's girls or do you work for one of the other fellas?" Eddie continued, keeping the conversation casual.

"Georgy G," Jackie sighed as she said the name. Eddie looked back at Cathy and she looked horrified.

"We got to get going Jackie. Stay safe!" Mike yelled out the window as they drove off.

Nobody said a word in the police car. Mike drove another few blocks until he was back again on Leitrim Street. He pulled over at the foot of Popes Road. Mike was elated when he saw Georgy Galvin's old green Volkswagen van parked in Rockwell Terrace.

Mike turned around to speak to Cathy. "Do you see that van parked by the curb about block down? You know who owns that van, don't you?"

"It looks like George's van," Cathy answered.

"It is Georgy's van. It's the only van in the city that looks like that. Do you know what he's doing there? He's watching HIS girls to make sure he gets paid when they turn a trick. That's what Georgy Galvin does. Pull your hood up, we're going to drive past him and I guarantee you, there will be at least three girls standing at corners very close by, including that girl Jackie. And Georgy is watching all of them."

Mike put the car in gear and drove slowly towards Georgy G's van. Cathy didn't argue and pulled her hood up as instructed. As they approached the rear of Galvin's van, Cathy could clearly see him sitting in the driver's seat. There was another man in the passenger seat and a girl who looked a total mess in the back. After they passed the van, sure enough they passed four more girls standing at corners. Each of them was, without a doubt, an exploited sex trade worker.

Mike drove out of the area, stopped the car and again turned to Cathy. "That's what Georgy Galvin does. Those are the women you want to help. Now you got to make a choice here. You are either part of the problem or part of the solution. Eddie and I know that Georgy told you about something that happened a few months ago. Something very serious that his friend did but he was part of it."

Cathy did not speak but nodded in agreement.

"He told you about this, the night he went to your house and locked his keys in the van," Mike added.

"How do you know about that?" Cathy quizzed.

Mike smiled but didn't answer her question. "He is correct in what he told you. He will go to prison for a while. Maybe a long while. But you'll help every single girl we saw today and twenty more like them that are crashing in the trap houses and crack shacks right now until their next deadly shift starts. Tell us what he told you Cathy," Mike said with such sincerity that Cathy's eyes started to fill with tears.

Twenty seconds of silence in the police car felt like two hours. The detectives let the silence linger. It was up to Cathy to make the next move.

Then she sighed, "He called me late on Saturday night. He said he had to speak to me because he was going to go away for a long time. I told him I would meet him outside because my dad doesn't like him."

Mike knew all this from listening to the recording of the phone call to Cathy. It confirmed to him that Cathy was being truthful.

"I don't know why he got out of his van but he did and he locked his keys inside." She smiled as she remembered. "He had a newspaper in his hand. He showed me the headline and said, 'That was us. We're going to get caught and go to prison for a long time.' I asked him what he meant."

Mike nodded but did not interrupt.

Cathy continued, "The headline was about a boy who was killed after a New Year's party. George said he was at that party and another gang attacked them." She paused, took a deep breath, let it out slowly and went on. "His friend got an old shotgun that was in the house and shot that boy and a couple of others. All the people they shot were attacking them and George said they were trying to get into the house and there were children sleeping inside."

"What else did he tell you about that night?" Mike pushed.

"I don't know," Cathy mumbled and fell silent. The detectives also stayed silent and Cathy felt she had to continue. "Some girls George knew helped his friend change his clothes, then George and his brother took the clothes and the old shotgun away before the cops came."

"Did he say what happened to the clothes and the gun?" Eddie asked.

"They burned the clothes. I don't know what happened to the gun."

Before Mike asked Cathy to come to the station and provide a formal statement, he decided to further win her over to his side. "Do you know who owns the house Georgy and his friends were partying at?"

"Some girl's place," Cathy answered.

"Do you know who this girl is, and who the girls who helped his friend are? Before she could answer, Mike continued, "The girl is Trish Langford. She lives with her mother and her three children. She has a husband but he doesn't live with her all the time. Her husband is Georgy Galvin and the kids are all Georgy's!"

Cathy looked up at Mike, angled her head slightly as if trying to comprehend what he had just said. Her eyes welled up with tears. She tried to say "No" and she shook her head but it was just a stifled sound that came out.

Mike knew he had disillusioned the girl and didn't hold back. "Trish Langford has been an associate of the Independent Posse her entire life. She has three kids, under seven, with George Galvin. George comes and goes and does his own thing but he does provide for his kids by working that string of girls who we saw and by selling drugs. Trish knows what he does and helps him the best way she can. By protecting him! You can let this go on and on and play second fiddle to Trish Langford and God only knows who else. Or you can do the right thing! You can come with us now to the station and give us a formal recorded statement. You know, Cathy, that is the right thing to do."

Mike did not wait for an answer; he started up the engine and began to drive in the direction of the Garda Station. He looked in the rearview mirror and saw tears streaming down Cathy's cheeks. When he was a block away from the station Mike spoke, "Are you going to do the right thing?"

"Yes," Cathy answered, loud and clear. She was determined.

Mike parked the police car in the detectives' parking area at Garda Station. Mike and Eddie accompanied Cathy up to the second floor. Mike apologized for having her wait in the stark and depressing Interview Room # 1. Cathy requested a cup of coffee and the detectives left her alone while they hung up their jackets, unloaded and put away their pistols.

John was sitting at his desk. "Any luck with Cathy?" he asked.

Mike Williams grinned and said, "She's here and has a great story that's she's ready to tell."

John raced out of the office into the monitor room so he could watch and record Cathy's statement.

Fifteen minutes later, when all the formalities were out of the way, Cathy told the detectives exactly what George Galvin had told her. She identified him from a photo lineup of ten photos of men of a similar age and appearance. She told them that George's brother was called Mike and the man that shot the kid was called Johnny. Cathy didn't know Mike or Johnny so there was no point in showing her photographs for identification purposes.

John could not stop smiling while he listened to Cathy's statement. He knew now that this case would be over very soon and charges would be authorized against three of Cork's most notorious gangsters.

When her statement was concluded, Cathy told the detectives that she was going to break off all communication with Georgy Galvin. "He makes me sick to my stomach that he can do that to other human beings. How dare he put those poor girls through that. He is nothing but a monster!"

Mike Williams and Eddie Jenkins drove Cathy home and asked her not to discuss her statement or her involvement with police with anyone until arrests were made. "Not a single person knows you came to our station today. Nobody knows that you gave us a statement about what Georgy Galvin told you. Eventually he will find out but by then he will be in prison awaiting trial. Are you okay with that?"

"Am I in any sort of danger?" Cathy asked, beginning to realize what she had gotten herself into.

"Cathy, you know how dangerous these people are. They shot and killed someone and maimed two other kids. This was not one gang attacking another gang. This was the Independent Posse acting the maggot and opening fire on a bunch of kids at a New Year's Eve party. If you feel in any sort of danger at any time, call 9-9-9 right away. Don't hesitate. If it turns out to be unnecessary, that's okay, better to be safe than sorry. After you call 9-9-9, call me day or night any time. I'll answer and help you out the best I can. Do you understand that?" Mike Williams promised as he held Cathy's gaze.

Cathy Clancy walked towards her front door. She reached in her pocket for her key but before she arrived at the door, her mother opened it and looked beyond her daughter at the detectives. Cathy walked past her mother and went straight to her bedroom. "What have I just got myself into?" she wondered as she sat on her bed.

John reviewed Cathy's statement. "I need a little bit more to make this stick," he thought. Superintendent Paddy Collins walked into the monitor room. John told him what they had so far. "I definitely have enough to charge and prosecute Johnny Johnson. But I also want those other two. Do you think we have enough?" John asked the superintendent.

"We have enough to lift all three of them. We probably have enough to get Georgy too. His girl says he took the gun from Johnny. But we are weak on Mikey. Do you have anything else in your bag of tricks?" the superintendent asked, sounding a little disappointed. "We must get Mikey G. He's fucking Teflon, nothing sticks to him. He's way too clever to give anything up in an interview. Those other two eejits will probably implicate themselves and each other. But they are all afraid of Mikey G."

"That's a good point, Boss. If we can get him in prison for a few months, we can probably convince some of the witnesses to come on board. I'll put the evidence together and maybe we can go and sell it to the prosecutor in the next few days," John replied as the wheels were turning and a new plan formulated in his mind.

Later at home, during the usual evening debrief on West Beach with Jules, John discussed the developments in the case. It was hightide and a full moon shone down on the calm Atlantic Ocean. The only sound were the tiny waves falling on the sandy beach. The dogs were off leash but were only interested in sniffing through the seaweed.

"I'm going to see the prosecutor in a couple of days. I'm ready to present both cases," John said. "If he likes the evidence of Ron Glowden, then Ken Rolland is going away for a long time. I'm hoping he'll give Ron a deal on his charges. That and the D.N.A. evidence that we have should be enough to put it over the top," John stopped and took a breath. "I got enough to charge and convict Johnny Johnson with murder and probably enough to get Georgy Galvin for manslaughter. But I'm really weak on his brother Mikey," John told his wife as they gazed out at the vast Atlantic Ocean, watching the lights of a large container ship sailing by, several miles away on the dark horizon.

"If you don't get him this time, I'm sure there will be another time in the future." Jules squeezed his hand as she expressed her support..

"Yeah, but Mikey is the worst of them. He'll terrorize all the witnesses and we might never get it into court. I have a plan. I'll run it by you and tell me what you think."

Chapter 21

J ohn spent the next few days in the Monitor Room on Stable Lane, listing all the evidence they had for both cases. Although he was looking forward to closing both these cases, he had to be meticulous. He could not afford to miss anything. It was imperative that the prosecutor saw the entire picture and was willing to take a gamble. He focused on the strengths of both cases and glossed over the weaknesses. If the prosecutor picked up on them, he would try to answer any questions that arose.

The strongest evidence in the double homicide near The Lough was Ron Glowden's statement. However, Cecilia Rolland's hair on the blood-stained jacket also linked Ken Rolland to the scene. All the police had to do was convince the prosecutor that Glowden would be a perfect witness.

The evidence for the Manor View Estate homicide and other shootings was more complex. No doubt the best of the evidence was Cathy Clancy's statement but there were valuable comments recorded over the wiretaps and probes. All together it was a neat package.

After a week of wading through over thirty thousand intercepts, John had his evidence for both cases in a chronological, readable order. He called up the Office of the Public Prosecutor and was told that Brian McCarthy, a young lawyer, was assigned to review both cases. Despite his youth, McCarthy was smart and brilliant at his job. He had the ability to see the value in the smallest piece of evidence and knew how to put a strong indefensible case before the court.

"That's very positive. I like Brian. He's not afraid to take a case to trial. Have you called him?" Paddy Collins asked John when he learned that McCarthy had been appointed to review the cases.

"No, I'm going to call him up now. I'll tell him we need to meet in person. I'm not going to let him talk me into sending everything over to his office. I'll tell him this is urgent and we need to get these assholes off the street. Also, it will be a lot harder for him to say 'No' to me in person, if he doesn't like the evidence."

John made the call to Brian McCarthy at Prosecution Services; five minutes later he was smiling. "I have an appointment at nine-thirty tomorrow morning. I told him it would take a few hours to go over everything."

"Good man! Do you want me to come along with you?" the superintendent asked.

"That's a good idea. He might be a bit intimidated by your rank. Okay, you start it off and then hand it over to me. All you have to do is back me up in everything I say. We got two decent cases here. We just have to convince McCarthy to take them to court."

The following morning John walked into the Anglesea Street Garda Station. He was feeling nervous about his meeting with the prosecutor. It was like he was going for a job interview. He sat at his desk and fired up his computer.

Tim Warren arrived, sat down and looked up at his boss. "You're quiet. Is everything all right?"

"Yeah, I am grand. I'm a little apprehensive about selling these two packages to Brian McCarthy later this morning. We've done an awful amount of work on these two investigations and there's more we can do. I just hope he thinks it's enough."

"Can McCarthy make that decision on his own?" Tim asked

"He can probably tell us to pound sand if he thinks it's not enough but if he wants to proceed, he'll have to recommend it to a committee. But his recommendation carries a lot of weight."

"What do you think he'll do?"

"Most of the lawyers in Prosecution Services want their cases on a silver platter. But I think McCarthy isn't afraid of a challenge. At least I hope he's not," John answered.

After coffee, John and Superintendent Collins made their way to the Prosecutor's Office, near the court house. Brian McCarthy met them at the elevator and directed them into a boardroom. There was a large oak table surrounded by an assortment of old office chairs. Paddy Collins made a mental note that none of the chairs matched. Stacked against the wall were a row of cardboard banker boxes. Collins recognized some of the names written on the boxes as homicide cases from over a decade earlier. John sat at the center of the table with Paddy Collins opposite him and Brian McCarthy at the head of the table. John was well prepared with folders containing intercept transcripts, notes on interviews, and reports. He laid it all out on the board table in front of him. He knew these cases back to front and inside out. All he had to do was convince this man that there was enough evidence to go to trial and secure convictions. Everything was strategy and John hoped he had strategized correctly for this important presentation.

As planned, Superintendent Collins took the lead. "We have two cases to present to you today, Brian. The first one is a double homicide that was discovered on New Year's Day. Alvin Pomeroy, twenty-two years old and Julian Hodnett, twenty-four years old, were both brutally stabbed to death at Hodnett's girlfriend's apartment near The Lough. I will let the inspector give you all the details.

Brian McCarthy produced a pen from his shirt pocket, opened a notebook and made a few notes. He looked across the table at John and said with a subtle grin, "Bring it on!"

John described this case and the evidence in chronological order. He started with Ken Rolland going out to celebrate New Year's with

Hodnett and Pomeroy and walking back to their apartment from the night club. He noted that the front door was broken down to gain entry and then he slowed it down to describe the horrific violent attack that took place on both victims. John described the long strands of hair located on the floor near Alvin Pomeroy. He concluded this part of the briefing with the stolen television and failed fire to destroy the evidence.

John stopped, allowing McCarthy to catch up. McCarthy had no questions up to this point. Then John described the first interview of Ken Rolland in Galway and how Rolland denied any involvement in the homicides. Next he addressed the forensic evidence starting with the mitochondrial D.N.A. tests on the loose strands of hair. He continued moving on to the hair from Cecilia Rolland on the blood-stained coat in the garbage bin. This was the same jacket Ken Rolland wore on video in the nightclub club and on CCTV on the walk back to the apartment. The blood on the jacket belonged to the two victims.

McCarthy digested this information for a few moments and jotted down a few more notes. He looked across the table at the detective and said, "Keep going."

Now it was time for the inspector to play his trump card and introduced Ron Glowden. He provided McCarthy with a copy of Glowden's criminal record and his police profile, outlining his background and criminal associations. John provided a synopsis of Glowden's statement, highlighting the description of the television that he helped move and later sold. John concluded with the recovery of the television with the assistance of Glowden.

When he was finished, John put his pen down symbolically and let out a sigh of relief. McCarthy kept writing frantically in his notebook. Paddy Collins looked across at his inspector and gave his shoulders a slight shrug as if to say "What now?"

McCarthy finally finished writing. He put his pen down but continued to look at his notes. "What does Glowden want?" he asked as he looked from the superintendent to the inspector.

"He wants a deal. He's is in jail on guns and drugs charges. His trial is set for six months time and he doesn't want to do anymore time. He wants to get out and he wants protection."

"Does he now?" Brian McCarthy muttered. "Can we trust him to come through for us?"

"He's motivated to cooperate. One of his kids is getting into trouble and he wants out so that he can keep an eye on him. Glowden's health is crap too. He can't do a long stint in prison. It will kill him," John replied with confidence.

"I like this case. I think I will recommend murder charges for Rolland with premeditated circumstances. What else have you got? I hope it's as good as this one," McCarthy said smiling.

"Well, Brian, we said we would soften you up with this one first. The next one is bit more complex. We had to do a wiretap project and you will really have to wrap your head around all the pieces of the puzzle to connect all the dots," Paddy Collins answered, in his thick Kerry accent.

"In other words, it's a piece of crap with a pile of circumstantial evidence and innuendo!" Brian McCarthy responded as he turned over a new page in his notebook without making eye contact with the two officers.

Paddy Collins took a deep breath and introduced the next case. "This also occurred on New Year's Eve. There was a brawl at Manor View Estate as two parties met on the street. One party was supporters of a local soccer team and the other party was a bunch of Independent Posse members and their associates. The Posse guys were taking a bit of a licking and they produced a sawed-off shotgun and fired a variety of rounds into the brawl. Jason Kimberly, twenty-three years old, was killed instantly. Chelsea Brown, nineteen years, was hit by a slug that smashed her right upper thigh and Kyle Healy, twenty-five years old, was also hit by a slug in the hip. Brown and Healy survived but have life altering injuries. Over to you, Inspector."

John closed his eyes for a couple of seconds, gathering his thoughts. He took a deep breath and started. "We are talking about an all out, free for all brawl in the middle of the road here. We had to get a bus to get over fifty witnesses into the station for interviews. As you can guess we got sweet fuck all out of the Independent Posse members and their associates." Brian McCarthy smiled and shook his head at John's description of the interviews.

"We learned from a reliable source that Johnny Johnson was the trigger man. But Mikey and Georgy Galvin were the ones giving the orders that night. Here are the injuries for the other two victims." John passed a document to the lawyer and continued reading from his notes.

John described the meeting at the hotel where they unsuccessfully tried to get Johnny Johnson to open up to an undercover officer. John explained the wiretap tap and the listening devices in the homes and vehicles. He outlined the scenario where they convinced the local paper to run a story on the shooting, describing Johnny Johnson right down to his limp. John read passages from the transcripts of recordings that were captured after the newspaper story. Brian McCarthy was frantically making notes trying to keep up with the inspector.

John paused to breathe and allow McCarthy catch up. He stole a quick glance at the superintendent. Collins shifted his eyes towards McCarthy and gave a conspiratorial wink at John. The story continued and John described the call that Georgy Galvin made to the unknow female identified only as Cathy. He told it in such a way that McCarthy was expecting the golden nugget...when Galvin would tell Cathy about the shootings and it would all be recorded inside the vehicle. Then John let him down when he threw in the twist about Georgy locking himself out of his van and they were all left hanging. McCarthy looked as frustrated as John did the night it happened.

Before Brian McCarthy could interject, John introduced Cathy Clancy's statement and recounted her story of how Johnny Johnson was told by Mikey Galvin to get the gun and then shot three people. He concluded with telling how Georgy and Mikey G ordered the clean up of the scene and got rid of all the evidence.

When John had completed his presentation, McCarthy reviewed his notes. He didn't speak for a few minutes but it felt like an eternity for the two policemen.

"You have a lot of circumstantial evidence and one decent witness who got a confession from one of the three suspects and not even the main suspect who is your shooter," McCarthy said condescendingly. "It's weak. In fact, it's very weak," he continued. "There must be more people that can put the gun in Johnny Johnson's hand that night and also the Galvin brothers getting rid of everything afterwards. If you can get me that, we have some chance of a conviction."

"Based on Cathy Clancy's evidence and the wiretaps, do you have enough to authorize a murder charge on all three of them right now?" John asked, trying to put the lawyer on the spot.

"Well, yes. I can authorize a charge but we have almost no chance of convicting them. I cannot see any member of the Independent Posse pleading guilty," McCarthy answered.

"Authorize the charge, Brian. If I can take the three of them off the street, I WILL get you more," John promised.

"Hmpf," McCarthy grunted. "I don't like playing that game. It isn't quite ethical. IF you fail to get more evidence, I'll end up staying the charges and we will all look bad."

"Fuck ethical!" Paddy Collins barked. "This is our opportunity to shut down the Independent Posse. If we don't lock these three up, they'll continue their massive crime spree and the body count will just continue to rise. Can you look at yourself in the mirror when they kill another kid or someone's kid dies from an overdose? This is our one and only chance. We must take it." The superintendent's face reddened from his rant.

Brian McCarthy took a deep breath in through his nose and slowly let it out through his mouth. "I need to think about this one. Go ahead and pick up Ken Rolland and charge him with two counts of murder. I will let you know about Manor View tomorrow.

The superintendent and the inspector walked back to their car. "What do you think, boy?" Collins asked in his thick Kerry accent.

"I think he was going to shut us down until you told him the blood of the next victim was on his hands. That rattled him and made him think,"

"I hope so. We'll get nothing else unless the three of them stay in prison," Paddy Collins sighed.

Chapter 22

The next day John obtained an arrest warrant for Ken Rolland while Mike Williams arranged to go to Galway to bring Rolland back to Cork. Once the warrant was entered on PULSE, the National Police Data Base, Paddy Collins called his counterpart in Galway and requested the Garda in Galway pick up Rolland.

"It shouldn't take too long to get Rolland in custody. He is not on the run and he thinks he's free and clear. I would love to be a fly on the wall when they slap the handcuffs on him and tell him they have a warrant for his arrest," John told Mike Williams and Eddie Jenkins. "Do you think he'll give it up when he knows he's being charged?"

"I doubt it." Eddie grinned. "He's a cocky bugger who thinks he's smarter than everyone else."

"I'm glad we've a good case against him. I would hate to be relying on a confession. I doubt he'll say more that 'NO COMMENT!'" Williams added.

As the day dragged on there was no word from Prosecutions on the other shootings. However, that did not stop John from making his plans for an arrest.

He paid a visit to the Technical Surveillance Unit in the rundown building on Stable Lane. Colin Spence was at his desk when John walked in. "Hey Colin, are you busy?" he asked.

"Never too busy for you, Inspector. What do you need?" Spence said smiling in anticipation of one of John Cahill's infamous schemes.

And John did not disappoint. He laid his plan out for Colin who salivated at the thought of doing something out of the ordinary using their technological toys. "I'm confident that Prosecutions will authorize charges on all three of them. Once they do, I'll l call you and you can get things in position. We'll round them up within twenty-four-hours of receiving the green light."

"I can't wait," Colin Spence replied, while wishing more of the detectives had the imagination and the drive to go all out to get as much evidence as they could to secure a conviction.

At 3:30PM, getting close to quitting time, Superintendent Collins' phone rang. It was Galway. Ken Rolland was in custody. He would appear in court later that evening and have a forty-eight-hour hold put on him for extradition back to Cork. Mike Williams and Eddie Jenkins made plans to drive to Galway first thing the following morning. At 3:55PM John's cell phone rang.

It was Brian McCarthy. John put the phone on speaker and Tim Warren and Pete Sandhu walked up to John's desk and all listened intently. "I'm going to go out on a limb here," McCarthy said. "I'm going to authorize a charge of murder and two counts of attempted murder for Johnny Johnson." McCarthy paused, took a deep breath, and the three policemen at the other end of the line held their breath in anticipation of what McCarthy said next. "I am also authorizing those charges for Mikey Galvin and Georgy Galvin. When do you plan on picking them up?"

"YES!" John whispered loudly punching the sky.

"Well done, Boss," Tim Warren said quietly as he patted John on the shoulder.

Although wearing a huge smile, John kept his voice even and without emotion. He took the phone off speaker and put it to his ear. "We will try and have them all in custody by tomorrow afternoon. How does that sound?"

"That's fine," McCarthy replied. "Let me know when they are in custody and I will attend their first bail applications. But I must stress if you don't get me any more evidence, I will likely have to cut the Galvins loose. Like I said, I'm going out on a limb here."

When McCarthy hung up, John called Colin Spence. "Green Light, Colin, do your thing. We're looking at picking them up by tomorrow afternoon."

Colin Spence hung up and gathered his 'Geek Squad' for some electronic surveillance.

It was another restless night of tossing and turning in bed for John. When the alarm went off at 5:30AM, he felt like he hadn't slept for more than an hour or two. Jules got up to see her husband off and hugged him as he left the house, wishing him good luck. The wind had picked up over night and the waves were splashing over the sea wall as John drove along the coast road.

During the drive, John called Colin Spence. "Everything is in place," Spence said. "I've got audio and video in the cell in the lockup and I have audio and video in the transport van. We had a hell of a time getting good audio in that concrete box of a cell. The sound kept bouncing off the walls but we got it figured out."

"As long as I can understand what they are saying and not getting a load of mumbling...that's all I'm asking for," John responded.

"We've put six microphones in the cell and four in the transport van. They are all set to slightly different frequencies so even if we get low talkers and mumbling, we'll be able to mix the sound and get a good result," Colin answered confidently.

John's plan was ready to execute. All that was left was to pick up the three gangsters and have them in custody at the same time. After they were interrogated, they would be placed together in a cell in the police lockup for a couple of hours. Their conversations would be recorded while there. Any conversation they had while being transported to Cork Prison would also be recorded. He was banking on the fact that, no matter how stressed they were, they would talk about the crime among themselves once they got comfortable in their surroundings.

The next phone call was to Sean Harrington and Percy Jones. "Can you guys set up on Georgy Galvin and follow him around for an hour or so to see if he meets up with Mikey or Johnny Johnson. We're going to bring them all in today but it would be better if we got a few of them at the same time."

"We were waiting for your call John, and raring to go," Harrington said as he rose from his desk and called his team to action with a wave of his arm.

Once at the station on Anglesea Street, John and Tim Warren walked the few blocks to the Technical Surveillance Unit's monitor rooms where they listened for any phone activity that might tell them where their three targets were.

After half an hour, Johnny Johnson's mobile phone lit up as an outgoing call on the computer monitor screen. Half a second later, Georgy Galvin's mobile phone lit up as an incoming call on the same screen. Johnny was calling Georgy.

"Hey," Johnny said when his buddy answered.

"Hey, whatcha doing?" Georgy asked.

"Fuck all right now. Can you drive me to our shack on Spring Lane? I got to drop off a thing for Big E."

"For sure, I got nothing else going on. I'll be at your sister's in half an hour. Be ready."

At that point John heard a sound that was very familiar to him. It was the sound of the action of a pump-action shotgun being racked, "*crack-crack.*"

"HOLY FUCK! Did you hear that?" John yelled.

Tim looked across at him in bewilderment. He hadn't been listening to the conversation and didn't have his headphones on. The civilian monitors also looked at John.

"Quick, go back to the start of this call with Georgy and Johnny. Tell me what you hear! Right after Georgy tells him to BE READY!"

The two civilians and Warren all listened intently to the recording.

"I hear it," both women said. "But what is it?"

"I don't hear fuck all, Boss," Tim replied .

"Jesus Christ," John snapped, rolling his eyes. He unplugged his headphones and turned up the volume on the speakers.

"Well, I don't know what I'm looking for!" Tim pleaded.

John played the recorded phone call, and when Georgy Galvin said 'Be Ready,' John raised his finger and right after the '*crack-crack*' sound, he stopped the tape.

"Did you hear that? What does that sound like?"

"Fuck, Boss. I don't know, it's just a noise," Tim answered.

"Sweet Jesus! How many times have you racked a shotgun on this job? Doesn't that sound like a shotgun being racked?" the exasperated inspector asked.

John played it twice more for Tim. "Do you know what? That's exactly what it is, a fucking shotgun!" Tim exclaimed. "Good ear, Boss."

John called up Percy Jones who was sitting with the surveillance team waiting for Georgy Galvin to go to his van. John told him that Georgy would be coming out to his vehicle and driving to pick up Johnny Johnson at his sister's house. Then they would probably drive to a crack shack on Spring Lane. "We must take them down before they get to Spring Lane. They are going to have a shotgun in the van. I'll get Armed Support to take them down," John instructed.

After another quick phone call to the sergeant in the Armed Support Unit, everything was in place for the arrest of Johnny Johnson and Georgy Galvin.

Moments later the radio crackled, "T-1 is walking to V-1, he is on the driver's side, engine starting and he's holding. T-1 is the lone occupant. Copy?"

"Copy that." replied Percy Jones.

"BREAK! BREAK!" a voice over the radio called urgently.

"Go break," replied Jones.

"T-1's brother, Mikey G just walked past my vehicle, he is heading towards V-1. He did not look at me, or pay any attention to my vehicle. Copy?"

"Copy that," replied Jones. "Let's add Mikey G to the Target Sheet, he is now Target 3, that is T-3. Copy?"

Another voice came over the radio, "T-3is getting in the passenger side of V-1and they are away eastbound and out of my sight."

The surveillance team loosely followed Georgy Galvin to the rendezvous with Johnny Johnson. He did not deviate from the route so there was no need to get too close.

The radio crackled again, "Tac-1, Tac-2 and Tac-3 are in place. We'll take them down on your command Percy."

"Copy that, stand by," Percy answered.

John could feel the excitement and the tension rise in the pit of his stomach. If there was a shotgun in the vehicle it would be a huge bonus and great leverage in the interviews that were to follow. He also hoped the takedown would go off safely and without a glitch. Part of him wished he was there for the takedown. He missed those days when you did not know what was facing you when you took down armed gangsters. The potential for a shootout was enormous and the unpredictability of the entire situation was somewhat addictive.

The radio crackled to life again, "T-2 is out of the residence and running to V-1. He is carrying a black backpack in his left hand. He is in the rear passenger side seat. Engine starting, they're away eastbound and committed for a southbound turn on Killala Gardens."

"Tac-Teams take them down on Killala. We'll close off the block from any other traffic!" Percy Jones ordered.

Percy Jones's surveillance team blocked off the road ahead and behind Georgy Galvin. For a moment Georgy looked confused and thought, "What the fuck are they doing that for?"

"TAKE THEM DOWN! TAKE THEM DOWN NOW!" Percy Jones ordered over the radio and three black SUVs lit up their strobe lights and boxed in the old van. Six heavily armed police officers in grey tactical uniforms and Kevlar helmets surrounded the van while pointing their carbines at the occupants.

"FUCK, FUCK, FUCK!" Johnny Johnson yelled and he almost let go of his bladder. Georgy Galvin's eyes opened wide and he immediately raised both his hands from the steering wheel.

Georgy was ordered to shut off the engine, throw the keys out the window and keep his hands in plain sight. Johnny was ordered out of the vehicle from the side door and told to walk backwards towards the heavily armed policeman, who yelled clear commands at him. Johnny then lay face down on the cold damp road and was handcuffed. Georgy and Mikey went through the same routine. Only when all three men were handcuffed did the members of the Armed Support Unit slightly relax. One of them approached the van while scanning it for a possible hidden unknown occupant. Once he was satisfied there was no one waiting to ambush him, he opened the rear passenger side door and looked inside the black backpack. "SHOTGUN," he yelled.

John, who was listening to everything play out on both the radio and the listening device inside Georgy's van, stood up and punched the air. "YES! Fuck you, Johnny Johnson! Game on, three for the price of one!"

Three uniform patrol cars attended the scene of the takedown on Killala Gardens, took custody of the prisoners and brought them to Anglesea Street.

At Garda Headquarters on Anglesea Street, the three gangsters were led into separate interview rooms. Georgy went to Interview Room # 1, Johnny to # 3 and Mikey to # 5. They were searched by the uniform officers and their handcuffs were removed. They were locked in the interview rooms and the background music in the room was turned up. The background music was typical elevator light jazz instrumental that played on a loop. It became very very annoying. Maybe that was the plan when it was initially selected.

John called a briefing with his team in the Incident Room to discuss the upcoming interviews.

"I can tell you right now, we're not going to get anything out of Mikey," Jeff Rafter said. "Even if it were to help him out in the long run, he has never given an inch in an interview in his entire life."

"Yeah, I know. But I still want someone in there to have a go at him for a couple of hours, even if it's only to stress him out. We got to give it the old college try," John replied grinning. "Jeff and Len, you get Georgy. Try and have some fun with him. He is not the sharpest knife in the drawer. Tim and I will take Johnny and Travis and Larry, you get Mikey G. Just make sure to spend time with him. I don't want you going for supper after half an hour because you think its futile."

The detectives walked out of the Incident Room to begin their assignments. Once these interviews started, every word that was spoken would be scrutinized by some of the top legal minds in the country.

Back in the interview rooms, Mikey Galvin was pacing like a caged animal. His head was down and he was getting in the zone for a long and arduous interview. He would answer certain questions but only to try to find out how much the cops knew. Now, before the games commenced, Mikey swore to himself that he would not give up any ground. This was not his first rodeo.

Mikey's brother Georgy was sitting at the table one moment and then running the two short steps to the door. He could not see out the window on the door as the steel shutter had been closed. He pressed his ear to the door to see if he could hear anything outside, but the elevator jazz music cheated him out of that too. Georgy sat again, put his hand down the front of his sweat pants and began to masturbate.

Johnny Johnson sat at the table in Interview Room 3. His shoulders were slumped down. His head looked like it was too heavy for him and just hung there. He stared at the graffiti etched into the top of the steel table by those before him in similar circumstances. Johnny folded his arms tight around his chest, subconsciously trying to protect himself from the outside world. His heart was racing, he had a lump in his throat, his breathing was shallow and his bowels felt like they were about to let go. Johnny Johnson was scared!

Forty-five minutes later, the six detectives walked towards the interview rooms, notebooks in hand, focused on getting a confession or some sort of admission of guilt.

Pete Sandhu stepped out of the video monitor room and called Jeff Rafter and Len Benoit aside. "What ever you do, don't shake his hand. He just was jerking off in the corner." Pete's Indian accent made the disclosure sound hilarious.

"This guy is nothing but a pure savage!" Len Benoit said with disgust as his partner opened the door to the interview room.

John had not told the other detectives that after the interviews the three accused would sit together in a holding room in the police lockup, where they would be surreptitiously recorded, as they would in the transport van on the way to the prison. He decided to hold this information back from his colleagues so they would push the interviews to the limit.

Chapter 23

Mikey Galvin had been interviewed by police many, many times before and he knew what to expect and how much to cooperate without incriminating himself. He answered all the usual background questions but denied being the leader of the Independent Posse. In fact, he denied being a member of any gang. When Larry Vickers asked about the New Year's party, Mikey thought carefully before answering. He knew there was no point in denying he was at the party because numerous people would have put him there.

"Yeah, I was there for a while. Had a few drinks, met a few old friends. I heard the house was attacked by a gang some time after midnight. I had left by then," Mikey answered as he looked Larry Vickers right in the eye.

And no matter how many times the detectives tried to get Mikey to tell them about the brawl and the shooting, Mikey didn't budge from that story. He said the only knowledge he had of the fight and the shootings was what he had seen on the news.

After Jeff Rafter told Georgy Galvin that anything he said or did would be recorded and could be used against him, Georgy replied, "I'm not writing no statement!"

"I don't want you to write a statement, George. I just want to chat with you, okay?" Jeff answered.

Georgy relaxed slightly. His idea of cooperating with police was writing a statement outlining his involvement in the incident under investigation.

Rafter was a skilled interrogator and it wasn't long before Georgy was chatting away about his family, especially his kids. Before Georgy knew what was happening, Jeff had taken him back to the New Years party and Georgy had put himself, Mikey and Johnny at the scene when the brawl started.

"Yeah, it was a bit after midnight after all the hugging and cheering like, we were all sitting around, just chatting and having a few drinks. Everyone was happy and calm. Then all of a sudden Trish said there was something going on outside."

"Your Trish said that? Where were you when she said that?"

"I was in the kitchen, almost in the living room."

"Who were you chatting with?" Jeff asked casually.

"Ahh, let me think. Tyson, Darryl, Mikey, me brother, I think Johnny was there, yeah." Georgy thought he was being clever by giving everyone an alibi for the double homicide downtown. What he did not know was he had placed the key players at the homicide at Manor View Estate.

"Did you all go outside then, just to look?" Jeff enquired.

"We went to the windows and the doors like and looked out. We saw two fellas who were at our party earlier getting a licking. I don't know their names but they showed up at Trish's place for a bit and left."

"So ye all went out to help them?"

"No, no. I didn't go out at all, I think one or two went out to the garden to get a closer look. Then I heard the shooting and legged it out the back door. I knew the cops would be coming and I didn't want to be around for that. I knew we would be blamed."

"You didn't stick around to help protect Trish or her mother or some of the old folks that were there?" Jeff asked mockingly.

"Fuck that! You know Trish, she can protect herself. Her and Sam could clean up the whole street in a matter of seconds." Jeff Rafter asked a few more questions to try to ascertain a few more details but Georgy was sticking to his lies. Nevertheless, he had put himself and his co-accused at the scene at the time of the shooting. As Jeff was leaving the room, he told Georgy he could go back to playing with himself. Georgy blushed a bright red.

Johnny Johnson was slightly smarter than Georgy Galvin during his interview with John and Tim. Johnny put himself at the party but claimed that he left right after the New Year's countdown. He said he was feeling sick. He walked home to his sister's house and there was nobody there so he went to bed. After telling his interrogators this, Johnny shut down and only offered "No Comment" to further probing.

After almost six hours of hard questioning and getting almost nowhere, it was time to move the three prisoners to the holding rooms in the basement before shipping them off to the prison.

Mikey Galvin was led down first and placed in Holding Room A. The room was a basic concrete bunker with a fluorescent light in the ceiling protected by a grill. There were two concrete benches against two of the walls and the concrete floor sloped towards a drain in the center of the room in case the occupants decided to piss on the floor. There were several steel rings embedded into the concrete benches so prisoners could be cuffed to the bench if necessary. The walls and ceiling were painted 'institutional green' and the floor grey. Mikey entered the room and walked around the perimeter. The room was big enough for at least eight prisoners but he was the only one. Mikey looked closely at the ceiling and the walls; he was searching for signs of a hidden camera. He could not see any.

Ten minutes later, the bolt on the steel door slammed open and the custody sergeant led Johnny Johnson into the room. Sergeant Kevin Dorney was a short stocky man with a huge attitude. One could say he had 'Little Man Syndrome.'

"Are you two going to be okay with each other? I'm house full tonight and if I have to come back in here to sort out any of your guff, I can guarantee you it won't be pretty!" Dorney bellowed at the prisoners.

"Don't worry, we're good." Mikey smiled at Johnny.

Dorney stepped out and bolted the door shut. "Are ya all right?" Mikey asked quietly.

"Ya, I'm grand. I didn't say fuck all to them."

"Me neither," Mikey said with a sneer.

The two men sat in silence for a few minutes and the bolt on the steel door crashed back again.

Sergeant Dorney led Georgy into the holding room. "I know you two are brothers, but if I come in here for any problems, I'll chain your necks to the benches like rabid dogs. Got it?"

"We're all right, Boss, don't worry," Mikey said, laughing at the policeman's comment. Dorney backed out and locked the door.

"Ya okay?" Georgy looked at his two comrades and sat on the bench opposite them. The other two nodded at him.

Across the hallway in another room, John and Tim Warren watched and listened intently to everything going on in Holding Room A.

After a few moments of silence Johnny spoke, "Mikey and me didn't say fuck all."

"They didn't even ask me to write a statement. They didn't even make notes or nothin," Georgy chuckled.

Mikey immediately picked up on what his brother just said. "What the fuck did you tell them? What did you say? Tell me!" Mikey demanded in a loud whisper.

"It doesn't matter. I didn't write it out." Georgy sounded worried.

"Tell me, what the fuck did you say to them?" Mikey deliberately said the words slowly, while looking and sounding his most threatening.

"Nothing! I just said we were all having a good time when Trish said there was a fight outside and we just went to the windows to look out and then heard the shots and legged it out the back before the cops came. That's all."

"Oh fuck," Johnny whispered. "I told them I left before the fight."

"Fuck! Fuck! Fuck!" You told me you said fuck all. Mikey glared at Johnny and was fit to explode. "And you, ya fucking bolox, dopey fucking moron! You are after dropping us all in it," Mikey whispered threateningly.

"But I'll deny I ever said that," Georgy whined, now pleading with his brother.

"There's fucking cameras in all those rooms ya fucking ghoul."

"There was no camera there Mikey, honest!" Georgy was desperate.

"They're hidden in the ceiling, they look like screws but they're actually a camera lens, ya stupid dopey piece of shit! How many times have I told you to say nothing?" Mikey hissed.

At this point Georgy was sick to his stomach. He was trying to remember exactly what he had said to the cops and exactly what they had said to him. He was starting to sweat. Georgy spoke again, "Ah."

"Shut Up! Shut the fuck up, for all we know, they're listening to us in here too. Don't say another fucking word, you said more than enough already." Mikey got up and started pacing the floor.

Tim Warren grinned at his boss. "Not too bad, eh?"

"Not a confession but it helps put another nail in the coffin," John answered, also smiling.

Two hours passed and not another word was spoken among the three prisoners in Holding Room A. It was time to take them to Cork Prison where they would be held until their court appearance.

Sergeant Dorney and two of his guards came into the holding room. "Time to go to Remand. You're going to be handcuffed and shackled and driven there. Once your cuffs are on, kneel up on the bench. Okay?"

Once handcuffed and their legs shackled, the three men shuffled out to the transport van. They stepped up into the back of the van where they each had their own small steel cage to sit in. They strapped on their lap belts and the door closed. The lighting in the van was dim and the air was stale from the previous occupants. The three men still didn't speak. But John and Tim continued to monitor from a distance.

Traffic was light and it took less than ten minutes to arrive outside Cork Prison. The driver hit the buzzer. A voice crackled through a speaker, "Cork Prison."

"Garda with three new arrivals," the driver said cheerfully.

"We had a bit of an incident here. You'll have to wait outside for half an hour or so, Okay?" was the response

Earlier John had called the internal preventative security officer in the prison and arranged to have the police van delayed outside.

"No worries," the driver replied. Then he picked up his radio, "P-T-Zero-One, we're delayed outside the prison for half an hour or so, copy?"

"Copy that," the dispatcher replied.

The driver looked through a grill in the panel behind him. "Sorry lads, we are stuck out here for a while. If you need to piss, you'll have to hold it or piss your pants."

The two cops stepped out of the vehicle and lit up a couple of cigarettes.

"Fuck sakes. All I want to do is get in there so I can beat the fuck out of you," Mikey said to Georgy as soon as the cops were out of the van.

Georgy just sat there with his head down.

Mikey felt like he could explode. He was not suspicious of the van being wired and didn't think it strange that they had to wait outside the prison for half an hour. His anger got the better of him. "That strap the cops found today in the van. Was that the same strap?"

"Yeah," Johnny answered sheepishly.

"How many shots did you fire?

"That night?" Johnny asked. Mikey nodded his head. Johnny looked up to the ceiling. "Four, the shells were all mixed up,"

"I swear to God, brother or no brother, I'll fucking kill you, I'll fucking kill you tonight!" Mikey hissed.

"What did I do now?" Georgy asked defensively.

"You only picked up three fucking shells, you lazy stupid bastard!" Mikey spat.

"It wasn't just me. It was Big E and Bertie Flynn too. They gave them to me," Georgy was pleading with his brother.

Mikey rolled his eyes and then glared at Georgy with the utmost contempt.

Back in the police monitor room, John looked at Tim. "Holy fuck! That shotgun we found today is the murder weapon!" John said louder than usual because they both still had their headphones on.

"We got them now!" Tim laughed. "They can't get away from this, they've said too much."

"First thing tomorrow, we got to compare the firing pin off that shotgun to the shell that was recovered at the scene. I'll bet you a month's salary there's going to be a one hundred percent match," John responded jubilantly.

It was quiet in the back of the transport van. Mikey was too angry to talk, Georgy was too scared and Johnny just sat there feeling uncomfortable. The driver and his partner returned after another two cigarettes and drove inside the prison. John decided it was best to call the IPSO in the prison and advise him that the three should be kept separate as there was some in-fighting in the gang at the moment. It would not do to have Georgy Galvin strangled by his brother.

It was almost 4AM when John got back to the Incident Room. He flopped into his chair, leaned back and shut his eyes. He needed a peaceful hour and hopefully some sleep. Tim had gone to his police car in the basement, sat in the passenger seat, put the back down and passed out peacefully for his well-earned nap.

Earlier, in Galway, Mike Williams and Eddie Jenkins took custody of Ken Rolland. Ken showed no emotion when he was placed in the rear of the Cork Garda car for the drive back to Cork. He refused to acknowledge his captors and just stared out the window for the three-hour drive.

They pulled into the underground car park at Anglesea Street Garda Station in the mid-afternoon. When placed in the interview room, Ken Rolland provided his name and date of birth and answered "No Comment!" to everything else.

John suggested to Mike and Eddie that they not bother spending hours interrogating Rolland and presenting him with damning evidence. Their case was strong and he had already been charged with two counts of premeditated murder.

"Let him wait for his lawyer to get disclosure. Why are we feeding him with information? He is too hardened a criminal to say anything about who hired him to do this now. Maybe he'll want to make a deal down the road. Let him stew in prison until trial," John said, yawning with exhaustion.

Everyone agreed and Ken Rolland was transported to Cork Prison that evening.

It was time to go home; it had been an exhausting couple of days but everyone felt good. They had wrapped up three homicides that looked impossible to solve a few months earlier when they occurred.

When John eventually got home, he was greeted at the back door by the ever-faithful greyhounds, Lucy and Molly. He put his holdall bag on the step, called out to Jules to let her know he was home and took the dogs to the back paddock. The dogs bolted past him at warp speed. They ran around the paddock a few times, sniffed a few rabbit tracks, peed on command and faithfully followed their master back inside the house. John hugged Jules and she kissed him tenderly on the cheek.

"I'll heat up your supper, eat first and then shower. You look like shit!" she said grinning.

He walked into the bathroom, washed his hands and splashed water on his face. He did look like shit, he thought as he barely recognized the reflection staring back at him. Over supper he told Jules how everything had fallen into place and all the bad guys were safely behind bars where they deserved to be. The world would be a better and safer place for a while was the hope.

"Shower and bed!" Jules ordered after supper. "If your phone rings, I'll smash it with a hammer. You are NOT going in!"

After a long warm shower, John fell into bed and he was out cold as soon as his head hit the pillow. When he woke around ten the following morning, Jules had left for work. The dogs were following the sun around the living room and barely acknowledged him when he made his way slowly to the kitchen. After coffee and cereal, he read the news on his tablet. He was in no hurry to get to work and was not looking forward to the tasks ahead of him. The families of the three deceased victims had to be informed of the arrests.

Mike Williams and Eddie Jenkins met with Johnny Johnson's living victims, Chelsey Brown and Kyle Healy. They both cried when they heard about the arrests. Their lives had changed forever because of Johnny's indiscriminate shooting on New Year's Day. John and Tim Warren met with Jason Kimberley's parents. Jason's dad, cheered at the news of the arrests but his mother cried. She knew the arrest would not bring Jason back. His young life had been stolen away forever, almost three months earlier.

When they left the Kimberleys' home, John and Tim drove in silence to Crystal Mannering's new apartment. Crystal had aged ten years in the months since her boyfriend's slaying. She too would never fully recover. She cried when she heard it was Ken Rolland that killed Julian and Alvin.

Crystal looked at her kids who were playing on the floor in the living room. "They aren't Julian's kids, you know? But he was so kind to them."

"This is almost worse than telling them their family member is dead!" John broke the silence as they drove to meet an aunt of Alvin Pomeroy. This was the easiest notification of all. Alvin's aunt didn't really care. She shrugged it off and asked if she would have to go to court. When John told her it was highly unlikely, she said, "That's good then, thanks for news."

When they returned to their office, Jennifer Martens from the Forensic Identification Unit was waiting for them. "I got news for you," Martens greeted them with a smile.

"Good news? Or bad news?" John asked.

"I don't do bad news in person. I'd deliver that in an email," she joked. "The shotgun seized from Georgy Galvin's van, in a bag where Johnny Johnson was sitting, is the gun that fired the shotgun shell that we recovered from the front of Trish Langford's house on New Year's Day."

"You're the best Jen! You are the absolute best!" Tim said as he hugged the sergeant.

A blushing Sergeant Martens handed John her report and left the office not quite knowing what else to say.

John walked into Superintendent Paddy Collins' office and handed him the forensic report. This should keep Brian McCarthy over in Prosecution Services off our backs and take the wind out of the sails of the Independent Posse for a while.

He could not have been more wrong!

THE END

Alibi for an Alibi
A novel by John O'Donovan

Epilogue

PIERCE ALFONSO was convicted of manslaughter for the killing of Stuart Killen. Alfonso appealed his conviction on the grounds that he had made a false confession due to pressure from John Cahill during the recorded interrogation. Alfonso was granted a new trial after his appeal. Prosecution Services scheduled a new trial and Pierce Alfonso was convicted again. He was sentenced to five years in prison. Alfonso was a model prisoner and passed his time by sketching and painting pictures of cars, trucks and animals. Although he was a prime target for institutional bullying, the other inmates left him alone and looked at him as an oddity. Pierce Alfonso served a little more than three years and was released on parole. He never broke the law again.

Tony Connolly was charged with murder but convicted of manslaughter for the stabbing death of Chris Shorting in the park in Ballincollig. Connolly was sentenced to twelve years in prison.

Chelsea Brown (19 years), had her right leg amputated above the knee after being shot by Johnny Johnson. Life, as she knew it, had changed forever.

Kyle Healy (25 years), also suffered life altering injuries after he was shot by Johnny Johnson. Kyle's hip was shattered and had to be rebuilt. He also suffered irreparable kidney and bowel damage and was forced to wear a colostomy bag for the rest of his life.

Ken Rolland was convicted of two counts of murder, for the brutal slaughter of Julian Hodnett and Alvin Pomeroy. He was sentenced to spend the rest of his life in prison. Rolland boasted that he was hired to kill his victims and that he was an accomplished hitman. However, he never disclosed who he was hired by. It was a couple of years later when the police finally learned that the two events of New Year's Day were connected.

Johnny Johnson *pleaded guilty to the murder of Jason Kimberly and two counts of attempted murder for firing indiscriminately into the crowd in front of Trish Langford's house. He was ordered to do so by Mikey Galvin. Johnson was sentenced to life in prison for the murder and fifteen years to run concurrently for the other shootings. The presiding judge ordered that Johnson could not apply for parole until he had served at least eighteen years in custody.*

Tyson Rolland *and his henchman, Darryl Lyons ensured that the prosecution of Mikey and Georgy Galvin would not go smoothly. Some of the witnesses from the party at Trish Langford's home on New Year's Eve, were paid off with cash and drugs; however, most of them were threatened and intimidated. When it came time to testify in court, they all had amnesia and although their recorded sworn statements were played to the judge and jury, it just did not have the same impact. Luckily, the intercept evidence and the physical evidence of the shotgun matching the shell casing was indisputable.*

Tyson Rolland went on to become the president of the Independent Posse. Under his dictatorship, the city had no idea what was ahead of it.

George Galvin *was convicted of manslaughter for providing Johnny Johnson with the shotgun used in the shooting. The prosecutor argued that life in prison with no chance of parole for fifteen years would be a fitting sentence for the notorious gang member. The defence lawyer argued that George was a 'family man' who was uneducated and easily led. The judge sentenced George to fifteen years in prison with no chance of parole for ten years.*

Michael Galvin *was also charged with manslaughter; however, he fought it bitterly in court paying for the best lawyers in the land, with his ill-gotten drug money. After a long-drawn-out court case, Michael*

Galvin was eventually convicted of accessory after the fact and sentenced to seven years in prison.

All three gang members easily made the transition to prison life. Mikey Galvin took his place on the Independent Posse "In-Custody" Council. Johnny was a protected man inside, followed orders and Mikey had his back. The same could not be said for his brother, George. George was shown no favor by the I-P Counsel. He was given difficult tasks, like collecting drug debts from other prisoners and rival gangs. As far as Mikey was concerned, they would have gotten away with the murder if it was not for his brother's laziness and stupidity. The only reason Mikey didn't kill George or have him killed was because their mother had pleaded with him to let George live, at least as long as she was alive.

Gerry Campbell *was not required to testify in the court proceedings against Johnny Johnson. He continued to operate as an independent drug dealer.*

Ron Glowden *was accepted into the Witness Protection Program after he pleaded guilty to lesser charges and sentenced to 'Time Served'. He testified against Ken Rolland in court and moved from Cork City with his girlfriend and son. However, Ron's diminishing health failed and he died months after the court case.*

Detective Inspector John Cahill *and the other members of the Serious Crime Unit continue to carry out their mission of getting justice for the dead. Unfortunately, there is no shortage of work for them. It is an exhausting challenging task that brings a different type of satisfaction when they successfully charge a killer with the most serious criminal offence in the land.*

The Real John and Julia Cahill and Paddy Collins.

John Cahill was born in 1878 in the tiny hamlet of Rathbeg, in County Kerry. He joined the British Army and served as a Sapper in the Royal Engineers, in Gillingham. He left the military around 1911. For those who do not know what a Sapper is, it was probably the least prestigious job in the Engineers at that time. The Sapper dug trenches, tunnels and probably latrines. After leaving the military, John Cahill returned to Ireland and got a job as a porter in the Metropole Hotel, on McCurtain Street in Cork City.

Julia Crowley was born in 1890 in the hamlet of Ardfield near Inchydoney in West Cork. She moved to Cork City and worked as a maid in the Metropole Hotel on McCurtain Street, where she met John Cahill.

John and Julia married and had six children. They raised their family in a small red-bricked terraced house on Suttons Buildings, in the Rathmore Park area of Cork's North Side. In 1946 John Cahill lost his job in the hotel because he won a bet! Another porter bet him that he could not drink a bottle of whiskey in one gulp. John won the bet and lost his job. The year was now 1946 and at the age of sixty-eight, John Cahill returned to London to find work to support his family. The construction business was booming, as London was being rebuilt after World War 2. John found a job as a night-watchman on a construction site in Tunbridge Wells. John Cahill sent his meager paycheck home every week, until he died alone, in his room in a boarding house in Tunbridge Wells, London in 1947. John Cahill was buried in a numbered grave in London because his family could not afford a marker or to bring his body back to Cork.

Julia Cahill raised her family in Cork City. They all grew up to be hard-working law-abiding responsible citizens. Julia walked to the City Center three times a week until she was 85 years old. Laded down with a couple of shopping bags, Julia walked up Richmond Hill and then Rathmore Road, back to her home in Suttons Buildings. These are some of the steepest residential hills in Ireland. Julia passed away, surrounded by her family at the age of 87, in 1977 in Cork City.

JOHN AND JULIA CAHILL WERE MY GRANDPARENTS. They went about their very ordinary lives without fuss. This is my chance to honor them both.

I do not know much about Paddy Collins, because nobody spoke much about him after he died in 1970 at the age of 42. Paddy was married and had four children. The family lived on the Model Farm Road and Paddy ran a moderately successful insurance brokerage. In September 1970, Paddy took his family on holidays to Kerry. Paddy had a heart attack, in the bedroom of the guest-house, where the family stayed. He was found unresponsive by his oldest daughter, Mary. Paddy died a short time later. When Paddy's daughter found him, she was only ten years old. In 1970 nobody thought that Mary should receive any form of counselling or help to cope with the shock of discovering her father's body. Fifty years later, Mary clearly remembers the day she found her dad. Throughout her career as an Education Assistant, in a high-school, Mary was a fervent advocate for children who have been exposed to shock and trauma. Mary now volunteers with children at a Therapeutic Riding Center. PADDY COLLINS IS MY FATHER-IN-LAW. The few people who remember him, knew him as a kind, honest and fair man. I wish I had met him; I think we would have been great friends.

Acknowledgements

First of all, Manor View Estate is a fictitious housing estate that I created. If such a place existed, it would be situated in the vicinity of Knocknaheeney and Nash's Boreen. I created Manor View because it is a hell-hole and although places like it exist in every city on the planet, there are good and great people everywhere and they should not be judged or have their reputations tarnished by the gangsters that live among us, in every neighbourhood.

After "*THE DEADLY STEPS*" was published, in January 2023, I received many positive emails and phone calls from people who had read it. This made me extremely happy, because, without you the reader, this is just the ramblings of some retired 'oul fella.' And, although I have said many times, that I write to download the ugly data that is stuck inside my head, it is truly an inspiration to keep going, when I receive the positive feedback from you, the reader. From the bottom of my heart, I thank you for taking the time to read this book.

The inspiration to write the *'ALIBI FOR AN ALIBI'* came from the great people that I was lucky enough to work with during my twenty-five years as a police officer. The emotions that I try to describe here are emotions that we experienced while working through the most tragic of circumstances. I was so lucky to have worked for the best of the best. I took a little bit of your empathy and experience from each one of you, and used it, when it was my turn to lead a case. No matter what the outcome of an investigation, we could always say that '*WE DID THE BEST WE COULD!* There are very few careers, where you start your day, not only waiting for, but expecting something awful and tragic to happen. And when it does happen, (and it always does), the world looks to you, the cop, to fix it, right now! And you are the first one to be blamed, when it doesn't turn out perfect. That is why police officers everywhere inspire me and I am so proud to have been one of you.

There were others who also pushed me along with '*ALIBI FOR AN ALIBI*.' These were people that I worked with over the years and, I not only trust their opinion, I trusted them with my life more than once. I will name them alphabetically, Ron Bilton, John Burchill and Kelly Harrington. You guys were amazing and gave up so much of your time to read my story and point me in the right direction. From the bottom of my heart, I thank you.

I will continue to write the 'Inspector John Cahill' series. I have at least five books in mind, who knows maybe more. If you like them, please leave me a review and keep going through the series. If you hate them, tell me what you disliked.

I do not know how to thank my editor, Maureen Steinfeld, enough. Maureen has spent so much time, using her expertise and command of the English language to turn this document into a manuscript. Thanks for everything Maureen, what a terrific teacher and a brilliant friend!

I dedicated this book to my children. Mary and I are so, very proud of you. You have grown into wonderful people and now, looking at you, it was all worthwhile. Keep doing what you are doing. It's working and we love you all.

Finally, thank you Mary, my beautiful wonderful wife, partner and best friend. You are always the first to read what I write and your opinion and judgement is invaluable. You always encourage me to continue writing regardless of what other commitments life throws at us. I really don't know how you put up with me. I disappear into my 'cave' for hours on end, writing a few thousand words, or working on a podcast, or with one of the True Crime production companies that continue to find me, to work on their documentaries. Mary, you never complain. You always find time to read the latest story and point me in the right direction while you pick up the slack that is part of everyday life. You are my inspiration and my rock. Thank you, I love you.

Take Care and stay safe. O'.D.

THE INCIDENTS DESCRIBED in this book did NOT happen in Ireland or Northern Ireland. However, something like them may have occurred elsewhere.

Be On The Lookout For

B OLO
Be on the Look Out for the next book in the Detective Inspector John Cahill series, 'THE STONGEST WEB.' Gang leader, Tyson Rolland uses violence, intimidation and child soldiers to take over the drug trade in Cork City. Can the PSNI Detective Inspector, who is on loan to the Garda, stop this gang of thugs and their ruthless leader, once and for all?

Don't miss out!

Visit the website below and you can sign up to receive emails whenever John O'Donovan publishes a new book. There's no charge and no obligation.

https://books2read.com/r/B-A-OSGW-PBKMC

BOOKS 2 READ

Connecting independent readers to independent writers.

Did you love *Alibi for an Alibi*? Then you should read *The Deadly Steps*[1] by John O'Donovan!

[2]

The Deadly Steps, is a Police Procedural thriller that is set in Cork City, Ireland. Detective Inspector John Cahill is originally from Cork City but circumstances brought him to Northern Ireland in the mid 1990's. D.I. Cahill joined the Royal Ulster Constabulary and progressed through the ranks as the R.U.C transformed into the Police Service of Northern Ireland. After fifteen years working in Belfast, D.I. Cahill is presented with the opportunity to work with the Garda in his native Cork City. John and his wife Jules return to Cork City, where soon John finds himself investigating, what appears to be the unsolvable homicide of an innocent woman who is

---

1. https://books2read.com/u/bxr8gD

2. https://books2read.com/u/bxr8gD

randomly attacked by gang members as she tries to get home after a long evening at work in Cork City's North Side.

The author introduces the reader to the mostly unknown world of physical and electronic surveillance, and the murky world of wire-taps and undercover police work. Reaching deep into his own experiences as a homicide investigator, John O'Donovan lays out this complex investigation, step by step and makes the reader feel that they are part of the team.

Throughout the story, O'Donovan not only takes the reader through the beautiful old historic city of Cork, but he also brings the magical West Cork coastline to life, in this 300+ page novel.

Read more at https://johnodonovanbooks.blogspot.com.

Also by John O'Donovan

The Detective Inspector John Cahill Series
The Deadly Steps
Alibi for an Alibi

Watch for more at https://johnodonovanbooks.blogspot.com.

About the Author

John O'Donovan grew up in Dublin Hill, on the North Side of Cork City, in Ireland. He married the love of his live, Mary Collins, also a native of Cork City. John was never a police officer in Ireland.

However, in 1989 John, Mary and their young children emigrated to Canada. Five years later, John joined one of the largest municipal police forces in Canada. After a short period as a uniformed officer, John was transferred into a Detective Unit.

As a detective, John excelled and soon transferred into several different specialty units. John transferred to the Homicide Unit and eventually became the Supervising Officer. During his career, John has been involved in the investigation of over 255 homicides and hundreds of sudden and suspicious deaths.

John O'Donovan served as a police officer for twenty-five-years and served in a Government Investigative Agency for another three years. Like Jules Cahill, Mary O'Donovan supported her husband and helped him deal with the carnage and violence that became part of normality. Without Mary's support, John could not have been a successful investigator.

After retirement, people often asked John if he missed the job. John always said no. However, there were parts that he missed. He missed the joy of outsmarting the killers and the elated feeling when an arrest was made. He missed the energy that was required to drive a complex investigation forward, even when physically and mentally exhausted. And he missed working with a dedicated team.

What John did not miss outweighed these things. He did not miss the exhaustion from working non stop, for days at a time. Neither did he miss the horror of violent sudden death. He did not miss the agony and sorrow of the families of victims when they were told their loved one had died suddenly and violently. And he did not miss the sight of the mutilated corpses and the stench of death.

The writing of this series of books is in many ways cathartic for John, who has the utmost respect for Police Officers all over the world carrying out their duty under tremendous stress. Sometimes balancing several complex cases at once, as described in this book.

EVERY INVESTIGATIVE TECHNIQUE described in this book has been successfully deployed in an investigation that the author was involved in.

Read more at https://johnodonovanbooks.blogspot.com.

About the Publisher

Publisher of the *Detective Inspector John Cahill* series of Police Procedural novels.

9 798223 316039